Praise for A. ... Remic

"Hard-hitting, galaxy ......, no-holds-barred, old-fashioned action adventure."

The Guardian on War Machine

"War Machine ...... novel of the yea ...... every testostero ...... easily one of m ..."

Fantasy Book Critic on War Machine

"Non-stop blood-and-guts action thriller."

SciFi.com on War Machine

"...a free-for-all punch-up, relentless and breathless and hugely enjoyable and for no extra cost, it's all held together by a clever storyline. A good read? Most definitely!"

SF Revu on Quake

"A hard-talkin', hard swearin', hard-fightin' chunk of military sci-fi."

SFX on Quake

"A new writer who knows what a regular reader sitting on the bus wants—action. Pure Die Hard, pure Rambo. This has got to be a film, surely!"

LADSMAG on Warhead

Also by Andy Remic

Spiral
Quake
Warhead
War Machine

A COMBAT-K NOVEL

BIOHELL

ANDY REMIC

SOLARIS

First published 2008
Mass market edition published in 2009 by Solaris
an imprint of Rebellion Publishing Ltd
Riverside House
Osney Mead
Oxford
OX2 0ES
UK

www.solarisbooks.com

ISBN-13: 978 1 84416 650 3
ISBN-10: 1 84416 650 3

A CIP catalogue record for this book is available from the
British Library.

Designed & typeset by BL Publishing
Printed and bound in the UK.

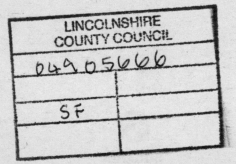

This bionovel is dedicated to Jim Rothwell and the Counthill Crew, all those fearless teaching squaddies who helped make my time educating little deviants bearable and even, sometimes, enjoyable.

And the kids! Never forget the kids! To all those unfortunates who suffered me over the years as their English teacher. You lucky guys.

PROLOGUE
HIGH OCTANE

KEENAN SAT HIS KTM crosser atop the volcanic cliff and gazed over fifty square klicks of disused quarry. Black rock aggression spread like an unravelled web filled with thousands of tunnels, dips, banks, drops and jumps. It would have been an adrenalin-junkie's playground—if it hadn't been so damned dangerous.

Keenan revved the bike hard, 1250cc LC12 titanium lekradite single-cylinder engine growling harsh, like a caged SPAW before its alloy breakfast. Sunlight glimmered on Keenan's piss-pot lid with raised black visor, and he lit a home-rolled cigarette and breathed deep on Widow Maker tobacco. The tip glowed. Smoke trailed from his nostrils. Keenan smiled, as he relaxed into the moment.

Reaching inside battered old leathers, he pulled free a flask and drank. Brown droplets of Galhari

Jataxa spirit glistened on his lips like a henna tat-too. His brain descended into honey, and he welcomed too readily the disturbing familiarity of an alcohol kick…

A distant drone cut through maudlin reminiscing and dragged Keenan kicking to the present. Three bikes slammed across flat, hard-packed earth at speed, sand pluming a wake of confetti streamers. He watched, cool and detached, from his high vantage point on the perimeter lip of the quarry. Dismissing the joyriders, he tapped down his visor and dropped the bike off the ledge in a sudden lunge… the engine screamed, and suspension juddered under clamped fists. Adrenalin rushed Keenan, wind smashing him, laughter filling his helmet. He crouched tight and fell down the vertical wall with tyres thudding and suspension pounding to level out some two hundred feet below in a valley of scattered volcanic cubes, heart in his mouth, balls in his pelvis. Keenan cruised the flat moonscape, regaining his heartbeat, then picked up his speed in sudden aggressive acceleration, leaning forward over the tank as the bike howled and climbed, low pressure tyres *digging* into rock and shale and propelling him up the incline. The bike leapt above the ridge, taking air, then hunkered down on suspension as Keenan's boot tapped down in a neat halt. He took the cigarette from his mouth, and with lazy contempt flicked free a narrow column of ash.

But…

They wouldn't leave him. Despite nicotine, adrenalin, alcohol, trikalla surges, and, sometimes, when the nightmares got too bad, something stronger... the *images* would not disperse. They followed, doggedly, nagging old ghosts prickling his spine with memory and making him shiver to his bloody, battered core. Words scrolled, ancient, staccato, stuttering, an old black and white movie filled with white noise and a billion-mile fragmented signal from a desolate world...

A world of betrayal, a world of hate, a world of the dead...

It can't be true.

I'm sorry, Keenan.

Why, Pippa? In the name of God, why?

You betrayed me.

I betrayed you? That's a fucking reason to kill my wife, my Rachel, my little sweet Ally? You fucking whore. You fucking disease. How could you do it to them? How could you murder my babes?

Keenan shook his head. Tears wet his cheeks. He rubbed them savagely, as if they were the enemy. He took out his flask. Sank another drink. "You bitch. I hope you rot in hell."

He heard the roar of engines, clearer now, brittle sounds cracking the stillness. He glanced back to the ridge he'd occupied only a few short seconds ago. Three bikes sat sky-lined. Matt black, with riders clad in black. The machines gleamed like cruel insects. And... something, some primal instinct slammed Keenan through his drug buzz and he screwed the KTM's throttle wide open as machine-gun fire roared across space and bullets whizzed and whistled around him. His bike leapt, front wheel clawing the air, engine spitting hot slivers of shaved cylinder fire which erupted from scorched exhaust cans. Keenan shot across the plateau with bullets flickering around him. Sparks spat from the bike, kicked spurts of dust and rock... but one— one found its mark, skimming through bike armour on its wormhole trajectory and carving a line across Keenan's flank, opening him like a sardine tin, like a zip. Keenan grunted in shock, felt a flush of warm blood. The impact twisted him, a sledgehammer blow. He hunkered forward, low over the tank, as the bike teetered across Devil's Brow, then skidded, slithered, and dropped off the violent, broken-tooth edge...

Keenan rode the KTM in a state of descending, cool fury. There was no pain and he gave a grim smile inside his helmet. That wasn't necessarily a *good* thing. The KTM roared and bounced inelegantly to the rocky floor, and stalled with a cough, rolling a few feet in silence. Tyres crunched loose gravel. Keenan grimaced, mind cold and analytical, breathing deeply, corroborating internal diagnostics—and the problem he faced. Three bikes. Machine guns. One probability. *Assassins...*

Sent for him? *Specifically*, for him?

For a long, long moment he sat there. *You could let them take you. Finish the job. It wouldn't be so bad. Wouldn't hurt. Go on, end the pain, sever the suffering, twist a lid on that jar of bubbling torment. What's the point going on, compadre? They're dead. Your girls are dead and gone and buried and dust... murdered meat, mate, and you couldn't even kill the bitch who slaughtered them in their beds, could you? Couldn't even finish that simple—final—job. You coward. You liver. You maggot.*

No, growled Keenan, teeth grinding.

Why ever not?

Keenan heard the bikes' screaming approach and their sudden drop off Devil's Brow close behind in a shower of raging thunder, suspension pounding, juddering, as they slammed down the slope. Through waves of surging adrenalin tinged with pain, Keenan loosened the strap on his helmet.

Why not? he thought, mind a savage tornado.

Because I'm still alive, fucker, that's why not...

The bikes howled at him. In one movement Keenan tugged free his helmet and whirled, the lid smashing the face of the closest rider as the group swept past. The figure was knocked back, bike veering right to smack a fist of rock. His body propelled like a stone from a slingshot, bike smashing end over end against the rocky ground; rider, with flailing slapping machine gun, tumbling to land heavily on his back, stunned into a coma. Keenan hit the starter, dumped the clutch and his KTM shot at the man, front wheel lifting. The man's hands rose in submission as Keenan's rear wheel connected, caving in the assassin's chest and leaving a long streak of crimson flesh vivid on black rock.

Keenan slithered to a stop. Glanced left. The two riders had halted, surprised by this sudden turn. As if through honey, they lifted guns and Keenan spun his bike on a slippery platter of geysered blood and—screamed at them. Bullets howled like needles, then he was past in a roar and through them and thundering down the valley floor, swaying left, then banking right to avoid priapic knives of rock. He hit a jump, soared over a deep crevasse known locally as Widow's Hook, landed light on the KTM's back wheel, and banked along a sloping wall with engine thumping rhythmically. He risked a glance back. The attackers were following. He watched them jump, land, and Keenan lowered his head and opened the throttle. The titanium lekradite breathed deep, breathed strong, exhaust note roaring with a metal purity of rawness and engineered savagery. Ahead, Keenan focused on the old mine tunnels, complete with timber barricade and huge signs displaying skull and crossbones alongside Quad-Gal symbols for heavy tox pollution.

Keenan roared at the barrier, feeling a fresh pulse of blood wash down his flank as he shifted uncomfortably in the saddle. He flicked the clutch, kicked the front wheel into the air and smashed through shards of wood—and on, into solid black.

Lights swept on, and the bike's roaring reverberated, deafening him. Keenan didn't slow, despite the insanity. The tunnel was narrow, winding, littered with rock. But... Keenan had been there, once before... years earlier. A self-confessed adrenalin junkie, he found the alluring danger of forbidden places hard to ignore.

Now memories flitted like teasing butterflies. The KTM slammed through darkness, Keenan's head low over the buzzing tank to avoid unforgiving overhangs. Sparks showered as he caught a footpeg on rock, jerking the bike.

Where is it? he thought. Alcohol tortured his senses. Mocked him. Jeered him.

Where is it?

Keenan feathered the brakes. The powerful head-light picked out the cone of a side-tunnel, and Keenan squeezed the front brake hard, went up on his front wheel and kicked the back of the bike wide around into the opening. He shuffled backwards, killing lights and engine. Stepping off the bike, he dropped to one knee and lifted a skull-sized rock. He could hear the pursuing bikes thundering close—fast. Keenan's eyes narrowed. Gone were pain and alcohol and bad memories; and fear. Here, now, everything converged on this moment of destruction.

Lights danced a strobe.

One bike flickered past, howling.

The second approached, and Keenan hurled the rock with devastating effect. The bike jigged, was slammed sideways, and rider and machine spun in a terrifying embrace of sparks and roars and high-pitched banging squeals. Flesh and moving machinery merged. Blood sprayed in thick streamers. Skin became spaghetti. Man and machine became one, spun in a wild dancing flur-ry of churning ripping chain and rock splinters and torn alloy. Fuel pissed over man and rider... as ignition *clicked* causing a bloom of fire to engulf this sudden thrashing unwilling cyborg. The explosion boomed. The assassin and his flaming steed were consumed, engulfed, explod-ing in a shower of fire and red-hot shrapnel, to come finally, slowly, to rest further down the tun-nel in a groaning lump of molten metal and flesh and flame.

The lead assassin slowed his bike, glancing back as his comrade disintegrated. Then his head snapped forward to witness walls disappear... and he was soaring over a high curved bridge only two feet wide, a slick cambered arc of smooth polished rock which fell away to either side, dropping into a deep and terrifying chasm. The killer slowed his bike, wary, then stopped, boot touching down, machine gun coming up and around as he looked ahead, then back, to the inferno raging in the tunnel mouth.

Keenan burst from the wall of fire, head low, KTM roaring. The killer drilled a short burst of bullets and realised Keenan's sudden, aggressive intention; he opened his own bike, shot off across the massive arcing bridge as Keenan's front tyre came within inches of the assassin's bike.

Together they howled across the chasm, symbiotes, bikes wailing, caressing, animal roars booming from high rock walls. The narrow bridge twisted, turned, rose and fell like an incredible roller-coaster. Tyres squealed and squirmed inches from a long dark fall into merciless oblivion.

Keenan, face grim, pushed his bike to the limit... then suddenly backed off, brakes on hard, leaving trails of juddering rubber as he hunkered down and back to give the bike more traction, more stopping power. The KTM slithered, and the assassin recognised, too late, the crumbling gap in the bridge. He hit brakes out of reflex, machine shuddering as it went into a spark-showering low-side... where it sailed silently off the edge, and down into the gaping maw.

Immediately, the bike vanished.

Dragged down by the bony fingers of the abyss.

The assassin slid along the bridge, leathers hissing, hands and boots struggling for grip. He hit the lip, where fingers snagged crumbled edges and he flipped, legs kicking over, to slam against the vertical rock wall. He hung there, breathing harsh, then panicked for his gun as Keenan edged forward.

The killer's gun was gone.

Keenan made a tutting sound, then seated himself cross-legged at the edge of the precipice. He smiled reassuringly at the assassin, and drew a long sleek blade from his boot. He toyed with it for a few moments, then tapped the blade close to the assassin's fingers.

"Who sent you?"

No answer.

"I'll ask you one more time. Then my patience dies. When that happens, I'll start removing your fingers. Who sent you?"

Laughter erupted, and Keenan was shocked to realise the creature before him wasn't human. Scowling, he reached out and tugged free the killer's helmet—to stare into narrowed, blood-red eyes in an oval face of... what appeared to be diseased, pitted metal, like old corroded iron. But this was no machine, it was a—

Shit, thought Keenan. *It's a junk*.

The corroded alloy nose was a small nub, and the lipless mouth opened like flowing liquid metal to reveal a dull silver interior and row upon row of tiny, triangular teeth. A forked tongue flickered against black, pus-oozing gums, and Keenan had to fight a primeval instinct not to take a hurried scramble back. This *junk* was a mutation of a once proud alien species; intelligent, noble, creative, the self-professed builders of a new utopia. Now junks were a degenerative pestilence from the diseased badlands and toxic wastes of the lethal ex-colony world of Twisted Eden. Or they had been, before their extermination.

Junks were terminally diseased, a living breathing biohazard with devolved brains and a dedication to nothing more than *death*. Across the Quad-Gal they were classified as vermin, a scourge, to be exterminated on sight lest they poison every living, breathing creature that walked and talked.

Now, however they were extinct.

Or so everybody thought...

The junk laughed, a hollow crackling sound. Its blood-red eyes sparkled.

"You want to know who sent me?" The voice was high-pitched, and hurt Keenan's ears like razors on glass. Keenan sat, shocked. Junks brought nothing but plague and death and desolation. They had devolved intelligence devoted to murder. They were a toxic *embarrassment*, and only a madman would employ them... for they were a plague, a pandemic, a virus... and to introduce them to a planet like Galhari was sheer bloody insanity. The junks were so utterly contaminated that, thousands of years earlier, they had been known to wipe out entire colony worlds by the simple act of breathing.

"Yes." Keenan was trying hard not to inhale. He studied the pitted, acid-etched face. There were no emotions. Nothing he could understand. It wore a blank mask.

"You will find out, my friend. Soon enough." The twisted alien met Keenan's gaze... as it released its grip, kicked itself back, and vanished into the dark...

Wearily, Keenan climbed to his feet and moved from the spot. He took a long soothe from his Jataxa flask, and with head down, thoughts tumbling, and the pain from the bullet score beginning to nag at him with grinding pulses, he headed back to the quarry.

KEENAN CROUCHED BEFORE the dead, chest-caved junk, studying the creature. Distantly, he could hear the drone of a chopper and the noise grated his senses like a garrotte. With his knife, he reached out and prised open the junk's crushed flesh. He gazed into the excised cavity with its broken, three-prong ribs and strange, brightly coloured internal organs which glittered like molten jewels. *I wonder if the history books were right?* With a swift cut he levered out the junk's miniaturised grey heart on the end of his knife, grasped it, and it squirmed, almost crawling, to nestle in his hand like a slimy, cold eel. He sliced the sausage-like heart down its fibrous centre, and squeezed free a small black coin.

"Shit. So it is real."

Keenan lifted the coin, staring at the smooth gloss disk. This was the junk's SinScript. It contained an encrypted list of the semi-sentient alien's *instructions*. Where it came from. Its destination and priorities. A program, of sorts. A puzzle for the brave and the foolish. Legend had it the SinScript contained not just the junk's *life*, but a ghost-scrawl of its *future*. What it would do. What it might achieve. A forecast. A damn *prophecy*.

Swiftly, Keenan sat back on his heels and used his Combat K PAD to ignite the corpse. As smoke rolled to the sky he moved away, crouching, and watched passively as the junk burned. Black fumes billowed, and there, amidst the barren quarry-scape of Galhari, amongst chunks of jagged stone, house-sized boulders, towering cliffs of diagonal sparkling lodes, this whole thing, this attack, these creatures, it just seemed *wrong*. Keenan shook his head. Junks. Filthy, toxic junks. What the hell were they doing on Galhari? What did they want?

Keenan shivered... his eyes lifting to the horizon where he could just distinguish a thick column of smoke. Something *clicked* in his soul and a coldness crept over him like ants. Keenan stood. Glanced down at his boots. He could see tiny stones vibrating, and suddenly the whole *world* seemed to tremble as a vast noise approached, a massive, mammoth booming which swept across the sky and Keenan looked up, back, as ten, twenty, *fifty* military K Freighters filled the sky with their offensive elongated bulks, cruising overhead and blocking the sky, filling Keenan with horror.

"No."

Keenan ran to his bike, fired the engine and screamed off across loose stone. The three junks he'd killed hadn't been assassins. They were a scouting party. This was an...

Keenan's grimace was darker than a junk's soul.

This was an invasion.

BIOMOD CAPSULES 0.2 mg
©NanoTek Corporation

KEEP ALL BIOMODS OUT OF THE REACH OF CHILDREN.

REMEMBER: Only a doctor or Biomod Sales Representative can prescribe this biomod medicine/ human/alien upgrade. It should never be given to anyone except the person it has been prescribed for. It may harm them in a grotesque and horrific way.

BEFORE YOU TAKE YOUR BIOMOD PLEASE READ THIS LEAFLET CAREFULLY. This leaflet contains a brief summary about your biomod capsules 0.2 mg. For full details please visit www.NanoTek.com/biomod

YOUR BIOMOD

Your biomod comes in the form of a capsule (although they can also be obtained in liquid suspension for oral or intravenous absorption, or in an anal application pack*). Each capsule contains 0.2 mg (including carrier) of the active ingredient **Trilidium ReXexate**. Each capsule also contains

---

*The anal application pack contains the newly patented Anal Viewing Console™ whereby the biomod contains a microscopic camera linked to your TV set so that all the family can gather round and enjoy the experience of seeing an anal biomod in anal operation! It's great family fun, and *the* recommended comedy application method for any biomod upgrade according to Renwells, Steiner and Steiner MD Ltd.

lactose monosodrate, ionising organo-starch and magnesium bio-stearate.

The capsule is made from gelatine and contains the colours Erythrosin (E127), Indigo Carmine (E132), Titanium Dioxide (E171) and Iron Oxide (E172). Biomod capsules are available in blister packs of 1 and 3 capsules dependant on genetic modifiers, and come with an external controlling console made from recycled hardcore plastic, called a Controller Pad. When you have completed your biomod (or the expiry date has been reached), please dispose of the console in the NanoTek Recycle Bins which can be found in most high-street shops and supermarkets Quad-Wide.

HOW DOES YOUR BIOMOD WORK?

Your biomod is a measurement of Nano Robots, called "nanobots", or Biological Modules, "biomods" which enter an organism and are controlled by a small programmable console. Most biomods are SF Grade—Specific Functional. For example, SF Grade FR biomods (fat reducer) are used specifically in the loss of weight for the patient, or an SF Grade PE biomod (penis enlarger) is used to increase the size of a patient's garbage. More expensive are the biomod WildMods—which are capable of multi-functional activity within any human or alien organism. For example, a WM Grade AC biomod (anti-cancer) can be used to kill cancer cells in all forms and operate within a system for a specified time period (usually on contract, and paid for by filling in the monthly direct debit mandate enclosed with this information pack) and will protect against further developments of cancer. The WM Grade VP biomod (vanity pack) can be used to change hair colour, reduce (or increase) fat content, increase or reduce sizes of body parts (including breasts, although this can be purchased as an SF upgrade single application 'tit pack'), improve skin tone, change skin colour, increase lip size, lengthen finger, nails, etc, etc.

The biomod robots operate at a molecular level and have two basic states called binaries. The biomods fall into the category of a *create* binary, or a *destroy* binary. To lose weight, destruction biomods are used. The same as those which kill cancer. Growth packs (for example, for body-builders) use create binaries to increase muscle mass. But *relax!* Most biomod tablets and injections have a balance of binaries to cover for every eventuality.

Biomod robots operate within the framework of a patient's DNA, so don't worry about your body rejecting things—in the old days an implanted organ could fail due to a body's own defence mechanisms. With biomods, the biomods themselves simply build a new liver, kidney, heart valve, etc adhering to an organic system's intrinsic DNA structure. Your body won't even know the difference! And once they're finished? Don't *worry!* Unless you have a time contract, the biomods will be easily and harmlessly flushed from your system with other natural waste. No fuss, no mess! And they're 100% bio-degradable, so they won't pollute the environment!!!

WHAT SHOULD YOU DO BEFORE TAKING YOUR BIOMOD?

You must tell your doctor or Biomod Sales Representative before taking your biomod, if:

- you have taken biomods before and suffered any unpleasant side effects
- you have taken biomods before and suffered really *nasty* and/or fatal side effects
- you are pregnant, intend to become pregnant, are gestating externally, or have inhabited another organism in the mode of parasitic invasion
- you are breast feeding [excludes GG5 spindlers with rotating mammaries]
- biomods have been prescribed to a child or hatched offling younger than 13 years of age
- you know you suffer from liver, kidney, heart, mental, or any internal or external problems not endemic to your race.

HOW SHOULD YOU TAKE YOUR BIOMOD?

Swallow your capsules whole. Do not chew. Take your capsules as directed. You can take them with water, alcohol and most common A Class and H7 Class drugs. Anal applicants should follow the anal application pack [form ANA1].

CAN YOUR BIOMOD HAVE ANY SIDE EFFECTS?

Very extremely occasionally and very extremely rarely, occasional rare side effects may possibly might be experienced whilst taking biomod upgrades. The side effects are:—stomach pain and cramps and skin reactions (such as itching, discolouration, peeling and the emission of curious bad smells), feeling or being sick (including the vomiting of blood and pus and internal organs), drowsiness, increases in urinary uric acid, dizziness and dry mouth (including the swelling of the tongue sometimes creating an incurable blockage of the airways). Swelling of the stomach, gout, constipation and paralysis of the stomach have rarely occurred, as have allergic reactions including swelling of the skin or severe skin rash, swelling of the joints and sexual organs, anaemia and other blood disorders, inflammation of the pancreas, liver, heart or kidney, other liver and kidney disorders, hair loss, muscle loss and muscle pain, convulsions, psoriasis, porphyria, vertigo, allergic reactions and fever, peripheral neuropathy, psychotic episodes, depression, anxiety, panic attacks, obsessive compulsive disorders and schizophrenia, visual disturbances including blindness, blocking of the arteries, myocardial infarction, liver and kidney failure, leukaemia, blood clotting disorders leading to possible bleeding from orifices such as eyes, ears, mouth and anus, brain haemorrhage, bone-marrow depression, hepatitis, HIV, all your skin peeling off, and the random snapping of bones. Consistent use may lead to brain tumours and various cancers including cancer of the breast, prostate gland, throat, lungs, skin, liver, pancreas and kidneys. Sometimes, instant death may instantly occur.

If you should suffer from any of these unwanted side effects or any undesired effect, then please tell your pharmacist, doctor or Biomod Sales Representative.

BUT... HEY!
DON'T WORRY!

If you DO suffer a side-effect we'll simply
prescribe another biomod <u>FREE OF
CHARGE</u> to counter the undesired effects!
You'll always be a winner! You can never
lose out in the genetic race for molecular
improvement!!!

SO RELAX.
SIT BACK.

YOU JUST CAN'T LOSE!

BIOMODS
THE WAY TO A HEALTHY FUTURE.

©NanoTek Corporation.

Product License Holder and Manufacturer: NanoTek Corporation (Sinax
Cluster, K1LL Subsidiary: [New York Clusters, San Francisco World, New
Tek London, Paris III, Old Athens, The Stockholm-Moscow Consortium,
POSH Town, Cairo, The Sydney Pipe, Cape Town Smash, Bombay,
Shaghai, The Dregs, Down-side, Low-Tek, Sub-City, SubC, Sub-City
Catacombs, NewLon, CoreCentral, DOG Town, Black Rose Citadel]

Manufactured by: NanoTek (K1LL Subsidiary) Pharmaceuticals Ltd,
D1RT1260 Vanløse, Black Rose Citadel HQ.

PART I

BIOCURSE

"Let us beware of saying that death
is the opposite of life.
The living being is only a species of
the dead."

Nietzsche.

CHAPTER ONE
TRUE ROMANCE

FRANCO HAGGIS WAS in love.

Love. Such a small word. A simple concept. Yet it happened so fast he didn't see it coming. It decked him like a right-hook, a well-aimed brick. Dropped him useless and gasping to the titanium-tox soil. Stomped on his head with bully-boy size 12 electrified boots. Ripped out his spine and beat him with the wriggling CPU end.

Love left Franco gasping and begging for mercy. But love *has* no mercy. Like God, love's victims are chosen indiscriminately. Without fanfare. A bolt from the blue.

Never happen to me, Franco always said. Well, it bloody had. He was smitten. She was called Melanie. Mel. She was a babe. A chickpea. A *peach*.

It all started, as these thing do, with Franco Haggis, Combat K squaddie (retired), rampant horny womaniser (active), voluminous quaffer of beer (guilty, m'lud) in the pub. The pub was, as SEC16 pubs went, a nice one. A good one. A clean one. A *cool joint*. A *place to hang*. A *place to chill*. It was one of the few SEC16 bars from which Franco had not yet been banned and *ejaculated*—such was his infamy: scarred knuckles and a tendency to launch furniture whilst singing about goats. Franco had a reputation. No, he had a *reputation*.

On this evening, however, Franco was having a quiet drink after a hard week at work. A quiet drink, for Franco, constituted ten or twenty pints, with a Vindaloo encore. A hard week at work constituted carrying out unsavoury acts—indirectly—for a certain Mr Voloshko, head honcho of a City-wide gangsta outfit named The Hammer Syndicate—one of the seven ruling Syndicates on the planet.

Now, The City was a planet. And the planet was a city. A *big* one. A synthetic mish-mash jungle of stone, concrete, alloy, a cacophony of contrasting architectural styles from every human, alien and basic *organic* life-form Quad-Gal side. The City had once been a planet; and the city had *consumed* the planet. Not an inch of the world in its whole had not been terraformed.

The City was the epicentre of wealth in the Quad-Gal. Nowhere could come close to the economic and private military *might* of The City. With a population of 112 *trillion* there was *nothing* that could not be bought, sold or exchanged, a situation perpetuated by the fact there were no regulations. The City had no written rules, laws or taxation on immigration, trade, import or export.

The City was mad and bad, trick and slick, hunter and hunted, killer and victim, a world of contrasts, a planet of anarchy, and Franco *loved it* with a raw energy and the embracing punk-gusto of all true slightly deranged nihilists.

Franco rested his elbows on the bar. The barman, a dude called Jed, waddled towards him with a pint of Greene King. "Ahh," said Franco, accepting this proffered gift. "Luvverly jubberly." He drank. A cream white moustache ingratiated itself with his short ginger goatee beard. "Ahh. Ahhh*hhhhhhh*."

"Not working tonight, Franco?" asked the ever-amiable Jed. He proceeded to polish a glass with a brown-stained beer-rag, not so much cleaning the vessel as spreading grease.

Franco peered over his beer. Shook his head. "No. The Boss is out of town. On a job. A mission. Worth a lot of cash, or so I believe." He grinned, showing a gap where one front tooth had been knocked clean free. Six pints had loosened Franco's tongue. This was probably *not* a good thing, considering Voloshko— Head of The Hammer Syndicate—was probably *the* most feared and revered gangster leader of all the 'families' in The City. His current *frag rate* numbered in the thousands. You did *not* dick with Voloshko.

Franco, however, was mad.

Admittedly, it was a sporadic and random madness, controlled by a cocktail of drugs, therapy, therapeutic drugs, beer and sex and chips and gravy; it was the sort of madness which could take him in its wings for long periods; or, conversely, leave him be—sane, or a close approximation thereof—for *years*. In his past life, Franco *had* admittedly been locked away at The Mount Pleasant Hilltop Institution, the "nice and caring and friendly home for the mentally challenged" under the watchful supervision of a certain Dr Betezh... but that had been a long time ago. It was a different story entirely.

Franco scratched his shaved head. "Business slow?"

"Aye," nodded Jed. "I think people are saving their cash for TQC. It's always the same vibe this time of year. We've only two weeks to go until the celebrations begin!"

"The Quantum Carnival," mused Franco, scratching his beard. "God, is it that time already? I should get me a proper calendar."

"An expensive time of year," nodded Jed, deep in thought.

"Aye. I usually do three months' wages."

"I know," said Jed. "You spend most of it in *here*."

"Well, I know you appreciate loyal customers."

"Just as long as you don't do what you did last year."

"What was that?" Franco frowned.

"You started a brawl."

"I did?"

"With seven drunk Justice SIMs."

"Ahhh. *That* brawl."

"Franco, a human can't take on *one* Justice SIM, never mind seven!"

"I was only fuckin' wit' them."

"They have no sense of humour, Franco."

"Yeah, I seem to recollect."

"Pure smashed the place up, they did."

"I remember!"

"You should, mate. They used *your* head."

The Quantum Carnival was a straight seven day run of parties and street-celebrations, fireworks and dancing and opulence, where nobody worked and the entire *planet* shut down for an annual orgiastic cacophony of *pleasure* and *pain* and *fun* and *depravity*. Everybody enjoyed TQC. Everybody joined in. After all, it would be rude not to.

Franco took another quarter-pint sip of Greene King, and realised his glass was empty. Jed poured him another.

"Hey up, look what the dog's dragged in."

Franco slow-spun on his bar stool, only half interested—he was in the mood for a serious drinking session, and it took a lot to distract him from that. However, the vision that met him quite literally *poleaxed* him. His jaw dropped. It actually *dropped*.

"Wow," he said.

Jed leant forward over the bar. He grinned, as he hissed, "Out of your league, buddy. By a billion parsecs."

Franco nodded aimlessly. Jed was right.

She was beautiful. Stunning. Perfection. A creature of gorgeousness carved from a block of gorgeousness. Petite and modest in stance, yet subtly athletic, Franco watched with a hint of escaped drool as she closed the door behind her, a precise movement, and her gaze swept the bar. She had green eyes, he saw that immediately. Long black hair. A beautifully deep brown complexion. And the most incredibly well-shaped and well-formed perfectly perfected *bosom* Franco had ever laid eyes upon. And he'd laid eyes on a few. After all, as Franco always said, *nothing's nice as tits.*

She walked across the room.

Franco's eyes followed her, beer glass touching his lips but no beer entering his mouth. It was too full of saliva. Brimming, to a point of embarrassing overflow.

And then, the incredible happened.

The woman, the vision of loveliness, the human goddess, altered her course of direction, moved economically to the bar, and hopped up on a stool beside Franco. Franco eyed her smart carbonised bamboo suit and even smarter briefcase. He smiled gormlessly, uneasy, as ever around women he wasn't paying for.

"Hello," said the beauty.

Franco nearly dropped his beer. "Hullo," he managed, then turned and fidgeted with a beer mat. *Shit* screamed his brain. *She's here, she came over and moved to the bar and sat next to me and said bloody hello to me so now so listen be calm boy-o you've got to act calm and not mess this up and just be real cool and show you're just not some low-down space-bum dirty no-good burned out ex-squaddie with a love of robot prostitutes and horseradish... show her you're a cool and gathered and hip and sophisticated kind of motherfucker dude. Right dude?*

"Right dude," said Franco, unintentionally aloud. His jaw flapped like a guppy fish at feeding time.

"Pardon?" said the stunningly stunning creature, tilting to observe the little ginger squaddie.

"Argh," said Franco, and spat a mouthful of beer down her cream silk&satin digitally enhanced blouse.

The woman stared coolly at the regurgitated beer.

"Sorry," said Franco, taking a napkin offered by a skull-grinning Jed and patting frantically at the beer stain *until hot shit, he realised he was patting all over her bouncing breasts and oh my God of Gods he* was *actually bloody mauling her tits and groping her and abusing her in public!*

Franco whirled about, face a platter of crimson shame, and fixed his eyes stoically on the back of the bar. He ground his teeth. Grunted a deep and disturbing grunt.

The woman plucked the napkin from Franco's shaking fingers and continued to pat at her stained blouse; she seemed unperturbed. "It's OK," she said, smiling with neat little teeth. Franco glanced at her. "Don't worry about it. Second hand beer?" She laughed like a tinkle of wind-chimes. "Absolutely *no problem.*"

"'S very kind of you," mumbled Franco, staring dejectedly into his murky pint.

"Hey, actually, wait a minute; you're Franco... aren't you? Franco Haggis?"

Adrenalin soared through his veins. Joy stamped-ed his mind into slurry. Hope clattered across the dusty plains of a wooden subconscious. Was this, perhaps, some ex-girlfriend he didn't remember come to re-engage his services as an amorous suitor? Or perhaps an admiring fan, high on the lust of seeing his picture in a newspaper some years earlier and intent on hunting him down and ravishing his weak and vulnerable rugged exterior? Or maybe *maybe* she was a long-lost childhood sweetheart returned to reclaim what was rightfully hers and sweep him away in a flurry of wealth and fast cars, penthouse suites and skiing with royalty?

"That's me," swaggered Franco. "Franco by name and, um, Franco by... *nature?*" He faltered. That had sounded *better* in his head. Damn that dirty beer!

"My name is Melanie. Mel." Melanie held out her hand.

Franco shook it. She had tiny intricate paintings on each elegant finger nail; entire scenes that wouldn't have been out of place in a gallery of fine art. *Class*.

Franco beamed, feeling an incredible urge to nod and drool. "Hi again," he said, oozing sophistication. He leant back on the bar, an action he thought *damn it he KNEW* made him look totally uber-*cool* and *available* and goddammit a downright hunky horny *stud-muffin*. It didn't help when his elbow connected with a slice of stray gherkin and his upper torso slid two feet across the bar making Franco recline like a heroin-chic model on a first-day porn-shoot.

"I'm employed by the Quad-Gal External Revenue," Mel said, the smile still on her face but now, *now* Franco noticed a dark gleam in her eyes and something shrunk and *died* in his breast as realisation kicked him. "I'm here to talk to you about your tax returns."

Franco shuffled upright, still beaming an optimistic smile as he peeled the gherkin slice from his elbow with as much panache as he could muster. He muttered through clenched teeth, "But... I haven't made any tax returns."

Melanie reached over, and shook his hand. "Exactly," she said.

"YOU'LL HAVE TO excuse the place. It's a bit of a dump."

Franco forged ahead, into his apartment as Mel negotiated the final staircase (numbering 68 out of 69), red in the face and wheezing like an asthmatic donkey.

Franco's eyes cast manically across the nightmare shit-hole he inhabited. It was, perhaps, worse than a dump. At least in a dump scavengers took the rotting food. This, however, was the place he called home.

It had seemed a good idea.

"I'll need to see your paperwork," Mel had said, back at the bar.

"Hey, come back to my place," swaggered Franco, ever the optimist. "I have all my documentation in my wardrobe. I can show it you. All of it. I can. In triplicate." Only... only *now* his home was one step away from fumigation and Franco hadn't really thought through this attempted seduction with clarity.

Ten seconds, screamed Franco's brain. *You've ten seconds to clean, tidy, mop, brush, vacuum, and generally turn a sloth-pit for sloth-slobs into a pristine bachelor pad worthy of any dream-girl's amorous lust. Yeah, I can DO THIS!*

"Sorry about the lifts," called back Franco, and taking a deep breath he dived on in like a blind, confused lesbian in a fish market. He leapt, scooping a plate of mangled week-old spaghetti in one hand and three pairs of rigid y-fronts in the other, landed on an old skateboard with three wheels, careered across the apartment, squeaking, as one outstretched sandaled foot hooked a crotchless PVC gimp-suit (used, don't ask) and the other strained to keep a wobbling half-drunk Franco upright. Three wheels jarred against the rim of the kitchen portal, Franco frisbeed the spaghetti mess into the sink, shot-putted the boxers into the overflowing laundry basket and stuffed the squeaking squealing PVC gimp-suit into the washing machine. With a stamp he flipped the skateboard into one hairy hand and whirled, skimming it sideways into the living room where it connected with the contents of the coffee table and efficiently blitzkrieged the surface of fifteen fungus-filled coffee cups, a pirated SONY Playstation 1000 Platinum with half its optic-wiring hanging free, and a pair of plastic devil's horns, in red. There was a clatter and crash of smashing cups. The table was clear. The skateboard landed neatly on three wheels and squeaked into a corner.

Franco put his hands on his hips and grinned. He nodded to himself in appreciation. "Looking good, looking fine. Hey hey, they don't call me Franco 'Efficient House Husband' Haggis for nothing!"

Melanie the tax inspector arrived at the door. She looked fit to be sick. She was pale and red-faced at the same time, and her knees wobbled beneath her finely-tailored bamboo-strand suit. It was only *then* Franco noticed her rather smart briefcase was in fact a rather smart *SIM-skin* briefcase. *SIM-skin!* Triple-class.

"Sixty-nine floors, and no lift?" panted Mel, attempting to regain her lungs. "Are you *insane?*"

"Keeps me fit." Franco puffed out his chest. "I'm a very fit bloke, I am. Not many men get to my age and can do the things I can do." His voice dropped to a conspiratory level. "It has been said in some circles," he paused, for effect, "that I'm a *sexual athlete.*" He beamed again, stepping back, as one sandal nudged a vomit-stained cardigan under a cupboard.

Mel wheezed, leaning against the wall. "What was that squeaking sound? Like... rubber, or something?"

"Mice."

"And the crash of crockery?"

"Neighbours. Would you like to sit down?"

Franco hurried to the sagging, split, bulbous example of his colourless stain-riddled settee. He grabbed the three porn mags (*"Inside This Month's Issue We've As Much Praxda Pussy And Alien Ass As You Can Pan-Handle!"*) and stuffed them down a crevice filled with old crisp packets. Franco sat down, back erect, hands on his knees like a naughty schoolboy. Mel stared at him, long and hard, suspicion gleaming in her eyes, then hobbled to the settee and took a seat at the opposite sagging end.

Franco's eyes scanned his apartment in horror. It was the first time he'd ever truly *looked* around. And he'd never realised he lived in such a *dump*.

Mel clicked open her SIM-skin briefcase. Shuffled through a ream of metal documents. Then looked sideways at Franco. He beamed amiably at her.

"By my calculations, you owe rather a lot of money."

Franco frowned. "But... I've been off the grid for a *long time* now."

"I've estimated. We're good like that."

"So... you don't know where I've been, don't know what I've been doing or what I've been earning—but you can still estimate my annual income and taxation on what you think I *may* have possibly might have earned?"

"Yes. I extrapolated from your early *army career* earnings, plus those monies accrued whilst in Combat K. Earnings which you also failed to declare and pay relevant tax." She smiled. It was neat.

"How do you know about Combat K?" Franco's voice had dropped low, and to anybody who knew him, levelled out at a dangerous tone. His brain was already working out distances to the nearest gun, bomb, or gun/bomb combo. Survival instinct was using his brain as a punch-bag. Sobriety ripped out his kidney and beat him with it.

"I'm from the Quad-Gal External Revenue." Mel smiled a teeth smile. "I know everything."

"Combat K is classified. Top level."

The gun which appeared in Franco's hand was small and black, and completely non-menacing. But to anybody in the know, the Heckler & Koch Kat.5 anti-terrorist microlite was a savage weapon. It could clean remove a person's head. Hell, a single round could remove an entire *torso*.

"I've been assigned to track you down," said Mel.

"For a mission?"

Mel frowned. "No, Mr Haggis. For you to pay your *tax*."

"We're in The City. Nobody pays tax in The City!"

"But you worked for the Quad-Gal Military. Quad-Gal Government. Gov6. And *that* had nothing to do with The City. You *are* in arrears, Mr Haggis. Franco. And, yes, whilst there are no official *laws* here, QGM can have you extradited. You owe what you owe. And that sum is *very large indeed*. I suggest you co-operate, or I'll be forced to initiate my PAB."

"PAB?"

"Panic Attack Button. There's a flier with twenty Battle SIMs just a couple of blocks away." She eyed the gun. "I believe the punishment for attacking a Quad-Gal Tax Inspector is, oh, instant death."

Franco deflated.

"OK. OK. I admit it guv'nor. It's a fair cop. I never paid my bloody tax to the bureaucratic penny-pinching, money-skimming daylight robbers we call *the System*. Go on. Hit me with it. How much do I owe?"

Melanie told him.

Franco went pale.

"However."

"Yes?" He raised an eyebrow above a face filled with despondency.

"There... might be a way out of this."

"Yes?"

"You were Combat K. Right? The best of the best. Elite. A super-soldier?"

"Yeah. Right. Fat lot of good *that* did me! Hah! Save the world, nay, the damn *galaxy*, and the bastards still expect 33%. Where's the justice in that, I ask you?"

"Do you... still have your uniform?"

Franco frowned. "Um. Yee-*ees?*" It was a long drawn-out answer. Wondering. Questioning. *Confused*.

Melanie smiled. It was a wide smile. Very wide. Very... *friendly*. She stood up and moved to Franco with undulating hips. She reached behind herself, undid the molecular zip, and stepped lithely free of her one-piece business suit. Full breasts filled a Glitter Web bra. A flat stomach greeted Franco's slack-jawed awe. Athletic legs rose from diamond shoes up to a micro-filament thong that could only be called underwear because it was *under there*. Franco stared at something slick and inviting.

Mel reached forward. She licked her lips. Her eyes were gleaming. She patted his arm. "Go and slip into your uniform," she said. "There's a good boy."

MEL HAD HUNTED Franco down for tax purposes—initially. But she'd volunteered for the job after seeing photos of him in his Combat K uniform, admittedly a *few* years younger, and a few pounds lighter, but still proud and erect and strong. As it transpired, Mel had a thing about soldiers. Especially uniformed soldiers. And *especially* Combat K uniformed soldiers. She acknowledged this was a character defect, but she was willing to work around it.

However, on that first evening, despite stripping from her bamboo business suit and dancing with Franco in his uniform, she had refused to "rush things". She left after an hour with a coquettish smile. Franco was left with an erection that could drill hull steel. Melanie departed with the promise she would return that night... with something special.

As Mel began her arduous sixty-nine floor descent, Franco, in his eagerness to please, like a puppy with a wagging tail, shouted, "I'll cook us a meal! I'm a good cook, I am!"

Mel laughed. "OK then."

As she disappeared, the enormity of what he'd said sunk in. A meal. Cooked. By. Franco. Shit.

Franco liked to eat. Hell, that went without saying. A gourmet chef, however, he was not. And he so desperately wanted to please! At first he thought about buying a fine meal from a restaurant and passing it off as his own... but he reluctantly admitted that a) his funding was limited, i.e. he had none, and b) his oven was darker than the fabled Black *Black* Hole of Black Sinax. He opened the oven optimistically on squeaking hinges, and poked around with a stick, but when something in that dark and greasy mess grabbed the stick, snapped it in two, growled, "I'm tryin' a sleep in here," and tossed the stick onto the floor with a clatter, Franco resigned himself *never* to venture into the oven again.

And so, with little option left, Franco decided that the one thing he could cook, something he was *good* at cooking, something which would be easy-peasy, a breeze... but which might well be his curse as well as his saviour... was chilli. A good, honest-to-goodness, wholesome fresh cooked chilli. Made to his own aged family recipe. With his own clean-ly scrubbed hands. And with the freshest ingredients his little money could conjure from an InfinityChef. And he knew, wow, it would blow her little socks off. It would knock her sideways. *And*, hopefully, guarantee him a *shag*.

Most people, when faced with this dilemma, would have simply summoned a meal from a local street-corner InfinityChef. But in reality, everybody knew the molecular-reconstituted food tasted like crap; the best way to cook was to beg and borrow as many fresh ingredients as possible. After all, only the *poor* or the *desperate* ate from a public Level 1 InfinityChef.

After a whirlwind stealing spree, which bagged Franco most of the ingredients he needed, he set to chopping leeks, onion, garlic, adding beans and strips of fresh beef (or as fresh as organo-construct auto-expanding meat could get)... and then moved on to the crème de la crème of his homespun dish. Chillis. Fresh chillis. Franco had to concentrate *really* hard, now. Because Franco liked chilli pep-pers. He liked *a lot* of chilli peppers. He liked the kind of amounts you could use to blast open a bank vault. So, careful not to overdo this culinary adventure, Franco chopped and chopped, and removed the seeds, and added the chillis to the bubbling pan.

Fast forward two hours.

A whirlwind cleaning of the apartment, good scrub in the bath, best silver glitter suit, neatly trimmed beard, (stolen) *Elvis Aftershave* dabbed at precise intervals about the body.

Franco was ready. No. *Ready, babee.*

The knock sounded exactly on time. Franco grinned. Tax inspectors, huh? Precise to the point of anal bureaucracy. It was in their nature. In their damned *blood.*

Franco flung open the door, half-expecting the whole thing to be some huge practical joke, half-resigned to seeing some fifty stone Blubber Stripper leering down with only half her own teeth and a spool of saliva connecting her from tongue to floor. But no. It was Melanie. Wearing a quite ravishing simple black dress, neck to ankle, tight as a body-stocking and showing off her perfect curves in a perfectly perfect curving way.

"Hi," said Franco.

"Something smells good." She held up a bottle of wine. Franco looked at it carefully. It was Chateaux du Tek-Paris. Thirty years old. *Very* select. "Come on, I'm ready for a drink. It's been a long week." *Wow. She liked a drink. A girl after his own heart! Could it get any better?*

Franco opened the bottle. Poured two glasses. They sat, a little awkwardly, one at each end of the sofa (newly covered with a quite garish floral covering which had, until recently, been next door's curtains).

They sipped the wine. It was divine.

Franco savoured the flavour, and didn't dare quite look at Mel. She was stunning. She had little silver flowers woven into her long dark hair. She smiled at him.

"You have a good—um—climb?"

"The stairs?" Mel laughed. Tinkling sunlight. "Like you said, it'll keep me fit."

"You look pretty fit as it is." Franco bit his lip. Blushed. *Don't be too eager you dumb-arse little fool if you're too eager she'll run a mile like they all do. Play it cool. No. Super cool. Sophisticated. Charming. Like James Bond, that most eternal of action heroes, 578 films and counting. Yeah. That's it. A ginger James Bond. You want ice with that sir? Ye-arse. Shaken. Not stirred.*

"What *is* that smell? It's sumptuous?"

"Chilli. Homemade. I nicked... *borrowed* all the ingredients fresh from the market. My mom used to make it." Franco beamed. "An old family recipe. You want to eat now?"

"Sounds good."

Franco disappeared in the kitchen, and when he returned with two plates of chilli, rice and tortillas, Mel had switched off the lights and lit two candles. Flames crackled. Soft yellow light cast pastel shadows over the walls. And, despite its designation as *shit-hole*, in the softening ambience of candlelight, Franco's apt was transformed into something quite romantic.

Franco sat down, a little closer this time. The plates steamed on the table.

Mel took a small, dainty mouthful.

Franco waited... if he'd made it too hot, it'd blow her damn head off! And bang would go his chance of a... well, he frowned. Not just a shag. No. This was… something more. Something *different*. Something *special*. His heart thudded in his chest. *He* felt different. This woman was… divine. Franco's face broadened into an almost relaxed smile. For once, sex didn't matter. There was no urgency. Franco— and he hated to admit this—well, he *liked Mel too much*.

They ate.

"So how *did* you find me?" said Franco.

"Quad-Gal External Revenue work closely with all other Government Agencies. I'm used to tracking people down. I'm efficient. I'm good at my job."

Franco placed down his fork. "Can I ask you something?"

"Be my guest."

"This isn't a wind-up, is it?"

Mel stared at him from behind long dark eyelashes. "Why would you say that?"

"Well, I'm only a little fella, but I've got a big heart. I don't like being messed about. And I'm not exactly…" he wrestled… "what some would consider a good catch. I'm not wealthy. I drink too much. I *can* be crude, or so my friends tell me." He sighed. "What I'm trying to say is, well, look, well, the thing is, just *look at you.*"

Mel laughed. "You think I'm such a great catch myself? Franco, I'm a *tax inspector*. We're like the toilet bacteria of the Quad-Galaxy. I've known war criminals get a better reception at a party than I do. The minute people hear where I'm from they usually run a marathon… but not you. You… you showed me kindness. You invited me back here, and despite it being a sixty-nine floor climb, I appreciated that." She shuffled a little closer on the couch. "And... I *do* like a man in uniform."

"Ahh." Franco himself shuffled a little closer.

Mel reached out. Put a hand on his knee.

"Ooh." Franco put his hand on her knee.

Again, they shuffled a little bit closer... until they were inches apart.

In a husky whisper, Franco said, "I really, really want to kiss you."

"Why don't you, then?" breathed Mel.

Franco leaned close, and their lips brushed. Franco's heart soared. It popped and crackled in his chest like an open exhaust on a 5000cc Harley.

They kissed in candlelight for long, long minutes. A gentle caressing of tongues and lips. A merging of inquisitiveness and building lust. A soft and sensual connection.

Mel's hand stroked Franco's leg, working its gradual way to his groin. Franco groaned. His own hand traced a delicate trail down Mel's arm, then came to rest on her flank. It was marble smooth. The dress was soft as fur under his fingers. He groaned again. Their kissing increased a notch. Mel's hand came to rest on his ramrod erection. Franco's hand found her leg... then worked down to the hem of her dress and his fingers walked their way up her calf, then onto the marble-smooth skin of her thigh. "Touch me," she breathed, a husky hot breath and they were kissing and breathing and moaning and Franco's hand slid up the inside of her thigh as she massaged him through his ragged combat shorts. She unbuttoned the torn shorts, tugged them free and Franco stood proud and huge and true. Her hand curled around him. They lay down together on the sofa, a mutual floating of magic, their meal and expensive wine forgotten. Melanie gave a little sigh as Franco's hand moved and he found the soft slick hot place. "Do it." He massaged her. Gentle. Firm. She squirmed in his hand, hot and wet and thrusting.

"Oh Melanie," breathed Franco.

"Oh Franco," said Melanie.

"Oh Melanie!"

"Oh Franco oww Franco oh, ow, ow bloody hell Franco, it's burning, it's burning!" She sat bolt upright, horror acid-etched on her face as she peered frantically down at her throbbing raw genitalia. She leapt up and ran for the bathroom.

Franco groaned in horror. "What? What happened?" Idly, he reached down and toyed with himself, keeping his proud Roger erect in the hope that whatever was burning his true-love's chuff would *bugger off* and allow him the pleasure of consummating their relationship with red hot fiery sex.

Suddenly, a shiver washed over him. Something was wrong. Something was *very* wrong. Something was warm. No, not warm, but *hot*. No, boiling! Burning! His cock and balls started burning furnace-hot. Throbbed, as if pounded in a door. Pain smacked him with waves of raw screaming heat and he kicked himself free of his shorts and ran feet-slapping to the bathroom where he stood side by side with Mel and together they splashed cold water on their bits, ululating soothing ums and ahs, and then, in a flash of inspiration, splashing water on *one another's* genitalia with cries of easing cooling soothing relief... until, after long and torturous minutes the hot and fiery sensations finally, ultimately, abated.

"What happened?" panted Mel. Sweat glistened on her brow.

"Well," scowled Franco, calming his breathing, a now very *limp* Roger in his hand, "I'd like to have said we were both on fire with lust, but it was something much simpler. I used fresh chillis in the cooking. I chopped them—by hand. Obviously, chilli juice doesn't wash off *that easy*. I am so, so sorry."

"So... you gave me a vaginal injection of red hot chilli peppers?"

"Ha! Only the best for you, my sweet."

Mel laughed long and hard. "I can see life with you is going to be far from dull!"

"Life with me?"

Their eyes met.

"Come to bed," she said, taking his chilli infected hands.

And for the remainder of the night, they really *did* experience a union of hot and fiery lust.

IT WAS LATER. Much later. *Four days* later.

Franco lay on his back, in the dark, staring at the ceiling. Beside him lay Mel, curled up against him, snoring gently. She was naked, and he touched her flank. Her skin was cool. Gently, Franco reached over and grabbed the thermal liquid-marble blanket, pulling it over Mel's exposed flesh. It hissed like a river over pebbles. Mel sighed in her sleep, and turned a little.

Wow, thought Franco.

Just… wow.

Said it would never happen. Love's for schmucks. Never happen to me. Take ten or fifteen girls to pin down this ol' wanderer. No single woman could possibly have all *the attributes this old dog's looking for in a gal. Never happen. Never ever* ever *happen. Shit.* Well, it had. And now it had, Franco was over the moon. He'd become a walking cliché. Now, he brushed his teeth *every morning* because he didn't want to be stinky for his new true-love. He even had a regular *bath*. And that was *not* Franco. In the scheme of reality in the universe, as all his friends knew, Franco did not *do* baths.

But it got worse.

Now, the air smelled sweet, fresh, *alive*, despite the toxic ash. Birds twittered in the trees and their annoying squawking was *birdsong*. Franco felt *lighter*. There was a spring to his step. He felt younger. Fitter. Stronger. Leaner. More handsome. When he walked with Mel, he walked hand in hand. Their faces shone with radiating *love*.

But it got worse.

Franco started to go *shopping*. He'd push the trolley, whilst Mel filled it with titbits for them to "snackle" on whilst watching late-night movies, curled on the floor of Franco's apartment in a liquid-marble blanket, scented candles lighting the air with romantic harmony. In the past, a supermarket was a dark and foreboding gateway to Hell as far as Franco was concerned. The only time he ever dared venture into a supermarket was to purchase a trolley of beer, much to the tutting soundtrack of mothers 'n babies and the disapproving scowls of smiley-uniform clad staff. Franco shuddered. No. Supermarkets had been a place of mystery. And misery. Until he met Mel.

But it got worse.

Now, Franco was prone to *cleaning* his apartment. He owned... wait for it... *cleaning products*. He had a nice set of marigolds. He did his washing up *after they'd eaten,* not on a six-monthly rotational basis when the mould threatened to take over the asylum. He cleaned the toilet. Not just that, but every *bloody* day... or even, even, even *after* he'd used it in response to a bad case of Vindaloo-arse! Franco had once thought a toilet brush was something for de-greasing his motorbike chain. But no. Mel taught him the error of his ways with a smile and a wink and slap to his rump. Now, Franco washed his clothes. In a washing machine. Dried his clothes. In a drying machine. He *even* ironed his *fucking shirts*. Franco never even used to *own* a fucking shirt, never mind *iron* a fucking shirt. But there he was, whistling along to the radio, applying steam here, squirting a jet there. Ironing, man, fucking *ironing*.

But it got worse.

This was the conversation as they sat out in the BubbleCrane which arched from Franco's apartment balcony on its skinny alloy arm, like the distended, synthetic limb of some giant old crone.

"Franco, my squeezy love?"

"Yes, sweetie pie?"

"I've been meaning to mention something."

"Yes, my angel flowerpot?"

"It's a bit personal, honey wunny."

Franco strained, peering down at the thick ribbons of flesh which filled the streets far below, winding like an albino snake between towering skyblocks. Millions of people. Thronging. Weaving. Jostling. The noise was a dull roar, muffled by the BubbleCrane's aural.field. "That's OK, chipmunk."

"It's about your tooth."

"My tooth?"

"Your missing tooth."

"Oh, my *tuff*. Yeah. Got it knocked out in a bar brawl hmm *hmm not that I do that sort of thing anymore oh no I is a good boy now a reformed character a man of improved moral fibre. Oh yes.*" He smiled. It was a noticeably *gappy* smile.

"Well," embarrassed pause, "I thought you might like to get it done."

"Get it done?" The smile froze and cracked Franco's ice-lake face. Below, a tiny percentage of The City's vast titanic population seemed to be laughing, and not just laughing, but laughing *at him*. The sound of a trillion organic life-forms from a thousand different planets chuckled in parallel with his horror.

"Yes. You know. A cap. A false tooth. A *denture*."

"Why, *in the name of Hades,* would I want to do that?"

"To please little old me?"

"Oh. That. Yes. Aha. Haha."

"I've arranged for you to visit the dentist."

"The dentist?"

"Yes. The dentist."

"Why would I want to visit a dentist?"

"To get your tooth done."

"Ahhh. Right. I see. OK. No problem. Grasped that idea. Got it."

And so, like a good and wagging dog Franco went along to the dentist. He sat in the sterile room sniffing the sterile dentist stink and when the needle slid into his gum, Franco's 9mm H&K nudged under the dentist's chin. The man's eyes bulged, tongue sticking out alarmingly from between *perfect* white teeth.

"Fuck this up," growled Franco, "and I'll shoot out *all* of your teeth. Yeah?"

Franco didn't like dentists. Never had. Never would.

"Yes. Yes. Yes yes!"

"Good boy. Get on with it."

He'd walked home a new man. Smiled a full-tooth smile. Mel had hung on his arm and giggled as they planted flowers in a window box on the balcony (she'd made him shift the old 3250cc Ducati engine he'd been restoring, which had sat there on the balcony for a good two years, untouched, sump full of old stinking oil, a project that'd never be) and as the sun shone across the vast, jagged-tooth skyline of The City, life seemed suddenly oh so *idyllic*. So *perfect*. So goddamn *nice*.

But.

It didn't last.

These things never do.

"It's The Quantum Carnival in four days."

"Yeah. TQC is magic!"

"It was in the paper. Loads of people are getting married!"

"What a romantic time to get married! Perfect!"

"Yeah, that's what, y'know, I was thinking."

"Is this a proposal, Franco Haggis?"

"I, um, suppose it is."

"Oh Franco! I'd love to! It'll be perfect! It'll be wonderful! It'll be a chance of a lifetime! My answer is yes!"

"I love you."

"I love you too."

AND SO THE day and the time were set—for the final, explosive finale of The Quantum Carnival. Mel invited her family with pink flowery invitations. Franco sent out two messages. One to Keenan asking him to be his best man, and one to Pippa, asking her not to kill anybody. Franco bought a ring and a wedding-bind suit. Mel bought a dress. It was big and white, and looked like a meringue.

"DO YOU THINK I've got a big nose?"

"*What?*"

"My nose," smiled Mel. "I've always thought it was *too big.*"

They lay in bed amongst sex-scrambled sheets. The sweat was still cooling on Franco's back. Like a true bloke, he wore nothing but his socks. "No no *no,*" he said, hoisting himself onto one elbow. "Your nose is perfect. Your nose is *beautiful.*" He tweaked it, as if his tweaking would give her beauty more emphasis.

"I've never been happy with it," she sighed.

"Well *I* think it's lovely. Like a pixie's. Scrumptious."

They lay, listening to the sounds of roaring city life. In The City—even at night, which only came once every three days—it was never quiet. 112 trillion people made sure of that.

"I've been thinking of getting it done."

"Done?"

"Via biomod. For the wedding. Apparently I've got just enough time to sort it out before everything shuts down for the parties! And I'm sure you *want me looking my best.*"

"Whoa! I know you're on good money working for the Quad-Gal External Revenue—we *all know* you tax inspectors are loaded, minted, greased—but NanoTek are fucking *extortionate* love."

"Franco!"

"Sorry." Sheepish. Mel didn't approve of swearing.

"I *know* it's a lot of cash. But… well, it's something I always wanted, it's all the rage now, and it just seems *the right time.* After all, you only get married once. Ha ha ha."

"Yeah. Once. Ha. Ha."

"I never fancied going under the scalpel of a surgeon before, but now this biomod technology has come of age, it's as safe as safe can be!"

"That's a line from the TV ad."

"So? Everybody's *raving* about it. Biomods are *cool,* now, hun. Hip. Happening. Even Sylvester Slyvester, the famous heart-throb actor, has had his penis done."

"His penis?" Franco raised an eyebrow. He was 10% interested.

"A biomod size *reduction*. Said he owed it to the ladies. Said they shouldn't have to suffer so much pain during pleasure." Melanie swooned, eyes fluttering.

Franco shivered. "No bollocks. Well, I'd rather go under the knife than take a biomod. Personally speaking."

"Would you? *Really?*" Mel was staring at him. Watching him in that way that freaked him out just a little. *Monitoring* him. *Reading* him like a book. Shit. Trust him to get an intelligent girlfriend. Why couldn't she be dumb as a doughnut?

"Listen love, I don't believe those NanoTek boys know what they're doing. Letting millions of bloody little robotic buggers run around inside your veinstreams. Urgh." He shivered. "It's unnatural. Alien. *Freakish*."

"They're called *nanobots*. They're harmless!"

"Harmless? Hah! How can something that rearranges your molecular structure from the inside out be classified harmless?"

"You are such a backward heathen, Franco Haggis! Nanobots help people," said Mel. "All the hospitals use them now. Our Jenny's cousin's boyfriend's mum's stepfather had a new *heart* built for him—inside his body—by the nanobots... by an injection of biomods! It was a pioneering operation! Everything was perfect! Newer than new, the adverts say. Grown or grafted from your own DNA. And now, NanoTek are filtering it down to smaller stuff!"

"Yeah, I heard."

NanoTek's rise to power had been incredible. An awesome stampede across the world known as The City... a thundering onslaught on the Empire of Finance... a left uppercut against the chin of every Global Corporation which had existed before it.

NanoTek was single-handedly responsible for all major advancements in biomods. Nano-technology. This technology consisted of the creation of tiny robots—nanobots—able to operate at a molecular level within the human or alien body, and capable of following simple instructions to devastating effect. But the magic of NanoTek, the major deciding factor which had catapulted this fledgling technology company above the now festering remains of its competition—thus turning NanoTek into an almost immediate Quad-Gal Major Player—had been the simple premise of *user-friendliness*.

NanoTek biomods were user-friendly; they came with a small colourful plastic console (with a massive variety of clip-on fascias and downloadable polyphonic tunes). The console was a user interface, its intention that of making the application of biomods a *breeze*. Easy-peasy lemon squeezy. It was so damned easy that even kids could use it... despite it being—technically—illegal for anybody under the age of 13 to swallow a biomod capsule, except in medical emergencies, or with a note from parents.

Biomod pads became a fashion accessory. A pad equated to wealth; for only the wealthy could use biological upgrades on a regular basis (although a huge array of dazzling and dazzlingly crippling finance packages were available for the discerning "bodder"). Cars were bought on credit; houses via a mortgage—why not a spectrum of easy-to-manage finance packages for the development and enhancement of that decrepit human shell the average soul inhabits?

"It's too expensive," said Franco, finally.

Mel smiled. "Well, I heard about this guy. This guy who can get the *pirated stuff*." She whispered *pirated stuff* as if somebody close-by might be listening.

"No, no and triple no," said Franco. "That's even worse. At least when you let the NanoTek butchers maul with your genetics you've got some legal come back and you can sue their arses. If you buy an illegal one—shit Melanie, I thought you were more intelligent than this? What legal comeback have you got against a guy on a street corner?"

"At least the illegal ones are *cheap*."

"Nothing in this world is cheap," said Franco sourly.

"I just wanted to improve myself. For our wedding! For you!"

"You're perfect."

"No I'm *not*."

"I think it's a bad idea."

"We-*eell,* you got your *tooth done!*"

"You bloody arranged that!" shouted Franco. "I was quite happy being gappy! God, can't you see? As long as the world is full of vain people then NanoTek and other vanity butchers will always grow and expand and end up ruling the damn world!" He calmed himself. "Look. Look. I'm sorry. I just… I saw the mess some of those early biomods made of people. It was horrific. Genetic experiments gone wrong. An explosion in a morgue. Something hideous from a horror flick."

"That was *decades* ago, Franco. Keep up! NanoTek have advanced since then. There are all sorts of safety precautions *built in*. I saw a programme about it. The other night."

"Well, the bastards tried to cover up their early mistakes," snarled Franco. "If it hadn't been for BBC Quad-Gal exposing them on that TV documentary programme…"

"All water under the bridge," said Mel. She smiled. "They're safe to use now. Proven. It said so in Cosmospolitan."

Franco held up his hands. "OK. OK. If *you* say so."

"Good." She snuggled up to him. Nuzzled him. Nibbled his neck. "Glad we got that sorted."

Franco frowned in the gloom. *Got it sorted? Did we? When?*

IF THAT WASN'T bad enough, the beginning of Franco's *real* problems started—as is often the case in life—with his job. Franco worked for a man called Mr Voloshko, Grade 1 Minister, Head Honcho, the Big Guy, Headman, Boss and Dude, the one and only true Guv'nor of The Hammer Syndicate—one of The City's seven major gangland mafia-type ruling families. The Seven Syndicates were huge in terms of man-power, finance, political acumen and military might. They traded and trafficked in everything from people to guns to drugs to money: the basics. They had a finger in every criminal pie on every damned planet across Quad-Gal—which made The City a criminal hub for pretty much everything dodgy that went down.

Franco, being ex-Combat K, ex-military and, technically, being unskilled with anything *other* than guns, bombs and his fists, had tried a variety of jobs. He tried to be a waiter. However, he thumped the customers. He tried working in a shop. However, he thumped the customers. He tried working in a factory making component sliver-boards for robot dogs. However, he thumped the robot dogs. Then thumped his boss. *Then* thumped the customers.

At first, Franco thought the problem was *everybody else*.

Eventually, it dawned on him that the problem lay with *him*. And, with a bit of psycho self-analysis, he realised that—well, Franco and idiots—hell, they just didn't get on. And there were *so many idiots* out there! They had all sorts of jobs! Doctors! Dentists! Teachers! Idiots! Millions of bloody idiots! Everywhere! You'd think it'd be illegal, or something.

And so Franco (through a friend of a friend of a friend, no?), managed to get a job with Mr Konan, which in time led to a job with Mr Voloshko. Franco was big (well, he had big *fists)* and acted dumb and didn't ask too many questions. He kept his mouth shut, usually (and when sober).

His jobs usually comprised standing and scaring people, collecting or delivering packages, watching and tailing other people in or around the casinos which Mr Voloshko—and The Hammer Syndicate as an organisation—operated, or simply driving a variety of people to a variety of places either in Mercedes groundcars or BMW fliers. It was a cushy job. No violence (mostly), no worries. And because nobody treated him as an idiot, nobody got thumped. And so he retained gainful employment, and didn't have to brave the horror of the Unemployment Office. After all, he was barred. For burning it down, that time.

"I'm off, love."

"Can you pick up some fireworks on your way home?"

"Fireworks? What for?"

"The Quantum Carnival starts tonight!"

"Hot damn, so it does. I forgot."

"How could you forget *that*? It's a global phenomenon!"

"Other things on my mind," mumbled Franco. "Such as our impending wedding."

"Of course. How sweet. Can you also pick up some jasmine oil?"

"*Jasmine oil?*"

"I bought some candles to float in our stimulant-bath when we have one of our bubbly wobbly bath moments. Just wanted a little something to spice up the water my cuddly little lovable teddy bear." She came through, wiping her hands on a synth-towel which made a little hissing sound as it sucked water moisture from her skin. She gave him a big cuddly wuddly hug.

"OK, will do, my sweet, my little puff pastry pixie," said Franco with a tight teeth smile, and climbed down the sixty-nine flights of stairs muttering, "*Jasmine oil? Bloody jasmino oilo? What the hell is a squaddie's life coming to when he has to buy bath oil on his way home from work? It's because my life's too great, right? Because my life has become perfect!*"

He needn't have worried.

Things were about to get bad.

CHAPTER TWO
DIRTY DANCING

LONDON. NEWLON. TEKCITY: a wonder of the modern world, a pinnacle of human and machine evolution, a climax of science and electronics and modified building genetics. Constantly re-built, re-structured, re-moulded, it was a colossal empire of steel and alloy and glass, skyscraper upon skyscraper upon skyscraper soaring like a mammoth dark phoenix with raised and threatening wings—poised, static, above the seemingly cowering landscape for a full two kilometres in height. London. NewLon. TekCity: a *showcase* for what contemporary architects and engineers could achieve with a little imagination and a bucketful of cash. A template for progression. A blueprint for the most advanced in all technologies and synthetic materials. London. NewLon. TekCity: Global Sales Centre of NanoTek Corporation.

THE WTS–OR World Technology Show—was held every year at Joker's Hall in NewLon. The world's largest trade event for contemporary advanced technology, the guest speaker on this humid afternoon which promised a violent storm was none other than Dr Oz, the sole owner—and singular share-holder—of NanoTek Corporation.

As Dr Oz took the podium, walking the length of lacquered bubble-stage to grasp the gleaming polished wings of the platinum eagle, a low muttering swept the gathered sixteen thousand tek-people who had congregated to witness this monumental event.

Dr Oz.

Dr Oz was legend; a near-mythical figure who rarely ventured into the public domain and never— not since the early days of NanoTek's fledgling uprising decades earlier—gave public appearances. He did not agree to TV, kube or media interviews, was never photographed by the paparazzi, and most of the people who worked under the banners of the NanoTek technological evolution and *revolution* didn't actually know what he *looked like*.

Dr Oz was a small delicate man, slim of stature and completely bald. His face was neat; an extremity of paleness, oval in shape, well-proportioned, the nose just the right shape, the eyebrows slim and waxed, the eyes brown, flecked with gold and just the right distance apart. He was not particularly handsome, nor ugly—and combined with his modest stature he was what some would call a *grey man*. He could blend with ease into groups of people. Nothing big, nothing clever, a statement of understatement. Dr Oz wore a simple black glass suit over a white shirt with blue silk tie. His shoes were slightly pointed, and polished to a deep sheen that would make any military man proud.

And then Oz smiled, and everyone present witnessed that simple face turn from blandness into one shadowed with—what? Just a hint of menace? Or simple vanity? Oz's teeth were small and pointed. Perfectly pointed—like those of a piranha. They gleamed red. They were carved from rubies.

Dr Oz's gaze swept the gathered thousands and a total silence descended in a swift rippling wave—so that a clichéd pin would have made a cacophony. Oz gesticulated at the people before him, and his glass suit *tinkled*. "Welcome, O my brothers and sisters," came a rich, rolling voice—the voice of an operatic singer, or maybe a classical Shakespearean actor. It was a voice that was a touch misplaced, almost out of synch with the vision of the ordinary man at the platinum podium. And yet, everybody present *knew* that one of the unique factors which set Dr Oz apart was that he did not *do* biomods. He did not use his own vanity mods on his own physical frame. He didn't "dick with his own slime/ you don't need that grime", as back-street slang-dreg children chorused.

"We find ourselves at a cross-roads of a technological highway. We find ourselves at a junction: a junction where one path leads down the road to salvation, to a bright future for the human and alien races of this planet, to a new Eden! And yet, down the second road lies a dark and dormant future, a junk-like representation of Toxic Hell... where technology falters, atrophies, fails, and the human races and alien species wither and regress to the primordial soup from which they first crawled.

"Now, all of us, those gathered here today, and those out on the streets, in the skyscrapers and cubeblocks—all can see these two roads, and they can see them clearly. NanoTek leads the silver-bright path to salvation, and the pirates drag us kicking and screaming down into the Toxic Furnace. What confuses me, friends, is that we are slipping; sliding slowly down the Dark Path... and we *allow* ourselves to be dragged by using the pirated biomods which have so recently flooded the streets, the markets, the Quad-Gal Net—in an uncontrollable tidal wave of abuse and immoral deviation!"

Dr Oz paused to take a sip from a glass of NanoTek SterileW™ self-purifying water. When the glass touched down on the podium, there was a tiny *clink*.

"Now, NanoTek have fashioned a proposal for The City World Council, and I think you will agree it is a very important proposal. At NanoTek we have been working hard on the VitaMod Triple C additives which we propose be added to water supplies of this fine global city. Like fluoride and calcium before it, this additive would enter a general consumer system, a mass-absorbed agent base which would bring *en-masse* benefits for the whole of organic kind! Think about it... Triple C—anti-cholesterol, anti-cancer and anti-canker biomods which would become a regular systemic additive. On a *global* scale! Free to all! Think about it... a world where the majority are protected wholesale from diseases and conditions which have afflicted mankind and alien species from the earliest of times. Think about it... the right choice for all our mingled species! The right choice in order to promote the longevity of so many citizens of this noble city!"

Dr Oz took a step back.

Applause and cheers thundered around Joker's Hall.

Dr Oz took a small bow. "Questions?"

"Sir, *Daily Fuzz.* Shouldn't we have a choice in this matter? A choice whether we consume NanoTek's biomod technology in our very water supply?"

"A choice? Whether you live or die?" Oz laughed. A cold laugh. "What sensible choice is that, boy? Another question?"

"Dr Oz, *The Weekly Vulva.* I'm not being funny, but what's in it for the aliens? Your biomod is aimed 80/20 at the human and human derived species. There's a lot of other flesh out there! You seem to be pandering to the largest common denominator and practically ignoring the alien minorities!"

Dr Oz smiled. "The Triple C additives would be a simple pioneer of the technology. As you know, all biomods are linked to the GreenSource Mainframe and can be subtly tweaked. We have planned stages of tek evolution to integrate *all* species on The City into our upgrade platform. Yes, for now the bio-mods are predominantly a *human* upgrade; but that is our base technology platform from which to *extend*. My friends, NanoTek strives for the improvement of *all species*."

"Sir? *War Machine Inc*. You mention all biomods being linked to the GreenSource Mainframe. Does that framework include pirated biomods? Do you have tags on the mods which have been cracked and smashed and pumped?"

There came an embarrassed silence which swept Joker's Hall like a tsunami. Dr Oz smiled, but his face was gargoyle stone. A non-animate. "Not—as such," he said, finally. "But we have people working on it. Now, one final question." He faced a sea of hands from the gathered media peeps. He pointed.

"Mr Blue. *The Shag Town Times*. Is it true that NanoTek have secured contracts with Quad-Gal Sec5 Military? And are developing new technology such as processor types, AI scripting and molecular weapon enhancements which will eventually filter down to civilian level?"

Dr Oz peered at the man in the sea before him. He smiled. "That is a rumour circulated by *you journalists*. NanoTek do not, and I repeat, *do not* have dealings with the military. We are a simple and ethical organisation interested in the extension and technologically enhanced longevity of the unified organic species of Quad-Galaxy. Now, I thank you for your questions. I bid you good night."

Another round of applause. A few cheers. That was *good*.

Dr Oz turned to walk from the stage. As he turned, a man entered from behind silver curtains and made his way swiftly across the platform. The man's walk turned into a run, another two men appearing from opposite sides as knives appeared glinting in fists and the three large men rushed the defenceless figure of Dr Oz who seemed— suddenly—alone and out of reach of his security.

Dr Oz's pace faltered. He glanced right.

The first man to appear, a huge and heavily mus- cled mercenary with a brutal scarred face and hooked nose, lunged with his blade; Oz side- stepped with clinical precision, the knife slashing past his heart as he slammed out, hand snapping down to break the assassin's arm at the elbow. The attacker screamed, his limb flopping and dangling useless as Oz whirled, fast, to meet the other assas- sins. With cries they leapt and Oz ducked a blow, ramming outstretched fingers into one attacker's eyeball which flicked free of an anger-skewered face to dangle, jerking useless and spasmodically against his cheek like a slug on a string. Oz flicked himself left, rolling, scooping up the long slender dagger from the first assassin and slamming it into the third man's heart. Blood fountained, soaking the man's long curly dark hair, and as he fell, ten secu- rity men charged the stage and grabbed all three assassins, dragging their bleeding, screaming and, ultimately (after several silenced bullets) *limp* fig- ures from the stage.

Dr Oz turned, mechanically, then moved back to the podium. He wiped his blood stained hands on a cloth, straightened his tie, lifted his head and swept the hushed audience once more with a gold-flecked gaze. He smiled, a slow easy smile. "I do apologise for this intrusion. As you must acknowledge, when you are in a position such as I, threats from extremist minority groups can sometimes embarrass a situation. I hope this has not ruined what is to be a superb World Technology Show, and beg that you enjoy yourselves in what has traditionally become known as the opening event leading to The Quantum Carnival." As if on cue, a billion fireworks detonated outside. Through the liquid-glass ceiling, the sky fizzled with colours and explosions. "Thank you. Goodnight."

Oz bowed once more, and travelled the long lacquered stage on a palanquin of cheers, screams and tumultuous applause. Not only was he the most powerful and wealthy sole owner of the Quad-Gal's most prestigious and technologically advanced technology company, but he could *kick ass* as well.

SLICK GUINNESS WAS tall, powerful and *fit*. His broad shoulders tapered to a narrow waist. He was the epitome of the natural athlete. He wore his gold-blond hair to his shoulders, a delicate fan of subtle hues, an olfactory treat of hinted-at perfumery. Slick's face was oval, strong-jawed, perfectly symmetrical and unblemished in tone. His nose was straight, a natural addendum to the precision of Slick's masculine, yet rugged beauty. When he smiled he lit up like a pinball machine on a $10,000 payout.

Slick was a beautiful man. A *heroic* man. It could be imagined they would carve statues of him in the future. Here was a man who oozed pheromones and had crowds of women flocking to catch a hint of that deep musical voice, to share a moment of *connection* with those profoundly philosophical turquoise eyes, to share an intimate moment of humour from his deeply witty repertoire. And to ride him senseless.

However.

Here, and now, Slick was in a *world* of pain.

He sat, naked, strapped to an alloy chair, his Adonis features crushed, his fabulously rich pelt matted with blood, his lightly tanned skin crusted with saliva, snot and vomit. Six large men stood around him in a tight semi-circle, panting and wearing shawls of sweat under the glow of the simple energy saving bulb on its coil of elasticised cable dangling limp and solitary from a high vaulted ceiling veiled in shadow.

Slick coughed, leaning to one side and hawking up phlegm mixed with swirling crimson. He coughed again, then rocked back on the chair and blinked, trying to clear his pounding, thundering head. His ears were ringing from heavy blows. His vision had become worryingly blurred.

"Enough," he managed to spit, and manoeuvred a broken sliver of tooth to his lips. He pushed it out with his tongue, but no longer had saliva enough to eject the piece of bone shrapnel. "What..." he coughed again, then forced himself to breathe deeply, carefully, smoothly. "What... have I done? What... do you want?"

Five of the grim men took several steps back, fading into shadows, as one was foregrounded. Slick's vision cleared and he deciphered a stocky bull of a man wearing a frighteningly expensive New-Italian suit and with close-cropped black hair. His eyes were intelligent, his face lined with the early contours of middle-age. His tan denoted wealth, for only in the Upper Reaches could a tan be freely obtained—either via sunshine, or with biomod vanity upgrades. Both routes to the pleasures of the sun were incredibly *expensive*...

Whereas *here*—

Here? Slick gazed around the damp cellar, the moss-riddled stones, the greasy, blood-slick floor with its history of violence and vermin. He breathed deep the sickly sweet stink of putrefying dead rats and piss, and an eternity of human detritus.

Here could only be one place.

The Dregs. Down-side. Low-Tek. Sub-City SubC. The hunting playground for criminals, the diseased, the whores, the biomod pirates and hackers and B-grade pushers. The final resting place of all the Non-Credits. The home of the Poor.

Slick breathed deep. Mentally, he retraced his steps...

A beautiful woman, swaying atop him, writhing and groaning as nipples brushed his questing lips and he thrust harder and harder, buried himself deep and drowned in her ambrosia nectar depths. His tapered fingers slid down her writhing sweat-streaked flanks as—shit, as she was *smashed* aside with a helve and men swarmed the room and blows came raining, crashing down; pounding Slick Guinness into an immediate mine-field of glittering unconsciousness...

Slick's eyes opened. He did not recognise the men, but by his stance the lead 'gangster'—for that was all he could be—expected recognition. *Craved it?* Slick smiled. That meant he was small fry striving to jump from the little pond to the ocean. The only *real* problem was that the ocean was a *very* dangerous place.

Man, when I get out of here I'm gonna *seriously* fuck you up, ran Slick's internal dialogue. He composed himself and lifted his bloodied face to meet the man's iron gaze. Despite Slick's pain, and his beating, he made no sound of weakness. He focused with turquoise eyes.

"I'll start again." Slick spoke, voice slow and measured. "I'll start at the beginning. Do you know who I am?"

The bull-necked gangster nodded, once, a curt movement. Then he smiled, and it was the smile that did it. Messed with Slick's brain. It was the smile of the knowledgeable. The accepted. The Big.

"My name," came the bass rumble, "is Mr Konan." He paused, a long and arrogant pause.

"Never heard of you." Slick was satisfied to witness a twitch at the corner of Konan's mouth.

"I am the avatar of Mr Voloshko."

Slick's heart skipped a beat. He felt the temperature of his skin plummet. His balls shrivelled to pips. Slowly, he allowed a breath to exhale on a jet of apprehension. He took a tentative lick at bark-smeared lips.

"OK. Voloshko I *have* heard of. Can you tell me what I've done wrong?" Shit. Now it made sense. Slick became finally and terminally aware he was in some pit of depravity for a crime he did not comprehend. He was in what had become notoriously nicknamed Voloshko Cellars. *Torture* Cellars. Down south in The Dregs.

He chuckled—but the chuckle fell from his *soul*. This was serious. This was *bad shit*.

Mr Konan sighed, stepping closer. His boot squeaked in a puddle of blood Slick's flesh had deposited when his head connected with stone. "Up there, Mr Guinness, up above us elevates the perfect world, glass and alloy, gleaming, an immaculate rejection. The Tek-World. The City. It is a pinnacle of human and alien evolution, an entity of organic construction over natural chaos, a mish-mash blend of organics and genetics ruled by money, ruled by the biomods, ruled by NanoTek. But down here, Mr Guinness…"

He frowned, heavy brows darkening. The henchmen approached from the shadows; they carried helves and steel truncheons. One—the most intimidating, in all his slim ferret-faced efficiency—carried a steel-panelled briefcase. Somehow, this was even more terrifying than any obvious weapon.

"Down here, NanoTek doesn't give a shit what The Seven Syndicates do. We rule, Mr Guinness. The Dregs, the Sub-City Catacombs. They're ours. Our Land. Our World. Our *Dominion*."

Slick nodded, heart racing. He agreed. I agree, he thought, *I agree!* Just let me out of here…

You did not mess with The Syndicates.

You *could* not mess with The Syndicates.

The Seven Syndicates ruled. And Mr Voloshko was Grade 1 Minister of The Hammer Syndicate.

The Man in Command. 1ic. *Hell. Slick was in trouble!*

Konan produced a photograph on a thin piece of photo-plastic. He held it before Slick's face. It was set to [cycle]. Slick watched the images impassively as blood drained ever further from the already undead flesh of his face.

The statics depicted Slick linking arms with a beautiful woman, and they were both laughing// they ate in a restaurant, Slick complaining about the soup, the woman touching his arm in an intimate fashion// walking to a plush hotel, arm in arm// taunting one another with fresh strawberries in the lift // Slick moaning with need, eyes fixed on her face, lips wet and gleaming// the woman dancing provocatively as she undressed, face lit with an open, primal animal lust// squirming naked together, bodies writhing on sweat-streaked sheets// the woman's face, a parody of pain, mouth open, tongue firm against teeth in a deep sex-need hypnotism of repeated moaning shuddering gun-shot multiple-orgasm// [end].

Slick's eyes stared at nothing. Then, his gaze sidled carefully to the left.

Mr Konan was shaking his head.

"Who is she?" ventured Slick, finally, when he realised Konan did not have the charity to break the silence.

"Melissa. She is Mr Voloshko's *wife*."

"But he's..."

Slick bit his tongue. He *was* going to say *"he's ninety-six years old!"* but, obviously, being a Grade 1 Minister to one of the largest biomod piracy

Syndicates in the Quad-Gal meant Voloshko had access to a billion human upgrades. Age simply wasn't the handicap it had been. And who needed Viagra when a simple biomod could fashion a wealthy customer with a permanent penis upgrade? Length, girth, strength and endurance? All yours for a few dollars more.

"You abused the wrong woman, Slick. And, despite Mr Voloshko's recent… *interest* in more esoteric forms of passion, of enjoyment, of lust, you tampered with Mr Voloshko's *bitch*."

Slick Guinness considered this. And the truth of the situation finally penetrated his ego like syrup working patiently into a sponge. He was dead meat. This Chamber was not a child's playground… he wouldn't get a lolly and a contented ride home in the back of the car. No. This was a Torture Pit. A Death Hole.

Slick wasn't going to leave this room alive. He met Konan's dark and steady gaze. "My one consolation," Slick sighed, trying to buy himself more time, trying to put off the inevitability of fate, his face a picture of hang-dog sorrow, "is that Melissa Voloshko *enjoyed herself*. She howled like a whore. Fucked like a dog. And she tasted real sweet, my bully-boy friend. Like sticky toffee. Like syrup and cream. A personification of *orgasm*."

Behind the chair, Slick was rubbing at his thumb. There came a tiny *click*.

"Yeah?" Konan was shocked. He relaxed into a smile, a lizard smile showing nasty, coffee-stained teeth. "OK then, tough guy. Mr Voloshko wants to offer you a gift. A present. A valuable and hard-earned *lesson."* He pulled free a sleek alloy shaft and flicked free the tapered razor at its peak. It gleamed... a slice of steel, a splinter of raw and promised *pain.* Konan twisted the razor knife slowly from side to side, allowing light from the yellow bulb to play along the finesse of the glittering, sterile implement. Tiny rainbows danced like fish.

"He offers you a lesson you will never forget."

Konan glided forward. His eyes gleamed. Like glass.

Slick's heart seemed to stop beating as he watched that terrible blade descend...

FRANCO PARKED THE Mercedes groundcar and with a *whine* the seat deposited him on the pavement. Immediately he was amidst the heaving throng, and he pushed through the crowd of humans and proxers, and the occasional SIM, and up steep steps of a nameless, faceless steel-fronted hundred storey block. He eased through revolving doors which reflected the snake of flesh on the pavements, nodded at the two black-suited men bearing machine guns and dark glasses, hair slicked back, stance professional, and ambled down the corridor to the gate.

Once scanned and through, Franco stepped into the canteen. Keg and Tag were already there, Keg's huge figure squeezed into a small plastic seat, each man bearing a steaming coffee before him. Keg was an ex-gunrunner, a huge man with a tattooed forehead, tattooed forearms, and a body that was as wide as it was tall. He was a giant of a man, spiky black hair glistening untidily, stubble smeared like grease across a square-jaw you could break paving slabs on. His small eyes glittered in permanent challenge, and he watched Franco advance.

Tag, in contrast, was slim and tall, his face thin and pointed, his eyes narrow, almost oriental. Clean shaven, he wore heavy gold rings on each finger and a swathe of gold chains around his neck. Tag had risen the Hard Way from the Dregs; he was a rough and tough streetboy, a king of backstabbing, a master of the mashed beer glass.

"All right, lads?" smiled Franco easily, slipping into a chair opposite. His eyes took in the three heavy D5 shotguns gleaming on the table surface. Keg and Tag were staring at him fixedly.

"We've got a job come in," said Tag. His lips gleamed. He seemed... too eager.

"Oh yeah?" Franco was cool, but his mind was racing. Up until now the jobs had been... regular. Non-violent. That was good. That was fine. But here were two thugs with gleaming new guns and a need to make a name for themselves; they were out to impress, out to climb the ladder of a hard to recognise internal ranking system. And that always meant bad shit. It usually meant somebody had to die.

Franco sighed. Why couldn't things just carry on as normal?

Why did it always have to get so complicated?

I fear change, he thought morosely.

Tag leant closer. Coffee steam made his brow glisten. "Word's come down from Konan. We've got a pick-up. We've got ourselves our first *execution*."

Keg grinned. Most of his teeth were black. It was an ugly sight. "We've finally got the chance to prove ourselves, Franco. We're being given some responsibility! No more shitty little errands—we're dancing with the big boys!" He slid a shotgun across the laminated worktop to Franco. "It's time to start the killing."

Franco stared at the gun. His face screwed up. Carefully, he said, "I'm not really sure I like this idea, boys."

"Hey!" snapped Tag. "You're either with us... or against us." His eyes glittered. And his face said it all. There was no mercy there, no humanity. Not even for a fellow *roughboy*. Tag was out for pro-motion. Recognition. Acceleration. Notoriety. *Respect, man.* And woe betide anybody who got in his way.

Franco picked up the shotgun. It was a heavy, solid piece of engineering. It took sixty collapsible shells, and had a 25gig bandwidth mark. Auto-aiming. Dig-ital trigger. *Expensive.* Designer *killware*. Franco *hated* that. Murder *and* fashion combined. Dolce and Gabbana for the diseased. Versace for the vulgar. Prada for the perverse. Sick sick *sick*.

He watched Tag and Keg climb to their feet and roll shoulders to ease tension. They were nervous, Franco could smell it. They were hairline triggers waiting to be caressed. Somebody was going to suf-fer in order to banish their insecurities.

"You coming, little guy? Or do we tell Konan and Voloshko you lost your balls? *Maybe* they were never there in the first place. *Maybe* all those tall stories of life in a combat squad were just bullshit."

Keg sniggered.

Franco stood, cracked open the D5 shotgun, checked the payload, and slammed the weapon shut. Keg jumped. His nerves were shot to shit. Franco stared levelly at his two accomplices in mediocrity; his face was suddenly a gargoyle carved from tek-stone.

His voice, when he spoke, was dangerously quiet. "Well then, let's go kill somebody," he said.

SLICK GUINNESS OOZED pain. Not just from the beating—although it had rattled his cage and brought home the prolonged mental torture of a good physical pounding—but also from the tiny, emergency Nail_blade which even now was cutting the hardened titanium_nylon cable which secured his hands to the chair. It was also making a terrible mess of his own flesh; but that would be a problem for another day... if he survived.

The Nail_blade was a device reserved for military special forces. It nestled in a PTFE organic sheath within a finger or thumb nail, and could be teased free for a variety of useful purposes: opening tins of B&S, slicing the detonation cords on HighJ bombs, or severing titanium_nylon bindings when tied to a chair suffering serious physical torture and maiming.

"He offers a lesson you will never forget." Konan approached, razor knife outstretched, as Slick felt his own bindings part and he leapt forward, right fist slamming Konan's forehead, left taking the blade neatly from the gangster's flapping grip, right boot lifting to connect with Konan's chin in a side-kick that sent the man sprawling upwards and backwards to land with a grunt of shock. Slick dropped to a crouch by Konan's side and rammed the blade savagely into the man's heaving chest.

It slid free easily as the other, heavy-set men started with shock at this spurt of high-speed violence from a man who had—nanoseconds earlier—been constrained by chair and wire. Blood pumped and eased from the narrow wound in Konan's chest, and blood bubbled, staining the corners of the gangster's twitching mouth.

Slick uncoiled slowly and stood, arms by his sides, the bloodied knife and his bloodied fist— immobile. He smiled then, smiled at the five large bulky men who had just spent the best part of thirty minutes beating the shit from him.

"You *bastards*," he snarled.

One gangster went for his inside pocket—a gun— and the action triggered Slick into a dance of death. He cannoned forward, the knife slashing left then right in twin splattered showers of horizontal blood; he ducked a clumsy steroid punch, dropped to one knee and rammed the dagger into the gangster's groin, leaving it embedded as the huge muscle man screamed and screamed and screamed and Slick took his matt black pistol: a German-built Heckler & Koch P227 taking 9mm Parabellum cartridges in an 80 round micro-clip. The gun lifted, and two shots rang out, dropping two men in twin fountains of purple, spewing gore.

Slick stared at the six dead men. Then, with a smile, realised Mr Konan was breathing, pink froth bubbling at his lips. Slick moved to kneel by the gangster's side and grinned down through his own inflicted punishment.

"Surprised, fucker?"

"Mr Voloshko will... have... you... killed for this."

"You don't say? Well, he wasn't successful today, was he? I'd keep my empty threats to myself, if I was you."

"How... how... how did—"

"Bit of a stutter you have there, my friend. Want to get that seen to. Some form of speech therapy might be in order. I believe it's extremely effective nowadays. But then, oh yes, I forgot... you have an urgent appointment. With Death."

Slick lifted the 9mm P227. His eyes shone.

"No," said Mr Konan. "Please, don't shoot..."

Slick shrugged, sighed, and pulled the trigger, spreading Konan's head across the cellar floor.

Slick stripped one of the dead gangsters, pulling on the flapping trousers and ridiculously large shirt. The boots, at least, were a good fit and allowed him to walk. Taking a long overcoat, he filled the pockets with guns, knives and several magazines of ammunition.

More noise rattled from the top of the stone steps, and Slick moved to the side of the doorway. Two men entered, heavyset and carrying Ruger P-85 pistols. They stared down, dumbly, at their fallen comrades as Slick put two bullets in two skulls, stole their 9mm ammunition, and took the stairs three at a time to pause in a crouch at the top, breathing cold night air and gazing up at distant stars. Several starships, Titan Class III freighters, sat in orbit, grey and foreboding in their hugeness. Slick glanced down the street. Several cars with blackened windows stood nearby, engines idling, but Slick couldn't make out if they had occupants. He glanced left and right. *Where the hell am I?* he thought—then *smelt* the sluggish, toxic waters of the heavily polluted Kruger River. West Dregside—deep down beyond and below the *money*.

Slick eased himself along a wall, then darted right down a narrow tunnel between the concrete and alloy slab bases of titanic skyscrapers which towered, gleaming and alloy and bright with wealth and honour and love and menace.

The Dregs—scattered across The City in patches and tunnels and spidering labyrinths, like a gnawing cancer, hiding, mostly, beneath the ground and the wealth. They were the scattered No-Go areas of the poor, the diseased, the low-lifes and the No-Creds. Above, the world was under ICE—but there were no such extravagant luxuries down *here*.

Slick moved carefully for a while and paused, turning. He'd heard something.

The street was deserted.

He turned back—into the butt of a D5 shotgun. Slick went down. He went down hard. Franco stared without emotion at the bloodied, battered features, then lowered his weapon and gestured to Keg and Tag, who lifted Slick and dumped him in the boot of the Mercedes groundcar.

"Well?" said Franco.

"Well what?"

"Check him for *weapons,* dickhead."

"Yeah. Sorry." They stripped Slick of guns and knives and bullets. Then Tag held up Slick's limp hand. "Hey, Franco, what do you make of this?"

Franco stared at the tiny, serrated knife protruding from Slick's thumbnail.

Franco shrugged. "No idea. Get in the car."

They slammed shut the boot. And with a scream of exhaust headed into darkness.

THE JUMPER DOCKSIDE was pretty much deserted on the outskirts of a contaminated TOX1C AREA; a disused, abandoned, derelict relic of fifteen, maybe twenty years ago when Jumpers would shuttle cargo to and from huge Class I freighters in orbit around The City, leapfrogging into the sky like giant metal insects. Now the transport was redundant thanks to SPIRAL PORT technology, and the land had not yet been reclaimed for building due to heavy localised radiation. It made a brilliant dumping ground for bodies.

Franco sat on the end of a steel pier, legs dangling over the edge, staring out across the Blood River. The waters ran thick, red, heavy with natural mineral deposits from deep beneath the rock—minerals which also ate flesh and bone to nothing within an hour. A natural, toxic solution for the murdered. A final baptism for the damned.

In the distance, The City's dawn haze filled the horizon and the world with a muggy smog. Background noise, a constant buzzing and hissing, a low-level cacophony of trillions at work and play, imbued the distant ambient air with background level annoyance.

Franco cradled the D5 and spat into the river.

Dumb bastards, he thought, eyes narrowing as he remembered the short journey. Tag and Keg—ever the wannabe gangstas—poking him and cajoling him. Tell us another story! Tell us what it's like to go to war! Tell us what it's like to shoot a SIM in the face! Franco shook his head, wondering if he'd lost his raw edge, his killer instinct. Maybe he'd just got old, lost his fire, lost his *need* to fight and hurt and kill. The very qualities which had earned him a place in Combat K. Or maybe it was Mel; the new love of a good woman? A gradual, dawning feeling that one day, and one day soon, he would like to settle down. Yeah, get married, but there was more. Children. Harmony. Equilibrium. OK, Franco knew that to many, marriage and kids were outdated concepts, scoffed at by a street-savvy society. Kids? Ha! More trouble than they're worth. Instead, why not buy a poodle and save your money for interstellar exploration and adrenaline adventures on Ket?

But Franco? He shivered. He *longed* for simplicity. He longed for calm. And peace. An end to violence. An end to madness. "Shit." Franco wondered if he was going soft. Developing a cheese brain.

"Kick him. Not like that, like this." Tag kicked the unconscious body on the ground, and Keg cackled like a kid with a new toy. Slick's unconscious form jiggled under the heavy pounding from the two men's boots.

"Enough!" roared Franco, heaving himself to his feet and standing, back to the Blood River, dawn sunlight glimmering behind him and placing him neatly in silhouette.

Tag and Keg stopped, staring at Franco with open mouths.

"What's the problem?" scowled Tag suddenly. "It's only a bit of fun. Right? We're going to kill him anyway."

"Yeah," snorted Keg. "Bastard's going in the river. He'll be mush in an hour."

Tag gestured with his D5. "There's something wrong with you, old timer. You're not with the programme anymore, are you? Go on, admit it! You've lost your *fucking* bottle!"

Franco sighed. Then smiled wearily, nodding. Both Tag and Keg were squinting, the rising sun dazzling their eyes.

"Our instruction is to kill the man. Not torture him."

"And what's wrong with a bit of torture?" snarled Tag. "We should be allowed a bit of fun! It's playtime!"

Franco shook his head. "No. No. No. You've got it all wrong, lads. You see, I believe in this old concept—it's called *honour*. You don't kick a man when he's down. You always promote a fair fight. Mate, I just *hate* gangs, ten on one, unfair odds, it makes me fucking *sick*. And… you defend the weak against the strong, good against evil. It's a simple concept— some might say old-fashioned, an outmoded idea, but it's something I believe in." He took a deep breath. His voice was low, a tame growl. "I believe in basic honour, I believe it's inbuilt. Part of your genetics, you might say. However…"

The shotgun lifted and twin snarls screamed across the steel jetty. Tag was picked up and hurled backwards with incredible force. He slammed the dockside wall, leaving a huge red smear on alloy bricks, and with eyes filled with questions and tears as he scrabbled at his own destroyed chest he slid to the ground and was, eventually, finally, still.

"... if you have bad blood, you have bad blood. And there's no educating some people."

Keg rounded on Franco. He was shaking—with fear, and rage. A bomb awaiting detonation.

"What you doing?" he screamed.

Calm, Franco moved forward and stared down at Slick. "He deserves better than this."

"He's a scumbag!" bellowed Keg, and Franco watched as the man's edge of fear was replaced by anger; like a vessel filling to the brim. "He's a dreg. A lowlife zero-cred nobody. And I'm going to kill him..."

Keg lurched forward.

Franco's shotgun lifted, and Keg stopped.

"I think you were right." Franco's voice was soft. Low. Dangerous. "For a while there, I did lose my balls. Went soft. Lost some of my *fire*. But not in the way you understand it. To you, ten blokes kicking shit out of an unconscious man is... heroic. To me, that's just feeble. Weak, you understand? The mark of the true coward. Gangs." He laughed. "I *spit* on them."

Keg lifted his own shotgun. Ten metres separated the two men. Franco's eyes gleamed.

"I'm going to murder you," breathed Keg, lifting his own D5 with threatening menace.

"You ever been under fire, son?" Franco smiled.

Keg pulled twin triggers, and the shotgun snarled, shells pounding the air and whistling over Franco's shoulder. Franco did not flinch. Did not *blink*.

Franco's shotgun *boomed*, and Keg's head was taken clean off leaving a headless corpse standing, fingers twitching as blood fountained and pitter-pattered onto the steel jetty. First, Keg's gun clattered to the ground. Then his legs folded at the knees, and he hit the docks with a damp slap.

"I have," muttered Franco, "and it ain't a nice feeling. But hey, you get used to it. Right?" He holstered his D5 on his back, bent, and lifted Slick in stocky, powerful arms. He carried the unconscious man to the back seat of the Merc and laid him out.

Slick's eyes opened in puffed slits. He forced a grin through his broken face. "Thanks, man," he croaked.

"Anytime," nodded Franco.

"Why did you do it? Why save me?"

"The Nail_blade. You're Combat K."

"Yeah. Slick Guinness."

"Franco Haggis."

"I've heard of you. You're..." he coughed, and struggled into a seated position. "You're a *legend*."

"Am I?" Franco nodded. "Yeah. I suppose I am."

For the next few minutes Franco checked Slick over. He gave him some adrenalin and vitamin boosters, a drink, and a stab of painkillers from the Merc's first-aid kit. Franco moved to Tag, dragged the man by his boots and tossed him into the Blood River. The body sank instantly. Franco dragged the headless corpse of Keg, tossing this in as well. He found Keg's head, and with a mighty kick sent it sailing out over the blood-red waters.

He returned to Slick carrying spare D5 shotguns and an ammunition pouch. Slick was standing beside the Mercedes groundcar now, breathing deeply, and rolling his neck. Franco tossed him a weapon; which Slick caught in lacerated hands.

"Why did Voloshko want you dead?"

"I shagged his wife."

"Ahh. But… he's about a *hundred*, ain't he?"

"Maybe that's why she needed my sport," said Slick. "Listen. Franco. Really. Thanks. You don't know me, and you've stuck your neck out. I just want to tell you… I'm a good guy. I just hope you don't end up regretting the help you've kindly offered…"

"Nah! It'll be reet," said Franco, beaming. He pulled out a small bottle, removed a white pill, and swallowed it with a wince. "You're Combat K. That's all I need to know. And as for those two dreg chickenheads… they had it coming, mate. Believe me."

Time to move on, thought Franco. Time to take Mel and start a new life. Away from this insanity. Away from this hell. He shook his head, and nodded to himself. Shit. I'm definitely going soft.

Distantly, fireworks fired the sky. They sparkled, exploded in showers. And then—the darkness of the short city night was unzipped and showered by a billion explosions shooting to illuminate the horizon. Crackles, zips and pops echoed and reverberated. Smoke filled the sky in a 360-degree rotation. Franco spun around, eyes taking in the superb extravagance of opulent fiery celebration which seemed to cover the entire *world*.

"And so The Quantum Carnival begins," said Slick. "Man, I'm just glad I'm alive to see it."

Franco nodded. It was like... a sign! A sign that his life had changed, been ripped apart like the night sky before him! And yes, *he* had changed. He no longer wanted to live on The City. No longer wanted to work with violence. And Syndicates. And guns. He twitched. He felt an unerring desire to start gardening.

Inside the Merc, the kube buzzed.

Franco and Slick looked at each other.

It buzzed again; louder, more urgent.

"You going to answer that?" said Slick, voice low.

Franco lifted the kube. "Hello?"

"Franco. This is Mr Voloshko. I don't quite know how to say this, so I'll just say it. Because this was your first kill mission, we were monitoring the event—you know, for future training exercises, your own health and safety, etcetera. However, it would *appear* that you've killed your two work colleagues and teamed up with the man I want dead. Would you say this is a fair appraisal of the situation?"

"Ahh." Franco frowned. His eyebrows wiggled a little. "Yeah. I suppose that sums it up nice."

"You have one last chance to redeem yourself, Francis. Kill Mr Guinness. Now."

Franco considered this. "Fuck you?" he suggested.

"As you will." Voloshko's voice was crushed ice. The kube went dead.

"What now?" said Slick; he looked quickly around, eyes reflecting the coloured crackle of fireworks.

"Ahh relax," said Franco, waving his hand. "Voloshko's just some tired old ponce who can't please his wife. All we need to do is…"

An engine roared, loud even above the sounds of a billion firecrackers eating the sky, and over the nearby dockside buildings rose an Apache F52 Gunship, gleaming in its urban camouflage cloak, rotors whining and twin minigun eyes spinning with the distinct clicking sounds of a building fury.

Then, there came a different roar, and a missile detached and Franco and Slick sprinted with arms piston-pumping, to dive, landing and sliding on their bellies in the dirt as the missile slammed over them, connected with the Merc groundcar and pounded it upwards into oblivion. A fireball exploded with a cackle, and purple smoke rolled into the sky blocking out the carnival fireworks.

Slick glanced at Franco. "You were saying?"

"Run for it?" suggested Franco.

"Sounds good to me."

They sprinted through the smoke, Franco's sandals crunching Merc debris as miniguns roared and bullets chased them spitting *puffs* of concretealloy at their heels. The two men slammed between towering warehouses lining the old Jumper Wharf.

Behind, the Apache bellowed like a caged beast.

Its nose dipped…

And slammed towards them, guns thundering.

CHAPTER 3
NANOTEK

KNUCKLES, SPACESHIP-THIEF, drugsmoke entrepreneur, wheeler and dealer and ducker and diver,
stood on a Sub-C street corner, leaning nonchalant-
ly against a concrete support stained with streamers
of rancid tox. Before him, the traffic was a solid
block of noise and mass and fumes. People writhed
down the pavements like flesh noodles. Noise filled
his head. Fumes and scents from a thousand stalls
filled his nose. The mass of people, of traffic, of
sheer exhilar8ting bustle filled his soul like a heady
perfume and he smiled, narrow sharp eyes focusing
on the slab of people in order to locate his next
sting...

There. Tourist. Blue hair. Mini-skirt. High glitter
boots. Briefcase. What gave her away was the large
map she carried, occasionally stopping and

gawping aimlessly around as if the very sky itself would proffer directions.

Knuckles pushed off from the wall and approached slowly, from behind; a predator. The briefcase was a slim white affair with anti-snatch cabling. As Knuckles approached, he directed the micro-laser and watched a tiny plume of smoke start to writhe from the cable; then, with perfect choreography, he leapt and caught the bag as the woman screeched in pain from sudden laser burn— and took off through the crowd, weaving and jigging, bouncing and dodging and followed by screams and wails and he knew he was good and gone, and escaped.

"Wicked!"

Five minutes later he'd rifled the contents. A thousand gem-dollars and five Good-Cred cards sat snug in his pants. *Christiane Solomonsson,* read the name on the cards. Knuckles shrugged, and discarded papers to litter the dark alley around his red gloss boots. And then, from the bottom of the case, in his groping hand he brought free a... a vial of *biomods*. He could see they had ZERO registration. They were unmarked. Untagged. Unconnected to GreenSource. The biomods could not be traced...

Knuckles, spaceship-thief, drugsmoke entrepreneur, wheeler and dealer and ducker and diver, rough and tough, wiser than a prophet, harder than hardcore, bitter and decadent and cynical before his time, grinned with his ten-year old face. Gr8, he thought. Th1s could be th3 start of a *n3w* car33r! O:-)

* * *

BLACK AND WHITE NEWS CLIP
The City's Premier News Delivery Service
[available in: print, TV, vid, mail, dig.bath, ident.implant, comm., kube, glass.wall, ggg, galaxy.net and eyelid transpose— all for a small monthly fee].

News clip GG/06/12/TBX:

It has been reported by the World Bank that NanoTek are losing as much as one third of their business to the illegal biomod industry which has grown over the last three months. In an astonishing press release to technology industry insiders, NanoTek allowed access to documentation highlighting financial losses and subsequent projected acceleration of losses. It would seem pirated biomod use is on the up and up. Dr Sweeney, MD for NanoTek (Old York) stated, "I cannot believe people are using the much inferior and highly dangerous illegal capsules which purport to be biomod technology. Here at NanoTek we follow stringent safety guidelines and our technology processes are the safest in the business. Illegal capsules are the equivalent of having a back-street abortion, or an amputation with a rusty saw. Dangerous, painful, life-threatening, immoral, illegal—and a threat to the safety and economy of our social structure! I would implore people to use only NanoTek branded merchandise." When questioned on the, some would say, extortionate pricing system for legitimate biomods and a therefore subsequent understanding for people of limited financial means turning to the much cheaper hacked versions, Sweeney expounded, "The current pricing structure for biomods reflects R&D and the expensive chassis components needed for manufacture. This technology did not invent itself overnight; as such the pricing of this still ground-breaking technology is high and does include a component of profit. NanoTek is, after all, a business. But as with all business models, as take-up escalates so the scale of production will increase and create a more financially palatable product. However, because of the pirated biomods this is actually moving away from the consumer. In effect, in the long run, with this heinous spate of piracies people are effectively cheating themselves."

News clip: END.

"HE'S STILL OUT there," said Slick. His voice was low and disguised the tremor. Sweat painted a sheen on his beautiful, battered brow. Franco nodded, and crept across the warehouse floor, boots crunching bullet-decimated, cubed glass.

Miniguns screamed and bullets slammed through the windows and walls of the warehouse, pounding the building into submission as Franco dived, sliding over glass and covering his head with his hands. Slick cowered in the corner, clutching a length of chain, and glanced right where ten holes had appeared in the powdered brickwork. He could see a swathe of distant warehouses far below.

The firing stopped, and Franco glanced up. His face was sour. He tilted his head and lifted his hand. In old Combat K infantry sign, he said, *They are using sonic monitors.*

Slick nodded. *You sure you can line him up?*

I'll do my best.

Franco eased himself across the floor, trying to avoid the broken glass until he was against the wall. Several storeys below, he could see warehouses stretching off as far as the eye could see. The rotors of the Apache thumped a sonic concussion as it banked and whined. Franco grimaced. Shit. How had he ended up in this predicament? A hunted man? *Again?*

He locked his D5 shotgun to his back, and checked his Makarov 9mm. A pistol against a thundering war machine? Franco shook his head, then grinned. Hell, he'd had worse odds.

He edged towards the window, careful not to make a sound. Voloshko's men were monitoring for even the tiniest of movements, hunting Franco and Slick like furry rodents in a burrow.

Franco reached the window. Outside, the sky was brightening. Fireworks still crackled through the heavens and The Quantum Carnival was now, officially, in full swing, despite it being the middle of the night, or 'night period' as it had become known.

Again the Apache unleashed a payload of bullets. Franco cowered as metal ate through bricks and spun on trails of red dust through the air. Suddenly, Franco lunged into the space where the window had been—and the Apache squatted, hovering, guns smoking and rotors flickering in a blur. The machine nudged forward and Franco started to fire, Makarov thumping his palm as bullets struck the cockpit and, behind the bullet-proof glass, the pilot smiled. Bullets zipped and whined, ricocheting off the machine. The pilot shrugged—as if to say, "Good try mate. Better luck next time."

"Now," hissed Franco.

As the Apache's pilot took up tension on the mini-gun trigger, so Slick appeared at a second window, heavy chain links in his hands, and watched the pilot's head snap right to focus on him. He hurled the coil of chain through smashed panels of glass. The chain sailed, uncurling like a huge metal snake, and looped over the Apache's short, stubby wing and left-hand minigun. In reflex the pilot jerked on his control stick, and the Apache's engines whined as it lifted, banking. The chain slid across the floor of the old warehouse chamber, Slick nimbly leaping over its fast-slithering length... which went suddenly taut.

Franco and Slick looked at one another.

There came a groan, deep and reverberating, and both men glanced to where they'd fastened the chain to a huge machine of old, rusting iron, bigger than a house, a squat ugly behemoth whose function was lost in time and degradation. It would take more than ten Apaches to lift the hulk. Slick's face broke into a nasty grimace.

Franco leaned out of the window, watched the Apache struggling, engines screaming now. Fire erupted from exhausts. The chain ground a groove against brickwork, and as Slick appeared at a second window both men watched the war machine sway like a kite on a line, then drop, crashing into the wall, runners folding like buckled toffee, spinning rotors connecting with stone and brick and collapsing in on themselves with a grinding smashing howling cacophony of destructing metal. The Apache compressed. Folded. There was a click of detonation and the machine was consumed in a raging fireball as Franco and Slick skipped back, a wall of fire slamming along the vertical flanks of the building.

Fire roared, and metal screeched.

"Merry Quantum Carnival Day," said Franco.

"You're a devious bastard."

"They don't call me Franco 'Devious Bugger' Haggis for nothing, y'know. Come on. Let's get out of here—before Voloshko sends some more of his goons."

"Amen to that."

PEOPLE WERE CHEERING in the streets. Dancing and singing and drinking. Franco and Slick hurried along, glancing regularly behind. They entered an alleyway, littered with burnt-out firework stubs. They moved cautiously, still checking their backtrail, Slick nursing his wounded and battered shell.

The two ex-Combat K men stopped outside a Dreg bar named The Fist Fuck. Noise rattled thin glass windows and light and smoke spilled from various bullet holes. Nice place, thought Franco as he sidled warily towards a huge 2400cc Aprilia TSV—a race bike which had been crashed and had its fairings stripped to reveal the brutality of the acid_alloy-cooled engine beneath. A high set of handlebars had been welded to the top yoke and fat bald tyres sat gleaming, oil-drenched, beneath quad sports cans. Franco fingered the wiring, looking around with his Makarov drawn and ready, then deftly made several cuts and twists. Being a bike already abused by the caress of thieves, the triple immobilisers had been bypassed—probably a professional job from one of the outfitters which specialised in stealing rich Tek-side equipment, circumventing advanced protection electronics and then selling it on in the Dregs. Bikes were the favourite mode of transport down in the Dregs due to the physically narrow and restrictive nature of Sub-C life. There were many localities and districts which could not be reached by car. This made Franco's current position healthier.

Franco fired the motor, revved the bike hard with a scream of raw engine ferocity, threw his leg over the hard sports seat and grinned as Slick jumped on the back. Dropping the clutch he left a line of rubber against concrete and zipped away into the hazy smog-gloom of Dregside early morning. Behind, a group of men spilled from the pub shouting abuse; Franco banked left between two narrow walls of concrete and wheelied over a long metal ramp, jumping with a roar of disengaged engine to land in a long narrow courtyard beneath towering cube-scrapers.

Franco fed more fuel into the Aprilia's hungry engine, and the bike bellowed as it stretched its legs and thundered down narrow alleyways, exhaust *booms* echoing from wall to wall to wall in a curious song of metal synchronicity. Revellers and whores leapt hurriedly out of his way and Franco watched with cool detached amusement as stocky branded men and gangsters with swirling overcoats danced for him at the right-hand blip of this howling weapon of mass corruption.

Left and right he cannoned, the Aprilia's needle dancing up to over 180 kph—an insane speed for the Dregs. He sped past crash-barriers at head height, protecting roads blockaded from the Dregs and carrying thick streams of city traffic beyond; under arched bridges the Aprilia spun, Franco's knee dusting the dirt as the Aprilia's powerful lights cut slices from the gloom pie.

"Franco, slow down!" shouted Slick.

"What?"

"Slow down!"

"I can't hear you!"

After twenty minutes of roaring insanity, Franco finally decided he'd put enough distance between the two men and impending murder. He slowed the growling motor and rolled to a halt, tyres crunching and sliding a little on gravel. People were dancing in the street, drinking and gyrating. They ignored the two men.

Franco killed the engine and kicked the bike onto its side-stand where it clicked as if in annoyance at being switched off; and the two men moved down towards the boarded doors of an old metro station, passing between poor ravers and winos getting jiggy into the jig of The Quantum Carnival. Smoke and steam billowed from the murky depths of the disused station, and three figures moved forward with battered scratched Uzis when they saw the approach—but Slick smiled and the men returned grim smiles through dirt-matted beards.

"You know them?" hissed Franco, twitchy, hand straying to his D5.

"Yeah. They're not bad men. Just your usual Dregside poorlifes."

"You OK?" asked one man, peering hard at Slick's battered face. "You look like you've been through the shit."

"I'll live." Slick took a proffered cigarette from the man. "Which is more than I can say for the other bastards."

Slick dropped the men some old dollars, slid through the doors and led Franco into the ancient disused tunnel network. Inside, even the roar of still exploding fireworks was muffled. He picked his way with care through a maze of corridors, and after an hour of walking emerged through more guarded barriers into TekCity Central. Fluttering Search PopBots came whirling over to the two men, little alloy globes with high trailing flexible antennas, and both Franco and Slick allowed them to give retina scans to check their Credit Rating.

The poor weren't allowed onto NewLon streets.

With tiny *blips* and green LEDs both men were allowed to move on. If they had failed the *test*—been found to have negative Credit Status—then Justice SIMs would have been alerted and intrusion from Sub-C logged. Whilst not breaking the law, it was... *frowned upon*. And people who strayed were persuaded otherwise. Normally with a laser tube.

Franco and Slick stood for a while, watching the insanity of the early morning party. The City had come... *alive.* Humans and aliens, SIMs and Slabs, all danced and sang in the streets, drank and fornicated in the gutters, huge walls of living flesh meandering and joyful and the feeling of celebration crept into them, into their veins and souls and Franco sagged, weariness slamming him.

"You OK?" Slick looked concerned.

"A long night," grinned Franco. "How you holding up?"

Slick, who had been analysing his wounds, shook his head. "Three cracked ribs, a broken finger, and torn ligaments in my groin and ankle. Plus the usual cuts and scrapes. But it could have been worse." He stared hard into Franco's eyes. Took the little man by his shoulders and smiled. "I owe you one, mate."

"Ach, think nothing of it."

"I still have contacts. Combat K contacts. You ever need a favour, you look me up."

Franco nodded. Sighed. "I'll keep it in mind, Slick. Now, you look after yourself."

"Be careful, Franco."

"Voloshko doesn't even know where I live. I faked my application. I've never trusted the Seven Syndicates. Bastards, to a man."

"Even so."

Franco watched Slick disappear into the throng. Music blatted around him, an irritant. And, despite Franco's usual party-animal nature, his love of sex and drugs and rock 'n roll, all he wanted now, amazingly, was a hot mug of cocoa, a kiss from Mel, and his comfy bed.

Franco trudged through the cheering, singing crowds, towards his rest, and only when he was on the fifty-eighth step leading to his apartment did he curse.

"Hot damn and bloody buggers!" He'd forgotten the fireworks. *And* the jasmine oil.

THE APARTMENT SQUATTED in gloom, black-out curtains killing early-morning light. A strange silence seemed to have enveloped the room, and Franco, remembering his action-packed night, shivered.

What if...

What if Voloshko *had* discovered where he lived?

What if Voloshko had sent killers, or kidnappers, for Mel?

What if they'd rumbled Franco, and linked him to the jewel heist of a few years previous? Five of the Seven Syndicates had money in on that deal... which meant Franco had *now* made enemies of six of The City's toughest criminal underworld organisations.

Makarov in hand, his weariness evaporating, he called out in a wavering warble. "Mel? *Mel?*"

"In here."

Franco scowled, but his racing heart calmed a little. He holstered his weapon, locked the door carefully behind him, and picked his way across the rubble of his apartment.

Franco peered into the bedroom. "You OK, honey?"

"Mmm. Mmm." Mel turned, still half-asleep, hair tousled. "Hiya. You're back late."

"Busy day at the office," grinned Franco.

"Hope you didn't cause any trouble?"

Picturing the headless body of Keg, and the exploding inferno of the Apache F52, Franco shrugged powerful shoulders. "Nah. Nothing little old Franco couldn't handle. After all, they don't call me Franco 'Trouble Free' Haggis for nothing!"

Mel frowned. "Franco…"

"Yeah yeah, I know. They don't call me Franco 'Trouble Free' Haggis at all. But hey…"

"Did you get the jasmine oil?"

"Sorry. Slipped my mind. I'll pick it up in the morning." He yawned. "Listen. You go back to sleep, I'm gonna grab a few beers and wind down before I hit the AM pillow."

"Don't stay up too late. You *know* we're going to the Tek Central Carnival Opening with Jim and Sandra tomorrow afternoon. I don't want you yawning all the way through the presentations."

"I know. I *know.*"

Franco grabbed himself a ten-pack of Wife-Beater and slumped on the settee. Despite there being truth in what he'd told Mel, there was also another reason.

He cracked open a beer. Placed his D5 shotgun across his knees. And waited to see if he'd been followed.

Unlikely. But always possible,

Outside, millions thronged the streets, singing and dancing and drinking and drugging. The thump of distant music became a mantra. Screams and laughter the chorus. And the Carnival Song dropped a gear, wound itself up, and *trillions* really started to get jiggy.

* * *

FRANCO OPENED HIS eyes, slowly. Confusion was his master. Rat-spit his saliva. Tom-tom drums his skull. "Shit," was all he managed. Then his wandering blurred vision fell on the ten empty tinnies of Wife-Beater. Stupid. *Stupid*. And into the thunder of his skull intruded a white-hiss cackle of vacant TV broadcast.

"Ugh. What channel was I watching?" Most ran 24 hours. That meant it was a pirate channel. He reddened. That usually meant cartoon alien porn.

Franco sat up, his bones creaking, empty tins rattling from his body. His D5 shotgun hit the carpet with a *thump*. His feet were encased in his large fluffy comedy rabbit slippers. His tired eyes tried to focus on the clock. 11.17 AM. Hot damn, he'd overslept!

Franco climbed wearily to his feet, clutched his head in his hands, and wrenched his skull sideways. There was a sickening crack of crunching neck tendons. "Ahh," said Franco. "Ahh. Ahh. That feels better." Outside, the siren of an emergency vehicle wailed across The City.

But... he thought.

But but but.

But *why* was he still sleeping at 11.17 AM?

Why hadn't Mel woken him?

Why was Mel still slumbering in bed? That wasn't like Mel. Mel was a stickler for rising early bright and shine. Even after a *crate* of DOG Town red.

A million horrific scenarios galloped across his imagination. Franco sprinted into the bedroom, saw scattered, tousled sheets. But Mel was gone.

"Melanie?" he bellowed, panic giving his voice a bestial urgency.

No answer.

"MELANIE?" he screamed.

"I'm… in the bathroom." Her voice was weak, thick, muffled by the hefty bathroom door. Her tone held a wavering, ethereal quality. It sounded *strange*.

"Are you OK?"

"I just feel a bit… queasy."

"OK. I'll make you a coffee."

"That'd be great, Franco."

Franco staggered into the kitchen, scratching at his testicles. He switched on the CoffeeChef™ *(Coffee coffee you wanna nother coffee?*—although you probably had to be there to appreciate the joke). He lounged against the worktop, breathing deeply, and trying to work out any way in which Voloshko could find him. The bastard would certainly make *some* kind of effort. After all, Franco had made the head of a global Syndicate look like a dick.

From the bathroom, there came a *thud*.

Franco turned and stared at the door, languishing innocently at the end of the long corridor.

"Mel?" he called.

No reply.

"You OK in there?"

"Franco. I don't want you to get angry."

Franco sighed. That was bad, that was. Any dialogue which began *Franco I don't want you to get angry* meant he was, nine times out of ten, pretty much damn guaranteed to get angry. Taking care to keep his voice calm amidst his pounding headache and general feeling of unwell-being, he said, voice steady, and measured, "Why would I be getting angry, my love?"

"I just want you to promise me you won't get angry."

"How can I promise something, when I don't know what the something is, that might make me angry? That's unfair, that is. You're taking advantage of my good nature and prior ignorance to a situation I know nothing about."

"Franco!" she squawked.

"OK. OK. I promise I won't get angry."

"Good."

"So then? What's wrong?"

"Now, you promise, don't you?" Her voice had gone all wavery again.

"Yes," sighed Franco. Behind him, the CoffeeChef™ pinged. Franco poured two cups of steaming, frothing Heaven, and stood, a cup in each hand, facing the bathroom door.

"OK. I bought a…"

Here we go, thought Franco. A settee. A TV. Some curtains. A new dishwasher. For a tax inspector, Mel was awesomely lax when it came to inspecting the tax.

"… a biomod upgrade."

There was a crash as the coffee cup hit the floor. Coffee surged across the tiles. "You did *what?*" shouted Franco. "How the hell do you think we can afford that? We're getting married in a few days! They're bloody extortionate! We've already talked about this, and…"

"You promised, Franco."

His teeth snapped shut. He felt his new denture twinge.

"Anyway," continued Mel's wavering, "I didn't get a *proper* NanoTek one because they're too expensive. My friend Emily took me to the market and we met this lovely lad, a friend of hers called Knuckles, who sold me a cut-down pirated hacked model for a tenth of the price. Cheap as chips. A bargain!"

"That's even *worse*," groaned Franco, rubbing at his thumping cranium. What next? A head transplant? "Listen." He breathed deep, exaggerated breaths designed to halt impending palpitation. "At least, now, cheer me up here girl, and tell me you haven't taken them, it? Yet."

He waited. There came another, louder, thump. And a *strange* stretching sound.

Franco's head snapped left. There, on the worktop, was a tiny vial. On it, neat lettering read **BIOMOD 0.2mg**. He picked it up. Stared at it. Sniffed it. Frowned at it. Was it empty? What was he looking for? It looked empty. Shit and holy damn buggery, it bloody damn well looked bloody damn well empty! Franco spied the leaflet. His eyes raked the NanoTek instructions, expensive text on extensive vellum, the usual extravagant NanoTek way:

Patient Information Leaflet
BIOMOD CAPSULES 0.2 mg
©NanoTek Corporation

**KEEP ALL BIOMODS OUT OF THE
REACH OF CHILDREN.**

**REMEMBER: Only a doctor or Biomod
Sales Representative can prescribe this biomod medicine/ human/alien upgrade. It
should never be given to anyone except the
person it has been prescribed for. It may
harm them in a grotesque and horrific way.**

Franco stared at that last bit. *It may harm them in a grotesque and horrific way.* His scowl was crooked on his face, like a painting hanging not-quite-right on the wall. "Melanie?" he shouted again, still holding the single coffee cup. "Did you take the goddamned damn bastard bio-mod, or what?"

There came a roar so deep and monstrous and terrifying it shook the windows in the frames of the apartment. The bathroom door flexed and wobbled like a tree in a twister. On the floor below, and in the surrounding apartments, burglar alarms started to shrill, their high-pitched squeals piercing the relative silence.

Franco clutched his already throbbing head.

He glanced down at the coffee.

Glanced back up at the bathroom door.

And watched, mouth agape, as a fist the size of a plate smashed a hole through the heavy anti-intruder panelling and flexed long claws that belonged nowhere near a human hand.

The second coffee cup smashed on the tiles, sending another stream of dark brown soaking into Franco's comedy rabbit slippers. His head lifted. Oh my God, he thought. There's a monster in there! In there with Mel!

He sprinted for the living room, rolled across the coffee table like a true action hero, grabbed his D5 shotgun and pumped it viciously. He stampeded back into the corridor, and was just in time to see two of the long, armoured hands wrench the door from its quivering frame and launch it down the corridor. With a yelp Franco ducked, and the door hummed over his head and became half-buried in the wall above the front door. It quivered, like a large rectangular arrow.

The creature stepped into the corridor, stooping crookedly. It was eight feet tall.

Franco gawped, shotgun forgotten. The creature was slim and wiry, skin a dark mottled brown, spotted, corrugated, and slick with grease. The torso was a mockery of a human female body, with long, quivering, dangling breasts reaching almost to the monster's waist, and with nipples like plums oozing grey pus. The neck was long, curved, the head small and round and hairless, the lower jaw staggered out from a horrific face in a staccato jump, the nose two pin-pricks, the ears flaps of puckering anal flesh against more pus-oozing orifices. The neck crackled with plates of armour as the monster moved its head, rapping its skull against the ceiling. Fingers flexed like a newborn babe's. Franco's eyes dropped... to the long legs, and the pink quivering vagina, slick with gore and grey slime. It was distended, wobbling, and nearly made Franco throw up. It was probably the worst thing he'd ever seen in his entire life. A nightmare, for a man so fond of the female sexual organ.

"Don't worry!" bellowed Franco, suddenly. "I'm coming for you, Mel! I'm coming to save you!" Bravely, he charged at the monster, shotgun booming. Shells screamed down the short corridor and the monster moved with inhuman speed, twisting, charging at Franco as it swatted shells like flies. Franco skidded, thumped against the creature, felt his shotgun taken from him as he tottered backwards a few steps, like an old man on acid. He gulped. He stared up at the oiled face inches from his own, witnessed nose-slits sprouting thick black spider hairs, felt rancid breath coil across him like a disease-ridden oil-mist. The monster tossed the weapon to the ground in disgust, reached forward, and slapped Franco a stinging blow with the back of its hand.

Franco flew, hit the wall, and rolled into a heap with all wind knocked from him. The creature, in huge loping strides, was upon him and he screamed, screamed as that distended jaw hammered towards him and fetid breath invaded him abused him raped him and those long claws curled around his body, lifted him into the air and the room whirled around him, his familiar settee and TV and PlayStation 1000 turning into a blur as he was spun and whirled and thrown heavily to the floor. "Get the shotgun!" screamed Franco, to Mel in the bathroom. "Get the gun! Save yourself! I'll try and stall it!"

The abomination lowered its ugly pus-riddled face towards Franco. He heard the creak of its limbs, watched as those eyes moved towards his face and saliva and gunk dripped on him. He shivered, quivered in pure terror as he wondered how he would die... hey, he'd seen the movies, right? Jaws in the brain? Fist through the heart? Tear out his spleen and beat him with it?

The monster's jaws worked spasmodically.

Franco closed his eyes and covered his head with his arms.

"Aiiiiiiiie!" he screamed.

And...

Nothing. Nothing happened.

Franco opened one beady eye. Yep. The monster was still there. Staring at him. Breathing on him. Why didn't it just kill him monster him massacre him chew him break him crunch him hell, *shit,* just get it done and over with and let him die in a moment of pure-fire agony then enjoy an eternity of peaceful rest in a heaven of buxom half-naked vixen wenches.

"Do it, you sick bastard!" he screamed.

The creature, the beast, the monster... its jaws worked even harder. Saliva pooled in long strings that tickled Franco's face. And, well—it seemed to be trying to—

"Speak? Are you trying to speak?" snapped Franco in astonishment. Where the hell was Mel with that D5? If he could just stall this savage grotesque beast for a few moments, give Mel time to get to the gun, well, she was a plucky lass and she'd know what to do...

Maybe she'd save them yet!

"Ranco," said the beast.

"Eh?"

"Ranco. Is me. El."

Franco's mouth opened some more. He paused, unsure of what to say. Then he shuffled backwards, so his back rested against the settee. He stared hard and with a fearsome scowl at the abomination before him.

"Mel?"

"I ove ou Ranco." There were tears in the monster's eyes.

"Well—fuck me," said Franco.

Mel lurched towards him, and he held up a hand. "Whoa there girl, I didn't mean this exact minute. I mean, you've gone through a few changes since I last saw you, lass."

The creature formerly known as Mel let out a massive roar which blasted curtains from the rail, overturned the TV and blew-dry droplets of sweat from Franco's distended ginger beard.

There came a hiatus in time.

Franco scratched his chin.

"So, I'm thinking, maybe something went wrong with that there biomod, then?"

Mel roared again, and Franco scrunched his face up against the onslaught of acidic fetid breath. It was like rotting corpses. Dead dogs. Open sewage.

"OK, OK, don't get your knickers in a twist. I told you, didn't I, I said don't go buying pirated biomods because those bloody hackers and crackers and pirates don't know what they're damn well doing. They've buggered up the biomod, and now they've buggered up my bloody fiancée."

He stared hard at Mel.

She was not a pretty sight.

Franco sighed. "Bugger," he said.

Suddenly, there came a series of cracking sounds and Mel convulsed, her limbs twisting at impossible angles. Talons grew from her toes and her back arched, her neck distending yet further. She started to rampage around the room, smashing at the walls and furniture, a whirlwind of violence with Franco sat, cocooned in terror, at the core. Her claws cut lines through the brickwork. Her head smashed lights from the ceiling. Mel, it would seem, was pissed.

"Calm down, calm down," shouted Franco, flapping both his hands, palms outwards.

Mel screeched, her head punching through the ceiling and shaking, scattering dust and floorboards around the room.

Franco scrabbled to his feet, and ran through to the bedroom. He threw open his wardrobe and stared at the tumble of bombs and guns, knives and Kevlar-titanium vests. In a scramble he pulled out his old military kit in a spill, rummaging madly through the hardcore stash until he found...

There. "Baby."

A TitaniumIII leash, with a spiked silver collar dangling chunky from one end. Against the leather handle there was a small red button which delivered a jolt of electric shock through the collar. *Nice*.

Franco used to have a dog, a half canine, half alien blend of psychopathic muscle-riddled fighting machine. He loved that dog, Franco did, until it one day tried to chew his head off, and he'd donated the maniac bastard to the Urban Force to be used in tracking down alien *gugunga* smugglers. The TitaniumIII leash was good for 950,000 lbs of pressure. You could use it to moor Star Cruisers.

Franco returned, warily, to the living quarters. Everything was quiet. He peered myopically around the battered, splintered doorframe. Dust floated in layers. Mel hunkered at the centre of the room, head touching the carpet, eyelids drooping.

"There's a good girl."

Mel growled.

"Come on, don't be like that."

Mel growled again. Franco shook his head in confusion. Just what the hell *had* happened to her? A simple biomod injection gone wrong? Or something more... sinister?

He crept forward, the leash and spiked collar in one hand, dangling in what he hoped was a non-threatening manner. "Would you like a little treat? Of course you would, who's a good girl, come on, who's a good girl then." Franco held out his hand, wiggling his fingers and edging closer in a curious sideways crab-motion he sometimes employed.

Mel stretched forward with her long neck, and tentatively sniffed his hand.

Neatly, Franco looped the collar over her neck and compressed the mechanism. There came a click. Mel's eyes met Franco's, and he swallowed, hard.

"Rastard," she said.

Franco shrugged. "Look, I'm sorry love. Can't have you tear-arsing around the place and showing me up in front of the neighbours, now, can I? Not until we get you sorted." He stood up, puffed out his chest, and glanced around the devastation that was his destroyed apartment. He gave a deep and meaningful sigh.

What next?

A doctor. That was it. A doctor would know what to do! A doctor could *help them* and turn his girlfriend back into... well, a girl, for starters. Yes. A good old fashioned quack!

Franco picked up the kube. It was dead. Franco frowned.

Outside, distantly, a siren wailed. It was joined by another, and another. Franco moved to the window, peered outside, but could see nothing and he started to chew his lip. Behind him, Mel smouldered. Her stench made Franco's nose itch.

"Strange," he muttered, although what could be more strange than a girlfriend turning into an eight-foot mutated mangled abomination of a monster Franco couldn't quite vocalise.

He frowned. Something was missing. Out there. Down there. In the real world.

He frowned, even harder.

What the hell *was it?*

What was wrong? Out of place? Out of step?

And then it struck him. Like an anvil.

There were no *people*. No humans, no slabs, no proxers, no huggas, no SIMs. The street outside was *deserted*. More than deserted. It was a *ghost town*.

Another siren wailed, lonely and forlorn.

Franco watched an ambulance dash down the street, take a corner on two wheels, and disappear, stroboscopic lights flickering blue from the polished alloy and glass of cubescrapers.

Odd, he thought. It's the first full day of The Quantum Carnival. The streets should be thronged with a million party people. The City should be *crawling*—as it had only a few short hours ago. So… where had everybody gone?

He turned back to Mel. She was asleep, snoring, her small round head gleaming with grey and brown pus. Franco's eyes ranged over the body and limbs of his girlfriend, his fiancée, his woman, his true-love. The woman he wanted as wife. The chick he'd decided to finally settle down with and pump out a machine gun volley of bambinos.

Now, however, she was transmogrified into a personification of disgust.

"I mean," Franco muttered to himself, "you've been with a few beasts in your time… but this takes the biscuit barrel!" He shook his head. Sighed. Hell. What a day, he thought. What a *week*.

But he needn't have worried.

Things were about to get a whole lot worse.

FRANCO CREPT DOWN the sixty-nine flights of stairs, Mel following behind on the TitaniumIII leash. Her claws raked grooves in the concrete, but Franco pretended not to notice.

"What we'll do," he said, "is find you a good doctor. He'll be able to sort this out. No problem. I promise, sweetie."

"Grwwll," said Mel, and blinked back faecal-matter tears.

The descent seemed to take an eternity, and Franco reached the hall and peered around. It was curiously quiet. *Where is everybody? How can they have simply… vanished? Am I in a dream? A nightmare?* He glanced behind himself, stared at Mel, and suddenly wished he was.

He stepped onto the street. Skyscrapers soared above him. Cubescrapers hunkered and squatted further down the street, in a variety of architectural shapes and blobs. A wind blew cool air, disturbing several papers which gusted, soaring across the deserted metalled roadway and pavements, hissing along on a platter of disturbed dust.

Franco padded along the pavement. He stopped. Checked behind him. The D5 shotgun in his hands wavered. He shivered, as foreboding crawled up and down his spine.

"This just ain't right." His voice boomed, crashed, echoed loud and brash amongst the deserted towering blocks. He gazed up, looking for faces in the millions of windows all around.

He could see nobody.

"Focus. Doctor."

He padded on, Mel behind him, her claws clacking the pavement like an obedient hound. Occasionally, Franco glanced back at his fiancée, all eight-feet of muscled rangy monstrosity. He shivered in apprehension. Gods, what would happen if he couldn't get her changed back? Imagine the *food* bill.

The local doctor's was only a couple of blocks away, and as Franco turned a corner he stopped. There was a corpse, in the road. It had no head. Franco glanced about, and felt the hairs on his arms and neck prickle. He pumped the D5 and moved to the centre of the road, approaching the headless corpse with apprehension. Blood streamers led off across the street, swimming with a few lumps of vegetable soup gristle.

Franco's eyes narrowed. "Not good," he muttered, spinning in a slow wide circle, D5 primed as he eyed the many, many narrow alleys, dark doorways, perfect places where an enemy could hide and ambush unwary Francos.

He stopped. Heard a slurp. He blinked. "No," he said. Turning, he stared hard at where Mel had her disjointed muzzle buried in the corpse's open neck cavity. "Urgh! Gerroff! You dirty *bitch!*" He whacked Mel across the head with the butt of his shotgun, and she pulled free her muzzle and stared up at him with wounded eyes. As if to say, *What did you do that for?*

Franco held up a finger, his eyes wide. "No! No eating corpses! Bad girl! *Dirty* girl."

Mel whined, and a long brown tongue like a slug slurped blood and chunks from her tightly stretched mottled lips.

"Come on. Follow me."

Again they moved, Franco on a hairline trigger, his tension building with each and every footstep. There! He thought he saw a shadow move in a doorway. And there! He was sure he saw the flash of a pale white face. Franco accelerated, little legs pumping, until he reached the block where his doctor's surgery nestled. He stopped by the door, and glanced up and down the street. Distantly, he could see something and he squinted. It looked like... a pile of bodies? Franco shuddered. Prioritise, he thought. Sort Mel out. Get her back to normal. *Then* worry about the apparent disappearance of The City's entire population.

He moved to the door, shaded his eyes and peered inside. There seemed to be signs of a struggle. A smear of blood led to the lift. Franco frowned, and behind him Mel rattled the chain which tugged against his hand—like a dog straining against its leash. "Down girl," he said, without any hint of comedy.

He hit the kube's buzzer. It buzzed.

After a long pause, so long Franco was about to turn and walk away, a wavering voice said, "Hel... hello?"

"Hi," said Franco. "This is Franco Haggis. I've come to see Doctor Gentle. He's my doctor, he is."

There came a long, considered pause. Strange rustling and grunting noises came over the kube.

"What did you say your name was?"

"Franco Haggis."

"Are you one of them?"

"One of who?"

"What do you want?"

"I want to see Doctor Gentle."

"He's dead."

"*What?* How?"

"One of the *things* bit off his arm."

"The things?"

The kube went dead. Franco buzzed it again.

"Yes?" snapped the voice.

"Can I see *another* doctor, then?"

"What's wrong?"

"It's my girlfriend. She's..." Franco's brain worked fast. "... ill," he said. "Nasty virus. Laid her low. Made her... a bit odd."

Above, ten storeys above, a window opened. A head peered out.

Franco stepped back, staring up at the face.

"Is that *her?* Hell, man, you weren't bloody joking when you said she was a bit odd! She's had a biomod, hasn't she? Changed into one of the *things.*"

Franco shrugged. "What things? What're you talking about?"

"What the hell have you been *doing,* you lunatic?" said the head from the window. "Everybody went *crazy.* People—those people still normal—are saying it's because of the biomods. The nanobots have mutated people! Lots of people. Millions of people! It was on the news, until they took down Broadcast Central. Now all the TVs are dead."

"Let me in," said Franco.

"Oh no. You might be infected."

"With what?"

"The biomods!" hissed the head. "Haven't you been listening to a word I said?"

"Wait. Wait." Franco held up his hand. "Look at my girl here. Mel, she's called. She's like a little lamb. A little puppy." Mel growled. Franco kicked her. "She wouldn't do no harm to nobody. All I want is to be let in, we'll get a doctor to see her, sort her out, get her back to normal, job's a good 'un." Franco beamed. It seemed quite logical to him.

"There are no doctors *left,*" said the disembodied head. "They were all vain! They all took biomods! So they all... changed."

Franco put his hands on his hips. "Now listen here," he said. "This just sounds like a load of horseradish bullshit to me. Are you sure you're not drugged up from the partying? This hot damn bloody bollocks of a situation is all bloody ridiculous, so it is."

"Shit, they're coming back!"

Another head appeared. A woman. She looked worn out, bedraggled, even from ten storeys below. "Oh *no!*" she groaned, her voice low and bubbling with terror. "That's where they've been!"

"Where?" said the first head.

"For weapons!" hissed the woman.

Distantly, they heard the rattle of a machine gun. And an explosion, which *boomed*, a muffled detonation. Franco's ears pricked up. That was a G7 Frag Grenade. Military. His head tilted to one side. He frowned. A G7 shouldn't be used in urban developments.

"You'd better go!" snapped the woman, looking down at Franco with haunted eyes. "They'll rip you apart, eat your liver, tear out your spine! We've seen them. We've watched them!"

"Why don't you just let me in?" said Franco, persistent as a terrier, through gritted teeth.

The window slammed shut, and Franco heard the click of a high-tensile lock. He buzzed the buzzer, again, then rattled the doors. Taking a step back, he levelled the D5 and a *boom* rocked the street. The lock held. "Damn and buggery." He turned to Mel, but Mel's long neck was stretched out, her small round head focused on something further down the street. Her distended jaw worked noiselessly. Saliva pooled in long streamers, like thick tobacco drool, to connect her with greasy umbilicals to the road.

"What is it, love?"

"Grwlll."

And they came, stampeding down the road, hundreds, *thousands* of distorted, grotesque, twisted, transmogrified figures, monsters, beasts, abominations, flesh hanging from faces, eyes dead in disjointed skulls, many with missing limbs or bearing huge jagged wounds; they grunted and moaned and screamed and chomped, teeth gnashing; they stomped in a dark grey pus-oozing swarm, a tidal wave of rotting flesh preceded by a *stench*...

"They're..."

Franco paled.

"They're...!"

Franco's eyes went saucer-wide.

"They're...!!"

He turned, and with Mel on the leash, sprinted for his life, arms pumping as the fast-moving surge of deformed, twisted, ragged creatures swept after him, the stench of putrefaction and decay washing over Franco and making him gag, vomit splashing down his shirt even as he ran with all his might, Mel galloping alongside him on her chain, her head down, talons crashing the road...

Groans filled the air, a terrible moaning, wailing sound of agony and despair.

"They're *zombies!*" screamed Franco in terror. "Bloody *zombies!*"

He turned, stumbling for a moment, and they were almost on him. Hands clawed at him, raking his flesh and trying to find a grip, trying to put out his eyes and pull him down to the ground. And they moved... *fast*. Dangerously fast.

Franco slammed a right hook. Kicked a zombie in the crotch. Punched another, cracking its six-inch long grey-pus nose. The D5 *boomed*. A zombie's head was blasted clean from his tattered ragged disjointed body, but still he came at Franco who was stumbling backwards, Mel at his heels, the swarm before him, ululating. Franco's D5 boomed again, and the monster's legs were blown off at the knees. And still the headless, legless torso crawled after him leaving a slick trail of gore.

Franco stared into a sea of snarling gibbering hanging grey faces, many without ears or eyes, or teeth or hands, some with puke-green flesh, some the brown and black of necrotic leprosy. And he realised, in the blink of an eye, that this diseased and decadent mob carried...

Guns.

They sported shotguns, rifles, sub-machine guns, pistols, and Franco saw the gleam of a grenade. Weapons bristled amongst the decaying, flesh-eating ranks.

"Holy mother of God," whispered Franco.

He turned, and sprinted for his life...

As machine gun bullets slapped his heels.

CHAPTER 4
A KNIGHT AT THE OPERA

THE SOUND OF a 1250cc LC12 titanium lekradite single-cylinder engine cut through the Galhari morning, a high-pitched screech to the backing track of heavy industrial military might. Choppers swam through the distant sky. Infantry K Freighters hung on the horizon.

Keenan slammed the quiet roads on the outskirts of the city, Dekkan Tell. Dekkan Tell was a low-slung scatter of white stone buildings sporting terracotta tiled roofs, orange doors and shutters, and connected by wide paved highways and a pro-liferation of the bright orange Dekka flower which gave the locality its name. Whilst classified a city, it had a modest population which coincided with the solitude of Galhari as a planet on the fringes of the Quad-Gal in general, and made an ideal place for those wishing for a quiet existence. Until now, it would seem.

Head thumping, mind weary, and leaving a trail of dust in his wake, Keenan smashed down twisting roads in a controlled panic. He had to get a message to the Quad-Gal Military. If the junks *were* invading Galhari, Keenan was sure the quiet, peaceful, and easily outnumbered authorities would already have fallen. Keenan, however, being Combat K, had military-grade kit. He could kube for help on military channels...

He pulled from the main highway and roared down a dusty single-track road. Stopping beside his white-walled wooden house, he kicked the bike onto its stand and pulled free his lid. Beneath, his hair was sweat-streaked and he ran a hand through the tangle, then glanced off towards the sea. It glittered turquoise, and he could see boats with brightly coloured sails, bobbing. They seemed crazily at odds with the warfleet hanging ominously from the sky.

Grimly, Keenan ran up the path and steps, boots pounding. As he approached the door he palmed his Techrim 11mm and entered, dumping his lid and jacket on a low-slung leather couch. Keenan searched through his home methodically, Techrim by his cheek, a casual comrade in violence, and only when he'd cleared the final room did his powerful frame relax a little and he placed the Techrim back in its holster.

He moved to his study, with its low TitaniumIV furniture and business-like air. Opening a high cupboard, he dragged free a matt black box which looked distinctly battered, and of very little value. Keenan activated the power cells, and sent a PB—a Panic Burst—to the nearest Quad-Gal Military Sentry Ship.

A red light illuminated. Keenan cursed.

The signal had been blocked.

"Son of a bitch."

What next? Keenan had to get off the planet. If, as he suspected, the junks in massive numbers had performed a surprise invasion, it could be *weeks* before QGM might be alerted.

What do they want on Galhari?

Why invade this peaceful, modest, and modestly armed planet?

Keenan grabbed a pack and stuffed it with a few essential items, growling all the time that Cam, his little Security PopBot, had chosen a fine time to abscond for system upgrades.

Moving to the kitchen, Keenan paused, rubbing at his damaged flank. The bleeding had stopped now thanks to the application of WORM-strips, but the pain still nagged him. Against his better judgement, he grabbed a bottle of Jataxa and a glass, poured himself a generous measure, then stared at the amber liquid, shaking in his hand.

No.

He placed the glass down with a *clack*...

As the cold barrel of a gun nudged the back of his head.

"Where is it?"

The voice had the same kind of high-pitched buzzing the junk made back in the quarry. Keenan cursed himself. How could he have been so stupid? He dropped his pack to the floor.

"Where's what?"

"Don't be smart. The black disk."

"I've no idea what you're talking about."

"Turn around."

The gun pulled back, and Keenan turned. Five junks stood in his home, their bodies encased in black armour, their faces warped and distorted, old, pitted metal, disease personified. Keenan could almost imagine fumes rising from them. Their eyes were narrow, red, blood-filled emotionless discs. They all carried guns. Keenan felt his Techrim dig against his hip. He allowed breath to leave his body like a soft-knifed tyre.

"We witnessed the mess you made of our scouts." The junk tilted its head. To Keenan, it sounded as if the creature struggled to form human speech. "You burned us. You took the SinScript. The SinScript looks like a coin. A disk. But then, you already know this." Its eyes narrowed. "You know what we are... and so you know I want it back. *Need* it back. Or you'll suffer, scourge, like no other human ever suffered."

"OK. OK." Keenan held up his hands. "Listen mate," he laughed weakly, "it's not in the house." He slammed forward, smashing his left forearm against the gun which discharged, bullet whining into the ceiling. Keenan cannoned into the alien, head crashing against the pitted metal face, right hand drawing his Techrim and shooting another junk in the throat. The junk staggered back, blood flowing between scabbed fingers. The others lifted weapons… but to shoot Keenan was to shoot their commander.

Again Keenan smashed his head into the metal face, wrapped his arm under the junk's, locking it in place, and put his Techrim against the creature's skull.

"Tell them to lose the guns, fucker."

The junk shook against him, and Keenan realised it was laughing. He stared into those red eyes, only inches from his own. The stench of the junk was awesome.

Slowly, where his arm locked the alien in an iron grip he felt its flesh slowly melt away and turn and lock into a different limb, forcing his own arm painfully away from its body and almost snapping his bones. Snarling in surprise, Keenan fired his Techrim, kicking himself back away from the creature as blood sprayed from an 11mm gunshot wound and the junk whirled, blood splashing in a horizontal spray, eyes glowing in fury as it leapt at Keenan, bearing him violently to the ground. Both arms slammed Keenan's head with a *boom* and the junk took his Techrim neatly, tossing it, clattering, to one side.

Keenan groaned, blinded by the blow. Old alcohol tasted bad in his mouth. And he realised, with a bitter, nasty kick, that he was a shadow of his former self. A replicant. A dark and spineless ghost.

The junk, atop him, smiled down, tiny triangle metal teeth grinding together. Keenan watched the blood flow stop from the gunshot wound in its head. He swallowed, hard.

"Last chance, Keenan." The junk removed gloves. Its hands were minced flesh, sporting holes and gradual degradation. Keenan could see tendons operating through rotting gaps.

"OK." Keenan breathed heavily. He knew that to tell them would be instant death. He had to buy time. But how? And how did he *kill* these... creatures? Bullets were ineffective.

The junk gestured to his comrade, the one Keenan had shot in the throat. Blood glistened slick on skin and armour. It passed the commander an MPK and the barrel came to rest against Keenan's chin. The junk leaned close. The aroma of toxic flesh invaded Keenan's senses.

"Last time. Where is it?"

"I have a safe store. In the woods."

"For weapons?"

Keenan gave a nod.

"You will take us there."

The junk stood, dragged Keenan to his feet and put the MPK in his back. It pushed him out onto the veranda, towards rough-wood steps which led down to a gravel path. Keenan walked, sunlight dazzling him, the five diseased creatures following close and glancing nervously about. Distantly, more choppers howled. Keenan's nose twitched. He could smell burning. They were burning the city.

"What do you want here?"

"Walk."

"Why invade Galhari? We are a peaceful planet!"

"By the time QGM discover our little party, there will be nothing left to salvage. Now do as you're told, *Combat K* man, and retrieve the disk if you want to live."

"Down here," he said, moving across the sweeping gravel drive which ended at a fence by a small stand of dense rayga woodland. A narrow disused path veered right through the swathe of angular, gnarled trees with sparse orange leaves, and meandered down through the woods to the mouth of the ocean. Keenan climbed over the fence, glanced back. Sweat stung his eyes. Distantly, he could hear the roar of heavy machine guns, muffled, as if by fog. Keenan glanced right. He could see the junks' groundcar parked to one side, a battered all-terrain GWZ with blacked windows and six wheels. The junks followed him over the fence, covering him with automatic weapons. They knew: no man could outrun five machine guns.

Suddenly, Keenan's hackles raised. This didn't feel like him leading the group; it felt like an execution squad, taking him into the woods to die. A coldness descended on his soul. His mouth was barren, heart thundering in his ears.

Think. *Think.*

The group were swallowed by the cool silence of the rayga. Even the distant guns vanished as the packed trees absorbed noise. They strode over springy green moss until Keenan halted, and stooping, took hold of a large iron hoop. With a grunt he heaved and a large section of dulled alloy lifted on smooth hydraulics with a rain of soil. The group stared down at a second alloy panel.

"Open it."

The commander prodded Keenan unnecessarily, and he knelt, keying in a code. The panel slid to one side revealing a steep alloy ramp. Lights flickered into life one by one. A smell of cold air rushed out.

"Wait here," said the commander. He glanced at Keenan, and gave a smile full of nasty metal teeth. "On second thoughts, you go first. It might be booby-trapped."

"You got me there." Keenan stepped onto the ramp, striding down into gloom. The commander followed, and then the four remaining junks. The one with the hole in his throat left a trail of blood droplets sizzling on the moss like a chemical pestilence.

Swiftly, they were swallowed by the pit.

CAM'S HEART SANG with joy. *Going home! I'm going home!* It had been a gruelling month of upgrades under the watchful eye of Gunnery Sergeant Reznor. The training had constituted many different factors; from database uploads, technical and logistical testing, a physical replacement of bandwidth transmitters which was tantamount to torture and digital abuse, and day after day of physical and mental combat tests. Seven of the thirty withdrew after only a few days, much to the jeering of Gunnery Sergeant Reznor. The ruffled, indignant PopBots said they would put in official complaints, to which Reznor snarled, "Go on then, sod off and tick your little fucking boxes." He was obviously no fan of bureaucracy. However, Cam was proud to admit that he made it to the end of

Upgrade Training, along with twelve others, including Private Pyle, the 'maggot'.

Now, as the Shuttle docked and Cam found himself bobbing through immigration where his chip was stamped and he paid his 'entry visa' of ten gemdollars, much to his chagrin, he floated into the relaxation suite of Dekkan Tell's Shuttle Docks and spun, looking for Keenan.

Strange. Keenan had said he would meet Cam.

Unless—the Jataxa had kicked in again.

Annoyed now, but feeling a touch on edge, the small black ball bobbed along and out into the sunshine—as behind, machine guns screamed and a flood of junks swarmed the Shuttle Docks with guns yammering, bullets scything people like wheat and cutting them down in bright showers of blood and flesh cubes.

Cam jumped, shocked. His scanner slammed across the entire planet of Galhari. He saw the invasion force. Gave a digital *gulp*. It was big. Far bigger than a tiny, poorly defended planet like Galhari had a right to demand. And Cam sensed... orbital stacks blocking incoming and outgoing signals of all kinds. The junks had isolated Galhari. Cam had *just* squeezed in before the Big Sleep.

Cam cruised past a stream of black armoured military vehicles, which opened fire on him making him curse and accelerate at a phenomenal rate as bullets *pinged* from his shell. As air rushed by, Cam could smell the familiar aromas of home... mixed with fire, and hot metal, slaughter, and the pervading invading stench of the junks.

Cam approached Keenan's house warily, after again passing convoys of black armoured infantry carriers. He halted, hovering, spinning, lights blinking on his shell. Cam's sensors immediately picked out hot oil. So then... Keenan had been out on the bike? Then he detected cordite and the little Pop-Bot's sensors quickened.

Cam stopped dead. He orientated.

Scanned. Triple scanned.

With all his senses on full-scream, he remembered the words of Gunnery Sergeant Reznor. He had to be strong. Proud. Have courage in the face of adversity... even if that adversity was ten million invading junks...

Cam prepared for Battle.

He slowed his speed and kicked an adrenalin charge up to full. He eased into Keenan's house and there the stench of the *junks* was abominable. A reek so foul if Cam could have puked, he would have done so. He spun slowly through various rooms, audio-detection modules clicking in his metal case. There. *There...*

Cam shot from the house, straight through the wall, and towards the woods and the old stores Keenan kept for emergency situations. As he approached, buzzing with velocity, there came a high pitched shrilling scream and smoke belched from the opening in the forest floor. Suddenly a figure emerged, sprinting; it was aflame, huge billowing tongues of green and yellow leaping from clothing and face and armour. The junk was squealing and keening, sprinted straight at Cam—who settled into a grim spin and punched with vicious violence through the junk's chest, removing its heart with tiny snippers, to emerge from its flaming back holding the pumping, slick grey organ. The junk collapsed, dead and smouldering on the mossy path, and Cam sped to the opening and dropped into the confined chamber...

All was a confusion of flames and thrashing. The junks were attacking one another, trying to find Keenan, trying to *kill* Keenan. Cam scanned, then moved to the bomb screen and floated behind it. In the darkness, in their agony as they burned, the junks seemed almost blind.

"Nice of you to show up," snapped Keenan. His face was streaked with black, and Cam could see the man was struggling to breathe. Cam glanced down at the industrial flamethrower Keenan carried in battered, sliced hands.

"Looks like you didn't need me," said Cam.

"Be a good lad and put them out of their misery. Even junk scum deserve a better end than burning in oblivion."

"I'm not sure about that," said Cam, but emerged from behind the bomb screen and efficiently silenced the remaining junks. Using manipulators, Cam piled the bodies in the corner and watched as Keenan appeared and strode up the ramp, out into the fresh, free air.

He sat in the grass, coughing, then lit a cigarette.

"A little foolish?" suggested Cam.

"I just faced five of the toughest killers I ever encountered. Even a bullet to the head doesn't slow them down. I deserve a little hedonism, my metal friend."

Distantly, out to sea, a heavy engine droned. Dark junk boats sped across the waves, heading for the city docks. Keenan inhaled with shaking fingers, then glanced off through the trees. The sea sparkled.

"You did well," said Cam softly. "What happened?"

"I was out on the bike. Three attacked me, chased me into the quarry. I killed them, and took one of their SinScripts. I read somewhere, years back, that it carries their instructions and can be used to decode what the semi-sentient bastards are up to."

"You still have it?"

"Yes."

"You are right. It carries their instructions. Like a drug, it injects their codes straight to the heart."

"Insane," said Keenan.

"It's how they work," said Cam. "They're like programmable machines. They were on a mission." Cam lifted into the sky. "All ten million of them are on a mission."

Keenan tilted his head. An engine noise out to sea was growing close, at speed. "Shit." He climbed to his feet, checked his Techrim. "You fit to fight after all these upgrades?"

"Aye!" said Cam, "I am a new and improved model! I have been upgraded! I am *now* a GradeA+1 Security Mechanism with advanced SynthAI and a Machine Intelligence Rating (MIR) of 3450. I have integral weapon inserts, a quad-core military database, and Put Down™ War Technology. I'm a pretty damn hot cookie!"

"Well, you might just get the chance to use all that." Keenan's voice was a low growl. He ground his cigarette under his boot. "Look out there."

Through the dense smash of trees they could make out the bulk of a Styx Fast Attack Boat, or S-FAB. It could carry a hundred soldiers, and Keenan and Cam heard the clash of ramp in water as it ground up the shingle. Dark figures moved in the hold.

"Time to move," said Keenan. "We need to get off this planet. Warn Quad-Gal Military. Steinhauer will know what to do."

"Your old General? I thought you hated him."

"Oh yes. But I trust him. Listen, check all local and global transmission stations; see if you can find anything from before the junk lock-down."

"OK boss."

Keenan glanced behind; the Styx was disgorging its payload. He sprinted for the KTM LC12 and climbed on, firing the engine to thump viciously.

The junks came, flooding through the woods, hundreds of lithe, pitted figures in black body armour carrying short sub-machine guns and long Thump Rifles. The seething mass made Keenan blink; like an army of insects they filled his vision and only when the first opened fire, and a hail of automatic gunfire slammed across the clearing, was Keenan kicked into action. He slammed the throttle open, front brake locked, spun the KTM in a tight circle spitting gravel and shot up the track with Cam buzzing close beside him, the tiny PopBot's pacing immaculate. Bullets chased them, and Keenan risked a glance back. The junks had formed a tight phalanx beside his house, halted, and simply stood watching in stoic silence.

"Head left," said Cam. "Away from Dekkan Tell."

Keenan slammed onto the road and was nearly mown down by an armoured truck. Tyres squealing, he veered into a ditch and, standing the bike, powered up a hill and halted. The road to Dekkan Tell was filled with armoured vehicles—SlamTruks, infantry carriers, even some K-16 tanks. All matt black. And all peopled by junks.

"Cam? When you said ten million junks a few minutes ago, was that just an idle, random figure?"

"No. My sensors indicate this is the scale of the invasion force."

"I thought they were extinct," said Keenan, voice lost in awe.

"So did I."

Keenan stared off, shading his eyes. He saw the fires burning through the beautiful city of Dekkan Tell. Distant gunfire echoed, a rolling scourge. Smoke blanketed the underside of the sky like a parasite.

"Galhari has fallen, my friend."

Keenan nodded, lips tight.

Bullets whined overhead. A squad of junks were sprinting up the rocky slope towards Keenan and the burbling bike; again, he revved the vehicle and hammered free, heading down narrow trails into the hills. Behind, more bullets whined, along with the slow and heavy *thwack* of Thump Rifles. Keenan shook his head in disbelief. The bastards. Galhari was a quiet and peaceful planet; it was no threat to *anybody*, and had remained neutral during the Helix War. Galhari sported a tiny, local army, and had no natural wealth or resources of any real worth. Tactically, it spun on the fringes of Quad-Gal and was a technically useless staging post. To all intents and purposes, it really wasn't worth the trouble to invade. So why invade?

"The bastards," he muttered, eyes dark. He was overcome with a need to blast into the city, to kill as many of the invaders as possible. As he sat there, he knew people were dying, screaming with hot metal in their brains and hearts.

"No," said Cam, reading the man. "No."

Keenan nodded, and said nothing. His bitterness was tangible. He rode for an hour, away from Galhari civilisation; out into the bush. Occasionally, Cam picked up resonance from a flyer; but after a while even they vanished. The junks were concentrating on urban areas and military outposts.

Galhari, as a planet, was mostly uninhabited; a barren rolling expanse of mountains and hills, forests and lakes. It was deserted when compared to a heaving metropolis like The City. Quiet. Peaceful. That's why Keenan had chosen it to hide.

Finally, Keenan halted at the foot of a looming mountain, and hid the bike in a circle of rocks, camming it up with branches knife-cut from Splay Ferns. He considered building a fire, but shook his head in the negative. They might have to move again—fast. There was no point drawing attention to themselves.

Cam zipped off to check the local perimeter, and returned after twenty minutes, satisfied, to find Keenan sat on a rock, back straight, Techrim in his fist, face filled with thunder-storm.

"The Galhari government has fallen," said Cam, quietly. "They have issued a statement that all rogue army units should give themselves up. The junks are too formidable. President Taeoto has called for an end to violence. He said there has been enough killing for one day. All Galhari military must surrender arms."

"What, and be slaughtered? These bastards follow no codes of justice or honour." Keenan sighed. "Once the Peace Unification Army get a wind of this, Quad-Gal will rain down hell. You can't invade planets and expect no consequence. What the hell do they want? I thought we lived in a civilised age."

"Civilised?" Cam paused. His lights flickered in what Keenan knew was a smile. "There is no such thing, my friend. Civilisation is a utopia dreamed up by your warped species."

Keenan grunted.

"Anyway, this game is bigger than Galhari, Keenan."

"What do you think they want?"

"I truly have no idea." Cam buzzed into silence, his lights black. He spun closer to Keenan, who rubbed at his weary, blackened face and yawned, exhaustion finally kicking him in the spine.

"Get some sleep," said Cam. "I'll keep scanning, see what I can discover. I'll try to locate and contact

Steinhauer. The sooner QGM know about this debacle the better."

"Can you decode the junk's SinScript?"

"I will apply my considerable talent."

"Wake me if there's trouble."

"You won't need me for that," said Cam.

NIGHT FELL. KEENAN slept fitfully between the rocks.

He dreamt of his dead wife.

He dreamt of his dead girls.

And he dreamt of... Pippa. Combat K. Soldier. Killer. His ex-lover... And he spiralled down to Molkrush Fed. After the crash. Abandoned by the military... and it was real, in his mind, in his hands, in his soul... and he was there, on the beach, on a different world, in a different age, prostrate before flickering flames...

Red firelight danced over his face, glowing.

Wood crackled, warped, blackened, twisted, and the twisted limbs reached out for him. He'd shivered, then, wondering if he would ever see his little girls; wondering if he would die there on that empty planet with only Pippa for company...

"Hey, lover." She moved to him, snuggled beside him, pressed up tight to him with tiny wriggling movements. Keenan laughed, stroking her hair with affection.

"Now you're blocking the fire."

"I'm cold. I was out fishing."

"And now you're wet! Eurgh! *And* you brought back the stink of fish! Is that supposed to impress me? Am I supposed to fall head-over-heels in love with you?"

"Maybe," she growled, nuzzling under his chin.

"Did you catch anything? Or do we have to starve?"

"Yeah. I caught plenty. Enough for four days."

"That's excellent!"

Pippa pulled away a little. "Why's that?" She raised her eyebrows, frowning.

"It means I don't have to get out of bed."

"Why, you lazy son-of-a-bitch!" She smacked his iron bicep.

"Hey, less of the abuse. I'm a gentle soul, y'know."

"Could have fooled me."

They lay, cuddled, in comfortable silence. For long minutes Keenan thought Pippa was asleep. But she spoke, eyes closed, lips pressed against his throat so the words tickled him. "I was thinking... about later, when, and if, we get home."

"Yeah?"

"About me. And you."

"Hmm?"

"Your kids. Your girls. Rachel. Ally. Do you think they'd...?"

Keenan pulled back, looked down into Pippa's face. Still, her eyes remained closed. He gritted his teeth, wondering where this was leading and feeling suddenly like a stranded toddler atop the middle of a cracked and frozen lake. Helpless.

"Go on," he whispered.

"Do you think they'd ever... take to me? As a mother, I mean?"

"I don't know."

"You do think I'm maternal, don't you?"

"I do, my love."

"I'd like to try and be their mother. One day."

Keenan stroked Pippa's damp, black hair, watched her fall into a lulled sleep. Then his eyes moved over her, to the fire beyond and the beckoning twisted limbs of wood, scorched and seared, and being slowly, inevitably, consumed.

Just like me, he'd thought.

And in his sleep dream nightmare Pippa's face began to change and warp, morphing agonisingly into the face of a junk lying breathing gently in his arms and Keenan bit back a scream as he gazed down into that pitted metal face. Pippa opened her eyes, blood-red eyes, and she twisted, hauling him to the sand and pinning him violently down, cackling coldly as she drooled liquid putrefaction into his open, screaming maw...

"Shit."

He awoke before dawn, shivering, cold, his Techrim in his battered hand. He stood and stretched, spine crackling, WORM-strips pulling tight, but there was no sign of Cam. He peered from the ring of rocks, then sat and watched the sun rise, sparkling over hills and mountains. Such a beautiful, sweeping, majestic land, he thought. And now it had been taken by force. *Invaded.* He shook his head. I thought we'd left the dark behind.

Cam appeared. "You OK?"

"I've felt better," grunted Keenan.

"I failed to decode the SinScript. It is incredibly complex. But I found a manufacturer's identity mark."

"Where was it made?"

"What other planet would deal with immoral death-bringing toxic lifeforms? The City, Keenan, The City in all its glorious, humble decadence."

"Great. You found QGM or Steinhauer?"

"No, we'll have to break the signal blockade first. The good news is I've located transport via a pirate signal. We're about seventy klicks from a billionaire's extravagant PlayPad. Seems he has his own private Y Shuttle; I've made contact with the machine which calls itself the *Drunk and Loving It;* it won't be hard to crack." Cam sounded confident.

"I assume the junks have stuff in orbit?"

"They've some Cargo Hulker Class Is, and a few Marine and Offence Frigates. Most of their force appears to have invaded. From what I can scan."

"I hope you're right; if we leave in a damn Y Shuttle and the junks have Interceptors or Hunters—well, we're dog meat. You realise that? And I bet you a pretty penny those bastards will be watching. Like you said, there's a bigger game being played. They won't want muppets jumping planet and running crying to QGM."

"Well Keenan." Cam watched him carefully. "We'll just have to see what kind of pilot you really are."

Keenan barked a laugh, and scratched his stubble. He lit a cigarette, smoke from the harsh Widow Maker tobacco filling the clearing. The flare of an open flame gleamed against his dark, narrowed eyes. "If those fuckers cross me again, I won't be responsible for my actions," he snarled.

"Glad to have you back," said Cam, and buzzed a little tune.

CHAPTER 5
THE QUANTUM CARNIVAL

THE THEFT OF the Y Shuttle went without hitch.
They cruised up into the Big Blue, which gradually
eased into black. Thankfully, Cam's orbital scans
had been correct; the junks were focusing on attack
and their heavy-grade industrial military transports
were easily side-stepped.

Keenan wandered into the cockpit of the Y Shuttle *Drunk and Loving It*, and slumped onto a pilot's
couch. Cam was floating, immobile, with no case
lights showing.

"You awake?"

"Of course I'm awake. I'm piloting this craft."

"You don't look like you're piloting this craft."

"Well, I am."

Keenan pulled free a small flask of Jataxa and
wetted his lips; then, with a glance at Cam, took a

long gulp. He sighed, leant back, rested his head against the faux leather upholstery.

"Is that wise?"

"Are you my mom?"

"We've had this discussion before, Keenan. A thousand times. You said you'd stop."

Keenan laughed. "Yeah. Only to shut you up, you nagging little bastard. OK. OK. Listen, I'll try my best." He placed the flask on the cockpit controls. "See? There? I've put it aside. Won't touch another drop today. Scout's honour."

They slammed through the darkness of space, through trails of dust and endless void.

Keenan slept, hunched in the pilot's chair, trusting the PopBot implicitly with piloting duties. A Y Shuttle was basic, with no form of sentient control. For a PopBot, it was child's play.

Keenan yawned, opening his eyes.

"I've found a QGM Mobile Incident Unit. And General Steinhauer."

"An MIU? Where?"

"You're not going to like it."

"Hit me."

"The City."

Keenan chewed his lip. "That's... *coincidental*. Franco's down there. What's the little maggot been up to this time?" He laughed, but his joke fell flat. It'd take more than Franco Haggis to bring the might of a QGM Mobile Incident Unit into The City's post-orbit.

"I'm just scanning QGM beacons."

Keenan nodded, and pulled out his PAD. A PAD was a tiny mobile communication unit used by

Combat K special forces; it was superbly powerful and could be used for messages *Quad-Galaxy* wide. A PAD also had an assortment of tiny weapon mods and intricate devices which could be used in the many uncompromising situations a Combat K squaddie encountered. It was the basis of all Combat K missions.

Keenan tapped the blue screen, then MESSAGES. He stared at the text; it had been sent by Franco only a few days previous, and Keenan had been waiting for Cam's return in order to make the necessary travel arrangements.

Hey buddy, you'll never believe it! I'm getting married! As you know, you're my best mate, my only mate in fact, 'cos I'm mad, but I want you to be my Best Man! The chick's called Mel, she's utterly gorgeous, and even more mad than me! Has to be, or we wouldn't be getting wed. So, when you've got a free minute, get your arse over to The City and look me up. We've got a lot to discuss.

Keenan grinned. The text was Franco all over, ever the optimist, ever the wild man. But now he was... what? Trapped down on the city whilst God-only knew what sort of military shit was going on?

"OK. Got it. I've been granted download permissions." Cam's voice became suddenly bleak. "It would seem The City is under martial law."

"Why?"

"There's been an outbreak."

"What kind of outbreak?"

"We'll find out when we get there. You still want to see Steinhauer?"

"Yes. Have you sent them a report on the junks?"

"Doing it... now."

Keenan nodded, silent and grim, and thought about Franco.

PUSHING THE Y Shuttle's engines to the point of death, it took Keenan and Cam eight days of insane and merciless acceleration to reach the out-skirts of The City. However, the journey left half the Shuttle's engine pistons strewn across Sinax Cluster.

During that time, they received reports from Steinhauer on scouts sent to Galhari concerning the sudden invasion of junks. Other than that, commu-nications silence was enforced.

The City had no laws, no immigration, no cus-toms and excise. It also had no, official, police force—only a disparate group of privately owned agencies and armies, used for personal, political or financial gain on this, the Quad-Gal's biggest steaming piss-pot of decadence, debauchery and anarchy. As such, there was no single company to police immigration—or to stop unwanted landings, despite the "outbreak" emergency currently unfold-ing on the streets and alleys below. The City and its inhabitants expounded the moral stance of *free-dom,* a totality of no restraint. The City and its inhabitants had a core philosophy of *what will be, will be.* A shame, because what could happen, had happened.

Keenan whistled as they drew closer to The City, slamming past a Mammoth Class II cargo ship, in this case being used to run missions for Quad-Gal

Military. They cruised under kilometres of dull grey steel. Ion Gunships and Fast Attack Hornets zipped and whizzed around the exterior, like a million insects around a huge hive. A thousand times they were challenged, and a thousand times Cam secured them passage.

"What's going on, Cam?"

"We've just passed the EVH cordon."

"What's an EVH cordon?"

"An Event Horizon Cordon. Now, there's no going back."

"That's just... just great."

"You know Keenan, I've got a funny feeling in the pit of my... atomic furnace, that you're going to end up going down to The City."

"Ha! Yeah. So do I. Are QGM down on the city streets in force? Sorting out whatever problem's dragged the military kicking and screaming across ten billion klicks?"

"No. QGM have imposed a circle of restraint. But they're keeping their distance. Whatever's kicked off on The City, well Keenan, it's big time, my friend."

Keenan rubbed his stubble. "How much hardware?"

"Ten Mammoth Class IIs, and fifty Titan Class IIIs."

"Fifty? *Fifty?* Cam, that's enough flotilla to conquer a galaxy."

"Still scanning, Keenan. Give me a minute. I'm trying to discover what's going down."

"I've got a bad feeling about this."

"Shut—up—data—streams—painful."

Keenan clamped his teeth, pulled out his Techrim 11mm, slammed it on the console in temper, then rolled himself a Widow Maker cigarette. He lit the weed, annoyed even when the internal fans clicked on to extract pollutant. "Shit," he muttered, grabbing his Jataxa spirit and taking a huge swallow. "We leave one war zone just to enter another. The Gods truly are *insane*. And laughing and pointing at me."

There came a *buzz* from the small security Pop-Bot. It rotated, red lights flickering at Keenan. "OK. We're going to merge with Steinhauer; he'll be able to answer your questions. He seems… very keen to meet you."

"Yeah?" Suspicious.

"Yes, Keenan. QGM have a problem."

"I'm sure it's nothing fifty damn Titans couldn't sort out," he muttered.

The Y Shuttle slammed past a Titan Class III, and Cam gyrated madly as they were caught in a Boomerang. A Boomerang was a capture net of force-fields which locked onto a ship and brought it around in a gentle arc to dock… decelerating it in the process.

"Steinhauer's in there?"

"Yeah. They're waiting for you, Keenan."

"I knew it was going to be a bad day."

"Franco's down there on The City. He's your friend. You should help if you can."

Keenan stared at the PopBot. "I know that, Cam. I know."

Cam remained silent, and they watched grey fill their vision until tiny specks of light in the wall of grey became huge docking mouths which grew and expanded, ringed with emergency doors like rows of teeth. The Y Shuttle was sent like an unwilling sacrifice into a moon-sized maw, and behind, spirals of alloy whirled and closed, sealing the Shuttle in the belly of the Titan.

DOORS MESHED AND Keenan squinted out onto the ramp. Ten soldiers were waiting, uniforms crisp and smart, weapons tracked on him. He strode down the ramp, boots clumping, hands open palms outwards to show he was unarmed. A Widow Maker dangled from his lips and he squinted through smoke as he stepped onto the vast metal floor of the docking mouth.

"How's it going, guys?" said Keenan through a tight grin.

"Sir, please accompany us. Your counsel is urgently requested."

Keenan squinted at the badges of rank on the young officer's uniform. "Sir?" He laughed a hollow laugh. "And you would be?"

"Captain J. K. Neggra."

"This your ship, Captain?"

"Negative, Mr Keenan. This is a Titan III. I don't rank that high. I wish I did."

They walked, and with a squawk Cam found himself surrounded by a sudden flurry of BattleBots—far, far superior to a simple PopBot mechanism. BattleBots were machines *built* for war. They were matt green, and stamped with stencilled lettering. They growled and jostled Cam into a holding cage. Cam decided not to argue as the hotbars fizzed. Instead, he simply revelled in superior intellect.

Keenan was marched, smoking, through long corridors and up endless speedy lifts. Finally, he was ushered into a long low room glittering with terminals. The far wall was a sea of black looking out onto the gulf of space. Distantly, The City glowed.

A man stood, surveying the vista.

Keenan walked forward, feeling like a schoolboy approaching a headmaster. The man turned and smiled. He was large, grey haired, with square sideburns and pock-marked skin. His face was flat, jaw angular, eyes dark and unreadable. He was large-framed, and had put on some weight since Keenan last saw him. Fat disguised muscle, but Keenan knew this man was as strong as an ox. He had to be: he'd trained Keenan.

"How are you, old friend?" The man's voice was soft.

"You've heard about the junk invasion of Galhari, General?"

"Straight to the point, Keenan. As ever."

Keenan stared hard at Steinhauer. "It's a subject close to my heart."

"Then, yes. We have a Mobile Incident Unit on path. The problem is, the junks are highly toxic—as you know. And with ten million on the planet..." he let the sentence hang.

"It's infected. So you can't send in the infantry."

Steinhauer nodded, turned, stared back at the distant glow of The City.

"They've poisoned it, Keenan. And they poisoned you."

"I'm not infected. Cam checked me over."

"You have forty-eight hours to live. Unless I administer an antidote."

Keenan held up his hands. "Whoa. Hold on, Steinhauer. You forget—I know you, I know how you operate. You brought us Combat K boys up real good; you allowed us to *think*. I trust you, but I'm not sure I trust you *that much*."

"Yes!" hissed Steinhauer suddenly, "I trained you, so use your brain *now*, Keenan. The Quad-Gal fringes are awash with junks, millions of them, advancing, polluting, spreading their toxic wrath. We thought they were extinct. *Ten million,* Cam reported. Is that just the beginning? Where did they come from? What do they want? Keenan, Cam told us what you carry. An excised SinScript. This could be the key for us, the key to Quad-Gal Military halting the junks. And... we know about Franco Haggis down there; you were to pay him a visit." Steinhauer smiled. His eyes glittered. "I suggest you still go ahead with that journey. Catch up with your old friend. Have a chat. Things are... strained on the planet at the moment, but we will give you every bit of help you need."

"So this is a military mission, now?"

"We need to know," said Steinhauer. He stared out over The City. "The plague is coming," he said. "We've grown too big, too decadent. It would seem we are going to be punished."

"What do you want me to do?"

"I will heal your toxic affliction, Keenan, and give you co-ordinates where you can find a man down there who will decode the SinScript. We need to understand the junks. Keenan, the object you carry is like a gift from the gods."

Keenan took a deep breath. "This is official Combat K business?"

"Yes. Your Prohibition D has been lifted."

"No more sneaking around, then," grinned Keenan.

"No more sneaking," agreed Steinhauer.

Keenan moved to a settee, sat down, rested back, rubbed at his pounding temples. "What's going on down there, General? Why the heavy metal orbit?"

"We will get to that in a moment," said Steinhauer. "For now, be satisfied that we'll give you weapons. Bombs. Permatex WarSuits. A Fast Attack Hornet. Anything you need."

"All that just to find a man?"

"Get down there, link up with your old Combat K unit, and carry out this mission."

"My old Combat K unit? Ahh, so that's the Franco link. Convenient. For you."

"Yes." Steinhauer turned his glittering gaze on Keenan. "And Pippa. She is down there. We can locate her for you."

"And why would I want you to do that?"

"Combat K. Complete again. The perfect military unit." He sighed. "You're going to need everything you've got. It's a warzone, Keenan. A killzone."

"You still haven't told me what's going on."

"Things have taken a turn for... the worse, shall we say."

"Is it the junks?" Keenan's voice was hard. Bitter. He was thinking of the dead back on his home planet.

"No. It's the people."

"What, civilians?"

"Let me explain," said Steinhauer, leaning against the edge of his desk and folding his arms.

* * *

BLACK AND WHITE NEWS CLIP
The City's Premier News Delivery Service
[available in: print, TV, vid, mail, dig.bath, ident.implant, comm., kube, glass.wall, ggg, galaxy.net and eyelid transpose— all for a small monthly fee].

News clip GG/07/12/TBA:

The City is suffering under the iron fist of a terrifying affliction! Millions of people have changed from loving, happy, good and hard-working citizens into *creatures* from the deepest realms of nightmare. Everyday folk have transmogrified into flesh-eating gun-toting monsters, surging in swarms and packs and gangs across the now deserted city streets, massacring everyone they meet, and sometimes even eating the corpses! It has been rumoured that unfortunates who *have* changed are in fact innocent people or carbon-based alien-forms who took a dose of *pirated, hacked and cracked biomods*, the famous new technology from NanoTek, currently running at revision 1.4. Further speculation has revealed that there *may* be a basic flaw in the original nano-technological design, a major *bug* in the code found in every one of the single miniature *nanobots* which populate this supposedly wondrous new technology for human and alien improvement, or as NanoTek like to call it in their marketing manifesto, "The Organic Upgrade". NanoTek have vehemently denied any and all accusations that their nano-molecular technology is flawed, instead blaming it vehemently on the pirates, crackers and code-freaks. Within the next 24 hours they will issue a formal statement; probably vehemently. However, down at street level the massacres, the mutilation, the murder and mayhem *will not stop*. Seven independent private Urban Force groups have sent out large-scale squads of SIMs, Slabs and Mercs, but all of these quite hefty private armies have been overwhelmed in minutes and massacred to a pulp. It would seem the "zombies", as these mutated citizens are being affectionately called, are not just the dead risen, not just the walking dead or a rampaging *dawn* of the dead—they have, in fact, some semblance of *intellect*. This is a terrifying concept! The zombies can, for example, operate a D5 shotgun. They can replace a magazine in a H&K twin-barrel MP9. They can pilot a helicopter. And the millions of zombies across The City have *tooled-up!* Various governing factions on our lovable world have issued the following statement: "Stay off the streets. Lock and barricade your doors. And whatever you do, do not attempt to fight these creatures. Quad-Gal Unification Peace Forces have been informed, and are currently in orbit in an observatory capacity, working closely with NanoTek and other agencies to bring an end to this horror." Our only final worry is that of contagion. Can a zombie pass on this [suspected] hacked biomod infection to a non-infected person or alien? At this early juncture, all we can do is speculate. Be safe. Stay indoors. And whatever you do, carry a weapon—and shoot for the knee-caps.

News clip: END.

DR OZ STOOD, surveying the darkened world. Lights glittered and he turned, pouring himself a generous measure of antique brandy in the stygian gloom of this, the dimly lit upper reaches of NanoTek T5. He took a tiny and considered sip, moved across thick glass carpet, and past a wall of glittering hardware containing six bio-immersion terminals finished in a stylish and moody chrome. Dr Oz moved precisely, as if afraid to waste a single joule of energy. Carefully, intimately, he sat at his huge mahogany boardroom desk as his desk-kube purred.

"Yes?"

"Mr Ranger is here."

Dr Oz smiled, and peered off into a darkened corner of the T5 suite where... something... brooded. He gave a nod, imagining he could see *her* eyes (or was that just a trick of the light, his imagination, his *fear*?). The movement was an almost indiscernible dip of his chin. "Please, send Mr Ranger in."

The door opened and a huge figure blocked out the light. It squeezed awkwardly through the aperture and the only thing Dr Oz could determine was a silhouette wearing a wide-brimmed hat. Smoke plumed into the room, the heavy, acrid odour of cigar.

"I didn't think anybody still smoked those—or *at all*," said Dr Oz to the bulky man. They both knew smoking was dangerous beyond comprehension; an act, in fact, of educated suicide.

"I'm not just anybody," came a heavy drawl. The figure strode in, substantial boots thumping, and halted. He pushed the brim of his wide hat up, but his face remained dark, lost in shadow. "You have a job?"

Dr Oz ignored the omission of *sir*. It was something he did not normally tolerate. However, on this occasion, he would live with it. "Mr Ranger. You come highly recommended by my... contacts." Again, his eyes moved to the corner of the room. It seemed cold there. Colder than death. "It would appear I have a problem."

"Problems are there to be solved," drawled Ranger. He took a drag on his cigar, and another poisonous cloud of tox billowed out. Ceiling lights danced patterns through thick grey swirls. Somewhere on Oz's desk, a carcinogen monitor beeped.

Dr Oz coughed. He wasn't used to pollutants. "Take a seat. You want a brandy?"

Ranger moved hugely to the boardroom desk opposite Oz and eased himself into a chair, which buzzed, moulding to his large frame. He removed his hat, allowing light to spill over his middle-aged, unshaven face. His features were rugged, hair brown shot through with grey, storm-cloud eyebrows shaggy, eyes a piercing blue. Mr Ranger smiled—but it was a smile without humour. The smile of a predator; the smile of an unnatural born killer.

"I only drink the whisky nowadays. Good for the stomach, you understand."

Dr Oz ordered a decanter of whisky over the kube and Uma tottered in, long pink hair swishing behind her. She placed a digital jade decanter on the table before Ranger. She giggled, wiggling and looking coyly back over her shoulder as she exited the plush suite in a cloud of Minx Jinx perfume.

Ranger poured a slug of whisky and downed it. His piercing eyes fixed Dr Oz, who smiled, elbows on the table, fingers steepled before him, face set in a mask of concentration.

"You have, of course, heard of our recent explosion of biomod technology. And you must also have heard, newswide, of the massive hacking, cracking and piracy racket surrounding our premium organic upgrade device. A week ago, a Juggernaut Supply Train was hit by a *very* specialist outfit. Stole two million chassis units. *Two million!* If those sort of numbers were to flood the market..." Oz shook his head, sighing. But his eyes were hard.

"You want me to find out who robbed your components?"

"No."

"What then?" Ranger looked intrigued, sitting forward a little. He clamped his cigar between his teeth and squinted at Dr Oz through a cloud of cancer.

"I have a... *special*... job for you."

Oz pulled a large black case from under his desk, stood, and planted it firmly on the lacquer. There were twin clicks, and Ranger stood and moved to peer inside.

"Do you know what these are?" said Oz, as Mr Ranger's eyes were lit by a strange and subtle green light. Ranger leant forward, his hand bathed in green as he delicately touched the three tiny, intricate, black machines.

"They're controllers," said Ranger. "Latest military specification. Prototypes, in fact." He eyed Oz carefully, his lined face showing concern. "They control the new GKs—the most advanced AI systems ever built by NanoTek... or any other micro software-butcher. I didn't realise they were finished."

"You keep your ear to the ground," said Oz, neatly.

"I know my business," said Ranger.

"Officially, the GKs are far from complete." Oz smiled. "However, let us just say we are ahead of schedule. Now, the friend who recommended you... she claims you will know how to operate these machines? You can set them on a path to—kill. Yes?"

Ranger nodded, and closed the case. The green curled around his fingers, like mist, then gradually dissipated, evaporating. "I am *au fait* with all manner of mechanical and digital killing machines. They are, what you could call, my," he smiled with cigar-stained teeth, "my *speciality*. But first, I need to discuss money..."

Oz waved his hand, as if batting away an insect. "I will triple your fee." He sipped his brandy, which glittered against ruby teeth. Ranger's eyes widened, although his face showed no change of expression. "Do we have a deal?"

Ranger shook Oz's hand. Ranger's skin was rough and calloused; the hand of a *mechanic,* the hand of a *labourer,* somebody who labours to kill.

It was a harsh contrast to the soft, supple, ladylike touch of NanoTek's *numero uno*.

"Dr Oz. You've bought yourself a killer."

RANGER HAD GONE, leaving only the stale odour of cigar smoke. Tiny machines flitted from the ceiling and darted about, purifying the air. Oz reclined, placing his feet on the desk and forcing himself not to turn, not to stare, into that darkened corner.

He did not hear her approach, but his *other* senses, his intuition, told him she was behind. He shuddered a little, and when her hand touched his throat he gave a shiver of delight.

"You liked him?"

"Yes," said Dr Oz. "A fine addition to our army."

"So we are at war?" Her voice was deliciously dangerous.

"All business is war," said Oz.

"Indeed, as is all life."

Oz nodded, and gently the woman massaged his shoulders. He rolled his neck, savouring the iron-powerful grip, and the skill with which she released tension from his over-stressed muscles.

"Do you think he'll find them?"

She spun Oz around on his chair, a sudden, violent movement. Wheels squealed against the floor. He gazed up into the cold, grey eyes of his Chief Security Officer.

Pippa smiled, although there was no evidence of humour, just a cruel upturning of her lips. "He'll find Combat K," she said. "Keenan and Franco are dead men."

* * *

KNUCKLES, SPACESHIP-THIEF, drugsmoke entrepreneur, wheeler and dealer and ducker and diver, rough and tough, wiser than a prophet, harder than hardcore, bitter and decadent and cynical before his time... well, he wasn't having a good day. He'd woken to an astonishing silence, a deep and foreboding silence above and *beyond* the clash and clatter of water-streams. He crawled from his slumberpit in downtown Dregside, in the subterranean vault which nestled like cancer beneath The Happy Friendly Sunshine Assurance Company, and heaved his lithe form from the mouldy mattress, dodged streamers of leaking water and toxic effluvium, eased his way beyond crumbling concrete pillars to the child-sentries who guarded this, their secret underground domain. He approached Skull and Glass warily; they didn't respond, even when he gave a low warning whistle.

"Glass? Skudders? What goes down dudes?" he whispered.

Slowly, Glass turned and through the gloom, where white light painted shadows on the young boy's face, Knuckles could see... *terror*. Knuckles strode forward; he may only have been ten years old, but this was *his* damn outfit, his den, his gang, his *world*. He grasped Glass's shoulders. "What is it, bro'?"

"They... they, they..."

Knuckles stared at Skull. The lad hadn't moved. "Tell me!" he snapped.

"Outside! It's the people. They've been on a... a rampage. They've *changed*, Nuck. They've changed *bad*." He grabbed hold of Knuckles' arm, his grip so hard it made Knuckles' face compress in pain.

Knuckles moved to the Plexiglass sheet, stared up through an array of mirrors to the street a few feet above and beyond. It sat, deserted. A hundred groundcars lay abandoned. Five or six still had water-lithium engines running, fumes pouring from sub-tox exhausts. Many sported open doors. The scene froze across the lake of Knuckle's mind. It made him shiver, ripples cascading the shores of his imagination.

"What's going on? Where is everybody?"

Skull faced Knuckles. "They changed into zombies," he said. "We got a Black and White News Clip."

Knuckles barked a laugh. "Get to hell. What a load of shit."

"Seriously."

Knuckles searched their faces. "This is a wind-up, right?"

"Zombies," repeated Skull. "I was watching. There was a woman, in the street. She started twitching, squealing, then she ripped off her clothes and people gathered round, clapping and cheering and thinking it was a free peepshow! Then there was a *crunch* and her face exploded on strings of tendon." He shuddered. "It was horrible. Then other people started to twist and change and blood and stuff came out of their mouths." He fell silent, tears running down his cheeks.

"What happened then?" said Knuckles, placing a hand on his friend's shoulder.

"They started to fight, and eat each other, they jumped on the ones who weren't changing and ripped out their throats and brains. They used anything for weapons. Many had claws."

Knuckles stared up at the deserted street level. Squinting, he realised the scene was bathed in blood. Puddles of crimson glittered under dull grey light. Smears adorned the hoods and flanks of groundcars. Several limbs poked cheekily from behind tyres.

"Why didn't you wake me?" said Knuckles.

"We were frightened to move," said Glass.

"More importantly, now, where have these *zombies* gone?" Knuckles looked from Skull to Glass, and back again. Both boys shook their heads.

"We don't know!"

"What do we do, Nuck?"

"Hmm." Knuckles was frowning, hand dropping to a velvet bag attached at his belt. He reached inside, where ten small, smooth objects rolled over his hand with the tiniest of *clacking* sounds. He rubbed them thoughtfully, brow creased in concentration.

"This place isn't safe," he said, finally, with a nod. "We've got to get the gang and move them. Little Megan is still ill, but we can carry her between us."

"You think they might come here?" said Skull, wide-eyed.

Knuckles nodded, glancing around at the derelict cubescraper basement they inhabited. "It's an open freeway, mate. We have guards for early warning of other gangs and SIMs, but if what you say is true—"

"Don't you believe me, Nuck?" Glass's voice was tiny.

Knuckles patted him. "I believe you. Come on, I know a way to the roof. Zombies are dumb, right? We've all seen the movies. What was that latest one? Shaun of the Dead 29? The Remake Remastered Director's Final Cut v3.7? Ace film. Super. That scene with the undead zombie dog and the lamppost outside the Winchester. Genius! But... these zombies, hey, they'll never find their way up to the roof, right? We'll be safe there. You'll see."

A scream, high-pitched and chilling, echoed through the subterranean basement. It was inhuman, but quite clearly produced by a human voice. A girl ran into view between the grotty crates and grime-smeared cardboard containers; her hair was long and blonde and curled, bouncing down her back. Her arms and legs were smeared in grime. Her face was a mask of terror, eyes desolation.

"Sammy! What's wrong?" cried Knuckles, starting forward. And...

Something leapt from the darkness, it was long and sleek and naked, its body mottled brown flesh, eyes the yellow of cancer pus. It had once been a man, but there was very little human about this grime- and shit-smeared creature that landed lightly in front of the fleeing girl, its body curling and swaying.

Sammy stopped, terror rippling through her.

"Hey!" bellowed Knuckles, waving his arms and starting forward.

The zombie's head smashed left, focusing on him with dead decaying eyes. A flap of skin was open on his cheek showing yellow, broken teeth within the cavern of his mouth. Only then did Knuckles realise the zombie carried a vicious curved blade, maybe two feet long, serrated and black and stained with blood.

"Nuck?" wailed Sammy, pleading across the darkened vault.

"Urh," said the zombie, grinning with two mouths, and slashed the blade at the little girl who stumbled back, wailing. Knuckles stooped, hand closing over an old brick with brittle sharp edges and he threw himself at the creature which turned, faced him, and leapt to meet the challenge. The blade slashed past his face, and Knuckles dodged, rammed the brick into the zombie's face, knocking out several teeth which clattered across the concrete like dice. The zombie was flung backwards, where it rolled with a crack of splintering bones but came up fast and leapt again, immediately, with a savage screaming snarl which sprayed blood over Knuckle's face and for a moment froze him in terror. There was intelligence there, in that decrepit face, in those diseased eyes and the blade whistled a millimetre from his throat and he smashed the brick again, but this time the zombie ducked fast and kicked out, sweeping Knuckle's legs from under him.

It loomed over him, its body stinking and flaccid and streaked with excrement. Knuckles wanted to vomit, but terror held him in thrall. The blade lifted, poised above him at an arc of climax... then the zombie grunted, and keeled forward into a roll of flailing limbs, the head sliding free from a diagonal neck cut. Sammy stood, eyes wide, and she dropped the machete with a clatter of rusted steel. The zombie twitched, its severed head ululating, lips fluttering, calling out in low moans as its eyes rolled around in its skull like loose marbles. There seemed to be a hint of green at its severed neck stump; but Knuckles blinked, and the image dissipated. Limbs thrashed and twitched. Knuckles climbed to his feet, picked up the machete, and put his arm around Sammy.

"Thanks, babe," he said.

"What is it, Knuckles?" she whispered. "Why is it still moving?"

Knuckles shivered, remembering the intelligence in its eyes. Zombies were supposed to be dumb, right? All the vids and games said so. So what the hell was going down?

"I don't know, Sammy."

Skull and Glass joined them, and they watched the body thrashing. Then it went rigid, and crawled over to the head. Hands reached out, and started trying to affix the head back to the torso.

"That's just *impossible,*" snapped Knuckles, and with a snarl he leapt forward and hacked at the arms and legs. Black blood spurted out, covering his fine red gloss boots, and in a few seconds he'd chopped off every available limb. He stared up, to see the other three children watching him, eyes wild, faces contorted in horror.

"What?" he snarled.

"Look!" pointed Sammy.

The arms and legs were twitching, flexing disjointed fingers and toes, and they started to move following their own little individual paths, turning themselves around and trying, so it seemed to the children, to attach themselves back onto the torso. The zombie was trying to reconnect itself!

They can rebuild him, thought Knuckles sourly.

"Skull. How many of these things did you say there were? Out on the street?"

"Hundreds," said Skull.

"No. *Thousands,*" whimpered Glass. "They were everywhere. And after they killed all the normal people, and ate their faces and brains, they seemed to work like a gang. They all got up together, and ran off in a group. Like a... like a pack of dogs."

"We need to get the hell out of here," snapped Knuckles. "Skull, Glass, take Sammy and get the others. You know the back way? Up the blue-stair fire-escape? Head up there, I'll meet you on the roof. Try and find some weapons, anything, swords or knives. Guns, if you can. And try and get petrol or oil, and some sticky-lighters... and aerosols. Anything like air freshener or some anti-stink deodorant."

"OK. But Knuckles, what are you going to do?"

Knuckles stared grimly at the zombie, where two severed arms were trying to shove a leg into place on the rocking, squirming, blood-splattered carcass.

"Mincemeat can't fight," he said.

KNUCKLES' GANG, THE City Liberators, numbering twenty-five rough and tumble hardcore streetwise grime-smeared rag-tag orphaned kids in total, and armed with a variety of crude weapons, including forks and sharpened spoons, crept across the office space on Floor 13 of The Happy Friendly Sunshine

Assurance Company. Computers buzzed and hummed, a thousand machines showing a variety of comedy screensavers. Paperwork and metalsheet stacks loomed in towers in the eerily deserted office. Never had A4 looked so threatening.

"Where is everybody?" whispered Skull, as he led the group. He was armed with a long kitchen knife. It gleamed.

"They must have run, when they saw what was happening realworld side."

"Maybe they all turned into zombies? And they're waiting in the cupboards?"

The kids seemed to shiver as a singular entity at this idea. Their fear was palpable.

"Come on," said Skull.

They moved through the office, a unit in tight formation, past derelict beeping photocopiers, scattered office chairs, and temporary partitions which had been arranged to give a false semblance of privacy, when they in fact simply allowed an over-eager plastic management to keep a close eye on the shenanigans of underpaid employees.

"Shh!"

"What is it?"

"I thought I heard something."

They all listened.

A little girl whimpered.

And then they *did* hear it. A clawing, scratching sound.

It stopped.

The group moved forward again, towards the double doors at the end of the office. To the left of the doors, which in turn led to fire stairs, was a cramped interior office. The small, partitioned room had windows, but the blinds had been closed.

Again, the scratching sound tugged at the dark side of the kids' imaginations.

The group of kids halted, wary, eyeing their escape route, then staring fearfully at the office with its hidden secretive interior and scritchy scratching. It was just too damn close to where they had to pass.

"There could be a zombie inside," said Glass.

"Or ten zombies!" said Sammy.

"Maybe a hundred," shuddered Skull.

They stood, quivering, then Glass shook himself out of his fear and spat on the green patterned carpet. "This is silly! We're jumping at shadows! There's nothing in that office! Come on, or we'll never get to the roof and Knuckles says it's the safest place to be."

"I don't know," whimpered Skull.

"Don't be such a big blubbering baby!" snapped Glass. "I'll damn well show you!" He stormed over to the office, and flung open the door. Suddenly revealed was a deformed and mutated woman— once an office worker, for she still wore a neat black suit skirt, pristine stockings and smart, polished shoes. That was where the niceties ended; she was naked from the waist up, her flesh grey, breasts covered with some kind of thick fungus and sagging to her belly button; her neck was thick, *waist*-thick, and bulged with huge lumps and contusions. Her head was distorted, like an egg tilted on its side, and one end had erupted to show brain and green pus. Her nose was gone, the hole surrounded by deep impregnated teeth marks, and her eyes were yellow, gleaming with malevolence.

She scratched a long and perfectly manicured nail against the wooden doorframe. She grinned with pointed fangs dripping colourless, viscous fluid.

"Boo," she said.

The kids screamed, and charged back towards the stairs from which they'd emerged. The zombie snarled and leapt after them on all fours, drooping breasts brushing the carpet in pendular rhythm as she bounded, like a powerful cat.

The kids streamed, a swarm of screaming and confusion, the zombie close behind, snarling and spitting, finely manicured claws raking the carpet, fangs snapping at heels. The zombie suddenly reared, and pounced, bringing down Little Megan who grunted, rolling over to lie, foetal, staring up as the zombie reared over her.

"Please don't hurt me," whimpered Little Megan, eyes streaming hot tears down flushed cheeks.

The zombie office worker grinned, eyes glinting, and oversized teeth tried to form words. "Litt grl flsh tst swt." She grinned again, and opened her maw—

"Hey, bitch."

The zombie's head snapped up.

Knuckles ignited the aerosol can (*No-STINK STINKless Deodorant Kills the STINK You Don't Want!!*) and a four foot flame gushed from a slim metal canister, enveloping the zombie's head and grey-flesh breasts in fire. She screamed, stumbling back, hair and skin ablaze, and Knuckles leapt the fallen figure of Megan, pursuing the zombie and continuing to spray fire, rusted machete in one fist, face a grim realisation of what he must do to survive.

The zombie's hands were up in supplication. She stumbled back over an office chair, hit the carpet writhing, and Knuckles swung the machete, severing the flaming head. The body squirmed. Knuckles chopped the torso in half with three vicious strokes, then returned to the shivering, whimpering group.

"My hero," said Little Megan. Stooping, Knuckles picked up the little girl and she curled into his arms, head against his neck. Knuckles took a deep breath.

"We have to get up to the roof. *Fast.*"

Even then, they heard clamouring on the stairs. Snarls and screams and grunts and ululating moans. Skull, by the doors, had gone pale. And then, another sound intruded...

It was a machine, which revved high with a violent, metal song.

"What *is it?*" shouted Knuckles.

Skull stared hard. "Some of them have *chainsaws,*" he hissed.

"What? That just isn't right! *We're* supposed to chainsaw *them!* That's how it happens in the movies!"

They ran, past the smoking zombie corpse which lay, thankfully, still, and through the doors to the steps leading to the roof. Another eighty flights of steps. Grimly, Knuckles hoped they could make it. It was a long way up.

He stopped, shepherding the kids through the portal and grabbing a thick metal pole used normally to reach high window-hooks. Then he watched in horror as a flood of zombies invaded the office. They came, bounding and snarling, all manner of shapes and sizes and deformations. Skull had been right; three carried chainsaws, which they revved high and long and hard, holding them above their heads, eyes focused on Knuckles and the fresh meat he carried on young bones, fresh brain cradled in his ripe kid skull.

Knuckles dragged shut the metal doors, slotted the pole through the looped handles, and took a hurried step back as the weight of the charging horde slammed the portal. It rattled unconvincingly.

"Knuckles!"

He scooped Little Megan in his arms and fled as chainsaws started to buzz through metal-reinforced timber with clangs, and squcals, and showers of bright glittering firefly sparks.

PART II

MOD(ERN) CULTURE

"Death is nothing to us, nor should it
worry us a bit; we can't suffer after
death, since the nature of the spirit
we possess is something mortal."

Lucrecius

CHAPTER 6
THE ONE LAW

THEY WERE ON *him!* He could smell their stench. Feel claws raking his heels. Bullets slapped along the metalled road to his right. Franco flinched, staggering left, and something grabbed his foot and he went down, rolling, his D5 booming in large hands, Mel's lead lost in the confusion and madness. Zombies loomed everywhere, deformed, disjointed, lop-sided heads grinning at him with black tongues and yellow, diseased eyes. Saliva spat and dribbled, pus oozed, and Franco was screaming screaming *screaming* as this living nightmare this walking charging moaning mass of depraved and gibbering monsters tried to rip off his head and eat his brains...

"No-*ooooooo!*" screamed Franco, letting off another savage D5 *boom* which punched a hole through a female zombie allowing Franco to see through the gap, and watch a tiny tail-end of spine wriggling like a worm in the core of a rotten apple.

The D5 was wrenched from his grip, passed back amongst the horde. It was discharged into the air. Moans surrounded him. He could smell burning, feel their claws raking his flesh, smell their dead, putrid organics dripping from bones. It smelt like a ten-day dog corpse. The perfume of the zombie. *Eau du undéade.*

Claws tore at him, and he started to punch out, breaking jaws left and right with powerful hooks. Several jaws detached from faces and hung, swinging on elastic tendons against hole-filled, serrated chests. Franco dodged hissing talons, ducking and diving. He belted out a few savage straights... but the weight of the *crush* forced him to his knees, and they tore at his hair and face. A *slash* of claws opened a line down his jaw and Franco's blood spurted free in a pulse which made the zombies go suddenly wild, howling at this promise of fresh meat and bright blood and succulent *brains*...

A scream rent the air, high-pitched and metallic and keening. Franco shuddered—a moment before realising it was coming from *Mel*, his *Mel!* She had seen his jaw-line opened by a claw, watched his blood spurt free. And now her own jaws were clacking a curious drumbeat, her small black eyes gleaming as she pulled herself to her full height of eight feet plus—towering over the zombie horde— and with a blur and *slam* of violent acceleration she began to maim and massacre all around. Franco stumbled back, stunned, the zombies turning to face this new threat that pirouetted like a whirlwind of death amongst them. Claws slammed heads from bodies, cut arms and legs from torsos, punched holes through chests and ripped free hearts and spinal columns on ejected fountains of black and green blood. Mel howled, small round head bobbing like a bean on elastic as she whammed and slammed and mashed and maimed, turning and whirling, jigging and dodging. Guns rattled and boomed, dropping zombies to the left and right of Mel, but she growled and charged, and with a sudden howl the zombie horde turned to flee under the terrible onslaught of Mel's distended jaw and blood dripping claws. Boots and toe-less feet stamped down the road, and the horde sprinted away leaving behind a hundred slaughtered, dismembered monsters, some writhing on the ground, many just motionless and oozing blood and grey pus.

Franco, seated on his rump, coughed, and looked up as Mel turned and stared at him. Fury was her face, insanity her eyes. She lifted her claws and stalked towards him, a strange bobbing gait as Franco found himself scrabbling backwards in panic, eyes fixed on those terrible, natural killing blades.

Mel reared over him!

"Argh!" squawked Franco, terror in his heart and breast and soul, and fear eating what little bit of his manhood remained.

Mel slumped down, sighing, head pushing forward on her long slick neck and nestling in his lap. She crooned, and with a dawning horror Franco realised the eight-foot pus-ridden horror was fluttering her eyelids at him.

"Ove ou," came the disjointed words. Mel's jaws clacked, like badly fitting pincers. Her long muscular neck undulated, making a sound like a bag of marbles in a meat-grinder.

Franco reached out, and steeling himself, patted her head. "There, there," he said, voice cracked and weak and almost feminine. And at that moment in frozen, horrific time, he wondered which bit was worse: the fact Mel might try to kill him, or the prospect she might try to fuck him.

THE Y SHUTTLE swept down from towering, storm-filled skies. Rain pounded the hull, wind howling, the storm trying its hardest to thump them into the wrong side of oblivion. Keenan, now at the controls, skimmed towards The City's Freeport Range, but something made him decelerate rapidly and pull up at the last moment.

"What is it?" said Cam.

"Look," said Keenan.

They watched in ill-disguised horror as the huge swarm of zombies ambled across the Freeport Landing Zone beneath, eyes turned up, mouths hung limp. The group suddenly opened fire, and a thousand machine guns howled sending bullets scything past the Y Shuttle and Keenan twisted the controls, the Y Shuttle's engines screamed and it banked violently to shoot up into the storm with rain rattling off the cockpit and tracer dancing against armoured engine ports.

"I know Steinhauer said a large number of the population were a genetic malfunction, a transformation of humans and aliens into mutants; but he never said anything about them using damned machine guns!" Cam sounded affronted.

"Zombies with brains," said Keenan. Then laughed. "God does enjoy dicking with me. Cam, we've leapt from a junk-ridden war-zone into a cesspit of plague. What the hell are we doing here?"

"I never suspected it would be like this. And *you* agreed to come. Steinhauer played you like a xylophone."

"I can't leave Franco down here to have *all* the fun, can I?" Keenan fired the Y Shuttle low across towering skyscrapers. Below, huge tracts of The City were deserted. In other parts, fires raged and riots were in progress. Zombie riots. From their high vantage point, it appeared a vision of hell.

"Cheer me up. Tell me this mutation thing isn't contagious."

"Scanning now." Cam went silent for a while, as Keenan dropped down between tower blocks and skimmed low above the streets, watching in grim silence as zombie creatures hunted down screaming men and women. God, he wished the Y Shuttle was armed... and he suddenly regretted not accepting Steinhauer's offer of a Hornet. What had he said? Keep their entry low-key. Covert. Don't draw attention to themselves. But hell, he'd love to have sent a savage volley of fire to pulp the mutated bastards raging below. Instead, all he could do was watch in a brooding silence. Nothing burned Keenan worse than innocents destroyed by evil strong.

"OK," said Cam, eventually. "You were right to use that terminology. These things are... zombies. Of a sort."

"I never invented it; I read it, in the Black and White News Clip provided by Steinhauer," said Keenan. "But still, zombies... you're pulling my dick, right?"

"The mutations below are unfortunate people who took pirated, cracked and hacked biomod technology in order to improve their physical aspects. They call it a human upgrade. Very droll."

"You mean NanoTek?" said Keenan.

"Yeah. So you've heard of them?"

"I've seen one of these biomods go wrong before," said Keenan, voice a low drawl. "A rich bitch down on Galhari; holidaying on a yacht. They had to scrape her off the poop deck with a shovel. Her father wanted me to investigate—and I tried, but man, I've never seen a conglomerate as powerful as NanoTek. They put so many obstacles in my path I needed an army of lawyers just to take a shit. Eventually, I filed a lawsuit against the owner himself, I targeted the *individual* rather than the organisation. A guy called Dr Oz."

"What happened?"

"The rich bitch's father was paid off by Oz. It seems if you add a few more zeroes to any cheque then the after-effects of murder can be negotiated. The whole incident made me sick."

"Well, it's a lot *more* sick down there," said Cam. "It's a plague-town. Very dangerous. How many weapons did Steinhauer provide?"

"Everything I need. And I've still got my trusty Techrim."

"You understand that... if we meet resistance, it will be a tough gig."

"I didn't expect anything less," snapped Keenan. "I ain't here for a holiday."

They cruised for a half hour, and eventually located the narrow street—aptly named *Stud Avenue*—which led to Franco's apartment. Keenan had Cam check the location locks five times. "After all," he said, "we don't want to get stranded in No Man's Land."

Keenan lowered the Y Shuttle onto a Porky Pauper's Fast-Food Burger Emporium car-park. There were a few derelict groundcars, and the Y Shuttle compressed them with grinding shrieks and *bangs* into steel pancakes. The ramp clanged open just as the storm, growing in fury, unleashed its elemental payload; rain slammed, thunder grumbling across dark bruised heavens. Lightning stalked the skies. Keenan strode down the ramp, heavily tooled, and stood at the bottom in the shadow of the Shuttle. He lit a cigarette, Permatex WarSuit gleaming with spatters of rain, and peered out into the gloom. A huge glittering neon sign announced: "PORKY PAUPER'S TRIPLE CHILLI CHEESEBURGERS! GO ON, BE A PORKER! ENJOY FIVE FOR THE PRICE OF ONE!!"

"Looks like a bargain," said Cam, spinning close, red warning lights fluttering across his black casing. "Cheap as chips."

"Have you ever *eaten* a Porky Pauper's? There's so much fat you need liposuction before you've even *finished*. It oozes, like a thick white syrup, from the edges of the burger." He shivered. "Gross. Franco loves 'em, the gastronomic pervert."

"I'll scout for trouble."

Keenan glanced around at the shattered, battered, bullet-ridden war zone. "You're joking, right?"

"I never joke," said Cam primly, and spun away into the rain.

Stamping out his cigarette, Keenan cursed his existence and stepped into the heavy downpour. It was like walking under a waterfall. Externally, he was instantly soaked. The WarSuit monitored his temp and kept him dry and snug within. He moved out, jogging, senses alert, a slick Techrim in his fist. He followed Cam's bobbing unit through the gloom of high-rise scrapers. Up close, the streets were filled with detritus: broken glass, planks of wood, bullet casings. Blood smeared doorways and the battered spider-webs of impacted shop windows. Occasionally, Keenan thought he saw a body part. He looked away.

Cam stopped. "Up there."

Keenan peered through sheets of rain. The alley was narrow, very dark, and skyscrapers and cube-blocks teetered above him for as far as the eye could see, sending the already gloomy, sodden world into deepest intimate shadow. The skyblock flanks were slick with black rain. Windows watched, like the dormant opal eyes of some sleeping leviathan.

"Nice," nodded Keenan. "Well, nice *place* for an ambush."

"Zombies aren't that sophisticated," said Cam.

"These aren't zombies," said Keenan, "they're mutations. And from what I saw when we floated over this charnel house, I'd say they still had brains enough. And guns. Too many guns."

"Come on."

With a deep breath, Keenan hoisted his MPK and followed Cam into the jaws of the alley.

THE DOOR SLAMMED, and Franco stood, panting, weary, drenched to the bone, staring at a point at the centre of his battered, wrecked living room. Mel moved off, head whacking the ceiling to send plaster-dust drifting, and she disappeared into the kitchen. Franco heard the tap running, and he sighed, deflating. He was exhausted. Gods, he had been close—so close—to death! What in the world was happening? The City—once haven to every hedonistic whim—had turned into a circus. A freak show. And Franco was there at the centre wearing the star attraction on his sleeve: his beautiful girl.

"Mel, my sweetness?" he said, eyeing the kitchen nervously. He glanced down the savaged corridor to the bedroom—and the stash of dangerous weapons he knew lay in his wardrobe, under the bed, and in his battered brown leather suitcase.

Mel came padding back, small eyes squinting, oiled head glistening like an overripe olive, distended vagina leaking some kind of thick green ooze which bleached patches of Franco's carpet as he watched with an open, awestruck mouth. She grunted, and stood before him, skin rippling like a sack of stoats.

"Urrrww?"

"Hi love," he said weakly. "Look, I'm knackered, and I was just thinking of putting my head down. Getting a bit of much earned kip. What with all the recent excitement, and all that." It sounded lame, even to his own ears. He took a few tentative steps towards the bedroom. Mel grunted, and padded after him.

Franco stopped. Mel stopped. He looked at her.

"I thought I might sleep... alone. You know how it is. Just for a few hours, you understand?" He yawned theatrically, as if to say, *boy am I bushed and in need of some serious solitary sleep-time.*

Mel grunted and gave a little bubbling whine. She shook her head, a heavy, pendulous motion on a heavy, undulating, corrugated neck.

Franco, holding up his hands, started a wary retreat. "Hold on, now. Oh no, no, love, you've got the wrong end of the stick here. I'm really pooped. Exhausted, in fact. After all that being chased by zombies fiasco, and them trying to munch on my brains an' all. I's just ready for a good bit o' quality lonely one-man shut-eye."

Mel followed the retreating Franco, taloned claw-steps cracking the floorboards.

Franco gave an accelerated stumble backwards into the bedroom and ended in a heap. Mel leapt, catching in the doorframe and dragging the splintered, tearing wood with her, to straddle him, claws on sagging hips, pink and gesticulating vulva only inches from Franco's terrified and locked gaze.

How did I know it'd come to this? he thought sourly.

I meet my dream girl. The One. And I mean, THE FUCKING ONE! The gal I intend to marry. Quality. Class. Hard-working. Great cook. Stunning in bed. Stunning out of bed, in fact. And then she goes and turns into an eight-foot bloody zombie mutation. What did I do wrong? Which evil god did I annoy this time?

A name drifted in his distant subconscious.

Leviathan...

"Shit," muttered Franco, remembering *bad* times. "Ahhh. *That* god." He focused on Mel, who was squirming above him, trying to align their bodies.

"Can we talk about this?" Franco whimpered, as she lowered herself ponderously towards him, and her small, round head came close to his face, her neck constricted into a tight inverted U. She must have possessed only limited motor skills, because her distended lower jaw bumped Franco's chin. He laughed nervously.

"Ove ou."

"Yeah, yeah babe, I'm sure you do, only the *thing* is, now don't take this the wrong way, but you've lost a teensy weensy bit of your physical appeal. I mean, don't get panicky now, I still want to get married, still want you to bear me six strapping sons, but at *this very moment in time*, shall we say, your *excess* of pus and oozing orifices does little to inflame my libido." He smiled with the sort of shocked and stunned expression reserved for car-crash victims.

Mel reached around with a long talon. She sliced the buttons from his shirt, which flapped open in a betrayal of welcome to reveal Franco's hairy curly chest. Mel reached out with a blood-encrusted talon, and started to rub gently at Franco's flesh.

"Ha ha ha," said Franco, his voice containing a nervous, underlying whine, like the discharge on a greenscale sniper's scope. Franco coughed. "That fight back there. It made you horny, didn't it?"

Mel nodded, her chain and collar jangling.

"And you're not going to take no for an answer, are you?"

Mel shook her head, collar still jangling. To Franco, it looked a little like she was pouting. But it was hard to tell, through the sheen of pus, and what with that distended jaw, and blackened, twisted lips like curls of lightning-struck oak.

Franco closed his eyes. "Oh. My. God."

There came a discreet knock at the front door, and in a swift, deft, panicked martial arts movement, and with a twist and a slither, Franco rolled and squirmed from beneath Mel's stocky legs, grabbed her chain and looped it twice around the wooden bed post. Mel growled, leaping up, vagina swinging. The chain went tight. Franco backed to the door, hands up, palms out. "Calm down, honeysuckle."

Mel roared, saliva glistening on fangs. She tugged, and the whole bed moved like a tectonic plate.

"It's only while I answer the door, my little chipmunk-scented rose-petal."

Mel roared again, like a caged lion poked with a pointed stick.

Franco turned and legged it, slamming the door in the smashed and twisted half-frame behind him. In the bedroom Mel proceeded to charge around the room, dragging the slowly disintegrating bed after her. It bounced from floor, walls and ceiling, making the whole apartment shake and boom in a bass sonata.

Franco stood behind the front door, hands on knees, panting. He opened it. And stared at Keenan.

"Keenan!" he roared, and leapt forward, embracing his old war buddy.

"Franco," laughed Keenan, taking a step back. "How's it going, you mad ginger midget? Still drinking yourself stupid? Still picking bar brawls with women? Still, y'know," he twitched, "a bit mad and slick and bad?"

Franco's laughter boomed even louder, but was drowned out by the sounds of a crashing bed bouncing from walls fifteen feet away. Something roared like a wild cat with its testicles in a nut-cracker, and dust drifted lazily from the living-room's swinging light-bulb.

"Problem?" Keenan lifted an eyebrow.

"You'd better come in and meet the missus," said Franco grimly.

Keenan stepped across the threshold, Cam floating in behind him. Franco fought to make the door fit its frame, and eventually leant a crushed piece of furniture against the warped portal.

"Sounds like you've caught yourself a bear," said Keenan, slowly, eyes never leaving Franco's.

"No. No no." Franco laughed, voice weak. "Much more entertaining than that, I assure you. In a serious and psychologically bleaching kind of way. The stuff of nightmares, so to speak."

Keenan slapped Franco on the back. "So, where's this amazing girl, then? The one who's gonna stop my mate Franco doing exactly what he wants, ten... times... a night." He stopped. Franco's face could have sunk the Titanic. His chin was more brutally chiselled than any iceberg. "You OK?"

Mel roared again. The building shook.

"It's nice to see you Keenan, really it is, it's just I'm having these *teething* problems in the old relationship department. It's Mel, you see. She's not, um, not well."

"Touch of a cold, by the sounds of her," said Keenan with a totally straight face, as a roar like the colliding of worlds vibrated windows in twisted frames. "Want me to pop out, get her a few packets of *Wankers* Honey & Lemon Flu Cure?"

"You're fucking with me, aren't you Keenan?"

"Look. I'm honoured you asked me to be best man. There was an internal struggle, but my humanitarian side won. So, if you've got a problem with the lovely lass then don't be shy. Bring her out, and we'll all deal with the situation. That's what best men are for, right? Franco, buddy, we *have* been through the shit together. Remember Terminus5? Remember Leviathan?"

"I remember," said Franco dejectedly. "Only..." he squinted. "This is worse." He trudged to the bedroom door and kicked it open on the fifth attempt. Inside, everything was dark, quiet, still. Dust drifted through the gloom. "You can come out now, Melanie."

Mel charged, knocking Franco from his feet, her claws raking up yet more floorboards and head leaving a long jagged groove in the ceiling. She stooped, sliding to a halt with a rake of sparks, her out-thrust face mere inches from Keenan's.

Breath like a sewer rolled out.

Slowly, Keenan lifted a home-rolled cigarette, cupped it, and lit the weed. He lifted his head, drew deep with a bright glow of burning tobacco, removed the cigarette, and blew a ball of smoke into Mel's face. She blinked. And gave a little, feminine cough.

"Nice to meet you," said Keenan, as he took in the mottled skin, small round head with ears and nose-holes oozing pus, and the dangling, distended grey-flesh breasts which reached to Mel's waist and swung in a cumbersome, pendulous cycle.

"Grwwlll."

Keenan leant left, and eyed Franco as the little man picked himself shakily from the floor. He started brushing crumbled plaster from his clothing. Franco looked up at Keenan. He grinned weakly.

"You've had worse," said Keenan, leaning back to stare into Mel's small black eyes.

"Hey!" shouted Franco. "Now don't be like that, this isn't the kind of situation you think it is."

"What, that my old Combat K buddy has netted himself something from a Nazi's experiment laboratory? Where you getting married? Castle Wolfenstein?"

"Oh. Ha and ha, Keenan. Listen, my Mel is a beautiful creature, sleek black hair, slim and voluptuous—and a demon in the bedroom!" Mel turned and eyed him. "*Sorry* love. Didn't mean to give away the intimacies of our private life. However," he gritted his teeth, eyes narrowing, "as you can see she has recently been a victim of a series of unfortunate and badly coincidental accidents which have transmogrified her into the admittedly inelegant creature you see before you."

"You don't fucking say," said Keenan, smoke curling from his nostrils.

"She still has the same heart, the same brain, she is still my Melanie, deep down inside her soul. Only... only... to the casual observer, she may appear to have changed a little."

"Hello Francis."

"Oh, hiya Cam." Franco twitched. "Didn't notice you there for a moment, what with all the, y'know, frantic charging and destruction of rented property and such-forth."

"Francis. Have you noticed your girlfriend is a zombie?"

Franco's eyes glazed for a moment. "Whadya mean?"

"She's one of *them*, Franco. One of the mad horde who've been rampaging through The City tearing people limb from limb, eating brains and generally causing a riot in a bloodbath."

"Nah. Nah she ain't," Franco shook his head in denial, but his eyes betrayed his heart.

"Yes," said Cam gently, "yes she is. Look at her. She is a genetic mutation! She's a disfigured monstrosity! She's a pus-oozing, slimy-scaled, distended, quivering sack of shitty rotting flesh and twisted bones!"

"That's a bit harsh," said Franco dejectedly. "That's my bird, that is. The woman I intend to marry. The woman I... love."

Mel turned, a sudden movement. Her lower jaw crunched open like a breaking femur, and she was on Franco in a second, her disjointed maw wrapped around his lips in what could only be described as a suction snog; with full-tongue action.

Pus oozed into Franco's mouth as his arms flapped frantically, like a suicide jumper desperately trying to push away the fast-approaching ground.

Mel kissed him.

Franco swooned.

Keenan stood by, uneasily, and glanced at Cam, shrugging. He puffed on his cigarette, and only then realised he was holding his Techrim. Damn those reflexes, he thought.

Mel pulled free.

Franco spluttered.

Mel fluttered her spider-hair eyelids.

Franco gagged.

"Now then, when you two lovebirds have quite finished?" said Keenan, and stooping, pulled Franco to his feet. Mel growled, and Keenan shot her a dark look. "Not now, girl, we've got some important business to attend."

Franco slumped to his battered couch. "I can't get married to her like this," moaned Franco.

"Listen, there are more important matters afoot," said Keenan. "Have you stopped to wonder *why* Mel has been so afflicted?"

"I thought it might have had something to do with the biomod upgrade thing she took," said Franco miserably.

"You're damn right mate," said Keenan. "Her and half the fucking population of The City."

Franco's eyes went wide. "That's right. This thing is *planet-wide*. There are millions of zombies out there, all waiting to tear off your head and shit down your neck."

"I have to help her, Keenan." Franco's face was filled with pain. "I have to get her back to normal. It's my girl. My bird. My *woman*."

"Well, I have a mission down here. You help me with mine, I'll help you with yours."

"What's the gig?" Franco was suddenly professional.

"My home planet of Galhari has been overrun by *junks*."

"Them bastards? They're a toxic pollution. You're lucky to be alive."

"Tell me about it. I have one of their SinScripts, because these things are kind of semi-mechanical, semi-sentient; they follow a set of instructions. I need to decode the disk, find out what game they're playing… and more importantly, how to fight them, how to get rid of their toxic scourge."

"How many invaded?" said Franco.

"Around ten million. I liaised with Steinhauer. He's lifted our Prohibition D. We're back in business, Franco. Combat K is back in business. Together again."

"Rasta billy!" grinned Franco, suddenly.

"The only problem we have is that The City is now under QGM martial law. You—me—Mel, the lot of us, we're quarantined here, mate. We can't leave. Not until we find out what's going on." Keenan grinned, and slapped a woeful looking Franco on the back.

"You know," said Franco, "a fella goes to sleep with the whole world just fine, and he wakes up and the bloody galaxy is out to feed him a big shit sandwich. What's damn well happening? I feel like I missed a bloody decade."

"Don't you keep your eye on the news?"

Franco grunted. "I'm in love, ain't I?" He glanced at Mel. Shuddered. "I had *other* things on my mind."

Keenan sat down next to Franco. "Listen mate. We'll sort her out, you see if we don't. You said she took a biomod upgrade. Which clinic did she attend? NanoTek have got a thousand this side of the river."

"No. She didn't get it from a clinic. She said..." Franco screwed up his face, "yeah, said it was cracked. An illegal. Got it from a pirate out in the street. Friend of a friend, yeah?"

"A friend of a friend? Who?"

Again, Franco screwed up his face, wrinkling his nose and ginger goatee. Then he nodded. "Down the market, she said. A lad called Knuckles. Friend of Emily. Although I've never met Emily." Franco scratched at his beard. "You think that's the way to go?" He looked lost and lonely, forlorn in the middle of the couch. Like a little boy in a big room, kicking his scuffed shoes.

Keenan patted his shoulder. "We'll get right on it, mate. I've a Shuttle parked down the street at Porky Paupers. Come on, tool up."

"You think we'll meet resistance?"

Keenan eyed Mel warily. "I know it, bruv."

* * *

BLACK AND WHITE NEWS CLIP
The City's Premier News Delivery Service
[available in: print, TV, vid, mail, dig.bath, ident.implant, comm., kube, glass.wall, ggg, galaxy.net and eyelid transpose—all for a small monthly fee].

News clip GL/14/12/TBA:
NANOTEK
A CORPORATION AT WAR?

NanoTek is, as we know, the all-powerful omniscient and *friendly* face of NanoTek Corporation based here, in The City, in its alleys and gutters, skyblocks and cubeblocks, in the New York Clusters, New Tek London, Old Athens, The Sydney Pipe and Cape Town Smash and Shaghai and The Dregs, Sub-City, DOG Town and POSH Town right up to the Black Rose Citadel itself—NanoTek's heart and home and pumping core. NanoTek are *the* unrivalled and most affluent entity in Quad-Gal, single-handedly responsible for the ability to cure death! NanoTek are indeed God—achieving a technological apotheosis, for the biomods have brought the ability to cure any disease known to man, to alter any aspect of a human organism from finger nail and hair structure to factors such as weight gain and loss, facial restructuring, skin tone and texture... the list goes on. NanoTek, the saviour of modern medicine—able to rebuild organs on demand without recourse to opening the body with a primitive *scalpel*! Able to increase sexual appetites, decrease race hatred, *evolve* man to a God Platform from which he may look down and survey with pride all he has achieved. What God created, NanoTek perfected. 2-1 to NanoTek.

But...

There's a worm at the rotten core of the apple.

A chicken beak in the burger.

A severed finger, trailing tendons, in the cheese pie.

Despite only being available for three months on The City's streets, the biomod (v1.0) human and alien upgrade has been cracked, replicated and *pirated* by illegal and immoral code monkeys. Where once NanoTek with global government support could control the facilities of biomod upgrades and monitor activity via control pad dials and GreenSource links to CoreCentral and GreenSource Mainframes, now the pirates have stolen biomod chassis modules, re-programmed existing biomods, *deviated* and *twisted* the design from the original NanoTek blueprint and ethic. In differing Dregsides across The City, these SubCs are *awash* with pirated biomods... which allow humans and aliens to give themselves *immoral* and *perverse* upgrades never originally intended by NanoTek! Last week, one suspicious suspect was arrested by the Justice SIMs—when he resisted arrest, it took ten SIMs and twenty-four bullets to put him down, so fast, powerful and agile had he become. And all by the abuse of illegitimate biomod technology!

A month ago, a Dreg porn syndicate was raided—to find a man with three erections filming a movie with a series of biomod deformed women, the most modest of which had turned her anus *and* mouth into two extra vaginas, and the worst of which had grown her arm into a huge flopping clitoris so that a gaggle of biomod deformed sexual deviants could suckle their way to multiple biorgasm! And let's not start on the pirates' abuse of the biomods as a drug... the ultimate drug, able to give week-long highs without risk of going cold turkey, and with the programmable ability to live out twisted biomod drug-induced fantasies in differing periods of depraved history.

My friends, this catalogue of abuse goes on unchecked and, sadly, out of control. Where will it end? This sorry piracy and abuse of the biomod human upgrade escalates and degrades with each passing day. The GreenSource Mainframe reports more and more 'snatch' samples of pirated biomods being used. They are on the increase, my friends, and have infiltrated up through the Dregs and SubCs to mainframe life cycles. No longer a pastime of the Non-Credits, now our wealthy executives, doctors, teachers, bureaucrats, publishers, editors, inspectors, critics, thespians, all the revered in our modern revolutionary and *evolutionary* society are partaking in these pirated and dangerously *hacked* biomods with apparent disregard for their own health and sanity!

We are slowly becoming a society of the depraved: a circus act filled with freaks riding parasite-like on the back of NanoTek's abused and twisted technology. It must stop! *We* must stop this farce. NanoTek must take responsibility for their abominable creation and withdraw the biomod technology until it's made foolproof! We, the people, should not be subject to such a dangerous and out-of-control technological deviancy. It must be stopped. And it must be stopped now!

News clip: END.

THEY STOOD BY the door, Franco in armoured jacket and pants, D5 shotgun strapped to his back, Kekra machine pistols in his broad hands, a large variety of grenades clipped to his belt, and a long *sha sha* knife strapped to one thigh. He wore leather sandals on his feet showing toe-nails in serious need of a clipping.

"At *last*. Are you *ready?*" growled Keenan.

Franco nodded. "Just need the kitchen sink."

"Very funny."

"You think I'm joking? Great weapon is a kitchen sink. Once clubbed a Slab to death with one. Especially if you get a good hold on the taps. Gives you a bit of leverage, y'know?"

"Grwwlll."

Mel stepped forward, her chain jangling. Keenan glanced at her, then back at Franco, then back to the mutated woman. "Wait a minute," he said, as comprehension dawned.

"She's got to come with us," said Franco.

"Oh no. We'll go and find this Knuckles guy, then bring help *back to Mel*. We're not dragging an eight-foot slab of muscled zombie torso on a damned mission. And that's final."

"But *Keenan,* she's my girl, my woman, my chick, my bird, my bit of fluff. I can't leave her behind. Y'know. With all the," he shivered, "all them there zombie monsters wandering around. She might get hurt."

Keenan eyed the rippling muscles, the jaw which could chew through hull steel, the razor talons. "What, in the name of fuck, is going to hurt *that?*"

"Hey, she's a she, not a *that*. And you never know!"

"Franco, no."

"Yes."

"No."

"Yes."

"She'll compromise the mission."

"She *is* the mission."

Keenan stamped his foot. "Dickhead, listen, she'll draw attention to us like groupies to an arse-ugly rock star. She'll be fine here, just leave her... the TV remote. Or something."

Franco stared with puppy dog eyes at Mel. "Sorr*eee* love. Keenan says no."

Mel barked, a savage canine ejection. She bared her teeth and growled again. "Grwwll."

Keenan took a step back. He clenched his teeth tight, his Techrim not-quite pointing at Franco's fiancée. He bit back a flood of jokes about Franco's woman being *a dog*. "Come on Cam, back me up on this one. We can't drag an eight-foot mutant on a mission."

"Actually," said Cam, "I think Mel could well be beneficial to our very survival in this place. And having her aboard will actually *reduce* our mission time if we do happen find a cure for her, ahem, condition. Speaking logically, of course."

Keenan glared at Cam—just as a shuffling sound came from the stairwell. Keenan whirled, but Mel was already bounding past him, talons lashing out as the bulky zombie appeared, strips of skin hanging from its mutated face, pointed teeth bared with yellow mucus, hands like claws scrabbling at the pistol in its human-skin belt. Mel's talons hammered the creature, which toppled backwards down the stairs with a series of sickening, bone-breaking crunches.

Everybody froze.

Franco beamed. "See! See what she did! There's a good girl Melanie! Atta girl!"

"OK," said Keenan, grimly. He deflated. "OK. I relinquish. Melanie can come on the mission." She turned and growled at him, long drools of saliva pooling from her crooked maw. He eyed the black blood on her talons. *Dangerous,* screamed his mind. "Just make sure you keep her on a damned tight leash."

Franco bounded forward, and wrapped the chain around his fist. "Don't you worry you none,

Keenan, I'll look after her, she won't be one ounce of trouble, I promise! Just get us to that Knuckles lad and let's get this business sorted."

"Come on," sighed Keenan. "Let's get to the vets."

"The vets?"

"Sorry mate. I meant the market."

THE STREET WAS deserted. Rain pounded a torrent. Keenan led the way, with Franco and Mel close behind, Mel's claws raking the enamel-tarmac. Cam brought up the rear with sensors spinning.

"Something's affecting my gyroscope," said Cam.

Keenan halted, boots splashing puddles. "Which means?"

"There's a big power surge coming."

"What kind of power surge?" said Keenan, eyes narrowed in suspicion.

"I suggest," suggested Cam, voice smooth and calm, "that everybody hits the ground. Right about *now!*"

They hit the ground, and the storm-clouds above *crackled.* A cold wind smashed down the street. Below, the ground rumbled. The wind increased, pounding the rain horizontally as the two Combat K soldiers and their mutant accomplice crawled to the edge of the desecrated road and cowered below a teetering, wobbling skyscraper.

"What is it?" screamed Keenan over the roar of the wind. "An earthquake?"

"No. There's a surge pretty much as big as anything I've ever felt. It's rolling across the planet."

"A surge? Of what? What the hell *is it?*"

"Just scanning."

Franco grinned at Keenan, gripping his guns to his chest. "Just like the old days, eh buddy?"

"I don't remember crawling through puddles with an eight-foot monster. Which old days do you mean, exactly?"

"I meant, the facing of uncertain odds, Combat K out in the wilds again. Y'know? That sort of nostalgic bull-shit. All we need now is... Pippa." Franco saw Keenan's face darken, and he put a hand on the arm of Keenan's storm-drenched War-Suit. "I'm sorry, mate."

"So am I."

"Here it comes. Cover your heads!"

A roar filled the ground, filled the sky, filled the world. The streets shook. Distantly, three tower blocks crumbled and dust *whumped* into the sky in blossoming dark mushroom clouds. For a terrible, heart-lurching moment Keenan thought the Quad-Gal boys had nuked the planet to rid it of its zombie infestation; one quick succession of strikes, or maybe a single Halo Strike from a Titan IV, and bam. Game over. Dogmeat. For *everybody*.

A smell like acid washed down the street. Keenan's nose wrinkled as the powerful stench invaded his senses, burning his nostrils, scouring his throat...

And then—

The lights went out.

Like a dimmer switch on The City's orbiting twin suns, the world was slowly turned down into darkness. The rain still pounded, the storm howled, but now nothing more than an eerie glow shone from the sky. Distant stars glittered. It was...

"Night," said Keenan, crawling to his knees. Ozone filled his nostrils and he coughed on tox. He could feel every pore of his skin tingling. "What happened, Cam? Where are the suns?"

"The City has no self-sustaining climate. It relies on machines, what are known in the trade as Global Equilibrium Pumps; they come from the old days, back from the time of terraformers—before the Helix War blasted World Builders and Ion Platforms into infinity and beyond."

"A Global Equilibrium Pump?"

"Climate control. On a global scale. Stops The City *frying*. Now, I've tapped into the local news," said Cam. "It appears the zombies have taken control of the GEPs. It would appear…"

Cam paused, and Keenan and Franco climbed to their feet. Electricity sparkled down the street, leaping from skyscraper to tower-block to cubescraper.

"Ah."

"Ah's bad, right?" said Franco.

"The zombies have blown the main GEP, and now have control of all subordinate machines. They're in control of The City's climate. Its weather. Its day and night cycle. Its ocean tides."

"Why would they do that?" said Franco, frowning.

"They don't like the sun," said Keenan, voice soft. "Right?"

"I don't get it?"

Keenan's head snapped right. His eyes focused on Cam. "It's the biomods. They slow down in the heat. If the zombies can shield the planet from the sun—cool The City down…"

"They will become faster, more dangerous, harder to kill," said Cam.

"Great," muttered Franco.

Mel lifted her head, small dark eyes glittering, and emitted a long, mournful howl.

Keenan hoisted his MPK with a rattle, and checked the mag on his Techrim. "Come on Franco," he snapped. "And whilst you're at it, smack your bitch up. She's driving me barking mad."

"Very funny, Keenan." Franco scowled. "I'm laughing so hard I pissed myself."

THE BLACK PANEL groundvan sat at the corner of two intersecting streets, now bathed in gleaming darkness. The sparking, ravaging energy which had smashed down the freeway rocked the van on heavy suspension, then left, like a fast-vanishing mountain storm. The van clicked softly, cooling. Panels shone, reflecting ambient light, the van and its precision engineering at odds with the surrounding detritus and destruction. Several zombies ambled past, but took no interest in the vehicle; there was no heady, needful, lustful aroma of brains.

The doors slid back revealing a black interior. Cigar smoke drifted free, and Mr Ranger leapt from inside, heavy boots thumping the ground and crushing broken glass. He looked swiftly up and down the street, blue eyes raking devastation. Then he motioned, and the groundvan rocked and groaned on heavily up-rated suspension as...

They exited smoothly, as if fashioned from animate liquid. There were three GK machines, all humanoid in shape, black, glossy, thin-limbed, sculpted—almost works of art. Beyond the ergonomic and functional semi-hydraulic joints, the enamelled TitaniumVI casings, the long elegant powerful limbs, there came teardrop heads with dulled matt black eyes. Each head was swept back to a point, and long slim jaws gleamed revealing rows and rows of tiny needle-thin teeth, each capable of injecting a variety of terminal poisons.

Ranger stood with one hand on the controller, which emitted a soft green smoke, curling like oiled umbilicals around his fingers and integrating with his flesh, with his blood; his free hand sat in the pocket of his heavy overcoat.

Ranger watched the three GK machines stand their ground and survey surroundings. Newborns. They had to learn fast. Ranger smiled; there was no fear in the machines, just an inquisitiveness of new life. Ranger licked his lips. Despite their machine AI status, they were quite definitely *female*.

Ranger's smile was dark. "Nyx?"

"Yes, lord." Her voice was full, powerful, mature and sentient. The GK shifted, her head dropping and rotating to fix matt black eyes on the old soldier. Nyx was the leader, stockier than the other two AIs; her gaze made Ranger shiver just a little, and take an involuntary step back. These machines were new, untested, straight from the crate. More prototype than prototype. Nothing like these had ever existed across the starfields of Quad-Gal.

"Show me."

Nyx dropped to a crouch, rows of teeth widening in a silent roar as spikes rippled across her slick metal torso. They spread across her spine, her neck, her head, a wave of hypodermics undulating across arms and legs. Each of the five thousand points gleamed with the promise of a painful, toxic death.

"Good. Momos? Lamia? Special functions?"

Momos withdrew two long black yukana swords from thin metal sheaves on her back; each was fashioned from a single molecule and could cut twelve-inch hull armour. She spun the weapons idly, dark eyes fixed on Ranger, then went through a complex and stunningly fast choreographed kata where blades hummed and *sang*. Ranger stood, transfixed by the show of awesome skill. Never had he seen such fluidity, speed, skill or timing. He licked dry lips, and released a slow breath as Momos finally wound down from her display and sheathed the twin yukana blades.

Finally Lamia, the thinnest, most elegant of the three GK machines, drew herself up as if standing on metal tip-toe. Her dark eyes seemed to shimmer, and with tiny metallic crackles her elegantly sculpted hands and feet, her arms and legs, they rippled with scales of shifting, blending, blurring metal, shimmering as they became four long black killing blades. Lamia started to dance, a slow rhythmical movement, elegant, mournful, the TitaniumVI blades clacking and clashing on the buckled road with harsh discordant sound. Faster she moved and spun, the four long killing blades flashing and spinning in a haze of incredible deadly motion. To get within reach of the GK was to be cut into chunks of bloody meat. Then Lamia leapt and Ranger stumbled back as blades slashed faster than the eye could see around his head, his body, his own delicate frail flesh limbs and Lamia spun away, halted her dance, a curious smile on her metal face. She folded her arms, which blurred back into a semblance of machine normality.

Ranger nodded, lifted his hat, ran a hand through sweat-streaked grey hair. "Good. Your programming is efficient. You know where your loyalties lie?"

"To you, lord," came the three female voices.

"You must kill them. Combat K: Keenan, and Franco. And the deviated monster who travels with them. Not just kill them, but annihilate them from our plane of existence. Do you understand this directive?"

"We do, lord."

"Go. Do not leave any trace. Slaughter anyone or anything that gets in your way. Have no mercy, no compassion, no empathy; you must simply obey the One Law."

"Yes, lord. The One Law is to Kill. We will Kill, Lord."

Ranger watched the three machines lope off into the stygian gloom, padding through falling rain and mist with the tiniest of suppressed hisses. As Ranger surveyed, they passed a cluster of zombies, busy tearing at a fallen corpse. The six zombies turned, grunting and moaning with curiosity as the GKs approached. Without breaking stride the GK machines blurred into action and were through the zombies in less than a second leaving behind a scatter of body parts and heads, and streaks of tainted blood against buckled pavements.

Ranger climbed into his groundvan, and slammed the door with a solid *thunk*. It h ad been hard finding Franco Haggis, for the man was ex-Combat K and covered his tracks well. However, once Melanie had transformed into the... deviant (Ranger smiled at that) the trace had been narrowed and location easily pin-pointed through GreenSource. Keenan had been in the right place at the right time; Ranger's eyes scanned the tracers on the walls of the groundvan. Ranger had a hot pirate-link straight to the Quad-Gal Military database. Wherever Keenan went, Ranger—and the GKs—could follow.

Ranger lit a cigar, and with grim fascination looked out into an abused world through the eyes of his newborn AI killers.

"This should be... entertaining," he said.

CHAPTER 7
SINPLI(CITY)

"IT'S NOT THERE," said Franco.

"What do you mean, it's not there?" Keenan pushed past Mel and crouched at the corner of the street, chin on the barrel of his MPK, peering at where they'd landed the Y Shuttle *Drunk and Loving It*. Franco was right: the ship wasn't there. Porky Pauper's Fast-Food Burger Emporium wasn't there. In fact, the *street* was gone. All that remained was a pyramid pile of rubble over which stumbled a few lone zombies searching for meat and brains.

"This darkness is giving me the creeps," said Franco. Being a denizen of The City he had grown accustomed to pretty much constant daylight. The odd few hours of nightfall tended to pass whilst Franco lay deep in drunken slumber; as such, his night vision was underdeveloped.

"Don't be such a big girl."

Mel, crouching beside Franco, started to scratch behind an ear with her foot claw. A rasping sound, as of metal on metal, echoed down the rubble-piled street. One of the zombies looked up—a quick, unexpected movement. With a guttural snarl it leapt towards them, scattering bricks and shards of glass, using hands as feet as it pounded towards the group with a sudden burst of acceleration.

Keenan stood, and growled, "I'm sick of this shit." The zombie leapt, and Keenan unloaded ten bullets into the sagging grey flesh, each impact spinning and punching the marionette until it landed, rolling, rags fluttering, twenty feet away. Keenan glanced at Franco. He shook his head. "Looks like we're on foot."

Franco gestured past Keenan with a twitch of his head. Keenan looked back, to see the dropped zombie crawling unsteadily to its feet. Keenan could see clean through several holes, jagged with splinters of bone. He pulled a smile without humour as the zombie, snarling again, charged with a limping, wounded, tortured gait. Keenan leapt to battle, ducking a swipe of claws and side-kicking the creature in the chest. But it was fast, faster than Keenan expected; claws closed on his leg, catching him in steel manacles and he was spun horizontally, second boot hammering at the creature's face. It stumbled back, tripped, flailed as it hit the ground. Keenan landed lightly, leapt forward, placed his boot on the creature's chest and gazed down into yellow, feral eyes.

Once human, he thought.

It was once a person. A man.

"Shit."

He unloaded twenty bullets into the zombie's head until there was nothing left but a protruding shard of slick spinal column. Decapitation by machine gun. Keenan glanced up. Around. The activity had gained them some attention. He cursed.

"Neat," said Franco, watching the gathering crowd of zombies climbing up over the rubble pyramid and shuffling together, silhouetted against a bright sulphur glare of strobing lights from a nearby train-wreck, which rested on its side amidst the annihilation of the street. "You dealt with that incident in a perfectly covert manner. You didn't get us into no bother, no sir. No unwanted attention at all!"

"Quiet! Cam? Which way to the market?"

"Which one? The City has one hundred and seventeen thousand."

Keenan looked at Franco, as the background noise of groans and moans increased in volume. "Which market, Franco? To find this boy, Knuckles? Come on, the bastards are *coming*."

Franco shrugged. "How the hell do I know? I've no bloody idea where the damned woman shopped. Shopping is an activity for the female of the species!" He spat with aggression, face contorted in hatred, and growled, "I wouldn't be seen *dead* with a fucking plastic carrier bag!"

"You'll be dead pretty soon if you don't explain where we're going," said Cam, voice an atomic whisper.

Mel grunted, heaved her bulk to its taloned feet, and set off at a lumber down a street littered with broken glass, which glinted, sparkling like tiny, fallen stars. She glanced back, over one rippling shoulder, then continued, claws raking the ground.

"Where's she going?" rumbled Franco, eyeing the approaching horde of zombies.

"I think she's showing us the way," said Keenan. He glanced wearily at the buried Y Shuttle. "So much for weapons, bombs and the Permatex War-Suits I had stashed for you and Pippa!"

"Pippa? You mean we're meeting her?" Franco's face lit up. He had a *special* affection for Pippa.

"No. But I have a nasty suspicion she'll find us. I don't trust Steinhauer as far as I can piss. This little drama is starting to feel too much like a bad gig. Convenient. I'm only here because I want to know why the junks invaded my world; Steinhauer, on the other hand, seems to want Combat K together again."

Franco nodded, pumped his D5 shotgun ten times, and they set off at a run. Behind, the rag-tag collection of zombies pursued doggedly, but these were the slow, the lame, the injured, the deviant. The stronger ones had more important work to do.

DESPITE HER BULK, Mel ran quickly, talons pounding the littered city streets. Keenan and Franco kept pace, with Cam bobbing just behind, his haywire scanners trying their best to locate threat.

They halted by a wide-open plaza. Fires burned, and they could see where a collection of people— with a few proxers and Slabs thrown in—had built a high barricade. At the foot there lay a smattering of dismembered zombie bodies. Further out, in staggered arcs, lay the smoking, blackened corpses of the deviant.

"Flamethrower?" said Franco, dropping to one knee beside Keenan.

"Yeah. They're doing a good job in that temporary fortress."

Franco stared across the paved space, beyond several burning cars, and could see huge Slabs bearing what looked like industrial pipes but with flames flickering in holed barrels. They patrolled up and down the makeshift ramparts, which had been hastily built from sections of concrete and steel, and old steel barrels.

Slabs were genetically modified humans bred in Vats for an ancient game of war on a planetary scale, designed to amuse decadent game-head humans. They were, to all intents, genetically bred defects: huge, muscular, with cubic heads and flat faces, awesomely powerful in battle, but what Man—as God—had given them in brawn, he had taken away in brain.

"What you thinking?" whispered Franco.

"I'm wondering why Mel has stopped."

"Is this place in the way? Is she frightened of the fire, do you think?"

Keenan shrugged. "She's your girl, Franco. Ask her."

"Mel? Mel!"

Melanie turned, globular head dropping to within a few inches of Franco's face. She made a strange keening sound, and her chain dragged across the ground.

"Es?"

"Why have we stopped?" hissed Franco. "Do we need to get through here?"

Melanie shook her head. Her corrugated neck made strange hissing and popping sounds.

"Why then?" Franco frowned. "Is this the marketplace where you bought the biomod?"

Mel nodded, pea-head bobbing.

"But it's no longer here! How are we going to find this lad, Knuckles?"

"We'll ask the locals," said Keenan, who'd lit a cigarette. The burning fires reflected in his eyes. "With a name like that, I'm pretty sure *somebody* must have heard of him. Sounds like a wheeler-dealer type."

"The City has a population of *trillions*," said Franco, staring hard at Keenan. "Your optimism never ceases to amaze me."

"Any better ideas? After all, it's not my bird who's got fleas."

"Funny, Keenan, very funny. I'm laughing so hard my sides are splitting."

Behind them came a groan, and the sound of sodden limping in the darkness. Keenan shuddered. "If we don't move soon, that might well come to pass. After all, your sides are the quickest way to your kidneys. Come on."

"We can't take Mel in there," hissed Franco, clasping his gun. "They'll burn her!"

Keenan gave a half-smile, wrinkling his nose at the stench of smoke. "I'm sure they'll see her feminine side," he muttered.

* * *

KEENAN APPROACHED FIRST, and waving his arms, shouted, "Ho! In there! We're friendly, hold your fire."

A huge flat Slab peered over the jagged barrier of concrete. Small black eyes stared at Keenan without compassion. "What you want?"

"We're looking for information. On a lad called Knuckles, used to work the streets round here."

The Slab stared at Keenan for a long time. "You not one of them flesh eating boobies?"

"No," said Keenan. "Do I look like one? I have all my own arms, see?"

The Slab stared again and Keenan sighed. Slabs were hard. Rock hard. But intelligence didn't feature high on their list of employee attributes. In fact, you were lucky to get a stupid one.

"You *might* be boobie," said the Slab, slowly, face wrinkled in concentration. Keenan caught the whiff of a flamethrower held just out of sight. His hand tightened on his MPK.

"Look, what's your name?"

"I is Rappo, and I is no cherry spuke, nor a cheese in fact! Ha! I know your damned zombie games. You boobies, you sneak in, past this old spuke and try and eat my brains yes you would!"

"Rappo. Rappo." Keenan smiled, holding out the flats of his hands. "Is there a human there I can speak with?"

"No. Rappo in charge of EPF."

"EPF?"

"Exterior Perimeter Fence. No clever spuke getting past this cheery cherry Slab! Oh no! Rappo not have cheese for brain just cheese in his belly!"

"Listen, Rappo. My name is Keenan. I'm a soldier, look, with a gun. I'm a friend. I've served with many Slabs in my time; after all, would a zombie *really* know that you were born in Vats, that you feed in Troughs, and that a spuke is another name for *bastard*? Well?"

"Suppose not," rumbled the Slab. "Who that with you? In the darkness? You being clever cherry and trying get old Rappo to let you zombie motherfuckers in?" He growled a string of expletives in a language Keenan could not vocally replicate.

"No. No. Listen, just let us inside…"

Suddenly, Mel charged, leapt the high concrete barrier and Rappo let out a screech like nothing Keenan had ever heard. Flames roared, billowing into the sky but Mel was past, down in the trench, and there came a single solitary *thwack*. Something slapped hard against the ground. Keenan put his head in his hands, then with a mumbling Franco in tow, climbed the barrier of concrete, scaffolding and barrels, and jumped down into the trench. Rappo was laid out cold. Mel held the flamethrower like an interesting toy, staring down into the glowing nozzle.

Gently, Keenan prized the large weapon from her talons. "Better let me have that, love. Don't want you burning your own head off, do we?" Keenan prodded the Slab with the toe of his boot.

Franco was beaming. "A single punch! What a gal! Never seen a Slab laid out with a single punch before! Who's a good girl, yes, jubba jubba jubba, who's a pretty little girl then."

Mel rolled on her back, and Franco rubbed her belly.

"Franco!" snapped Keenan. "Mission. Biomods. SinScript. Knuckles. *Remember*, fuckwit?"

"Aye, Keenan, aye. Just giving praise where it's warranted."

"You stay here. I'll go and find whoever's in charge. Cam?"

"Yes Keenan?"

"Keep an eye on these lovebirds, will you?"

"Yes Keenan, although I fear the surges and pulses which rearranged the planetary weather and night cycles have damaged my scanners. I only see enemies a couple of seconds before you see them yourselves."

"Sometimes, that's all we need," said Keenan quietly. "Just do your best lad."

Keenan stalked ahead, down the narrow trench between barrels, H-section girders and plinths of shattered concrete. He soon heard voices, and keeping low, silent, he approached. The barricade had been melded to the front of an office block, the foyer changed into a CoP—a Centre of Operations. Keenan could see around thirty men and women, all heavily armed, and several Slabs, clustered around a heavyset man pointing at a digital map which glittered.

So, they've got power, thought Keenan.

And a leader.

Then Keenan's mouth dropped as recognition bit him. The man by the digital map was...

"Keenan!" roared the bald, black-bearded, short stocky warrior, and pushed past the gathered soldiers and Slabs, a beam hijacking his face. "I don't believe it!"

"The surprise is all mine," said Keenan, stepping forward. All eyes were locked on him. The stocky man approached, and gave Keenan a powerful bear-hug.

"Lads! Lads! This is Keenan, the one I was telling you about."

"From your Adventures With Leviathan That You're Not Supposed To Discuss, sir?"

"Aye lad, from my Adventures With Leviathan That I'm Not Supposed To Discuss."

Keenan laughed, then, releasing some of his tension. He eyed the savage Frankenstein-scars on Betezh's face, the small dark eyes, the predatory look of the shark. It was easy to underestimate the man. However, Betezh had proved himself in many a fire-fight.

"It's good to see you," said Keenan, at last.

"And you! Man, this city has gone insane! It's nice to get another gun on the parapet! We're fighting a losing battle here. Every single body helps, so to speak. Every gun another bullet in the eye of fascist zombie oppression. You dig?"

"You've organised all this?"

"Well, I did my best."

Keenan slapped Betezh on the back. "You did well, mate."

Betezh was former Combat K turned Internal Affairs—and several years previous had been set up by his employer, the politician Kotinevitch, to monitor Franco Haggis when the ginger-bearded soldier had been incarcerated in Mount Pleasant—a mental institution for the seriously unstable—after the military mission of Terminus5 had gone horribly wrong.

Keenan, Franco and Pippa now knew the Terminus5 debacle had been a set-up, but it hadn't stopped their subsequent imprisonment, and Franco's incarceration in a lunatic asylum. After a daring escape, Franco had gone on the run—closely pursued by Betezh who wanted nothing more than Franco's blood. Via a bizarre series of twists, and the comedy of fate, Franco had first stapled Betezh's face with an industrial bone-stapler, then was in turn rescued by Betezh from an organic lake on the bleak desolate planet of Teller's World. Betezh had, in the end, proved himself to be Combat K—proved himself true to his roots. And, whilst they could not really ever consider themselves friends, Keenan, Franco and Betezh could be considered brothers in adversity.

Now, here, Betezh had boosted these nostalgic memories until he believed, *believed,* they had been the best of buddies. Which went in some way to answer Keenan's confusion at this unexpected and over-friendly reunion.

"Listen," said Keenan, keeping his voice low. "You remember Franco?"

"Franco! Salt of the earth, a bosom buddy, what a guy!"

"Well he's having a few, shall we say, pre-marital problems."

"He's getting married?" Betezh cackled. "Is she a babe? A sex-monster? A lithe and buxom lap-dancer type? Is she? Is she?"

"That would be *one* way of describing her, yes. The thing is, we need to locate a lad who used to work the markets around here. Went by the name of Knuckles."

Betezh turned to his soldiers. He preened, for here, and now, he was able to publicly aid his old war buddy—the one about which he'd regaled his platoon in over-exaggerated tales highlighting his own over-exaggerated bravado. "Listen up! Good buddy of mine is in the shit, needs some help."

"Is he Combat K?" asked one rangy looking woman, her face unhealthy, hair like strings of barbed wire. And yet her eyes shone with adoration for Betezh, her charismatic leader.

"He is. He is," rumbled Betezh. "We are *all* Combat K!" Betezh beamed foolishly.

Keenan coughed. "I, um, wouldn't be shouting that out too loud, if I was you."

"Why not? I am proud of our military heritage!"

Keenan looked into eyes twisted from the path of sanity. "It's a clandestine unit," said Keenan, carefully. "Totally covert. A secret organisation within a secret organisation. Combat K is supposed to be a myth to the general population of Quad-Gal... so we can *continue* to carry out covert infiltrations, assassinations, detonations, that sort of thing. Yes?"

"Ahh, poppycock! We should be proud of our Combat K missions! We are the *elite of the elite!* Eh lads?"

The crowd of armed men and women gave a cheer, waving their weapons in the air, grateful to be led by such a wonderful military wartime hero, *and* given temporary honorary status in such a secret organisation to boot. The Slabs grunted and groaned in appreciation, like a bad aural rendition of horse sex. Keenan covered his face with his hands and groaned. *What's happened to the world? Am I truly surrounded by idiots?*

"I've heard of Knuckles," said one man, raising his hand.

"Good lad! Spill the beans, what do you know?" Betezh's shark eyes gleamed.

"He's a bad lad, a spaceship-thief, drugsmoke entrepreneur, wheeler and dealer and ducker and diver. He'll buy, sell and rob anything that isn't nailed down. The market-traders normally chase him with snap-sticks if they see the little terrier."

"And where might we find him now?"

The man shrugged bony shoulders. "I think he's part of a gang, one of the teeny bastards who infest this part of The City. They call themselves The City Liberators, I assume because they try to liberate cash from people." He gave a bleak smile, looking at Keenan. "If you find him, put a bullet in his head. He's a maggot in need of a thrashing."

"So, a nice guy," said Keenan, lighting a cigarette. "Anybody know where I can find these City Liberators?"

A woman pointed, across the raging fires and burning cars, to a dark narrowing of city streets. "Over there, Dregside, gangland. I think they eke out an existence on the edges of the financial district; lots of rich people to mug down that way."

Keenan nodded, staring out at distant streets that looked completely impassable, thanks to collapsed buildings, rubble, raging fires and plentiful zombies. "Shit." He took a deep toke on his Widow Maker. His PAD rattled and it clicked to his private frequency. It was Cam. "Yeah?"

"Have you made contact with the leader?"

"Yeah. Franco's gonna get the surprise of his life."

"Well, whoever is in charge, tell him we got trouble."

"That Rappo Slab wake up?"

"Worse than that. The zombies are coming."

"Set Mel on them, she seems to be adept at cutting heads from deviant bodies."

"No, Keenan. Tell the Big Man he needs to bring his troops. And fast. The zombies are coming. They're armed. Armoured. And dangerous."

"How many?"

But his words were drowned by a sudden deafening roar from across the barricades. Keenan and Betezh, followed by the rag-tag band of makeshift soldiers, sprinted along the narrow trench to where Franco was peering over a concrete balustrade. Betezh eyed Mel warily, eyes following the collar and chain to Franco's fist. Mel growled, but Franco patted her disjointed muzzle affectionately and her growl switched instantly to a *purr*.

Beyond the barricade, the roaring continued and Keenan leapt up, taking hold of rusted wire and hauling himself to peer over the edge. The zombies had spread out into what could only be described a *phalanx*. There were hundreds of them—*thousands* of them. They stood in ranks, sagging grey flesh illuminated by fires. Many carried machine guns and shotguns. The front ranks had...

Keenan blinked.

"They've got *shields*," he snapped, and glanced over at Franco.

"I never said they were stupid," said Franco.

"Yeah, stupid is one thing, but the bastards have organised themselves into a military unit. A battalion. An *army*."

"We've faced worse odds than this," grinned Franco.

"When?" snapped Keenan. "Tell me, when the hell have we faced worse odds than a three-thousand strong military-tooled zombie-army?"

"Ach, plenny of times Keenan, we'll be just fine. You'll see. Or they don't call me Franco 'Jammy Bastard' Haggis for nothing, so they don't!"

"They don't call you Franco 'Jammy Bastard' Haggis at all! Come on, Big Guy, what's the plan?" Keenan eyed the horde. It sent up another wailing roar, and the zombies started banging axes and lengths of pipe against their makeshift shields.

"Did you find out where Knuckles is?"

"A rough approximation."

"Then it's easy," grinned Franco. He waggled his eyebrows. "We're going to run away."

Franco wasn't the only one with the idea of fleeing, and as Betezh clapped Franco on the back with a booming laugh and a cry of, "Well met, Franco, you old dog!"—much to Franco's frowning consternation—Betezh looked around at his small band of fellow troops. "Listen up!" he bellowed. Below, the zombies had started a lumbering, staggered charge. Their rotten feet thundered sloppily across the plaza, leaving many a toe behind. "We can hold these walls, die, and become heroes! Or, as I now propose, we can squeeze out the back way and hot-tail it away in order to fight another day! That way, we will certainly come to face ever bigger odds on a more glamorous battlefield! And become even bigger heroes! Hurrah!"

The vote was instant and unanimous. As the zombies, screaming and frothing, clambered up the barricade in search of fresh brains, Betezh led the group—nervous now that Mel was in their midst—down through makeshift trenches and through the once opulent foyer of the office building. They sprinted down dank concrete steps into a half-flooded basement. Water and oil swirled about their legs, and with zombie screams echoing behind, Betezh led the group past concrete support pillars to a wide, low room, at the end of which squatted seven narrow tunnels guarded by heavy mesh grilles of TitaniumIII.

"We'll have to blast our way inside," said Betezh.

"I'm the man for *that* job," said Franco, puffing out his chest.

"This is just like the old days!" beamed Betezh, slapping Franco on the back.

Franco eyed the crazy scarring on Betezh's face. "Not the old days I remember," he muttered, and dragging his pack from his back, started to rummage for hardcore explosives.

"No need," said Keenan.

"Why's that?"

Keenan gestured to where Mel approached the grilles and attached her talons to metalwork. With a grunt, she heaved, muscles writhing across her powerful, mottled body. There came a long moment of locked tension, then a squeal as the grille gave way. Mel hurled it aside, where it buckled against the wall and clattered into swirling flood-water.

"Jesus," said Betezh. "I've spent the last couple of days trying to kill these bastards. Never thought I'd be running away with one!" He glanced over at Franco. "What a beast, hey? And ugly? Hell, you could crack bottles open on that face!"

"Shut up," muttered Franco.

"But why?" Betezh frowned. "It's not like she's your bird or anything." He roared with laughter at his own joke, and slapped Franco heartily on the back

Groans and roars came echoing down into the skyscraper basement. "Looks like they breached the walls," said Franco. Keenan simply nodded, wincing. "You OK?"

"Headache."

"Hangover?"

"No, Franco. It's not a bloody hangover."

"OK. OK. Don't get so tetchy."

Keenan clicked the narrow Mag-torch attached to his MPK, attempting to ignore the tiny, intrusive pain at the back of his skull. Bright light leapt in a steady beam. And, with Betezh and Franco close by his side, weapons at the ready, they waded into the flooded service tunnel—into the darkness—and into the unknown.

THEY CREPT THROUGH nigritude, with only a few torches to light their way. The tunnel roof was circular, smooth, and gleamed with damp under pencil-thin beams. Water sloshed around their knees, invading boots and making life uncomfortable.

Keenan and Franco were up near the front, beside Betezh who led the way. It seemed he knew the tunnels well, and when Keenan asked him why, he just gave a broad wink—which, on his scarred and disfigured face, and in the light of the torches, looked quite horrific. Certainly demonic.

"My God, what kind of monster did I create?" mumbled Franco.

Keenan gave him a friendly slap on the back.

Mel followed, in the midst of the soldiers, who continually *didn't-quite-point* their guns at her. Occasionally she growled, and snapped at anybody who got too close. A lot of makeshift squaddies came close to ND.

Far behind, the howls and groans and screams followed them through the haunted tunnels. It would seem the zombies, the mutants, the deviants, had not been fooled. And this new darkness, and sense of enclosure, did nothing but heighten primal fears.

Franco was reliving many of his own private nightmares. Not only was his woman a mutated monstrosity, but he hated enclosed spaces almost as much as he hated a quarantined brothel. He muttered in rhythm as he walked, words spilling out like a depraved marching song.

"Bloody dark. Bloody zombies. Bloody creepy gloom."

"Bloody water. Bloody sloshing. Bloody creepy shadows."

"Wish I had a rainbow pill."

"Wish I had a rainbow pill."

This last mumbled sentence referred to the days spent incarcerated at The Mount Pleasant Hilltop

Institution, the "nice and caring and friendly home for the mentally challenged". Franco had certainly been mentally challenged; now, he was merely mental.

"Ouch!" he screeched, doing a sudden jig in the water which sent waves lapping against slick walls. "It's there! Down there! In the water! It's a zombie! A zombie fish!" He unleashed a hail of bullets from his Kekra quad-barrel machine pistol, the roar filling the tunnel, the flash of fire illuminating his deranged features.

"Franco!" snapped Keenan.

Franco released the trigger. A metallic booming rang up and down the tunnel. Acrid smoke filled the air. Everything seemed suddenly much darker. Much more frightening.

"Sorry!" Franco held up his hand, glancing back at the other soldiers. "My mistake. Just a piece of old tyre."

"How the *fuck* can an old piece of tyre be misconstrued as a zombie fish?" snarled Keenan.

"Hey, look, I said I was sorry," snapped Franco. "Excuse *me* for not being an expert on zombie marine life."

Keenan tutted, and moved ahead with Betezh.

Franco pulled out his lower lip, trudging through the oily water, listening to the distant sounds of slopping zombie pursuit. Suddenly, there came a slapping of water, a few grunts and curses of, "Hey, what you doin'?", and Mel arrived beside Franco. He glanced over at her, and gave a weak and watery smile.

"Oh. It's you."

"Grwwlll."

"Oh yeah? Easy for you to enunciate."

Her head lowered, and she nuzzled at him, just as Betezh turned and grinned through the gloom, his face eldritch in the bobbing torchlight. "I think she fancies a slice of Franco pie," he said.

"Get stuffed Betezh."

"Don't be like that, Franco, we've been through some tough times together! Some *great adventures!* We're like brothers in arms, *compadres*, a rag-tag firm of muscular savagery and might!"

Franco stared at Betezh. "And you thought *I* was insane?"

"What's that supposed to mean?"

"Betezh, we *never* had any good times."

"Yeah we did!"

"What, like the fifty times you electrocuted my testicles? Or maybe the time I punched you out of a dive-bombing helicopter? Or what about the episode where I injected your brain with a syringe— direct through your forehead? Maybe you're referring to the incident when I used an industrial bone-stapler on your saggy face? Ring any bells? Notice any common themes of violence there?"

"Ach, that was just us fucking wit' each other."

"Stop the games," snapped Keenan, "we've got a split in the tunnel ahead."

They arrived at a large cylindrical chamber which rose above the group for about a kilometre. Far far above, against ink black, a few stars glittered.

"This is where we part company," said Betezh. He pointed. "Follow the tunnel that way, two or three klicks, it leads to a service chute and back onto city streets; keep your eyes peeled though, it's an easy entrance to miss. Narrow, with a tiny ladder poking from the tunnel roof. You'll be in the heart of gangland then—just find yourself a scumbag scrote-filled shit-stinking little hoodie and ask for directions. All the gang members know the other gangs. They spend most of their time trying to slaughter one another. Honour amongst thieves, eh?" He grinned, face like a devil's sick of sin.

"Where you going?" asked Keenan.

"We'll have to try and find another area to defend. Our barricade, whilst secure, was far too close to street level. A foolish move, I fear; although I never expected the deviants to form an army and attack *en masse*. I thought zombies were dumb and stumbled willingly onto your gun barrel!"

"Well, thanks for this," said Keenan. He shook Betezh's calloused, meaty hand. "We owe you one."

"Yeah, cheers," said Franco, a tad grumpy, a tad sulky. "Go on Mel, say thank you."

"Eers," rumbled Mel, and Franco gave her chain a tug. It jangled. Mel growled.

Betezh eyed the huge monster warily. "Hell, I'd get that ugly bitch put down real fast, if I was you. Can't have deviants stumbling around in the dark. Gives us all the heebie jeebies! Listen, we could do it now for you, if you like? As a favour?"

"We have it under control," said Franco, coolly.

"OK then. Well, so long!" Betezh saluted. "Hey, and if you ever have another mission where you need a brave and foolhardy accomplice..."

"Be assured, we won't call you," muttered Franco.

They moved down the tunnel, with Betezh's booming laughter chasing them. It would seem he was in his element, all animosity towards Franco gone and forgotten.

Silence closed in, and with it a heavier, more claustrophobic atmosphere. Franco felt himself growing ever more twitchy, goosebumps rising on his arms and neck as he constantly jumped at shadows.

"Hey Keenan," he said after half a klick.

"Yeah mate?"

"What do you think the zombie horde will do when it reaches a split in the tunnel?"

"I think our enemy is a damned sight more intelligent than we give it credit for." Keenan stopped, lit a cigarette, and the flame lit the tunnel in a globe of light for a few moments—then retreated. Darkness rolled back in, liquid ebony. "I think they'll divide, spread out, search all the tunnels."

"Why do they want us?" asked Franco.

Keenan shrugged. "I'm not sure what drives them. I'm not a zombie. Ask your girl Mel over there."

"Hey, she ain't a zombie, Keenan."

"Whatever."

Cam, who had been silent with damaged scanners doing their utmost to locate enemy activity, zipped in close to Keenan. "Kee, I'm struggling here. I need to locate some specialist circuitry and affect a repair. I am worse than useless. A few minutes ago, I located *eight* Francos in the vicinity."

"The *horror*," said Keenan.

"Exactly! Look, I'm afraid I'm going to have to leave you on your own for a few hours. Do you think you can survive down here? Maybe find your way to this Knuckles lad?"

"Well, I'm not staying put," said Keenan. "Until we find some help for Mel, then Franco's off-task. And when he's off-task, he's useless to me in decoding the SinScript. The more time I waste slopping around here in the grime, the longer I have to stay on this godforsaken shit-hole. You go and do what you have to do—me and Franco, we're going to sort out Melanie. We'll find Knuckles. Try and get her fixed. Ain't that right Francis?"

"Damn right bro'."

Cam coughed. "Yes. Very well. I'll be off then. It's starting to feel like an Arnie down here."

Arnie, a famous actor from thousands of years previous, had been *so successful* in action-movies during his life that, upon his death, several of the unscrupulous up-and-coming Ganger Agencies had genetically cloned him and sent his clones out to work making, ironically, clones of the famous movie-star's earlier movies. In uproar, the Arnie Estate had filed a litany of lawsuits prohibiting Ganger Agencies from genetically reproducing their recently dear and departed action hero. However, due to a technicality of small-print in a contract from an early Arnie movie, it seemed the Ganger Agencies had bought the rights to *him* from GPA Films—the very rights to Arnie's organic likeness. In effect, they owned his body, and his *reproduction*. The following uproar led subsequently to savage new anti-cloning laws, and despite the several thousand year legal battle which followed, unfortunately for Arnie, his likeness and DNA were owned not by himself, or his Estate, but by somebody else. His many clones no longer owned their own bodies, and had to pay *rent* to inhabit their flesh, which perpetuated yet more cloning and a continuation of movies... which eventually became known simply as Arnies: a cliché of art where a muscle-bound good guy beats up muscle-bound bad guys with a scattering of witty one-liners. Brilliant, in terms of cheap entertainment value; not so brilliant in terms of the poor man himself. As a clone, or *ganger,* a working Arnie had less rights than a Battle Slab. There had recently been a series of secretly filmed insider documentaries by the BBC on the terrible living and working conditions of movie-bred Arnies, and there had been a public uproar and cries for an internal inquiry into the depraved and unethical movie industry as a whole. Across Quad-Gal, Arnies were horribly mistreated. Kept in narrow cages, force-fed porridge, and only allowed out for an hour of sunlight a day. It just wasn't right.

Cam zipped off into the black, and was instantly swallowed.

Franco peered at Keenan. "Hey, now it's really spooky. We're alone together!" he said, and shuffled a little closer.

"Don't get any ideas."

Franco looked injured. "I was just, y'know, attempting a bit of brotherly solidarity. A bit o' bonding. Strength in union, an' all that."

"Well, give your girlfriend a cuddle," said Keenan, voice harsh, eyes sweeping the tunnel. "She looks like she could do with a bit of sweetening up."

They moved through the swirling water, warily, twitchy, constantly on the lookout for pursuing zombies or whatever hell else was down in the tunnels. Franco stayed close to Keenan, eyes wide, and Mel followed to the rear, head sometimes banging from the tunnel roof and smashing tiles to tumble with concrete pepper into the soup through which they trudged.

"What is this place, anyway?" asked Franco after a while.

Keenan shrugged. "Not sure. But look at the walls." He moved his MPK, which highlighted several horizontal streaks. Franco stared at the streaks, then back at Keenan.

"So, it's got streaks?" he ventured.

"No, those are marks left when the water level is higher, up near the top of the roof."

Franco considered this. "So it floods?"

"Aye, either it floods, or there is some kind of sluice. Draining water from somewhere to somewhere."

"So water could come smashing down at any moment and wash us away?"

"Yeah. Our dickhead friend Betezh forgot to mention that bit, didn't he?"

Franco nodded, chewing his lip. "I *definitely* do not like this place. It gives me the jitters, the creeps, the heebie jeebies. Come on, let's push on; get back up to the fresh air."

"Fresh air filled with zombies?"

"Zombies I can shoot," muttered Franco. "But down here?" He stared at Keenan, deadly serious, mouth a line which had lost all sense of humour. "Down here, well, it's enough to make a man mad."

"YOU HEAR IT?"

"Hear what?"

They stopped, water lapping lazy at the edges of the tunnel.

"It was a hiss," said Franco.

Keenan glowered at him. "Don't start jumping at shadows again, you mad midget. Zombie fish? Hah! I don't want any gunfire until a target's identified. Clear?"

Franco said nothing. He was staring past Keenan.

"You mean like that?" he muttered.

Keenan whirled to see three dark shadows moving fast along the edges of the tunnel. They gleamed, metallic, and were quite obviously designed as killing machines.

"They *don't* look like the sort of robots I'd want to meet in a dark alleyway." Franco licked dry lips. "Shit. I think we should, like, run." Franco sprinted away down the tunnel, water slopping his groin and chest. Keenan ran after him, struggling to move at speed through the high water-level, and he cocked his MPK ready for contact. Mel kept pace with the two men.

Keenan drew alongside Franco. "Look out for the service chute," he hissed.

Distantly, there came a deep, bass rumble.

"Hell's teeth, what are they, Keenan?"

"Advanced killing machines."

Franco glanced back. "They're gaining."

There came a series of metallic *shrings*. Nyx, Momos and Lamia were running in a tight, close formation, a dark, inverted V of water in their wake; Momos had drawn her yukana swords and the three machines gleamed, faces rigid, gloss black and terrifying in the gloom as they closed for the kill...

"There!" snapped Franco. Above, a chute protruded into the tunnel with ragged edges of twisted ladder barely visible. They stopped, and Keenan and Franco sent volleys of machine gun fire screaming down the tunnel at the pursuing AIs. Bullets rattled. Everything was chaos. Fire lit the darkness. Metallic screams charged the air. The three GKs ignored the spinning bullets which spat sparks from casings, deflected by hardy TitaniumVI armour.

"Get up there, Franco," snarled Keenan, pulling free a savage BABE grenade. So named because, as the military contract literature proudly proclaimed, *IT GIVES YOU A GOOD FUCKING!*

"I can't make that jump!" wailed Franco. "I'm only a little fella!" Mel was there instantly, and she hoisted him towards the roof where Franco grasped metal rungs, legs dangling and kicking. With a grunt he hauled himself up, and glanced back.

Again, there came a deep rumble. This time deeper, so deep as to not be heard, just *sensed*. The walls shook. Water sloshed wildly around Keenan's waist.

"Come on Keenan!" Franco bellowed.

"One minute," said Keenan, holding up a finger.

Mel followed Franco, squeezing herself into the narrow aperture with a crunching of armour, a tearing of concrete, a twisting of steel. Powdered concrete rained down on Keenan... as the tunnel began to vibrate.

Keenan pulled the pin from the grenade.

The three GKs were closing *fast*, but Keenan blinked, eyes narrowing as he watched the machines pursued by an increase in rumbling, thundering, shaking and he realised the tunnel water level was rising, swirling violently about him and he tossed the BABE, a small matt globe which sailed out towards the charging enemy robots as a wall of water slammed them from behind picking them up and spinning them and Keenan leapt for the ladder—but too late as a smash of frothing, seething liquid plucked him from his jump and pummelled him along with the flailing, shrieking GKs, and Keenan's MPK roared and spat under froth and foam, and somewhere, distant, as if deep down in a dream muffled by distance and the ocean, there came a terrible subdued *crack* and super-heated water and steam rushed past him in a terrifying violent surge and he thought or dreamt he heard a high-pitched metallic scream but everything was chaos and Keenan was pummelled and torn and smashed, he hit the tunnel wall hard, battered, slapped, was slammed along without control until something snagged his WarSuit, held him there under the onslaught of charging water like a fish struggling for life on a hook—

Water surged and pumped. The world was darker than dark, filled with violent random currents and bubbles. Keenan was slapped repeatedly against concrete, and each blow felt like it shattered bones. He could feel his WarSuit, so many times a saviour, this time betraying him, holding him ensnared with invisible fingers... holding him there *to drown*. He kicked out uselessly, trying his hardest to swim with the current; his MPK was lost and everything was dark and choking and suddenly so very, very cold. Keenan couldn't breathe, simply *could not* breathe, and pain slammed his brain with flowering stars as he struggled desperately, trapped under the flooded tunnel. A dawning realisation forced clarity like a burst of fireworks exploding in his mind.

After all the shit he'd endured, all the battles and wars and demons and AIs he'd faced and fought and killed... here, now, Keenan realised with an ultimate clinical certainty that he was going to die.

CHAPTER 8
CHILD PROTECTION

IT'S BEEN SAID a man's life flashes before his eyes prior to death. For Keenan, it wasn't his life—it was a single moment, a solitary incident stretching away unto infinity. It was a moment of beautiful simplicity, of honesty, of happiness. Standing in the park, in the sunshine, his two girls—Rachel and Ally—on the swings, giggling, squealing when he pushed them too high. To one side, on a bench, sat his wife Freya. She'd tossed back her long hair in the sunshine, and rays sparkled through individual floating strands. Her face looked so calm, so serene, so ultimately at peace. This image, a tableau, remained fixed in Keenan's mind as the powerful rage of the underground flood buffeted him, pounded him, and his burning screaming screeching lungs finally gave out and he breathed—breathed *in* water. Keenan gagged, choked, tried to vomit—and in doing so inhaled even more, desperately drawing more water into his oxygen starved body, arms and legs thrashing wildly and panic, a raging beast closing jaws over his brain, his sanity, his ability to *think*. Keenan fought the invisible foe of the flood; and for once, for one long and painful moment he realised this was a foe he could not beat. Tears fell from frustrated eyes to mingle with the flood.

And... he could see his girls.

His sweet, dead girls.

Waiting for him by the swings...

Something grabbed him, a harsh connection, violent in its suddenness, and he was jerked with a jarring pain back into a world of snarling reality. Everything was a confusion of bubbles. He was stunned. A blow connected with his jaw and he spat in anger, hatred and pent-up frustration and violence as he blinked and realised—

It was Mel.

She swam like an otter, undulating the entire length of her body. She circled him with powerful strokes, fighting the violent torrent. But even as her strong talons sliced through whatever had snagged Keenan and held him a prisoner beneath the flood, so he felt a dark fist of unconsciousness take him; the sun was shining strong and Freya looked so pretty sitting in the warm yellow light, sunshine diffusing her hair.

Mel dragged him by the scruff of his WarSuit up towards the chute, and forced his limp and failing frame up past the ladder which bubbled and fizzed with detergents, frothing a brown foam soup. Franco grasped Keenan from above, hauled him up onto the city street and slapped the man's soaked dead body onto the tarmac. Franco heaved on Keenan's chest, forcing flooded lungs to disgorge. Water bubbled from Keenan's mouth, ran like brown vomit across his face and into his eyes. Franco rolled Keenan onto his front, heaved on the man's back forcing yet more fluid out. Then he administered the kiss of life... as Mel squatted, small head weaving left and right, scanning for zombies.

Franco inhaled, exhaled, inhaled, exhaled. Pumped at Keenan's lungs. He checked the man's wrist. He could feel a pulse, fluttering weakly, and suddenly Keenan choked and coughed, rolling onto his side, foetal, and wracking as he choked out the remains of the invasive tunnel water.

There came a few long minutes where Keenan simply lay, panting, staring at the ground like a limp fish. Franco squatted by his side, D5 shotgun in his calloused, scarred knuckles, watching for zombies... and the three *things* which had attacked them in the tunnel.

What were they? A manner of AI Franco had never before seen, that was for sure. Extremely high-tech, not like the primitive GE Razor Droids of pre-Helix. No. These were fast, fluid, lethal. Franco knew killers when he saw them; and the things hunting them in the tunnel had been awesome.

Keenan sat up, breathing deeply.

"Cheers mate."

"No problem Keenan. Listen, I know you don't want to be hearing this right now, but we need to get moving. Those things from the tunnel—God only knows how far they were swept. I don't want to meet them again in a hurry."

Keenan nodded, allowed Franco to help him to his feet. "I lost my weapon." Franco handed him a Kekra quad-barrel, which he hefted thoughtfully. Then he turned to Mel, waiting patiently, her lead lying by her side. Keenan smiled. "And... thank you. Melanie." He met her gaze. There was pain there; a mixture of feral understanding, and... tears. Keenan nodded. She was trapped inside another shell. Yet she still felt... at least partially... the same.

Mel made a kind of low purring sound. Keenan bit back a comedy retort, and ran his hands through wet hair, spiking it. More rain was falling and he laughed, turning his head to the sky and roaring as loud and boisterously as he could.

Franco placed a hand on his shoulder. "You OK?"

"Yeah mate, never better. I just cheated death. But you know what? I wasn't afraid. My girls were waiting."

Franco exchanged a worried glance with Mel behind Keenan's back. "Come on Keenan. This way. We'll move slow to begin with. Your system's overloaded with shock and shot to shit."

"Franco, bizarrely, I feel as strong as a bull."

"Well, one step at a time."

They started down narrow, overshadowed streets. Skyblocks loomed around them, upper stories nearly touching high, high above in the imitation night sky. Mel padded behind the two armed men, eyes watching Keenan, head bobbing in rhythm to her raking footsteps.

"Listen," said Keenan.

"Yeah?"

"You gave me the kiss of life, right?"

Franco frowned. "Ye-*es*. To save your life."

"Well, don't be getting any ideas."

"Hey, I took no enjoyment snogging you, mate. Next time I'll fucking leave you to die, shall I?"

"I'm just warning you not to get frisky."

"Don't flatter yourself, Keenan."

"*And* your beard tickles. It's not something I've ever considered before, having never snogged a bloke."

"Fuck off," snapped Franco.

"Tetchy."

"You've answered that question, anyway."

"What question?"

"Did you suffer brain damage from oxygen starvation." Franco eyed him beadily, in the gloom. "Quite obviously, you did."

Keenan's laughter boomed between the buildings, and a cold rain fell like black diamond tears.

THEY WERE IN gangland. They could tell, because of the graffiti. It filled every spare inch of space at ground level, in every colour and every language conceivable, including various alien tongues written with Hydrogen Pens, which shifted eerily through several dimensions. Keenan halted, boots splashing an oil puddle, his confidence returned after his close brush with death. To Franco, he seemed somehow more... powerful. Fearless. As if he'd faced an internal demon: and conquered the savage beast.

"Why we stopping?"

Keenan pointed. Huddled in a doorway was a little girl. "She might know of Knuckles. Let me handle this."

"Oh no," said Franco. "I remember back on Ket, you scaring the shit out of all them little kiddies on the Gem Rig."

"What? Wasn't that *you*, Francis?"

"No, no," said Franco, holding up his hand, "I think you'll find I am the friendly face of the child population." He paused, chin tilted, and considered his position as humanitarian. "I am easily trusted, nay, readily confided in! I should be a Samaritan! They should put me on midnight suicide watch."

"Go on then."

Franco approached the young girl, who squatted, huddled in a blanket. He slowed his pace, stooped almost double, plastered a broad, teeth-filled smile on his goatee-bearded chops, and with a worrying gait, scuttled in an almost-sideways shuffle towards where she sat.

"Hello der liddle pumpkiny wumpkinny. Now don't you be frightened of big old bad Franco here, you funny wunny liddle girlie popsicle," said Franco, with a completely straight face.

"I'm not frightened." Despite her youth, her voice was guttural and harsh.

"Tsch! Wsch! And why's that, little bunny wunny girlie wirlie?" Franco was close now. Close enough to reach out and tweak the nose of the little bunny wunny.

The blanket twitched and Franco found himself staring down the twin barrels of a Heckler & Koch

Terminator5. A single round would blow his head clean off.

The girl smiled. She'd lost most of her teeth. "Because, after all the zombies I've slaughtered, a little ginger man wouldn't offer much of a fight."

Disgruntled, Franco scuttled back to Keenan, his face beetroot red, his hands clenching and unclenching.

"I thought you were 'the friendly face of the child population'?"

"Shut up."

"'Easily trusted'?"

"Shut up."

"'Readily confided in'?"

"Are you going to have a go," he growled, "or should we just go home now?"

"Temper, temper, Francis." Keenan strode to the young gang member. "We're looking for Knuckles. Part of The City Liberators. I can pay you for information."

"I know where he hangs out. What have you got?"

"What do you want?"

"Are those BABE grenades on your belt?"

"Yeah."

"I'll take five."

Keenan removed the grenades, and stooped, placing them at the girl's feet. She gestured down the street. "Five blocks down. You'll find a towering shit-hole. The Happy Friendly Sunshine Assurance Company. They live in the basement." She smiled. "With all the other bunny wunnies."

"You sure?"

The girl gave him a withering look, and pushed thick strands of greasy hair from her face. A small hand appeared, scooping the BABE grenades and placing them neatly into a canvas sack.

"Come on," said Keenan, and led Franco and Mel down the street. During the trade, Keenan had noted the girl had her Terminator5 permanently fixed on Mel. Keenan felt it wise not to point this out.

"One more thing," she shouted.

Keenan halted, and turned back. Rain ran in rivulets down his face, making the Kekra slick in his powerful hands. "Yeah?"

"Watch out for the zombies," said the girl. "They're like a plague down there."

Keenan nodded, turned, and headed through the rain.

"They spotted us, Keenan."

Keenan cursed, and the two Combat K men and Mel ran down a narrow alleyway, glancing behind. They stopped on a corner; ahead, a group of perhaps fifty zombies were moaning and hammering at glass doors. Many carried Uzis.

Suddenly, high above, gunfire rattled. Keenan shaded his eyes, watched windows explode and glass snowflakes rain from on high. A short battle raged. They heard the muffled revving of engines.

"Engines?" said Keenan.

"That sounds like chainsaws," frowned Franco.

"Just like in the movies." Keenan flinched as bullets smashed bricks by his head. He dropped to a crouch. Gloss brick dust settled over him in a patina, and he snarled, the Kekra pumping in his fist. Zombies were punched from their feet, three, four, five, in a flurry of perfect headshots. Keenan paused, watched the dropped zombies stumble back to their knees, then climb to their feet. The horde turned its attention towards the Combat K men.

"We need to get up from ground level," said Keenan. He fired off another couple of rounds. Zombies rolled with the blows, their decrepit flesh flying off in long curled strips. Even at this modest distance, they could hear the crunch of splintering bones.

"I thought these kids were in the basement?"

"Not with that zombie horde outside. They've been chased upwards. To the roof."

"I can't see kids using chainsaws."

"Yeah, well, that girl back there just relieved me of five BABEs. Don't underestimate the little buggers."

More Uzis rattled and Keenan and Franco retreated; they circled the building, eyes alert, Mel padding behind them in silence. Keenan found his lungs were screaming at him, his head light, and he stopped for a moment, leaning against a graffiti-strewn wall as lights danced behind his eyes.

"You OK?" asked Franco.

"Better, since I was resurrected."

Franco nodded, and they continued. Suddenly there was a snarl, and a zombie leapt from a darkened recess; Keenan's Kekra was knocked from his fist, bullets blatting skywards as claws and fangs descended on his throat and brains, bearing him to the ground. Franco's D5 shotgun boomed, and the zombie was flung like a ragdoll down the street. It rolled to a savage abrupt halt, slamming a wall. Franco ran forward, placed the D5 against its head, and pulled twin triggers. Half of the zombie's head splattered up the wall. Black blood ran along the gutter in the gloom. The mutation twitched.

"Thanks," panted Keenan, retrieving his Kekra.

"No problems, bro. You need a lie down?"

"I need a holiday."

"I went on one of them once. Cleaned out every damn brothel on the planet!" He grinned, and winked. "They don't call me Franco 'Horny Stud Muffin Gigolo' Haggis for nothing, y'know." Keenan sighed.

They moved on, Keenan filled with apprehension. He was in a greatly weakened state, he acknowledged, and it galled him. He had always been so strong, so fit, so unstoppable. But, first with the heavy drinking, the smoking, the continuous abuse of his body… and then his near-death experience, well, his Combat K reserves of seemingly limitless strength and endurance were being pushed to the brink of what a human body could endure.

Keenan halted in the gloom, boots thudding. "Here." He glanced up, and Franco followed his gaze. An old fashioned alloy-iron fire escape. Thirty feet off the ground, slick with rainfall.

"But… how do we reach it?" said Franco. "I'm only a little fella."

"Mel?" Keenan looked at her sideways. "Can you throw me up there?"

Franco puffed out his chest. "Better let me do it. You've had a recent brush with that Old Daddy, the

Grim Reaper." He coughed, nodding to himself. "I'm man enough for this gig."

Mel cupped her talons, and Franco stepped into the makeshift cradle. "When you're ready," he growled, and Mel tensed huge muscles, and hurled Franco flapping and squawking fifty feet into the air. The little ginger soldier flapped his way up and *beyond* the ladder, sandaled feet kicking as if he thought he could paddle himself to safety.

"I think you put a bit too much effort into that," said Keenan, voice soft.

"Grwlllll."

Franco reached the summit of his ascent—there came a long pause, as he glanced down and his eyes went wide—then flapping even more vigorously, he began to fall. There was a grunt and a clang as he connected with the fire ladder, bounced from a rung, scrabbled frantically for a second, and finally managed to get a grip. Franco sighed in relief. The ladder creaked. Franco's sigh turned into a wail as the ladder engaged digital rails and accelerated towards the ground, aided and abetted by Franco's considerable belly.

Mel leapt, catching Franco as the ladder hit its rubber stops. She cradled him in her arms like a babe. Keenan pushed past them, looped his Kekra to his back, and stared up at the ninety-three stories of ascent. "Better get to it," he said, coughing heavily and hawking a mouthful of tunnel water and phlegm into the gutter. He started to climb quickly, boots clanging rungs, and Keenan was eaten by the sky.

Franco stared at Mel from his safe cradle against her distended, rotting bosom.

"Thanks for catching me."

"Mewlll." She nuzzled him, drool leaving long slimy streamers across his skin and beard.

"Ahh. That's OK. Just a little slava accident. Not much mess at all. We can clean that up just fine... [cough]... you *can* put me down now, chipmunk."

Mel nuzzled him again. He could see his reflection in the pus-gleam of her mottled facial skin.

"Really. Honest Melanie. It's time to put me down. We have a job to do."

Reluctantly, finally, Mel deposited Franco on the buckled tarmac and watched as he started to climb the ladder.

After a few seconds, Franco glanced back from his perch, and went suddenly red with embarrassment as he realised *exactly* what Mel was doing.

"Hey, you can stop watching my arse *right now*!" he bellowed, huffing and puffing and acknowledging the utter irony of the reversal. Franco had spent a lifetime watching girls' arses. Now, he was on the receiving end, and it made him feel quite abused.

KNUCKLES AND HIS group of twenty-five gangland orphans, The City Liberators, had successfully reached the roof of The Happy Friendly Sunshine Assurance Company—barricading at least forty doors in their wake. The problem at first had been the zombies with chainsaws, cutting and hacking away at reinforced doors and allowing entry for the snarling, clawing creatures. The doors had at least bought the kids time—time they used to reconnoitre further floors, and then use a plethora of metal filing cabinets and kev-mesh firemats to further impede the chainsaws' progress. On Floor 80 it seemed the kids had won against insurmountable odds, and Knuckles led a hearty cheering session as they danced and punched the air, watching as chainsaw blades struggled and tangled and ground to a stuttering two-stroke halt on the kev-mesh firemats. Even Little Megan danced a little jig.

"Suck on that!" shouted Knuckles, gesticulating with hand-sign street-shit at the door. "You can't puk and ruk with the best! :-)."

The kids were barricading the door on Floor 81 when a detonation on the floor below signalled an end to their juvenile barricade. A curious silence settled over the children, like ash.

"No," said Skull.

"They can't have," muttered Glass.

The kids were all thinking the same. If zombies had access to *grenades,* or even worse, *High-J,* then no matter how thoroughly the kids barricaded the corridors and doors, the zombies would be able to follow. To hunt them down. And the children were fast running out of space, time, and *floors.* There could only be one conclusion if they reached the dead end of the roof...

"Knuckles, I'm *so* tired," said Little Megan.

"Come here. I'll carry you." Knuckles hoisted the little 'un onto his shoulders, and the group ran through flickering, deserted corridors, past water-coolers and dormant glowing computers. Up more stairs they sprinted, and heard another *boom,* muffled, behind them. The floor and the entire building shook. Little Megan started to cry, shaking in his arms.

Cursing, Knuckles led the charge to the roof. Flight after flight of stairs sped beneath boots and sandals; lights flickered on and off, on and off, and every now and then the building's entire power would go down... then surge on a boost of generation... then die again, plunging their world into a temporary, ethereal gloom.

They were panting, streaked with sweat, and brandishing makeshift melee weapons as they climbed wearily the final set of narrow steps to the roof of The Happy Friendly Sunshine Assurance Company building. Knuckles had thought they would be safe there; now, he was no longer sure. Fear gnawed at him, like a ferret in his belly.

The door slammed wide, and they were greeted by a black sky. A wind smashed this high precipice, and Knuckles gasped, breath caught in his throat. He staggered onto the flat concrete-alloy platform and fell to his knees. The kids fanned out behind him, and Skull gently closed the final door. He threw three thick bolts, but eyed the portal dubiously. It wouldn't hold against a detonation. What could?

Knuckles placed Little Megan gently down, and staggered to his feet, rusted machete in one fist, eyes dark and hooded. The wind howled. It smelled fresh, filled with rain—and a welcome drug after the stuffy confines of the assurance building.

"Are we safe here?" asked Little Megan, large brown eyes staring up at Knuckles, lower lip quivering.

"Yeah, sweetie. We're safe."

The door rattled. Knuckles glanced at Skull. Had it been the wind? *Surely* the bastards couldn't have caught them already?

The door rattled; harder this time. There came a moan, distant, muffled, but definitely the ululation of the zombie. Knuckles squared his shoulders, lifted his ten-tear old's chin, and scowled at the door. His hands tightened on the machete. He released a slow breath. "We're going to have to fight," he said. "If they get through the door."

"*Knuckles!*" hissed Glass, and nodded past the youth. Knuckles turned. From the deep shadows of the roof three figures had emerged; they were heavily muscled, yet slender, and would have been fine examples of the athlete if they hadn't been zombies. There were two men, one woman, and yellow and grey flesh hung in strips from their faces, gaps in cheeks showing working, gnashing teeth within. Their eyes were feral, glinting, dangerous. They spread out, moving smoothly, padding like hunters, almost like cats.

Knuckles took a step back. These weren't like the others. They seemed, somehow, more *dangerous*.

"You back me up, now," growled Knuckles and Glass, Skull, Sammy and some of the others lifted their assorted knives and pipes and makeshift clubs.

"We'll back you," said Glass. "We've nowhere to run."

The three zombies murmured, low soft sounds of appreciation. Their nostrils were twitching, lifting to the wind a little as if savouring this delivery of fresh meat, raw brains.

"Don't fight now," said one, suddenly. It was the woman, its voice low, a lullaby. It tilted its head, smiling with gaping fangs and holed cheeks. This did nothing to instil the children with confidence or trust.

"We won't hurt you," said another, flexing claws which shone like long daggers in the starlight.

The third, the largest, most heavily muscled, nodded slowly, methodically, saying nothing but running a fat red tongue over distended black teeth.

With snarls, they leapt to the attack...

KEENAN PAUSED ON the ladder as a boom rocked the building within. He glanced down. "Franco?"

"KEK5 blast," he said without looking up. "Antipersonnel, a mixture of splinter-barbs with a High-J coating and Honey-spunk with G6 trigger det. Definitely military sourced. Let's hope the zombies aren't using them." He laughed weakly.

Keenan carried on climbing, reached a low parapet and swung his legs thankfully over the ridge. He dropped into a dark trough of corrugated metal, then climbed up a slope of the same metal and crouched behind a low bank of cubic extractors. They hummed, vibrating under his steadying hands. He pulled free his Techrim, stowing away the Kekra—which he found too bulky and intrusive for his liking. He checked his weapon's magazine as Franco joined him, followed by Mel who formed a terrifying silhouette against the bleak skyline.

Mel grunted, pointed at herself, then at the sky.

"She's trying to tell us something," said Franco.

"You don't say," muttered Keenan.

Franco frowned. "Go on, Mel. What you trying to say, girl?"

Mel growled, and gave a little bark. She patted her breast, flexed her foot claws, then shook her head as if savaging a bone.

"Shit, it's like trying to decode Lassie," snapped Keenan.

"She's saying," said Franco, primly, "that the cold and the dark have speeded up her metabolism. We should expect the same from the enemy zombies we encounter."

Keenan stared hard at Franco. "You got all that from *that*?"

"We have a spymbi… a spiimbe… a connection." He tapped his skull. "A joining of minds. *Reet*?"

"OK. *OK*." Keenan peered past the cubic extractors. There was something going down. He watched the children disgorge from the door, bolt it, then turn in horror as three zombies appeared from a pool of inky shadows. "Looks like we've found… somebody," said Keenan.

"We've got to help them!" snapped Franco.

"They may not be critical to our mission," said Keenan, voice cool, eyes hooded, ever the professional.

"They're damn and bloody kids, and I won't stand by and watch no nasty zombies eat their brains!" Franco leapt to the attack; he charged, and with a mutter and a curse, Keenan padded after the powerful ginger squaddie.

When he was ten feet away, Franco's Kekra boomed in his fist and, with a blink, he watched the three zombies scatter, rolling apart fluidly like a combat squad, and coming up with claws at the ready. Franco skidded on his heels, tracking one. He fired, the bullet winging the female zombie in a splatter of gore as the gun went *click* with stoppage and Franco cursed and shook his weapon as the other two zombies snarled, drooling befouled spittle, and leapt at him—

"Keenan!"

Keenan opened fire, Techrim slamming his palm. Five bullets ate their way up a male zombie's chest—but did not slow him. The creature slammed Franco, bearing the powerful pugilist to the ground as claws slashed an inch from his face. Franco growled, slamming a right hook, then another to the zombie's head. A tooth flew free, and as Franco bounced, the zombie atop him, he grasped the zombie's ears to deliver a smashing head-butt—but the ears came away in his hands leaving him stunned, mouth open, a scream of horror welling and bubbling in his throat...

Keenan leapt, Techrim whipping against the second zombie's head. It rolled with the blow, ducking and spinning, leg sweeping Keenan's feet from beneath him. He hit the ground, rolled, as claws smashed the concrete where his face had been. The zombie reared above him, leapt at him but he rolled again, Techrim barking. Bullets scythed past the zombie, missing as it moved with awesome speed— then was atop Keenan, fangs open, bearing down on his face as he twisted, wriggled, then discharged his Techrim from hip-level. *Booms* slammed through the zombie, which twitched with each rapid successive impact; claws raked Keenan's flesh, from neck to sternum, slashing his WarSuit, and he felt blood pump from the wound at his neck. He wrestled free his arm, and the wounded zombie was snarling, clawing at him, his skin under its talons and its teeth lowered towards his face; he could smell the foul stench of sour acid breath and as the muzzle dropped towards his eyes he squeezed his Techrim under its chin and fired. The head jerked, glassy eyes staring deep into Keenan's with a sudden *connection* as the top of its head mushroomed in blood and rotting purple brain. The connection was simple: from murderer to victim. The zombie smiled, then snarled despite half its brain raining down over the roof concrete—and Keenan snarled in return, firing again. The top of the zombie's head lifted like a flap and the remains of its diseased brain flowered from the dark, blood-pooled cavity. Keenan pushed the flopping useless body from him, heard it slap the ground, saw Franco struggling, locked in his own personal nightmare—the creature atop him, talons locked in his hands, both straining but unable to break the grip. Keenan crawled over to Franco, poked his Techrim into the zombie's blood-ringed ear-hole, and sent its brain pissing from the cranial cavity with three slams of 11mm Techrim.

"Thanks, mate," panted Franco.

"Where's the third?" snapped Keenan. Both men stood, and stared over the group of shocked, silent children. The wounded female deviant stood to one side, swaying, a smile on its lips; it held Little Megan to its chest as if the girl was a protective ward. Her claws hovered over Megan's head, stroking her forehead, backwards and forwards, a gentle and threatening sawing motion.

"Put her down," growled Franco.

"No, you drop your weapons!" hissed the zombie, and both Franco and Keenan stood, stunned, astonishment plain on their faces. "Or I'll peel open her head like a can of beans and scoop out her brain in front of her little friends."

"It can talk!" stuttered Franco.

"Better do as it says," soothed Keenan.

"Throw down our weapons? Never! I'd rather die!"

"The little *girl* will die, dickhead," snapped Keenan, and kicked Franco on the ankle. He yelped, and both men threw down their weapons which clattered against the roof.

"What do you want?" said Keenan, eyes locked to the female zombie.

"I want to feed!" it hissed.

"No you don't," said Keenan, head tilting slightly. "You want something else. Something more. What were you doing up here?" He glanced around, then up. "Are you waiting for somebody?"

The female zombie smiled then, baring unnaturally long teeth. Pieces of dark flesh were caught between incisors, and flapped against her battered lips when she spoke.

"You would never understand."

"Try me."

"Move away from your weapons."

Franco and Keenan took several steps back, and Keenan glanced right. He saw the look of pain in the children who stood, frozen like rabbits in a spotlight, and it bit him. Terror was acid-etched onto every young face. Horror shone like a dark light in prematurely adult eyes. Keenan's eyes settled on a young girl; she had long brown hair, just like his Rachel. Just like his *dead* Rachel.

There came a sudden roar from behind the zombie as Mel reared, claws lifted high. The zombie dropped Little Megan, and in an instant the Kekra was in Keenan's hand and a *blam* roared across the space; the heavy calibre round took the female zombie between the eyes, punching her back towards Mel, who caught the body and stumbled as the female zombie twisted, claws raking Mel's eyes. Mel screamed in pain, temporarily blinded, her own talons slashing out ineffectively as Keenan sprinted forward, and the zombie snarled, hammering five blows into Mel's crumpling form as Mel shook her head, neck crackling, and grabbed the zombie in a powerful embrace. Mel threw the zombie, which flew, bounced, rolled and slammed into a cubic extractor with a crunch of compressing steel. Keenan tracked the zombie, fired off three shots. Two hummed overhead, but one caught the body and sent a *whump* of diseased flesh splattering over concrete. Mel landed, as the female zombie pushed itself to its feet and—amazingly—attacked. A barrage of blows forced Mel back, head bobbing, until she slammed a punch which again sent the female zombie spinning and rolling, slapping harshly against the roof. She hit a slope of corrugated steel, and slid down the V to the bottom of the trough. Keenan ran, leapt onto a ridge and sighted down his Kekra.

The zombie had already gained its feet, and it ran up the slippery steel as Keenan fired off five shots and bullets danced past the zombie's head. By God, he thought, it's fast! It reached the top—and the edge of the building—and turned, a smile on its distended, flesh-hanging face. Keenan's finger hovered on the trigger.

The zombie's eyes met Keenan's. Understanding passed between them.

The zombie jumped.

Franco sprinted down the steel slope, then slithered and slid his way up the opposite bank. He stood, teetering on the edge of the skyblock, and watched the zombie fall. Distantly, it hit the ground, and separated out into splattered component limbs.

"Ugh," said Franco. Then glanced at Keenan, who had picked up Little Megan. "What happened then? You shoot it?"

"No," said Keenan. "She jumped."

"You mean," Franco frowned, "*she* committed suicide?"

Keenan barked a laugh. "Yeah. She. It. What the hell. And that screams something more than a dumb lust for brains. These bastards were up to something, up here on the roof. Only now, we don't know what."

"Boy, they were hard to kill," said Franco, running back across the V of alloy. He patted Little Megan on the head, and cooed at her. Tears had streaked the dirt on her face, but she forced a beautiful smile.

"Thank you." Keenan and Franco turned, and stared down at the little boy who spoke. He had battered red gloss shoes.

"Our pleasure, lad," beamed Franco. He reached out to pat the boy's head, but the lad moved fast, dodging and grabbing Franco's hand and twisting it back against the joint. "Ow! Ouch! That bloody hurts, you little bugger!"

"Sorry," grinned the boy sheepishly, releasing his grip. "Just reflex. I'm a bit jumpy at the moment."

"You don't say," rumbled Franco, rubbing at his wrist. "Clever move that. You'll have to show me sometime. But whilst we're here, maybe you can help. We're looking for a gang member. A lad. Goes by the name of Knuckles. Can you help?"

Keenan saw the shutdown on the lad's face as internal barriers slammed into place. It was a revelation to Keenan: what was an innocent young lad one moment became a suddenly shifty, devious creature, and Keenan picked out tiny details which suddenly had him checking his wallet. This was no simple boy; this was a wise and street-savvy gang member.

"What do you want him for?" The question was innocent, but Keenan saw the lie in his eyes.

Keenan glanced down at the little girl in his arms. She yawned, snuggling against his chest. "If I put you down, will Knuckles look after you?"

"Mmmnn, yeah," nodded the girl, almost asleep.

Keenan glanced back to the boy. He smiled, but there was no humour there.

"Clever," Knuckles said. "What the hell do you want?"

Franco glanced between Keenan and Knuckles, frowning. "Hey, what happened then? Because, like, I'm good at following stuff normally but that was a bit weird that thing that went on and old Franco he say to himself, just listen and be patient Franco and everything will be revealed but I'm not quite sure it *is* so I'm going to ask all the same."

"Eloquent," said Keenan.

"So?"

"Meet Knuckles," said Keenan.

Franco stared at the lad. "I thought you'd be bigger. And *older.*"

"And I thought you'd be slimmer."

"But you don't *know* me!"

"I might do."

"Now I'm confused."

Keenan slapped Franco on the back. "He's messing with your head, Franco mate." Keenan squatted down, Little Megan now asleep in his arms. "Listen, Knuckles—we're not here for trouble. We've just got a very simple question for you."

Knuckles gazed at Little Megan's sleeping figure. He seemed to soften, and he released a breath. His face changed from a hard mask to soft, boyish features. He looked young again. "I'm sorry," he said, slowly, as if it hurt him to apologise. "You saved my life. You saved all our lives. You have a question for me? Sure, go ahead." He grinned sheepishly. "You killed the zombies. What have I got to lose, right?"

At the door leading to the roof, there came a sudden *boom*. Then another. Beyond, a two-stroke engine fired and revved high and long, shrieking. Chainsaws!

"More zombies?" sighed Keenan.

Knuckles nodded. "They've been chasing us through the building. We ran, up here, but they followed, cutting their way through the barricades we erected. And just when we thought we'd won, it seems they had some grenades." He eyed the door, which was now vibrating and squealing under chain-blade impact. "Looks like they ran out of bombs."

With a growl, Mel moved towards the door scattering kids out of her way. She threw back the bolts, and threw open the door—in which the chainsaw was embedded, jiggling. It tugged the zombie from its feet, and the deviant stared up at Mel with a look of stupidity and confusion. Mel planted a solid punch in the zombie's face, and it slammed backwards into darkness, the chainsaw finally stuttering to a halt. Mel pulled the machine from the twisted door with a squealing wrench of steal, stared at it for a moment, then pulled the cord. Fumes spat from exhaust. The chainsaw rumbled in her talons. She glanced back at Franco, a strange look on her face which may, with a lot of imagination, and even more hallucinatory drugs, have been a smile. Then she was gone. Below, growls turned to screams. Gurgles and splatters followed, fading into the distance.

"I've never seen *that* before," said Knuckles. "Lucky you brought your own."

"Our own what?" said Franco.

"Your own zombie. It must be awesome, having one fight for you, on your side. It'd make a great movie though, wouldn't it? Zombie chases other zombies with a chainsaw! Wow! Think of the gore-effects you could implement!"

"She's not a zombie," said Franco, woodenly. His eyes were a touch glazed.

"Hell, she looked like a zombie," said Knuckles. He sat down beside Keenan, and stroked the hair of Little Megan, who sighed in her sleep. At peace, at last.

"Actually," said Keenan, "that's why we're here. And that's what we wanted to ask you about."

"What have I done wrong this time?" said Knuckles, and part of the internal barrier came back.

"That zombie," said Franco, with tears in his eyes. "Well. She's my bird."

"Your *what?*"

"My girlfriend. My woman. My wife-to-be. She used to be normal, but she bought a biomod—from you—and apparently, it turned her into *that*."

Knuckles was silent, for a very long time.

"Oh," he said, finally.

"You remember?" said Keenan.

"I remember."

"Where did you get it?" said Keenan. His voice was soft, but his eyes were keen. They glinted in the glow of the few stars which managed to shine through the break in towering storm-clouds overhead.

"I stole it."

"Where from?"

"A woman in the street. I steal a lot of things. I've sold a lot of biomods before. But none of them ever turned their users into… whatever it is she is." He looked sympathetically at Franco. "That must be hard for you, Captain GingerBeard."

"It is," snuffled Franco. "And you should see her fanny!"

"Franco!" hissed Keenan. "He's only ten!"

"It's OK," grinned Knuckles. "I've heard worse. Much worse, believe me."

"How do I change her back?" said Franco mournfully. "How do I get my Melanie back?" He rubbed a streamer of snot from his nose, and Knuckles crossed to him, patting the broad and rotund pugilist on the back.

"There, there," he said, in a curious reversal.

"So," sighed Keenan, "it was a simple theft. You're not a hardcore biomod dealer, hacker or pirate. So—shit—we can't track your source."

"A dead end," nodded Franco.

"Did you steal anything else from the woman?"

"I got her cards." He stared at his red gloss boots, trying to remember. "I sold them on, as well. What was her name?" He frowned, squinting, then his face lit up in a smile. "Christiane Solomonsson. That's right. A proper weird name; even against the craziness of The City."

"Never heard of her," said Keenan.

"I have," said Franco. Keenan looked at him inquisitively. "You have?"

"Yeah," he said, rubbing at his temples. His eyes were closed. "She works for NanoTek. She's a top-dog military biomod engineer. A weapons designer. *Shit*."

CHAPTER 9
INFERNAL AFFAIRS

"THOSE ZOMBIES, THEY were deadly, dangerous, vicious... not like the ones we met before!" Franco's eyes were wide as he set up the burner and sat a big pan atop thin TitaniumII legs. He fished through his rations, tipping dried noodles, tinned CubeSausage, and salt into the pan. Knuckles arrived with a jerry can and Franco poured water into the soon-to-be-Franco-stew.

"They were different," agreed Knuckles. "But you... you fought well, Big Man. You were fast, fearless. A hero! You saved us all."

"A hero?" Franco scratched his beard. "I wouldn't go that far, lad, but yeah, you little, help-less children, you needed my support. Hey, hey what's that?"

Sammy, one of the young girls, was playing with a Scope.

Franco's eyes narrowed. "That's mine, you thieving little scumbag!"

Keenan slapped him on the back. "Kids giving you a hard time, mate?"

Franco grinned sheepishly. "Nah, boys will be boys an' all that. Listen, we was talking, about them damned dangerous zombies. It was like they were super-zombies, uber-zombies..." his lips quivered, eyes widening yet further, "even... wonder-zombies!"

"*Wonder*-zombies? Franco, are you still on your medication?"

"No, I am not!" Indignant.

"Well maybe you should be."

The PAD rattled, and when Franco managed to wrestle it from the iron-grip of Little Megan, *who just would not bloody let go,* he activated the machine and glanced up at Keenan.

"Hey Kee, it's Steinhauer—that stinking old flabby bitch of a donkey's bitch. He wants you."

Keenan nodded, lit his Widow Maker cigarette, and took the PAD from Franco. The wind howled across the high vantage roof top, and Franco went back to his pan and the promise of food for the orphans, the kid-thieves, the *gang.* Keenan walked to the edge of The Happy Friendly Sunshine Assurance Company's corrugated roof and leapt onto the low parapet, gazing down into the blackness of streets far, far below. Like a deep concrete ocean. A graveyard chasm. The wind rocked him, and he felt suddenly invigorated—a few hours earlier, he had been close to death, to a watery grave. Now he stood, a saviour. Yes, it was only a small victory;

but sometimes a small victory was all that was needed between survival… and extinction.

"Yeah, Steinhauer?"

"We have located the Professor."

"What's he called?"

"Xakus. An expert in codecs and all things bio-mechanical. He's currently holed up with an academic mob at The Great Malkovitch Library, about eighty klicks due south of your current location. He's an ex-NanoTek biomod engineer. And let's just say he owes Quad-Gal Military a few favours."

"We've lost our transport."

"Well, we'd fast-drop you a ship," said Steinhauer, "but it would seem the, ah, deformations have taken over a variety of military installations across the entire planet. They're shooting down aircraft like there's no tomorrow. The City has become a no-fly zone."

"You mean they're controlling SAM sites?"

"Yes, Keenan. They are showing far more intelligence and resilience than we initially gave them credit."

"Now there's a surprise," said Keenan. "Considered them a backward race, did you? Easy targets? A lot less technically advanced than QGM? Steinhauer, mate, after all the shite we've been through, you should have fucking known better."

"When you know the full facts of the situation, Keenan, then you may judge," said Steinhauer, voice icy. "But for now, just do your job. Did you link up with Franco and Pippa?"

"Franco, yeah."

"Not the girl?"

Keenan smiled at that. "If Pippa heard that, she'd cut your throat."

"Which is what makes her a perfect field operative. Do I need to reiterate co-ordinates..."

"No." Keenan's voice was hard. Too hard. He watched below as a fire blossomed, raging down the street to ignite a distant fuel tanker. Flames roared into the sky, billowing orange and purple. Even a hundred storeys up Keenan could feel the heat.

"You OK Keenan?"

"Yeah, I'm still here."

"You be careful. Every report we receive, well, our intel speaks of insanity, atrocity, murder and mayhem."

"And that's just the Quad-Gal infantry."

"You taking the piss, Keenan?"

"I don't need to, Steinhauer. You're giving it away—labelled in glass bottles for all to savour and enjoy. Did you sort out the mess on Galhari? After all, it's the place I call home."

"Get me that decoded SinScript information, Keenan. Then we'll talk about the junks."

The PAD died, fluttering with an EXTERMINATION command in Keenan's hand. He finished his cigarette, smoke whipped away by the promise of another storm; he flicked the butt into the raging inferno far below.

Franco approached, warily.

"You OK, bro?"

"Yeah. I don't know what to say about Mel."

Franco shrugged. "There will be a way to cure her. I will find it. Even if I have to waltz up to

NanoTek's major HQ and bang on the doors and demand to see their chief bio-engineer!" He laughed. His eyes glinted. "Now there's a thought."

"I need to leave," said Keenan. He lit another cigarette, and Franco tutted. He didn't approve of Keenan smoking. "I have the co-ordinates for the man who can decode this." He placed a hand against his ribs, where the SinScript sat in its protective case within his WarSuit; a tiny, inoffensive black coin. So small. Vulnerable. Yet holding the secrets to an extinct invading *race*.

"We will come with you."

"No." Keenan shook his head. "You see to Melanie. After all, at the moment her bite is worse than her bark."

"Funny, Keenan. You're getting better. We'll book you a spot at The Frog and Bucket soon enough. But, seriously, you helped us get this far; it's the least we can do to repay you."

"Perhaps. Listen, these people may be able to help Mel. They are professors, academics; the man I need to see is ex-NanoTek."

"Interesting." Franco rubbed at his beard, which made scritchy scratchy sounds.

"He's also an ex-biomod engineer."

"Well then!" roared Franco, "that's definitely our next port of call!"

"Can you get us transport?"

"You want a chopper?"

Keenan shook his head. "Steinhauer says the zombies have taken over the SAM sites."

"What, across the entire damn and bloody planet?"

"It would seem that way." Keenan gave a tight smile. "Mighty advanced, our little drooling, undead friends, aren't they? A bit more intelligent than fried chicken."

"Yeah. Just a bit. Well, give me thirty minutes. I'll knock us some transport together."

"And Franco?"

"Yeah mate?"

"Make sure it works this time. I remember the T5 Jeep you got us on Jeptune."

"Hey, that exploding engine wasn't my fault!"

"It sure looked that way at the time. It took me weeks to get engine oil out of my hair."

"This time, it'll be right mate. Or my name's not *Grease Monkey Mick*."

"But…"

"Yeah?"

"Nothing," sighed Keenan.

MEL, ARMED WITH a chainsaw and her talons, had successfully chased the zombies from the building— exterminating most en route. A few had escaped, mainly by jumping out of windows under Mel's furious violent whirlwind onslaught. Several had ended up in pieces, scattered liberally about the office locations. Thankfully, she did not come up against any more *wonder* zombies.

Securing doors, Mel had padded around the building with glowering eyes, like some futuristic Grendel. She activated security shutters, managed to get the lifts back online, and seemed happy (grunting and growling) that she was finally on a mission; doing something of good, of *worth*.

Returning to the roof, she squatted next to Keenan who sat, hands on his knees, head back against a wall, eyes closed, cigarette dangling from battered lips. He opened one eye.

"What can I do for you, love?"

"Grwwll. Ilding ecure."

"Is it? You sure?" Mel nodded, tiny eyes watching Keenan. "Listen," he said, "I appreciate you saving my life. I don't know what the hell has happened to you, but we'll do our best to help. We are going to see a biomod engineer... he should know how to revert you back to your feminine form."

Mel nodded, armoured neck crackling.

Why doesn't she look like the other zombies? Keenan thought idly, watching as she moved away, across to the group of children. They had grown used to her now, and even Little Megan—who had screamed the building down when she awoke to see Mel's distorted face looming over her, drooling pus—was happy playing between the transformed woman's thick, muscle-trunk legs.

Keenan shook his head, wearily, painfully. "What a weird world we live in."

"Talking to yourself?"

"Shit. Lad, you move quietly."

"Practice," said Knuckles, sitting cross-legged before Keenan. "Franco's downstairs. Got us some transport. Wait till you see it!"

"*You* are not coming," said Keenan, eyeing the young thief.

"*Yes* I am. I know this part of The City better than anybody. I know all the back-routes to The Great Malkovitch Library; I know the best places for ambush, for robbery, and I know the best escape routes if the shit goes down. I'm a wheeler, a dealer, a ducker and a diver. You see only a ten year old boy in front of you; but I am experienced far beyond my years. You saved my life, Keenan." Knuckles's eyes were filled with tears, but his face was a defiant snarl. "Let me do this for you. Let me help you."

"And who will look after your... gang?" said Keenan. His voice was soft, an understanding of sorts registering in his mind. Knuckles was proud, defiant, an adult in all but physical age. Keenan had been the same when he was young, and he felt a bond grow between him and this skinny little orphan with red gloss boots.

"Mel is staying here. She'll protect them. Can you think of anybody better?"

"She has agreed to this?"

"She suggested it," said Knuckles. "I think she wants to play at being mommy. And Franco said we'd move faster without her—find her help, and bring it back."

Keenan nodded, grabbed his pack and stood, stretching his back. The recent bullet score from the junks in the quarry nagged at his flank, like a bite of internal acid, and the more recent knocks and bruises had left their mark across his flesh despite the protection of the Permatex WarSuit. "Well, we can't leave your group unprotected; one of us would have to stay until we can arrange transport out of this biohell. It may as well be Melanie." He smiled. "She does draw a lot of attention to us out on the road." He slapped Knuckles on the back.

"Come on lad. Let's see what new toy Franco's found."

"WHAT, THE FUCK," said Keenan, "is *that?*"

"It's a Corvette Scrambler," said Franco proudly.

Keenan's eyes roved over the flared arches, the huge knobbled tyres, the thick triple exhaust pipes poking from the roof. It was like a steel-girder cage mounted on an engine and H-section chassis. It was, without doubt, a serious off-road tool. Or may have been, once, perhaps sixty years previous. Rust had eaten long jagged holes in the metal flanks, which had once born a proud paint-job of roaring, searing flames.

"Flames?" inquired Keenan.

"I thought it added a touch of panache," said Franco, face straight.

"The panache of the pimp?"

"Look Keenan, it's the best I could do at short notice. I'd like to see *you* rustle up some serious off road shit, so stop moaning and get in. It takes a while to start."

Grumbling, Keenan turned and gave Mel a small wave. He watched Knuckles leap into the stocky vehicle, then climbed in himself. The suspension dipped only a little, springs squeaking.

Franco moved to Mel, stared into her tiny black eyes. "I won't be long, love," he said.

"'e 'areful."

"I will."

There was a moment of uneasiness, and Mel stooped closer, distended, slime-covered lips puckering. Franco gave her a peck, wiped a handful of slime from his mouth, which slithered, pooling in a long stream to the rubble-strewn ground, then he leapt into the Corvette's driving seat and fired the starter.

The engine turned, making a noise like a bucket of bolts in a tumble drier. Franco gave an apologised grimace. "Sorry. Sorry! *Soreee*. It just needs the right bit of love and attention." He slammed his fist into the console, muttered, "Start, you bastard bugger," and the engine roared into stunned life. Black fumes poured from the roof exhaust, and Keenan groaned.

"Great. We'll be seen for miles around."

"Keenan! Stop it!"

"Sorry mum," he grinned.

"Let's go." Franco's gaze fixed ahead, on the crowd of zombies that were gathering, milling, moaning, frumping, at the end of the street, some pointing towards the rumbling Corvette, the smoke fountain, and the advertisement of sentient life within.

Behind, Mel slammed down steel shutters.

Franco stomped the accelerator.

They roared towards the zombies... and The Great Malkovitch Library beyond.

COMBAT K CRUISED, slowly, through decimated, rubble-strewn streets, the Corvette rumbling and belching, Keenan hanging over one side with a loaded Kekra and his Techrim close to hand, Knuckles sat on the back seat, his machete in his lap, his eyes cold. "Turn left at the end of this street," he said, voice low. Franco nodded.

An eerie silence had descended on the group, and indeed, across the cold desolate world in its entirety. A mournful wind blew down the street, bringing with it a smell of fire. Franco shivered.

"What have they done to my home?" he said.

"Who?"

"Whoever turned all these people into zombies. This was supposed to be The Quantum Carnival. It was supposed to be party time for the entire bloody city; instead, it turned into a big bloody massacre by deviants. It's a bloody disgrace."

"Best time to catch everybody," mused Keenan.

"What?"

"It's a coincidence that this plague, this scourge, whatever the hell happened here; well, a coincidence it happened at *just the right time*. Yeah? As The City had a large influx of tourists for the carnival. Wouldn't you say it was convenient?"

"You think it's man—or alien—made?"

"I guarantee it," said Keenan, eyeing the domineering buildings as the group cruised past. His eyes lifted, staring up at blank glass walls, vast obsidian cliffs towering high above him and exuding *cold*. "Whatever happened here—well, it stinks of expediency. And whether the hackers and the pirates intended it or not, *if* this thing was caused by the biomods, then it's a fucking scandal."

"I always said people should take more care of what they put into their bodies," nodded Franco.

"No you didn't," frowned Keenan. "I've watched you shovel mountains of shit into the charnel house that is your belly. Everything, mate, from the mangiest kebabs ever to hang from a ten-week skewer of disease-riddled grease, to that odd alien lager which used to turn your piss black and made your skin erupt in orange pin-prick blotches."

"Ahh, *Ye Olde Burklewurts*. A fine pint of alien ale." He smacked his chops. "Could just do with a pint now. Anyway Keenan." Franco fixed him with a baleful stare. "I heard you'd stepped up your drinking regime, partaking of the odd litre of Jataxa between meals."

Keenan spluttered on his cigarette, and laughed. "Hell, Franco, ever the discreet diplomat, hey? Where did you hear that?"

"I just heard it."

"Where?"

"Here and there. Knocking about. You know how it is. So then? Are you a mess?"

"Don't worry mate, I'm not a raging alcoholic."

"The mantra hiccupped by every raging alcoholic."

Keenan fixed him with a hard stare. "I stepped up my drinking. Yeah. I fucked myself up on regular occasion. I have that right. What happened with Pippa... and my kids..."

Franco slowed the Corvette. "Listen Kee, I know it's none of my business, nothing ever is, but I haven't let that minor indiscretion stop me before. You have to let that Pippa shit go, bro'. You have to let it pass. To die. Before it kills *you*."

"Pippa murdered my kids."

"I don't believe she did," said Franco, slowly.

"What do you mean?"

Franco tapped his skull. "Hey man, you're talking to the expert in psy... pscolog... head problems, here. I'm the guy who spent years at Mount Pleasant having my testes zapped and my brains subjected to every form of mental narcotic on the market. I know a thing or two about craz*ees*. Betta believe it."

"So… explain it to me." Keenan's eyes were rock.

"OK. You were married, with two beautiful kids. Pippa was your lover, and your wife found out. Then, whilst we're all stuffed in prison, your wife and kids are murdered before you have time to explain. Pippa felt guilty about all of this… she felt like, somehow, it was her fault. She imposed blame on herself—so hard, it tortured her, and she ended up believing it." Franco nodded to himself. "People do it all the time. Tell themselves something over and over again until they believe the bullshit. Either with denial, or in this case, with Pippa, an act of murder she did not, actually, physically, commit. But she still felt responsible. Because she was shagging you, and in her head that led to their deaths. You dig, yeah?"

Keenan stared at Franco. The smell of fire was getting stronger. The Corvette rumbled.

"A possibility?" said Franco, eventually, looking sideways at his partner.

"Do you have any proof?" said Keenan. His voice was barely audible over the roar of the Corvette's belching exhaust.

"No-*oo*," said Franco. "And I might be wrong. But it *is* possible, right?"

"I don't know."

"It's *possible*," snapped Franco. "You never gave Pippa a chance to explain, and when we blasted out of Teller's World, and performed that—I might add—insane K Jump which led to all that shit in the Dark Zone after we put down Leviathan, well," Franco rubbed at his ginger beard. "You two never got the chance to talk."

Keenan gave a single nod. "I'll think on it."

"Stop here," said Knuckles, and reluctantly Franco halted the Corvette in the middle of the road, amidst abandoned vehicles, many of which had been burned.

"You see something?"

Knuckles stood on the back seat, holding on to the Corvette's cage, head poking out into a cold wind reeking of fire. "I think our route is blocked."

"By?"

"Burning zombies," said Knuckles.

Keenan and Franco both stood on their creaking seats, staring down the ominous road. There was indeed a distant glow, filling the street like a sea of molten lava. The wind gusted, again, with a raw stench of fire. And it carried with it a low grumbling sound, an undercurrent of bass dissension.

"But hot damn, you've got good eyesight," snapped Franco.

"How close are we to this library?" said Keenan.

"A few kilometres."

"Is there another way round?"

"Yes." Knuckles nodded. "Straight ahead, for a few hundred metres; I'll show you a maze of alleys we can cut through."

The Corvette rumbled on, weaving between burned out cars and the occasional dismembered body, either of a human or alien, regularly showing the head slit open, cranium removed, and all brains scoured out. Sometimes, they saw the carcass of a zombie. Many had been burned into blackened husks.

"Seems there's some resistance," said Franco.

Keenan nodded. "Maybe some areas were hit worse than others?"

"Down there," snapped Knuckles.

Franco steered the Corvette into a narrow network of alleys between decrepit buildings. This was an older, more original area of The City with far less glass and alloy on display, and more ancient, blackened, crumbling brickwork, sometimes stone, and even wooden buildings. Here they weren't high edifices, but short stocky buildings, rimed with filth and centuries of pollution.

"Nice place," sneered Franco.

"This is where I was born," said Knuckles.

Franco shut up. He'd started to sweat, despite the cool breeze rampant in the streets. It was getting more and more narrow, with frequent blockages of groundcars, barrels, lumps of masonry, abandoned market stalls; sometimes Franco guided the revving, spewing Corvette high onto a mound of rubble or wood, huge knobbled tyres crunching and grinding and spinning, his hands sweat-slippery on the sturdy wheel of the off-roader. Once, as they breached a rise of loose white stones, the engine stalled and they slithered back towards street level, wailing, tyres locked and sliding without control. The Corvette thumped onto the road, suspension clanging, and Keenan glared at Franco.

"You dick."

"Hey, it wasn't *my fault*. Mary just cut out on me."

"Mary?"

"A car's gotta have a name. And I'm not getting inside a bloke ten times a day."

"Very droll. Remember your biting point, Franco. Control is everything."

"I tell you, it wasn't my fault! Mary's a contrary mule!" Franco pouted, a bit primly. He fired the old engine on the tenth attempt, revved it high and slammed hard up the slithering slope of stone, leaping a little from the top and cannoning down the opposite side where they suddenly slewed through a shop-front, skidded sideways through ten high shelving units, and slid to an abrupt halt, thumping the far wall. Ceiling beams, plasterboard and dust rained down on the cowering inhabitants, and everybody coughed long and hard as dust continued to rain, then drizzle, then trickle, and finally stop. All around lay a shop hit by a bomb.

"Right," said Keenan, eyes steel. "Time for me to drive."

"But Keenan..."

"No arguments, Franco, get the hell out of the driver's seat."

"But *Keenan*..."

"No!"

Franco stood forlornly on a pile of smashed planks and battered shelving as Keenan reversed the Corvette Scrambler and, with thuds and crunches, managed to extricate the huge, iron vehicle from the crushed and battered mess. He rumbled outside, and Franco gazed around at the shop's interior.

With sudden realisation it hit him like a new day. He was in a pharmacy. A drug store. Filled with... *drugs*.

"You OK in there, Franco?" came Keenan's drifting voice.

"I need a toilet break," said Franco, eyes shining. "Last night's sausage has worked its way through my sewage system. Hey, you guys, enjoy a quiet cigarette, I'll be out in a few shakes of a cat's whisker."

"Don't be long," snapped Keenan, voice muffled.

Franco gazed around. Through gloom he could see shelves lined with boxes, bottles, tubs and tubes. He rubbed his hands together. His face beamed.

"All *righty* then!"

He ran to the counter, rummaged around and located a canvas pack. Then he stalked quickly between the shelving which still stood—miraculously—erect, grabbing at tubes and potions, boxes of pills and rolls of medication. He paused, reading a packet's contents, then tipped ten boxes into the sack. Then he moved to the counter and eyed the locked door *behind*. It had a one way mirror. Franco grinned. In there, he thought to himself, you keep all the pretty drugs, the special drugs, the drugs I might really need, don't you? He rubbed his hands together. Found a plank of wood. Hefted it thoughtfully, and hammered it into the mirrored door.

After a few whacks, the portal disintegrated and Franco stepped through falling dust—into a punch. The blow lifted him from his feet, spat him back ten paces, and deposited him on his behind. Stars fluttered in his head, and blood spurted from his nose.

He coughed, stunned, and stared up through swirling dust at—

At a towering, bulging, power-house of a, a, a…

"A *woman?*" he snapped.

"I am Olga!" boomed the heavily-muscled, strapping beefcake of a lass. Her hair was tied back in a tight black bun, and layered with a fallout of debris. "You fool! You have broken my door! I was hiding! Now I have nowhere to hide from ze zombies!"

Franco climbed warily to his feet.

"Hey, listen, I'm sorry about…" he began, as a second punch whirred like a partridge through the gloom and lifted him from the ground a second time, sending him flailing over a still-standing shelf unit, in which he caught an errant sandal, and both Franco and the shelving unit cannoned into a second shelving unit, and the whole sorry mess went down in a tangle of limbs and galvanised metal planks which clattered and clanged amongst wood and dust.

Franco groaned, then struggled to extricate himself like a fish from a bucket.

"I hide from ze zombies!" insisted Olga. She stood over him, fists like spades on her meaty hips. "What I do now, huh? You take me with you! You protect Olga!"

"Protect you from *what?*" snapped Franco, struggling from the carnage. He stood, staring up at the bristling woman. She was… titanic. Shit, he thought, rubbing his bruised jaw. She must weigh three hundred pounds! His eyes followed her rippling, fatty curvature. Huge breasts filled a shapeless smock which billowed down to a rotund waist and stocky, hairy legs like tree-trunks.

"You staring! You like Olga? You like a bit of what you see?" Suddenly Olga smiled. Her huge football head broke into a cracked-egg of appreciation as she eyed Franco up and down.

"Whoa girl!" said Franco, holding out both his hands. "Just wait a minute! I need to rummage through your drug store, and then I'll be on my way. I ain't giving you the beady eye!"

"You take me with you!" insisted Olga. She tilted her head, in what she must have thought was a coquettish pose. "If you help Olga, if you take her with you, protect from ze zombies, Olga show you where ze special drugs are." She smiled. She had three teeth missing.

"OK. OK. OK." Franco struggled over broken shelving, and entered the narrow room behind the counter with Olga close behind. His hand stayed on the butt of his Kekra, and Olga's hand strayed perilously close to Franco's butt.

Franco eyed the dilapidated, dust-spewing ceiling. "Why me?" he groaned.

KEENAN LOOKED UP and down the street, finishing his cigarette and grinding the remains under his heavy boot. He was just considering whether or not to go in after Franco—not a decision he took lightly, because he had seen Franco heave and strain his way through a good ten-pounder before now—when a sheepish and slightly more battered version of the little stocky squaddie emerged, carrying a canvas sack, and closely followed by a woman whose clothing could easily accommodate three.

"Franco?" came Keenan's enquiring stare.

Franco avoided Keenan's eye. "Don't ask. Long story. Woman in distress. I said we'd take her to safety."

"*Woman?*" hissed Keenan, his voice low. "Franco, we're not a fucking charity. We've got a mission! We can't go picking up every stray waif we come across."

Franco frowned. "Hardly a waif, Keenan."

"Dick*head!* What's in the sack?"

"Provisions."

"Food?"

"Drugs."

"This ain't the place to get fucking *high*."

"No, but it's the place to get fucking *sane*. I can feel the twitching coming on, Keenan. It's the stress. The stress of seeing a loved one rendered into a terrible horrible monster!"

"I'll render my fist in your terrible horrible face in a minute." Keenan breathed deeply. He loved Franco, he really did. But sometimes he simply wanted to put the shaved ginger head between a door and jamb, and slam it a few times. He gritted his teeth. He knew what Cam would say, probably in an AI whine. *He's your best friend. You know he's mad. If you don't want his help, don't damn well ask!* Keenan rubbed at his brows. "OK," he said, releasing a breath of aggravation. "Knuckles, get in the front. You can help me navigate. And Franco?"

"Yeah Keenan?"

"Get in the back with your girlfriend. You can keep each other company."

"I resent that implication! I'm soon to be a happily married man!"

"What, to an eight-foot mutation?" barked Keenan.

"Things could be worse."

"How so?"

Franco considered this, as he watched Olga heaving her huge body into the Corvette. It strained, springs squealing in protest. One side of the vehicle listed, as if carrying a very great weight; which it was.

"OK, things couldn't be much worse," he conceded. "But don't keep rubbing it in. I'm sorry about Olga. I'm sorry about Mel. I'm sorry about the car crash. And I'm sorry about the mess. There. I've apologised." He bristled.

Keenan laughed, rubbing at the back of his head. "Shit, Franco. You are just one insane motherfucker."

"You got another headache?"

"Mm."

"I got some painkillers! In the sack! You want me to dig you out a pill?" Franco's eyes gleamed.

"It's a headache, Franco; the last thing I need is one of your psychedelic drug trips. No, I'll pass, thanks. The pain's not bad, just there, nagging at me like a wife with a new credit card."

"That's not politically correct," snorted Franco.

"But correct," said Keenan, baring his teeth. "You'll learn, mate. When you marry one of your two, ahh, chosen ladies. Unless, of course, you marry them both."

Franco eyed Olga warily, then climbed into the Corvette beside her, scrunching his frame into the narrow slot now available. Olga shuffled, with a big toothless smile. Then, she lifted an arm and placed it ponderously across Franco's shoulders, nearly buckling the small chap under the weight of her bicep.

"You gotta be joking," mumbled Franco, eyeing Olga's tattooed knuckles as he tried to get comfortable beside her titanic, heaving bosom; and tried his damnedest not to meet Keenan's chuckling, over-critical stare.

"IT'S BLOCKED," SAID Knuckles, as the Corvette stuttered to a halt, tyres grinding loose rubble. They stared at the alley, where two low apartment buildings had collapsed into one another, merging, to form a three-storey pyramid of rubble.

"Other ways?" said Keenan. They could still smell fire. It smelt stronger now, and tangy with a secondary, acid stench. Keenan was sure he could hear the moaning of zombies.

"Yeah. One."

Keenan reversed the Corvette, struggling to see past Olga's width. They skidded into a narrow cross-roads, and the hackles on Keenan's neck suddenly lifted. Behind them, advancing swiftly and in complete silence, was a wall of zombies.

"Keenan!" wailed Franco.

"I see them," he growled, and slammed his foot to the floor. The Corvette cut out with a grunt, and a backfire *crack* of unspent fuel. The zombies, seeing fresh meat stranded, accelerated.

Keenan turned the starter. It grumbled, rattling like a spanner in a turbine.

"Keenan!"

"We go now," said Olga, eyes wide, brows furrowed. "Ze zombies come! Oh my!"

Keenan turned the starter again, pumping the pedal. Fumes exploded from roof exhaust as zombies flooded past the vehicle, several leaping to grasp the back. Wheels turned, tyres spinning, as Franco struggled to drag free his Kekra and unloaded a hail of bullets into twisted, elongated deviant faces...

A roar went up, from all around. It was like a battle cry, the roar of an advancing army, a war host of terrifying and epic proportions. To Keenan, it sounded a million miles from the simple zombie moans of the movies... the simple cackle of brainless undead.

The Corvette lurched, engine screaming, and sped down the street. Five zombies clung to the Corvette's tailgate, and Franco unleashed a hail of bullets into their faces, destroying eyes, eating away grey, sickening flesh, but still they hung on with the tenacity of a yappy terrier. Franco clambered over the boot and started hammering at grey-flesh fingers sporting long, twisted talons with the butt of his Kekra as Olga grabbed the back of his pants to stop him toppling from the bouncing, juddering vehicle.

"That way!" screamed Knuckles, pointing—

As another horde of zombies flooded, like a rampant evil enema, into the street before them, hands bearing weapons which flexed and opened fire. Bullets whined and zipped everywhere as Keenan dragged on the steering wheel, and tyres squealed, squirming on warped rims. The arse of the Corvette slammed a wall sending a shower of sparks over the thumping Franco. Franco squawked, almost tossed free. Only Olga saved him. He glanced back into her wide, brutal, flat face. He could see sweat gleaming on the stubble of her upper lip. "Thanks!" he breathed. She winked at him, and his insides lurched like a lard-fried breakfast on a hungover wedding morn.

Keenan fought the Corvette Scrambler as it thundered down another alleyway. The huge bumper smashed through barrels and crates, then slapped the flesh of a zombie, tossing the body into the air like a broken ragdoll. More zombies stumbled into view, several opening fire. Keenan hunkered down behind the wheel as the Corvette's bumper whacked and smacked, crushed and tossed. Zombie bodies were hurled into the sky, crunched against dirt-smeared brick walls; were flung up and over the thundering Corvette. One flipped, caught a foot in the front bumper, and slammed onto the bonnet, inverting metal, its head cracking the windscreen. Keenan watched, heart in his mouth, as the skull gaped like a piranha's mouth and black brains oozed free, dribbling. The zombie looked up, grinning a long-fanged grin at Keenan and he felt it, his sanity, teetering on the brink of an abyss. "Hold the wheel," he growled at Knuckles, stood in his seat, and slammed five bullets into the grinning face. The body flipped to one side, leg torn free and slapping like a heavy rag against the front of the Corvette. Keenan tried to ignore it, but it nagged at his peripheral vision like an obtuse drunk in a posh restaurant.

"Not far now," said Knuckles. "Around the next bend."

Keenan nodded. "How you doing back there, Franco?"

"The bastards..." he slammed his Kekra against the last of the fingers, which finally parted with a soft squelching of necrotic flesh, "just don't know when to let go." He turned, panting, cheeks flushed red. "Shit Keenan, this ain't a fun gig by any stretch of the imagination."

Keenan glanced in his mirror. He tapped his chin. "Better see to the beard, Franco."

"What? Why?" Franco frowned, and combed fingers through the ginger monster. He knocked free a grey severed finger which tumbled into the footwell. "Aiiee!" he screamed. "A finger! A finger!"

"Let me soothe you," rumbled Olga, and took Franco in a bear hug.

Keenan grinned sombrely, and focused on driving. Clouds of heavy smoke were filtering into the street. He slowed his speed, veering suddenly to thud over another zombie. Tyres crushed flesh, and Keenan blinked, trying hard not to think that these devourers of flesh had once been human.

The smoke thickened.

"OK, up ahead," said Knuckles, "be ready!"

The Corvette slammed round a tightening bend, rear tyres squirming, and Keenan almost hit the brakes in shock. Ahead, stood a massive ornately carved stone edifice, a circular building filled with pillars and wide buttresses of stone. It sat on a raised plinth at the head of broad sweeping steps of finest gold and white marble. High long windows looked down over a plaza of manicured lawns and trees, an extravagant luxury in a place where every square inch was worth billions to developers. It just went to underline how affluent The Great Malkovitch Library really was, but then, it was an addendum to The Great Malkovitch University, and that was renowned as being academically elite to the point of farce through the Quad-Gal in its entirety.

And... the library burned.

The sculpted, tree-lined plaza before the library was filled from edge to edge with thousands upon thousands of zombies. Every creed, colour, shape and size was catered for. Every wound, deformation, amputation and decapitation was on show. It was a fairground of freaks. A party for the forcibly deformed. A unity of unwilling undead.

"Hell," breathed Keenan, lost in awe. Already his foot was lifting from the accelerator...

"Keep driving!" howled Knuckles. Keenan glanced in the rear view mirror to see a charging wall of snarling, growling, hate-filled faces only inches from the Corvette's rear bumper. He slammed his foot, and the bonnet lifted, engine surging, the Scrambler slamming towards the massive gathering of zombies filling the street, the plaza and the whole *world* before them.

Closer, they saw a pyramid of flammable materials had been stacked against the front wall of The Great Malkovitch Library—a bonfire of terrible proportions spanning perhaps two or three hundred metres. Flames roared, and the zombies cheered, waving guns and chainsaws at the sky as fire scorched stone and ornate pillars.

Knuckles grabbed Keenan's arm. Pointed. "Down the side. There. I know a way in."

"You been a busy boy, here?"

"I was a busy boy everywhere," smiled Knuckles, face grim.

The Corvette approached the wall of zombie flesh, and Keenan saw where a few over-eager, partying zombies had got too close to the flames and self-ignited. Still they danced and jiggled, waving flaming hands above flaming, blackened heads. Engulfed in fire, and seemingly celebrating some unrecognisable victory, this sight of denial and sub-animal stupidity chilled Keenan to the core and cemented in his mind that these were nothing like the zombies of fiction. Whatever these creatures were, they were different, the product of some terrible experiment perhaps, some disfiguring virus, or even the deviated biomods blamed by the press; whatever, the results were very, very dangerous.

The Corvette skidded at speed, rearing on two wheels like some unstoppable juggernaut. Tyres squealed and deformed to the brink of detonation. The zombies close by, those that had spotted the Corvette, roared and waved weapons, many opening fire. Bullets pinged and zipped from heavy calibre guns. Keenan prayed, keeping the motor revving high, as the Corvette touched down, ramming the necrotic wall with its front left bumper and sending figures toppling like skittles. For a moment Combat K ploughed through ranks of zombies, bodies falling and bouncing from the charging Corvette. Then they were free, rear wheels skidding and squirming in blood and pulped flesh, and sending the groundcar slewing on aged suspension.

They shot down the side street, the library rearing to their left, pillars *thum thrum thrumming*; they were level with a high windowless wall which formed the library's bulk. "Stop!" screamed Knuckles, and Keenan slammed the brakes, pitching the group forward in seats. Franco grunted, engulfed for a moment by Olga's flesh.

"Why here?" Keenan was loathe to leave the vehicle. It was sanctuary.

"We've got to climb," said Knuckles, rubbing at his skull. "I was going to take us in by the front door, but twenty thousand zombies kind of put me off the idea."

Keenan nodded, and watched Knuckles leap free, search for a moment, then locate a practically invisible handhold. He started to scale the building, hand over hand, red gloss boots digging into narrow horizontal slots which, due to their angle of cut, blended nearly perfectly with the wall. To Keenan, it looked like they had been expertly chiselled. A professional job.

"You don't like heights," said Keenan, glancing at Franco.

"I'll be fine. But what about Olga?"

"Olga climb!" boomed the huge woman. "Olga strong! Olga fit! Olga triumph!"

"OK," said Franco. "But... no offence meant, you can go last. I wouldn't want you on my head on the way down."

Olga smiled slinkily. "Yes, little man, but on *my* way down on *your* head I make *sure* you come last! Har! You do make sexy chit chat with Olga, you naughty little man! Har har!"

Franco paled, then glanced up to where Keenan was scaling swiftly after Knuckles, who had stopped, shouting down instructions on how best to climb. Franco dug in fingers, and began his ascent. Within seconds his fingers were sore, his sandals finding scant purchase on the sheer stone wall. Olga followed close below him, not quite blocking out the ever-expanding view of the flood of zombies making their way down the alley. A few errant bullets whined past the climbers and Franco ducked, feeling suddenly, incredibly, vulnerable. The zombies seemed to be sniffing around the Corvette Scrambler, and glancing about—but not, most importantly, *up*. Franco kept this keen in his mind as he ascended and used it as a mental helve to urge him to extra speed. Amazingly, Olga stayed with him.

Keenan, halfway up now, gazed down—and out—over the darkened city streets spread beneath. His stomach lurched, and he glanced down at the hard concrete six storeys below. To fall now would be instant death, despite his WarSuit. And even if the fall didn't splatter him into component atoms, the deviants would converge on his wounded frame and eat his brains. He shivered; then grinned a wild grin. Shit, he thought, but wasn't this what life was all about? If you never experienced danger, then you never had anything by which to grade safety, and security, and happiness.

Half way. Another six storeys. And Knuckles was already leaping ahead, monkey-like in his agility and sure-footedness. You could tell he'd done this sort of thing before; probably many times.

Franco, on the other hand, was suffering badly. His fingers felt like blocks of lead. His toes and feet were rigid with cramp which made him want to cry out, but he didn't dare, for fear of a rapid hail of bullets from below. And, worst of all, he needed a shit. Shit, he thought as he climbed, I don't bloody believe it. Of all the times the human body can dump on you, halfway up a building with a horde of flesh-eating zombies below armed with Uzis and D5s has to take the chocolate biscuit. Hot diggity dog. Cabbage and bloody bollocks! He surged on, body screaming, bowel pummelling, thinking about the drugs in the canvas sack stashed in his pack. He would gorge himself at the top, yes! And the thought of a drug-induced heaven pushed him on...

Olga, also, was struggling. She was incredibly strong, with fingers that could crush any windpipe. But her huge bulk and weight were conspiring against her. And despite being surprisingly manoeuvrable for her size and girth, she was tiring. She glanced down. The zombies held little fear for her, despite her earlier protestation. Neither did the drop. Never a woman blessed with an incredible imagination, Olga had achieved most of her goals in life and, when push came to shove, accepted what fate had to deliver. Her main motivation, as she glanced up at Franco's surprisingly muscular arse, was where this sudden impromptu meeting of boy and girl would conclude. Yes, he had spoken of another woman—his 'girlfriend'. But Olga merely smiled at that, her huge, multi-poundage mammaries wobbling with an almost innate and frightening AI. In Olga's experience, there were few men who, when drunk enough, could refuse her charms. Like a Venus flytrap, once you were inside her powerful muscular embrace...

Well hell, there was no getting out.

The group climbed.

Below, the zombies worked diligently at detonating the Corvette.

KEENAN REACHED THE summit of the library a few minutes after Knuckles, and with a groan he crawled over the edge and slumped to rain-slick organo-glass. His stomach lurched again, for as he peered down he could see through *every single* internal floor and he felt like he was toppling forward and down, down and falling...

Knuckles grabbed him. "It helps if you close your eyes. Orientate yourself gradually."

Keenan tried it, and felt stability return. He breathed deep. Steadied himself against the stone to his left, which was rough, textured, grainy under his glove. "I didn't expect that. Twelve storeys, straight down. Shit. Glass floors. What a stupid *idea.*"

"I think it's a security feature," said Knuckles.

"Do you see anybody?"

Knuckles crouched, peering in different directions. "It seems mostly deserted down there. There's a group of men, I think, near the main entrance at ground level. Probably worried about the fire eating through their defences."

"Well, the damn deviants want something from in here. That much is obvious."

"Yes," said Knuckles, eyes stoic and older than myth. "Fresh brain."

KEENAN HELPED FRANCO over the ridge, just as the Corvette, far below, detonated with a *boom*. Fire rushed upwards, and with a squawk Olga accelerated and, her great behind aflame, toppled over the ledge and onto the organo-glass floor which rippled softly under her weight. There came a hiatus. Then she squawked again, and Franco ran over, patting at her flaming rump with hearty slaps that sent many a pound of rolling flab quivering across her great bottom.

Franco hopped about, patting and blowing. "I can't believe they blew up the Corvette!" he scowled. "A mighty fine vehicle, that." Pat pat, blow blow.

He stopped.

Keenan gave him a weak smile.

"What?" said Franco. "*What?*"

Keenan shrugged, and Franco turned to meet Olga's eyes. His hand was still touching her long extinguished bottom. She was smiling, showing crooked teeth, broken from far too many bar brawls.

"Please, carry on, Olga *like*," she purred, although it was more the purr of a sabre-tooth tiger than that of *felis silvestris catus*.

"A ha haha," said Franco, withdrawing his hand just a little too quickly.

"No, you continue, Olga much enjoy!"

Franco skipped backwards, and bumped into Keenan.

"Come on lad, we're moving."

"Yeah, Keenan. What we gonna do for transport now?" He gazed over, where they could see from their vantage the gathering of thousands of zombies in the alleyway. His implication was obvious. The game was getting more and more dangerous by the minute. Locating a groundcar was no longer going to be easy. Their mission had, it seemed, led them further into the heart of darkness. And there would be no Conrad to write a conveniently neat ending.

"We'll sort something out. Let's find this Professor Xakus. If he's still alive."

"I never thought of that," rumbled Franco.

"And *if* he's not mutated."

"Ahh. Bugger."

"Exactly. Let's move."

They worked their way down through the library, past shelves of books, digital tomes, organo-glass reading cubes and plasti-sheets. Shelves upon shelves upon shelves, millions of tomes containing billions of words, knowledge, entertainment, the history of a hundred alien species; all contained under one transparent semi-living roof and huddled amidst stone walls which harked to a distant age, long gone from the reality of physical memory.

Keenan led the way now, Knuckles and Franco following, Olga to the rear and strangely silent. Down organo-glass stairs and ramps they moved, not trusting the lift system due to flickering lights and other strange electrical occurrences. Keenan carried his Techrim 11mm, preferring its discreet bulk and short-distance killing power to the over-heavy Kekra. Franco carried both Kekra quad-barrels; they were his weapons of choice. Knuckles had his rusted machete, whereas Olga simply had her fists.

Down they moved, through silence punctuated by distant roars of the besieging foe. Occasionally, The Great Malkovitch Library shook. And, despite organo-glass ceilings, it got darker as they descended, gloomier, as if moving warily into an undersea tomb.

The first man they met, old and crooked with a shock of bright white hair above circular spectacles, simply screamed and charged away, bent back and walking stick forgotten in his eagerness to escape the perceived enemy.

"Did I say something?" said Franco.

"I think it's more the way you look."

"Cheers."

They followed the stampeding octogenarian, guns still drawn, until they emerged from a broad sloping ramp onto thick red carpets and the central entrance hall. There, gathered with a variety of bristling weapons, was a group of men, not one under the age of seventy. As Combat K and their companions appeared, weapons levelled with a rattle of machine-gun alloy.

One gun slammed, and a bullet whined over Keenan's head to embed in organo-glass with a soft *plop*. A large man at the centre of the group slapped another man's weapon down, scowling. "Sorry, ND." He poked the responsible OAP in the chest. "We only shoot the zombies, Henry, you hear me?"

"Shoot the what?"

"The *zombies*. TURN YOUR HEARING AID UP! YOU UNDERSTAND?" The large man mimed his instruction, but the OAP with the H&K P5 semi-automatic wasn't listening, instead, taking a few tottering steps towards Olga... or more precisely, the huge woman's huge breasts.

"I'm looking for Professor Xakus," said Keenan, stepping to the fore.

"Well, you found him," said the large man, who despite his age still had a bearing of power, of innate strength. Keenan studied him; Xakus was a touch over six feet tall, with jet-black skin and a bush of white, frizzy hair atop a cubic skull. His face was square-jawed, wrinkled with age despite the latest anti-ageing drugs flooding the market, and deep-set brown eyes studied Keenan with a glittering, bright intelligence. Keenan immediately liked the professor; he felt comfortable in the man's presence.

"We are on a two-fold mission," said Keenan.

"You military?"

Keenan considered lying, but dismissed the thought instantly. "Combat K. Well, me and the little ginger one, Franco. The lad is Knuckles, a local gang-lad; don't leave your wallet lying around. And the woman is, ahh, Olga. A *lady friend* of Franco's we seem to have picked up on the way."

"I didn't invite her," muttered Franco.

"That's the way it looked to me," snapped Keenan.

Professor Xakus gestured to the group, numbering perhaps thirty and sporting the largest variety of home-knitted cardigans City-side of Quad-Gal. "Meet The Professors. We were here for a simple frag-sesh when the whole zombie fiasco escalated. As professionals, we are often entrusted with the keys to the library; all the staff had left for The Quantum Carnival. We were celebrating in our own way."

"What's a frag-sesh?" asked Franco.

"Gaming. Networked computers. You all connect to a game, and run around trying to kill one another in a digital representation of whatever battlefield you choose." He smiled. "You get to blow the shit out of those you love without actually resorting to caving their head in with a crowbar. You see him over there?" Xakus pointed to a bent and crooked man, who must have been a hundred years old to the day. He sported shaved white hair, a short white goatee beard, and piercing blue eyes. He was clasping a D4 shotgun in gnarled hands the texture of old tan leather. "That's Rembo. He's the reigning champion on Quake Fortress, Age of Vampires *and* Battlefield Quad-Gal. This library had become our digital battlefield until the zombies invaded!"

"Well, it's for real, now," said Keenan, voice soft.

"Yes. Unfortunately. It's one thing fighting in a digital representation; in reality, the experience is a lot more sobering."

From outside, there came a mammoth *boom*. The huge, towering doors shook, along with the walls. Behind the group, books—proper, old, leather-bound paper books—rattled from shelves and clattered across the floor. Xakus clutched his hair, his frustration obvious. "They're priceless!" he whispered.

"They're trying to burn their way in," said Keenan, rubbing at weary eyes. "You seem to have attracted a fair horde out there. Have you any idea what they want?"

Xakus shook his head. "I have no idea, Mr Keenan. But they'll never burn through those doors; this library could withstand a serious blast. Its cargo is precious indeed."

"Yet it's not designed for war," said Keenan.

"You are, of course, correct. I expect it's merely a matter of time." Xakus sighed, rubbing at his chin. His face was set in deep thought. "Quickly now, tell me who sent you, and why you seek my help. I think, soon, we will be heading for the back door. MICHELLE is waiting."

"Steinhauer sent us. My home-world of Galhari has been overrun by a race known as junks—the organic, germ-ridden toxic shite of Quad-Gal. I retrieved one of their SinScripts; Steinhauer seems to think you can decode the information therein. Can you do this?"

"Yes. Given time, and the right equipment. I need a CryptorBox. And I cannot do it here; CryptorBox decryption requires large reserves of power. So, the junks are on the move, are they? So many researchers thought them extinct. Were there many?"

"Millions," said Keenan, quietly.

"Ha! So it is true. Leviathan lives."

"Leviathan?" Keenan felt his heart turn cold. Ice rippled through his veins. His soul crumbled into ash.

"The World Eater," said Xakus, eyes distant. "The junks are his slaves. They do his bidding. The SinScript is formed in an ancient digital language, long forgotten by most of the so-called sentient beings in the Quad-Gal. Leviathan, the junks—they do not originate from this life arm. They come from somewhere else; somewhere far distant we could never imagine."

"This is your area of study?" asked Keenan.

"What? No, no; it came as a by-product. I worked NanoTek as a biomod engineer. I worked on some of the original blueprints for the biomods in current circulation; we studied hundreds of different organic races in the initial blueprint stages of biomod design. The junks became a little bit of an obsession for me. This is why Steinhauer sent you. Why he thinks I can help."

Keenan nodded. "This leads us to our second problem. Franco here, his wife-to-be, Mel, has been seriously affected by a biomod; it's turned her into an eight-foot mutation."

"Like the creatures out there?" said Xakus, eyes glittering.

"No. Different. Bigger. More dangerous. You were an engineer, yes? Can you help change her back?"

"I would need Level 1 equipment. I no longer have that kind of authority."

Out of the corner of his eyes, Keenan saw Franco deflate. "But if we could get you to this Level 1 equipment, you could change Melanie back?"

"Yes, theoretically. Anything is possible. But look outside, around you, Keenan. The nanobots have gone haywire; the biomods have deviated a population. It is horror made real. An abomination of science."

"So it's true, then?" blurted Franco. "The biomods *have* changed everyone into zombies?"

"On a basic level, yes," said Xakus. His face was filled with thunder. "I warned Dr Oz. The algorithms were too loose; there was too much scope for evolution. And then the pirates, the crackers, the hackers—they stuck their fingers into the pie and turned what could have been a saviour of so many organic races into a living, breathing nightmare. Boy, Dr Oz will be *pissed.*"

"For causing so much death and destruction?" asked Franco.

"You're kidding, lad, right?" Xakus boomed laughter, and slapped Franco on the back. "No, because of the bad PR it'll cause. Think what this little incident will do to global Quad-Gal biomod sales. Would *you* buy one after you'd seen a zombie army rampage across an entire planet?"

"I suppose not," muttered Franco, feeling like a naïve little boy.

"Could you stop this large-scale mutation?" asked Keenan, head tilted to one side, eyes fixed on Xakus. Suddenly, a crazy plan started to form in his whirling brain—a plan which would no doubt be incredibly, awesomely, frighteningly dangerous... but which could, if it worked, put a stop to this insanity. Once and for all. "After all, you helped design the biomods."

"Not these incarnations," said Xakus. "But... yes, technically, I know how to shut them down."

"You mean you can switch them off?" blurted Franco.

The professor smiled. "Nanobots are machines, Francis. Like any other machine, they can be powered down."

"But it's not easy, right? Or NanoTek would have pulled the plug."

Xakus nodded. "Or maybe NanoTek have been shut down by the biomods—the zombies—themselves? Maybe the machines became self-aware; maybe the monster turned on its maker?"

"More and more questions seem to lead to NanoTek. I assume they have a HQ?"

Xakus nodded, as another *boom* rattled the building. Franco's nostrils twitched as he recognised the scent of explosive; Knuckles turned, heading off to get a look at the situation outside.

"Yes. The Black Rose Citadel. A fortress island. Impregnable. Anti-aircraft. Anti-nuke. The NanoTek HQ descends beneath the island, and beneath the ocean for two or three kilometres."

"You think the zombies have taken control?"

"A possibility," said Xakus, licking his lips. "It is the logical source from which this flood of deviancy poured. It is there NanoTek have the GreenSource Mainframe. Without that, so I believe, the biomods would not function. NanoTek would have pulled the plug by now if they could. And the zombies outside... well, they just wouldn't work without GreenSource."

Keenan rubbed his temples, then turned to Franco. "Listen mate, if we can get Mel and Xakus to the NanoTek HQ, there's a chance we can do something—not just for Melanie, but for all those poor bastards out there. Otherwise..." He shrugged. "We sit here and twiddle our thumbs."

"I thought you were here to decode the Sin-Script?"

Keenan shook his head. "It's all fucked up, Franco. All connected—somehow. I'm just trying to work out the puzzle; but this shit going down here in The City, the biomods, the zombie deviations—they're linked to the junks and the invasion of Galhari." He grimaced. "I can feel it in my fucking *bones.*"

Franco gestured to Keenan, and they moved away from the group. Again, a detonation rocked the Great Malkovitch Library. More books toppled from shelves. Tutting and clucking like mother hens, the aged academics started picking the tomes from the ground as if they were rare and expensive crystal.

"Listen," said Franco, out the corner of his mouth, "he said *that name.* The bad one. The one we agreed never to discuss."

Keenan nodded, eyes locked on Franco's. "Xakus said the junks are the servants of Leviathan. But we killed it. Didn't we? We blew the singularity chains—watched it annihilated by the black fire, then sucked into that bastard black hole."

"We didn't see shit," said Franco. "Did we really understand what was going on—on that screwed-up world? Teller's World—the devourer of millions? It was alien to us, Keenan. Truly alien."

The two men were discussing their last, and most devastating, adventure. Keenan, tortured by the memories of his murdered wife and children, had taken a mission to locate and steal a fabled artefact called The Fractured Emerald—which could prophesise the future, but also see into the past. Keenan was promised the name of the killer who murdered his family in return. Only The Fractured Emerald turned out not to be a jewel, but instead, a woman—or at least, a *female*. An alien female named Emerald, from an age-old extinct race—the *Kahirrim*. Emerald wanted to go home, to be strong again, so that she could finally elect to die—to discover ultimate peace. Keenan, Franco and Pippa had escorted her to the dangerous and prohibited planet of Teller's World, a barren desolate ball of soul-devouring rock. However, travelling far beneath the world, towards its core, Combat K soon discovered the world was far from conventional, and was in fact a prison-sphere holding an incarcerated *being* in the cage of a stabilised singularity. The alien being was Leviathan, classified a GODRACE, one of the original Five Great Creators. Only, Leviathan had gone bad, turned sour, become The Eater, The Devourer of Worlds. Unwittingly, Combat K helped Emerald to free him from his chains; only to swiftly put a spanner in the gears of the plan, detonating the prison cage—and Teller's World in its entirety—and consigning Leviathan to a bleak and final extinction. Or so they had believed.

Now, it would seem, Leviathan's slaves were expanding, invading, conquering. That could only be a *bad* thing.

"We saw him crushed in that black hole," said Keenan.

"No. That's what we wanted to see. Pippa pulled that illegal K Jump and we got the hell out. To see Leviathan drawn down into that place..." Franco smiled, and it was cold, twisted and angular on his face. "Well, to see that through to its finale, Keenan, we'd have to have joined him."

"What now?" Keenan took a deep breath. "If Leviathan exists..."

"One step at a time, compadre." Franco patted him on the back. "We're not supermen! Well, at least you're not. First we sort out Mel, and this SinScript. Hopefully it will tell us what we need to know about the junks. Maybe they have nothing to do with Leviathan. Maybe they fancy a bit of conquering all on their own. When we decode the SinScript, then we'll see what threat lies beyond."

"Yes."

Knuckles appeared at the top of the slope leading down from the higher tiers of the library's unconventional internal structure. "Keenan!" he shouted, voice just a little too high, tinged with panic.

"Yeah lad?"

"You'd better come and see this."

"Is it important?"

"It's the zombies. They've brought tanks."

KEENAN, FRANCO, OLGA and Xakus ran after Knuckles up the ramp, which sprung softly under pounding boots. They were followed by a straggled line of limping, geriatric academics brandishing a bristling array of weaponry that would make any platoon weep with promise of wargasm.

Knuckles led, and Keenan, sprinting, soon felt the effects of too much booze, too many cigarettes, and a few years of gross physical abuse. He was tired. Exhausted. Filled with pain, and taunted by angst. As Franco would say, this gig was turning into *a proper hell mission from hell!*

They reached the fourth floor, and Knuckles powered ahead, out under an ornate archway with a thousand intricacies of gothic carving, across fake alloy-stone flags to a curled balcony. Outside, the flames had died down, the zombies presumably having either exhausted their fuel, or readying themselves for another stage of onslaught.

"There." Knuckles pointed.

Keenan reached the balcony, with Franco, Olga and Xakus. Heavy smoke filled the air, along with an acidic stench of fire. The balcony stone beneath their hands was hot. Embers glittered in the dark like fireflies. Keenan squinted.

Below, the zombie warhost stood arraigned in eerie silence. Many heads were turned, staring back across the once picturesque plaza. They started to part, shambling aside as deep, booming engines revved and a massive tank came belching from the rear, down a narrow street between towering black skyscrapers. It had a 45-degree sloping glacis leading to a flat hull top. Twin 250mm canons stared with evil, oval eyes.

"That's a Mammoth Mk13," said Franco, voice quiet, reverent, almost unheard over the still crackling fire below.

Keenan nodded. "No flesh shall be spared," he said. "That's some damn hardware."

Belching thick smoke, the tank thundered from the street, engine reverberations booming between towering blocks. Quad tracks ate rubble, mounted a ground car and crushed it easily into a pancaked bean tin with organic squeals.

"The thing is, can it get through the armoured doors below?" said Franco.

"Maybe not on its own," said Keenan. "But look."

As the Mammoth Mk13 rumbled onto the plaza, churning plastic grass and mowing down small trees, from the smoke of its inelegant wake came another Mammoth, then another, another, until six units spread out and halted, rumbling, twelve guns pointing directly at The Great Malkovitch Library.

"Haha," said Franco, without a smile. "I think it was time we made a sharp exit."

"How the hell did zombies learn to drive tanks?"

"Remembered genetics?" said Franco.

Keenan looked at him sideways. "That's quite good. For you."

"Hey, I'm not just some uncouth, misogynistic, beer-drinking, heterosexual power-house, with no appreciation of the finer points of science, literature and art." He farted. "Am I?"

"You could have fooled me," said Keenan, eyeing the tanks. He glanced at Xakus. "You mentioned a back door? A way out?"

The tanks revved, and suddenly one fired, rocking on heavy suspension. Twin booms filled the plaza, and 250mm armour-piercing shells slammed across the clearing and connected with the library. The building shook. High up, stones detached from roof ledges and clattered like cobble rain around the group. They sprinted back to the sanctuary of the interior, and Xakus nodded as more shells smacked the library and the world was filled with noise and violence and heavy metal aggression.

"It's not exactly a back door," shouted Xakus over the screams of fire and detonation. "But MICHELLE *will* help us escape."

"Who's Michelle?" shouted Franco.

"You'll see!"

The library was in chaos, pounded by the six tanks. The front of the building was crumbling, disintegrating under a howling onslaught. Outside, zombies were clawing at the rubble... a little too eagerly, for the tanks continued to fire and many zombies were blasted to merge with stones and marble. As the group sped back down ramps to ground level where the main doors—incredibly— were still holding, although battered and limp and allowing flames to lick through, so more explosions rocked the building and several flaming zombies were catapulted through gaps leaving flaming trails through the air to connect with walls, limp and bloody, and rolling to a stop where they set scattered books alight. The group of aged academics had a quick conference, leaning on shotguns, and Keenan glanced from the old men to Xakus.

"What's going on? We need to move."

"They will not leave."

"That's crazy," snapped Keenan. "This place is about to be overrun!" Even as he spoke, they could hear zombies dragging at the flaming debris stacked against the building. Many zombies caught fire, and blazed merrily through the gaps in the armoured doors. Not one screamed.

One old man, with wispy white hair and watery, rheumy old eyes, glared at Keenan. He loaded a D4 shotgun with liver-spotted hands, and grinned with a mouth of missing teeth. "Just because we're old, doesn't mean we don't still have fire! You young 'uns get gone, MICHELLE couldn't carry us all anyway... we will stay here, protect the library... protect the books." He looked incredibly sad, for a moment. "We won't let those bastards burn 'em. This ain't nineteen-forty-four."

Keenan nodded, filled with a sadness and respect as the old academics formed a shuffling line and readied themselves for the zombie charge. Again, bombs rocked the building. Debris smashed and splattered from armoured doors, revealing widening gaps through which the zombies started to squeeze, grey-flesh hands brandishing machine guns and pistols. The line of old academics opened fire, decimating the first row of snarling zombies...

"Time to go," said Franco, softly.

Keenan nodded. "Xakus?"

"Follow me."

They ran, back through narrow, wood-lined corridors which smelt strongly of musty old tomes. Thick carpets lined the way, and ancient oil paintings hung at intervals, stern faces staring down disapprovingly at the fleeing group.

"What did he mean, nineteen-forty-four?"

Xakus gave a cold smile. "Only the insane burn books," panted the old black man, stopping for a moment, sweat rolling down his face. "Give me a moment, lads, I'm not used to all this excitement."

"Is this back door at the back?" said Franco.

"A classic question," said Keenan.

"Actually, no," said Xakus. "It's beneath us."

"Not back to the tunnels!" groaned Franco.

"This is something different," said Xakus.

They ran on, as gunfire and screams echoed behind. The zombies had flooded the library's foyer, many leaping past the old men who had formed a circle of guns, and were killing with ancient cackles and the madness of the doomed.

Zombies spilled into corridors and lecture halls, storage rooms and high-ceilinged halls. They galloped, teeth gnashing, and several picked up the strong scent of *brains* and *fresh meat*...

Xakus stopped by a keypad in the wall. His gnarled hand flickered, and the floor suddenly opened at their feet, a ramp hissing down into a subterranean vault on heavy hydraulics. Lights glittered into life as the group peered down at what appeared to be an underground runway.

"MICHELLE's down there?" asked Franco, peering warily into the ice-chilled gloom.

"Follow me."

They were alerted by snarls and moans, and Keenan and Franco whirled, guns booming and cracking. Two charging zombies were caught in the hail, smashed up and back, limbs flailing as black blood and pus splattered out in an arcing gore rainfall. Behind, more zombies were advancing, yellow eyes narrowed, broken teeth bared in menacing snarls.

"Get moving!" roared Keenan, as his Techrim destroyed a zombie's head and sent cubes of skull thumping across plush carpet.

"We've got a problem," said Knuckles, voice edged with a filigree of panic.

Keenan glanced back at their escape route, down the long metal ramp to where tiny lights flickered like stars. At the bottom, standing patiently, were the three alloy GK AIs, thin gloss black limbs motionless, matt black eyes fixed on the group above. Keenan's mouth dropped. The three GKs spread apart, the central one drawing twin yukana swords from metal sheaths on its back. The one to the left suddenly sprouted a thousand gleaming, shimmering needles which rippled across alloy limbs and back and head. The one to the right transformed arms and legs into long killing blades which clattered at the foot of the ramp, kicking up sparks.

"Holy duck shit!" boomed Franco, as a flood of zombies from behind, punching and kicking and snarling and scratching, fought one another to get down the corridor leading to the stinking stench of pumping meaty brain...

Keenan stood, frozen, between hammer and anvil.

The spiked AI's eyes swivelled to lock on Keenan. A moment passed between them—in which Keenan felt himself totally ensnared, fixated by a graceful example of a beautifully advanced prototype technology. In a simple, measured, elegant female voice, the AI spoke.

"Combat K." She seemed to smile, giving a single nod, glossy hydraulic jaws hissing as they worked in a sad mimicry of human speech. "It's time to retire."

CHAPTER 10
HURT

MELANIE ROCKED BACK on her haunches, watching the children who had gathered round the small fire on the rooftop of the Happy Friendly Sunshine Assurance Company. They were singing softly, a lilting ballad led by Little Megan, with Skull and Glass crooning in the background as Sammy tapped out a rhythm on an old tin can with a long, dangerous looking stiletto dagger. Drool pooled from Mel's distended jaws, ran down her chin, and formed a long, sticky umbilical to the floor. She glanced down. There was a large oval puddle, from the recent torrential opening of the heavens, and Mel shuffled herself to the pool and gazed at herself. One taloned hand lifted, the arm slim and wiry, skin a mottled dark brown and spotted with black, rippled and corrugated in places as if her own skin didn't quite fit her, like a badly oversized rubber jacket. Her skin was slick with grease, and it shone. Her small black eyes moved down the shimmering reflection of her own body, past the obscenely dangling breasts with massive, pus-oozing nipples, to the angular and bony disjointed legs with knees that worked the wrong way and large, flapping, taloned feet. And then she gazed at her face, and let out a little whimper through her stepped-out lower jaw. Her head, small and round and hairless, sat atop a long neck with crackling armour plating.

What am I? she thought.

You are Melanie.

What have I become?

You have always been this way...

No, no, I was different. Before. I was a... woman. A human. With white flesh and long brown hair and gentle eyes. She closed her tiny black pin-pricks and focused *internally*. Somewhere, in her confused and raging skull, an image forced itself clear of the mire of hunger and hatred and blood-red rage; Mel concentrated on that image, held it strong in her mind, and holding its hand brought it to the fore of consciousness. She could see herself. As she had been. When she was...

Normal.

I was normal.

So what am I now?

Her eyes opened, neck crackling as her head moved and lowered, staring into a rippled reflection of organic horror.

I am a monster, she realised with shock.

I have become a deviant.

Sorrow washed through Mel, and she felt herself slipping down a slick greased slope into the broiling pot of turmoil and anger and hatred. Grinding her teeth, her stepped-out lower jaw clacking, she dragged herself back up the mental slope and touched again a world of humanity, a world of remembrance, a world of normality.

So... what happened? How did I come to this?

She remembered her job. A *tax inspector*. She smiled. It was so gratifying.

And she remembered...

Mel frowned. *Francis*. Her boyfriend. Her lover. The man she wanted to...

Marry.

Where had he gone? Had he abandoned her?

Melanie felt tears well within her mottled, distended breast, and she breathed deep, triple lungs rasping air through teeth more titanium than bone. Memories danced just out of reach. Images, blurred, of a childhood, of friends, of a job, a love-life. Emotions raged within her, and she felt herself slipping back into an uncontrollable pit of rage and despair... where a demon lived, a demon that wasn't her, filled with the need to hunt and feed and rip and tear and kill...

"Mel?" It was Little Megan. She touched Mel's grooved talons; tenderly, like a child touching its mother. "What are you doing sitting here all by yourself? Come over to the fire, where it's warm."

Mel nodded, eased herself to her feet and towered over the tiny girl. She lolled to the fire and all the children glanced up, smiling as they huddled together. Little Megan patted a space on the ground and Mel squeezed beside the kids, feeling huge and cumbersome, ungainly and suddenly very, very ugly.

Who did this to me? she thought idly, as the singing resumed.

Who changed me into this horrorshow?

Little Megan rested her head against Mel's arm, ignoring the slick grease on the deviant's skin. The orphan girl gave a little sigh and closed her eyes, and Mel started to croon, a lilting noise that rose in volume and joined with the children's sad, steady rhythm. And Mel sang, sang to the sky, sang to the stars, sang to the children, a song without words and yet which conveyed emotion—that of love, and sympathy, and sorrow; a song about loneliness murmured in dreams; a song about life. And, ultimately, death.

Mel did not know that she'd fallen asleep, only that she awoke.

The fire had gone out, was nothing more than glowing embers, lava etched on charcoal. Her nostrils twitched, at the woodsmoke, and at... something else. Something alien to her surroundings.

She scanned the group. The children slept, peaceful, breathing deeply in their little comfort circle. Peaceful, at rest, safe in the knowledge that they were protected by an eight-foot deviant mutation who had successfully battled zombies and expelled them from the Happy Friendly Sunshine Assurance Company.

But, ultimately, how much am I like the enemy? thought Mel.

Am I a zombie... as well? Am I undead? A nonperson? An eater of brains and flesh?

She frowned. More and more *human* thoughts were starting to cascade through a mind she now acknowledged as bestial and base. What was happening? Was she *learning*? Learning to be human again?

There came a tiny sound, of steel on wood. Her head slammed left—and there, not ten feet away, crouched a man. He was bulky, tall, his face aged but handsome, with neat black hair and a neat black beard. But his eyes were hooded, brown, bottomless windows to a soul twisted with pain and degradation.

The man smiled. "Hello, Melanie."

"Grwllllll!"

"Do not be alarmed." The man was holding a stick and a knife. Again, he shaved a sliver from the stick, watched it curl to the floor, then tested the point of sharpened wood with his thumb.

Mel wanted to say, *what do you want? I warn you, I'll rip off your head, rip out your spleen, chew through your face and spit out your eyes!* But the rage waned, and something cold settled across her soul. The man exuded power. And his eyes... his flesh was young, the prime of health and youth. But his eyes were *old*.

The man tutted, and glanced down at the length of wood in his powerful, thick-fingered hands. "It's a very great shame it has come to this, Melanie. You do not know me... only *of* me. You are the pretty, transmogrified girlfriend of Franco Haggis. Franco Haggis has done me a very great harm. However, it is you I seek. And you have been *very* difficult to track down."

Mel surged to her feet, talons clacking, but the man put his finger to his lips. His old eyes were smiling. "Shh. Be calm, my sweet. This won't take long."

From out of nowhere three Apache F52 Gunships roared from the false horizon of the skyscraper's roof, veering up from their rapid smashing vertical ascent and dropping, levelling, engines screaming and groaning with leashed power behind the brown-eyed man. He stood smoothly, tossing away the stick and sheathing his knife beneath his coat. He placed hands in pockets, coat tails flapping in the awesome downdraught of three thrumming, enraged war machines with miniguns primed. Mel took a step back, glanced down at the sleeping children who were stirring now, and gave a growl so deep and guttural it went unheard.

The Apaches disgorged a swarm of Battle SIMs, heavily armed and armoured, mechanical eyes glowing faintly as boots hit the ground with synchronised *thuds*. Their armour clicked and whistled, like a platoon of insects; the SIMs spread out behind the man.

"Forgive me." He smiled, but not with his eyes. "I am being rude. Let me introduce myself. I am Mr Voloshko. I own The Hammer Syndicate, one of the seven largest ruling conglomerates on this decadent and rocky ball of shit. You have been a *very* naughty girl, Melanie."

Mel launched herself in rapid acceleration to the attack, talons up and hammering in a dark arc for Voloshko's throat. He flipped to one side with surprising agility for one so large, and five of the SIMs lowered broad-barrelled guns... and fired.

No bullets, but TitaniumMesh, a living, organic biomerge of wire and AI threads. It ensnared a suddenly growling, hissing, thrashing, struggling Mel.

Her talons lashed out, but could not penetrate the fibres. Sparks crackled along web circuits. The TitaniumMesh stung her, and she yelped, a base canine sound as five layers merged and slid and oozed and tightened. They slid around her struggling, slapping body, constricting her; within seconds she fell, her limbs pinned to her sides, her head locked in a vice-like grip.

There was a *slap* as she hit the rooftop.

Voloshko strode forward, leant down, ran his hand along Mel's trapped jaw. Then he turned to the SIMs, waved them in. "Take her back to Hammer HQ."

SIMs ran forward and hooked the TitaniumMesh to an Apache. Rotors thrummed, engines roaring, and the machine leapt into the air. Cables pulled taut, and Mel was hoisted violently up, away from the roof of the skyscraper, into the freezing cold of sudden high altitude.

She gazed down at the children. Watched Voloshko turn his back on the waking group, and glance purposefully at the emotionless group of insectile Battle SIMs. He smiled a broad smile, showing a single gold incisor.

"Kill the kids," he said.

"GIVE ME THE shotgun," said Keenan, voice barely more than a growl. He did not shift his gaze from the rigid AIs at the bottom of the ramp. He felt the touch of barrels against his glove, the proximity of Franco close behind. He heard the click of Franco's Kekra quad-barrel machine pistols as he took the D5, cautiously, in one fist...

"Leave the zombies to me," growled Olga, turning with Knuckles by her side. The young lad grimaced, and brandished his rusted machete in sweating hands.

Keenan twitched a look behind, at the snarling, charging mass. And back, to where Nyx was moving like flowing liquid metal...

Keenan leapt down the ramp, D5 booming. Nyx was caught in the blast, spun, and fired backwards with a screech of stressed alloy. Franco charged with Keenan, both hands firing Kekras. Bullets howled and whined. Sparks flew. Nyx, blasted, curled into a ball, rolling with the D5 onslaught. Momos, with yukana swords whirling, was punched back, along with the twirling blades of Lamia. But even as Keenan pounded the steel, so Nyx turned the roll into a move which defied physics, spinning, and like a globe of needles she rolled at Keenan. The D5 snarled again. Franco halted, dropping to one knee, Kekra tracking Momos who circled in the dark underground vault. Franco fired, but quad-shots hissed over Momos' head.

Behind, at the top of the ramp, Xakus ran for the small console on the wall. Olga and Knuckles ignored him, for the wall of charging zombies were almost on them. One leapt to the attack, and Olga caught its grey flesh in powerful hands. With a crack, she snapped its spine and tossed it aside. And she howled, her huge jowls wobbling as her face changed into a mask of basic animal fury. Knuckles leapt, his machete swinging with the anger of the condemned. A zombie head rolled, the body collapsing sending arcs of black blood spurting. Some zombies tripped, slipping on blood. Knuckles hacked at them blindly, furious, sure now he would die here and it would all have been for nothing! His entire, pointless pathetic young existence, all for nothing! Teeth bared, he hacked and slashed, cutting hands from arms, feet from legs. He felt zombie blood wash over him. He laughed maniacally, lost from sanity as the world became this moment, this wail of hating snarling flesh and... he slipped, on gore, fell back under the weight of zombies and watched, frozen, as they fell towards him, their stench on him and in him, and he breathed in their deep slime and pus and blood which ran thick like black honey over his face and into his mouth and he screamed...

Keenan's D5 boomed again five times in quick succession, and Nyx was sent spinning away—as Momos leapt, yukana swords whirling for Keenan's head. He ducked, stumbling back as the blades hissed around him. One slashed his WarSuit, which buzzed a warning. Keenan unleashed the D5 in Momos' face. He heard a low feminine chuckle, followed by the blasts of Franco's Kekras. Keenan's boots slammed Momos, and she staggered back. Again Franco's guns boomed, and the force sent Momos skittering across the base of the ramp, yukanas showering sparks over alloy—as Keenan turned, into the frenzied whirl of Lamia, her arms and legs glittering blades, and Keenan and Franco scrambled back up the ramp in hasty retreat, slipping, sliding, guns snarling, bullets whining and smashing and everything, all discipline, all procedure forgotten under that panic of bright whirling attack of blades too fast for the eye to follow—

Knuckles gurgled on zombie blood like engine oil, which ran down his throat and into his belly and he tried to scream but nothing would come and he realised he was drowning. He felt claws caress his skull. This was it. Realisation hit him like a brick. They would eat his brain... then Olga was there, her bulk pushing the mass aside as huge shovel-like hands punched and slammed, fists smacking faces, cracking noses and cheekbones, breaking jaws, crushing skulls, lifting and throwing and snapping backs and arms and legs like brittle firewood. She reached down, lifted Knuckles, tossed him away, back to Professor Xakus who was tapping furiously at the wall console. It buzzed at him, red lights flickering. Knuckles rolled to a halt on the cold, hard metal ground, stunned.

Both arm blades slammed down, and Keenan slipped back, his D5, held in both fists, stopping a blow from cleaving his skull like ripe fruit. Pain and vibration shuddered down his arms, nearly dislocating his elbows. Again Lamia cut down, and the D5 buckled in Keenan's grasp, barrels bent, the shotgun useless, and Keenan snarled, boots kicking out uselessly at Lamia's elegant and perfect machine body. Lamia's blades slid, grinding sparks over the D5, and down, agonisingly, towards Keenan's face. He grunted under the effort, straining against the bent shotgun, the only thing between him and decapitation. There came a *clonk,* and Keenan saw Franco's hand withdraw. Lamia looked down. Keenan's boots smashed her chest, and she took three steps back. Franco's Kekras boomed in her face and she whirled away, blades flashing... as the funnelled BABE—now attached to her abdomen— detonated. Fire and smoke screamed, roared, and

Lamia was flung like a metal ragdoll across the dark underground chamber, away, clattering with sparks into the shadows. Nyx rolled, leapt at Keenan who hurled the battered D5 and drew his Techrim. Nyx uncurled, at the base of the ramp. She was smiling, head tilted to one side. Her jaws worked, and Keenan saw poison gleaming on thousands of needles which protruded from her metal skeleton. Keenan realised his mouth was dry. Fear was something to which he was unused, but as he watched Lamia stroll from the darkness, only a few scorch marks on her black casing—evidence of a *full* BABE fucking—he knew the weapons they carried were ineffective. They could not kill these GKs. The machines were far too advanced. The smile fell from Nyx's face, as Lamia and Momos closed ranks behind her. Nyx stepped onto the ramp, lowering her head, and readying herself for a final charge Keenan knew they could not withstand…

Olga lifted her head to the ceiling of The Great Malkovitch Library and roared. The zombies cowered for a moment, yellow feral eyes glittering, many of their fallen, deviant kind littering the floor, broken and bent, many squirming, trying to crawl with snapped spines, broken femurs, crushed heads; Olga charged them, a sudden movement from the huge woman, and talons came up, slashed out, but Olga batted them aside as she powered into the mass, fists slamming, pounding, beating, pulping, every blow a devastating jackhammer, every head-butt crushing deformed noses and skulls. She was a mighty powerhouse, an unstoppable bear of a woman, growling and roaring, her fists her weapons. She forced the zombies back into the narrow corridor, where they could only attack her two abreast, and she slammed them down, broke them down, until they were crawling over their fallen to reach her brains and wobbling, plentiful fresh flesh.

There came a high, ululating call, and suddenly the zombies fell back. Olga stood, her hands and arms covered in gore as if she were some bizarre butcher caught ripping a carcass apart. Olga stared at the snarling, spitting mass with contempt, a sneer forming on her lips. "You filth! You cannot beat Olga! Olga triumph, yes?"

The zombies parted, and from their midst came three with a brightness in their eyes, an intelligence Olga recognised. They moved smoothly, almost feline in grace, and the other zombies seemed to show reverence to these creatures which now faced the great woman...

One lifted its hand, and Olga tracked talons. And realised with a start it carried a small black gun. The gun *slammed,* boom echoing, and the bullet caught Olga high in the chest, punching her back scrabbling at the gunshot-wound, then slipping on the spilled gore of the fallen.

"We are the New Breed," said the zombie, eyes glinting. It half-turned, to the growling, urgent mass. "Eat her!" it commanded.

Nyx charged Keenan, as Professor Xakus hit RETURN. There came a *click,* and the ramp slammed upwards, catching Nyx in mid-charge and pinning her by her abdomen between ramp and frame. Motors whirred, straining, cogs grinding and clicking against powerful ratchets.

Keenan deflated a little. Relief flooded him. He moved forward, where Nyx glared up at him, struggling, matt black eyes clicking, her hands flexing as they tried to grab his soft human flesh. Keenan halted just out of range and dropped to one knee. "Who sent you?"

"Keenan... the zombies!" snapped Franco; he turned, and charged at the zombies which flooded the chamber from the corridor above, charging at the fallen figure of Olga, who lay with eyes fluttering, blood spreading across her punctured chest...

Keenan turned and ran after Franco, and they opened fire. Bullets tore into grey flesh and zombies were kicked spinning backwards. But the two Combat K men realised in an instant; they could not hold the flood. There were too many of them.

And then Knuckles was there, the young lad struggling under the weight of a fire canister. It was red, and down one side, past signs of a skull and crossbones, of toxic danger, biohazard and horrible bioreaction, it read: **DANGER—PERMAFROST BIO FIRE EXTINGUISHER***

[*NOT TO BE USED BY MINORS].

"Stand back!" screamed Knuckles, aiming the nozzle. There came a buzz, a click, then a HISS as a cloud poured from the PERMAFROST BIO FIRE EXTINGUISHER's wide cone nozzle, shuddering in Knuckle's hands. Like raw chemical ice the cloud slammed the charging zombies, freezing them solid. Screaming, Knuckles advanced, the canister rumbling and spitting as the stream of chemicals gushed and billowed over the zombies, turning them instantly white and crisp. He reached Olga, fell to

his knees by her side, and only then did he release
his grip and the chemical cloud evaporated leaving
a silent wall of rigid zombies, a frozen tableaux of
unyielding aggression.

"Reminds me of the last time I saw the football,"
said Franco, turning, scanning, checking for any
other dangers that might emerge to bite them on the
arse.

"See to Olga," said Keenan, replacing the mag in
his Techrim. He turned, nodded at Xakus, who
grinned weakly and gave a *thumbs up*, then strode
back to the still-straining ramp. Gears were whining. The ramp gave little rhythmical judders, still
trying to feed its mammoth weight into its accept-
ance grooves. Nyx was still struggling to break free.
She looked far from impressed.

Keenan crouched, just out of reach. Still, Nyx
grappled for him, inches away from his living flesh.
The GK's jaws worked, soundlessly, and Keenan
could see its legs kicking beyond entrapment in the
heavy ramp snare.

Keenan sat down, cross-legged, placed his
Techrim on the ramp with a *clack,* and lit a ciga-
rette. Nyx watched him. Beyond, he could see
Momos and Lamia pacing. He blew smoke into the
GK's face.

"Who sent you?"

"I will not answer your questions." The voice was
beautiful; a lilting, female voice. Keenan stared into
emotionless matt black eyes, and shivered.

He poked the Techrim in its face. "Do you have a
name?"

"I am Nyx."

"Well Nyx, I'm Keenan. You already know I'm Combat K, so we'll skip the fluffing and get right down to hardcore pornography. Why do you want to kill me?"

Nyx said nothing. Keenan fired a shot into the GK's face; the shot screamed, bullet ricocheting. Keenan peered close. One of the hydraulic valves which operated the mouth was damaged; it bubbled a thin white oil.

"Next, it's your eyes."

"Go to hell, little man," said Nyx.

"I'm already there," whispered Keenan.

"Keenan, get up here!" snapped Franco.

"It might take a while, but this gun," he waved the Techrim, "can eat away at your face. I've never tortured an AI before, but an old *ex*-friend of mine once said it could be a lot of fun. I'll be back in a minute, love. Don't go anywhere."

With cigarette dangling, Keenan strode up the gentle slope of the ramp and eyed the chamber. Franco had bound Olga's wound and stopped the bleeding with a D-PACK. She sat, pale and obviously in some agony. Knuckles held her hand. Xakus and Franco stood by the wall console.

"What is it?"

Xakus has tapped into the Library's monitoring cameras. Come have a look."

Keenan stood, smoking, staring at the scene of devastation outside the library. More Mammoth MK13 tanks had arrived, with thousands more zombies.

"Can you see them?" said Franco.

"I can see we're in the shit," said Keenan.

"Look, from where the tanks *came*. When we were up on the balcony. *Look.*"

Keenan stared, then dropped his cigarette with a curse. The alleyway was full of dark-armoured SIMs. Battle SIMs. Armed, armoured, silent, immobile. A waiting army.

"So the zombies have proper military backup," said Franco, with a grimace. "This gig just gets better and better."

"We need to get out of here right now," said Keenan, taking a deep breath. "Those bastards could advance at any moment. And a fire extinguisher won't halt SIMs. Olga, can you move, love?" Olga nodded, and Knuckles helped her lumber to her feet, grunting. "Xakus, we need to get to this back door. We're pinned down here. Are you sure the only exit was down the ramp? And we need transport. I'll even risk a chopper." He eyed the monitor again, shaking his head. "This puzzle gets more and more twisted the longer we play. We're being fucked with. Again. And I don't like it."

Professor Xakus rubbed his white beard. "The only escape route is down that ramp. That much is for sure. There's no other way out of this building. But that's OK, because MICHELLE is down there. I'll let her out of her cage."

"But what about the AIs?" hissed Franco.

"I'm sure MICHELLE will make short work of them. It's just, I couldn't release her whilst you two were on the ramp; without me, she gets a little too frisky."

Keenan frowned. "Actually, just what the hell *is* this *MICHELLE?*"

"Perhaps I should explain. I used to be an engineer at NanoTek. This much you know. Well, a leopard never changes its spots. Just because I left NanoTek, didn't mean I stopped building, inventing, creating. MICHELLE is my... my *pet*. My little project, shall we say. A way of whiling away the long winter evenings here on The City when your wife is dead and your children have grown up and travelled six billion miles to university."

"You never answered my question," said Keenan.

"MICHELLE's a Military Grade bio-mechanical transport vehicle slash war machine. A Mechanically Integrated Killer. A MIK *HELL*. MICHELLE. See? And she ain't pretty, so don't get excited when you see her. She might just rip off your damned head."

"So she's... organic? *And* a machine?" Franco frowned.

"Better just watch," said Professor Xakus, patting Franco on the shoulder like father to son. "And don't say anything. *Nothing* at all. MICHELLE's pretty temperamental; she gets upset easy. And when she's upset, she starts to kill things."

MICHELLE SLEPT. SHE slept more and more these days, and she was suspicious Xakus was putting drugs in her food. But then, why would he do that? Why would he want her to sleep? After all, he loved her, he nurtured her; he had *created* her. MICHELLE nodded to herself in slumber... and was gradually awoken by the whistle. It was tuned specifically to her command nodes; it brought her a subtle sexual pleasure.

MICHELLE awoke. She stretched, huge metal claws clanging off the sides of her cage. The place she loved. The place she liked to call *home*. MICHELLE stood, clanging her square head from the roof of the cage, and waited patiently as the twin blast doors opened; they could withstand a Grade 2 High-J blast. Huge knuckles of steel unmeshed and lights flickered on in the underground gloom. MICHELLE strode out, square metal boots clanging, but as she approached the ramp something was not quite right and script flowed fast through her half-organic, half-machine brain.

MICHELLE stopped. She could *sense* danger. Something you only got from organics. This meshed with computer instructions flowing at billions of instructions per nano-second.

The ramp was up. And *there*. Tiny metal legs kicked.

MICHELLE's sensors hummed at her, and she saw the two tiny AIs dancing down below. One carried twin swords, the other had blades as arms and legs. Flicking on dazzling HalogenV lights she flooded the chamber with brilliance, then stomped forward in huge lurching hydraulic motions.

"Xakus?" boomed MICHELLE's metal voice. The whole chamber reverberated. And then she... *clicked* with him, flowed with him, could smell his thoughts. Huge metal nostrils quivered.

I hope you slept well, my sweetness. Could you please do me a favour? The three robots, they have been causing me some pain. Trying to kill me. Could you please dispose of them?

Certainly, thought back MICHELLE, smiling at Xakus's use of the word *please. After all,* she thought, *it's so important to have manners in this day and age.*

The six hundred and fifty-eight tonne bio-organic machine took a couple more steps forward, huge iron boots clanging, and bent, motors whirring, pincer claws reaching down towards the GKs. The first danced at her, and tiny swords slashed, opening metal runs across her pincers. A signal flashed pain in her brain and MICHELLE gave a howl, taking an involuntary step back. This little robot had hurt her!

Script turned red. Her organic half flared in anger, whilst her computational half calmed her irrationality. She switched on electro-magnets with a *hum* that would have blacked out five square kilometres of The City's Global GRID, and the two GKs were sucked from the ground and pinned to her pincers, swords and blades immobile, heads twitching under a seemingly unstoppable force. Clanking and whirring, MICHELLE turned and strode clomping back to her cell. She hurled the two GKs into the chamber, and with a heave and a grunt, pushed shut the blast doors. She stomped back to the closed ramp and surveyed the wiggling black metal legs.

What about this one? she thought.

Put it with the others. Thank you, my little flower.

MICHELLE preened, reached out, plucked the GK from the clamp of the ramp with a *pop.* Thousands of highly toxic poisonous spikes failed to penetrate MICHELLE's metal skin; even if they had, they would have had little effect. MICHELLE was alive with billions of nanobots which would have negated the poison—any poison—within seconds. MICHELLE was military grade. Designed for the army. MICHELLE was Hard to Kill.

She strode back to her cage, opened the blast doors, and tossed the tiny GK inside. Nyx rattled from the back wall, limbs flailing, and lay still. With a grunt, MICHELLE heaved the blast doors—each weighing several hundred tonnes—back into well-oiled grooves.

MICHELLE grinned. "I am MICHELLE. Hear me roar!" she said, and roared. It was so loud, many of the light bulbs in the underground vault popped and shattered, littering the floor with broken glass.

Well done, my sweet, said Professor Xakus. *Now I'm coming down with some friends. We need transport to another location. Would you please try and not hurt anybody?*

Sure thing, thought back MICHELLE in smell-thought.

With a groan, the ramp juddered, and started to descend.

KEENAN HUNKERED DOWN, peering into the gloom. Lights fizzled, beams glittering from shards on the concrete-alloy floor. The booms, crashes and clangs which had filled the underground vault had Keenan and Franco exchanging worried glances, whilst Knuckles, still shaken from his near-death encounter, backed away brandishing his machete stained with congealing zombie blood.

"Follow me."

Professor Xakus strode down the ramp, boots crunching slivers of twisted alloy where Nyx had been trapped and forcibly wrenched free, leaving long smears in the metal. He stood at the bottom, hands on hips, a broad smile hijacking his features as he gazed up at—

Keenan looked up. And up.

Shit, he thought. It's *big*.

MICHELLE was a good fifty feet in height. She was built around an endoskeleton of high-grade military armoured TitaniumIV-alloy. Her hands and feet were huge cubic clumps of steel with braided piping coming from ankles and wrists and feeding into limbs. The trunk, arms and legs were a kind of blended, Kevlar-glass flesh, which looked a little like metal matting but, Xakus assured the Combat K men, was 100% organic matter. A short, squat powerful neck supported a head that was—

"By God, that's bloody ugly!" snapped Franco, staring up at the biomechanical behemoth.

MICHELLE clanked, took a step back, and lowered her face to within inches of Franco. Her head was as large as he was. He stared into glittering, silver eyes, many-faceted, like those of an insect, each tiny plate fashioned from high polished alloy. The panels and plates slithered and adjusted with the tiniest of metallic grating sounds. The eyes were large, like dinner plates set in the face of a human-insect. MICHELLE's face was the same alloy matting skin as on the torso, arms and legs. She had no nose, only a horizontal slot for a mouth—which she opened, showing row upon row of razor-sharp teeth.

"They are, actually, industrial standard razors," said Xakus proudly. He stepped past Franco and patted MICHELLE on the face where her nose should have been. Steam hissed from vents behind her vertical metal ears. It seemed to be a sign of pleasure. "There, there, who's a good girl?"

MICHELLE beamed, the horizontal slot somehow transferring the idea of a smile.

"So it's... alive?" rumbled Franco.

"Yes, biological and mechanical. I built her. She is mine."

"You're crazier than me, crazy fool!" snapped Franco. "You's a lunatic, mate. Why, in the name of all that's holy, did you build that damned monstrosity? And *why* did you make it so big? And *why* did you make it so bloody donkey-ugly?"

MICHELLE moved, so fast she was a blur. Her mouth was open, razor teeth inches from Franco's face. Her breath eased out, smelling of hot oil and ozone. She could have quite easily removed his tiny head. In fact, his entire being.

Franco stared into jaws of impending death. He snuffled a little. "OK," he managed, after a few moments of careful contemplation. "I retract what I just said. And I... 'pologise."

Clanking, MICHELLE stood to her full height, limbs whirring and rotating. Guns appeared along her forearms. Missiles ejected from the sides of her boots.

"She's a Class H military droid," said Xakus. "I was researching her for QGM under license to

NanoTek. But like all armies with an eye on the cheque book, the miserable whoresons pulled the plug when costs became too great. So... I worked at the university. And built her in my spare time. It would have been churlish to waste so much invested research."

Franco stared at Xakus. "A regular Doctor Frankenstein, aren't you pal? What's your encore? Raising the dead?"

"Franco, shut up!" snapped Keenan. He turned to Xakus. "You said MICHELLE was some form of military transport? Will she carry us? It just seems treacherous to be perched up on her shoulders like some estranged sci-fi hobbit as rockets and bullets whizz around our heads."

Professor Xakus stroked his white beard. His eyes gleamed. "She is far more ingenious than that, my friend. OK. Listen up." Olga and Knuckles had moved down the ramp, both staring in awe at the giant biological machine. Knuckles was holding Olga's hand. In her other, she carried one of Franco's Kekras. "MICHELLE stocks 7.62mm stowable miniguns in each ankle. She carries Hellcat 55 SAMs, and a wide range of anti-tank shells. However, in battle she is untested."

"I'm not surprised," muttered Franco. "If you let her out for a game of fetch, she'd damn well destroy half the city! *Then* they'd lock up the loony creator."

"You're a fine one to talk," said Keenan, eyeing Franco. "You might be a dab hand with a D5 shotgun in a shit situation, but I needn't remind you how many missions you've put in jeopardy because you can't keep your parrot in your trousers."

"Hey! A guy's got to spread his seed, right? It's a primitive thing. Part of my genetics."

Xakus coughed. "Due to MICHELLE's design brief, and to keep things compact and give her utmost agility, you will notice she resembles a human in physical contours. However, to actually get inside her, you need to traverse a simple rearward injection cylinder."

"Like a syringe?" frowned Franco.

"More like a tube," said Xakus. "Don't worry, once inside her chassis you'll be completely impervious to bullets and rockets. Her armour is incredibly thick. It's a bit like being a baby cradled in a mother's womb. You'll like it. It's comfortable."

Franco was frowning. "Where is this tube?" he asked, suspiciously.

"It's part of the rearward undercarriage assembly. MICHELLE? Please adopt the position."

MICHELLE clanked down onto all fours, and the ground shook. From her rear chassis oozed a smooth ejection of a narrow tube. Franco stared at it, then back at Xakus, then to Keenan, then to Xakus again.

"You're kidding, right?"

Xakus gave a tight smile. "It was the only place to put it."

"I ain't climbing up her *arse*," said Franco.

"It's not her arse, Franco, it's her undercarriage," said Keenan. "Her rearward assembly. Part of her chassis. She's a machine, mate. Now get up that pipe before I give you a size 10 persuasion."

"Actually, she's part *biological*," said Franco, taking a step away from the wide and disturbingly quivering tube. "That's means she's alive. And *that*, in my book, makes that thing her damn arsehole. And I ain't crawling up it. Oh no."

"Why not?" said Keenan dryly. "I'm sure you've been up a few in your time."

"Amusing, Keenan. You are a comedy maestro. However, I've had my fair share of arse problems in recent years, everything from simple straining injuries to bloody damn well buggering alien arse viruses! It's a place I think of as being a holy place, a place of quiet calm, somewhere to be respected and revered. Now, it can't be nice for liccle MICHELLE there having lots of strange blokes climbing up her pipe."

"Keenan," said Knuckles, who was looking up the ramp. "We got company. I think the zombies are back." Snarls and moans drifted down from The Great Malkovitch Library chamber.

Keenan nodded. Glanced at Xakus. "After you, mate. Show us how it's done."

Xakus approached the tube, lifted his arms, and was sucked into the biological machine's cabin. Olga followed, then Knuckles, with another requisitioned PERMAFROST BIO FIRE EXTINGUISHER in gloved hands. Keenan and Franco stood alone.

"After you," said Keenan, gesturing.

"Oh no, no, no." Franco shook his head. "You first, Keenan. I bloody insist."

Zombies lined the top of the ramp now, glaring down with feral yellow eyes. One lifted an Uzi, and bullets whined, howling down at the two men and spitting sparks on the ramp.

Keenan ran to the tube, lifted his arms, and was accepted into the bowels of MICHELLE.

Franco stood alone.

He stamped his foot.

"Damn and bloody bollocks!" he shouted, sent a round of Kekra fire at the zombies, smacking several from their feet with wet blood showers, then turning, he grimaced, screamed, and took a sprint towards the quivering tube...

He soon discovered violent, rearward entry hurt just as much as he thought it would.

FRANCO OPENED HIS eyes. Inside MICHELLE it was cool, and the machine hummed softly around him. The others were seated in front of a large screen—the view from MICHELLE's eyes. As she stood, clanking and stomping a boot to the concrete-alloy, so the interior cabin rolled smooth, keeping them constantly upright. Gyroscopes buzzed. Tiny computer readouts on the walls blinked and flickered.

"Wow!" said Franco.

Keenan turned. "You OK now, Big Man?"

"I kinda thought we'd be covered in shit. Or something."

"It's a *machine,* Franco. Get it in your head!"

"Yeah but, like, when her bio side *does* need a shit, where does it come out? I'm guessing this chamber can get a bit a stinky after she's had a few beers and a kebab."

The zombies streamed into the underground chamber, and MICHELLE whirled, ducking, one huge metal arm smashing through their ranks and sending ten flying through the air to compress with crunches against the metal wall. Her cubic fist slammed down, crushing another three. Yet still more zombies appeared. Guns whined, bullets flashing and screaming. MICHELLE punched and stomped, killing and crushing and breaking. She stomped, clanking, backwards and miniguns in her ankles ejected with neat whirrs. Bullets scythed through the zombies, cutting them in half. Within a few short seconds the chamber was a charnel house, thick with rivers of black blood pooling the floor, walls plastered and splattered with gore and zombie gristle.

"That's savage," said Franco, quietly.

"Better them than us," said Keenan.

"Damn right," snapped Knuckles. He still held Olga's hand, and his eyes carried a strange, haunted look.

"Time for us to get out of here," said Professor Xakus. His eyes were gleaming, as, for the first time in history, he tested his sparkling new toy.

MICHELLE turned and stomped across the chamber. Reaching the wall, she lifted mighty alloy fists above herself and grasped a thick, swinging chain. She pulled with a tremendous effort and there came a grinding of distant heavy gears. Before their eyes, the wall opened with a rugged shuddering of steel and stone panels. Night air flooded in, and within their cocoon they could smell the freshness of the night, still laced with a scent of smoke from recent fires.

MICHELLE stomped up massive blocks which formed steps, and out onto the street. Dark cube-scrapers towered around them. Zombies were milling everywhere, like insects. MICHELLE stepped on a few, whirling and whirring, and Keenan leant close to Xakus. "I'll give you directions," he whispered, feeling somehow that inside this creature, this machine, this metal foetal sack, it just seemed the right thing to do.

"No need," said Xakus. He pointed at a small display. "MonkeyMan Sat-Nav. The Happy Friendly Sunshine Assurance Company, you say? We're on it. *Come on MICHELLE, baby, show us what you can do.*"

And Keenan caught it. Heard it. Like a whisper on the wind. A ghost-voice. A communion of spirit. *Yes, Professor Xakus. Anything you ask my love.* Keenan shuddered, and decided that in this life, in this world, in this teeming, confusing, whirlwind Quad-Galaxy in which he suffered some kind of existence, there were some things he would never understand, and even if he was offered the key to such knowledge, would happily decline. Some things, thought Keenan, were better left undiscovered. He glanced back at Franco. "You OK, buddy?"

Franco nodded, but looked far from OK. He looked like he was going to be sick. Exorcist sick.

"Travel for one kilometre, then take a left," said the MonkeyMan Sat-Nav.

Keenan reached out. Touched Franco on the arm. "It's just like a tank," he said, kindly.

"It's messing with my head! We're in its—her—belly. It's rank, Keenan. Just totally gross. What kind of nutcase builds something like this? What kind of warped and freaky freaked-out fucking individual?"

"Yeah Franco, but what kind of maniac built the atomic bomb? Or the BABE grenade? Or the Halo Smash? Our history is littered with those who only desire to kill. It's in our nature."

"And what about us?" said Franco, as MICHELLE stomped across the city, squeezing between towering blocks of endless, blank-windowed skyscrapers. His eyes looked distant; his demeanour wounded. "We're just part of this terrible machine, aren't we?"

"We fight for a greater good," said Keenan.

"And you believe that?" said Franco.

"I have to. Or I'd surely go mad."

"That explains my affliction, then," muttered Franco, and suddenly remembering something, dragged his pack to his knees and rummaged inside. He found something, and placed it on his tongue without looking at Keenan.

"What's that?"

"Something to help."

"Something to keep you sane?"

Franco shook his head. He grinned then. "You've got it all wrong, Keenan, my friend. You have a twisted perspective. A deviated standpoint. This world. This life. This nightmare." He chuckled. "I'm the only sane thing in it. It's *everybody else* that's mad. The pills just make *your* insanity bearable."

Keenan stared at Franco. Stared hard. Trying to understand the little ginger soldier was like trying to walk on a razor, or cycle on water, like trying to peel yourself with a spoon. And Keenan realised; in Franco's bubble, he believed in *himself*. And that worked for him. Made the world make sense.

I wish I could be like you, he thought.
I really do.

"PLEASE TAKE THE next right. Take the next right. Take the next right. Take the next right. Take the next right."

Xakus thumped the MonkeyMan Sat-Nav.

"Please take the next right," it said. "Oo."

"Why did it say oo?" frowned Franco.

"It's a MonkeyMan," said Xakus, as if that was explanation enough.

MICHELLE clanked through The City with a heavy, weighted, rolling motion. Huge swathes of urban sprawl now seemed strangely uninhabited, and for an hour they met no resistance, MICHELLE's scanners picking up little or no localised zombie activity. It was as if the creatures had clubbed together, for strength in numbers; either that, or simply vanished. Keenan pointed out that this trait, again, indicated intelligence, a need for survival, a common goal. Not activity usually associated with the undead—even if they were a nanobot deviated zombification.

Franco managed to calm down after a while, and Keenan fell into a brooding silence, a half-sleep of exhaustion, no doubt reminiscing on his past, his dead wife Freya, and his slaughtered girls. They filled his thoughts often, and Franco caught him reaching for a Jataxa bottle in his inside pocket; a bottle that was no longer there.

Eventually, Keenan drifted in and out of sleep. And in his dreams, he remembered Freya. He remembered his girls. But most of all, he remembered Pippa...

As a Combat K squad proficient in infiltration, assassination, demolition, the original unity of Keenan, Franco and Pippa had been tighter than tight. They were a finely honed fighting instrument working for the Quad-Gal's Peace Unification Army with the original intent of ending the Helix War. However, events transpired to reveal that his love of Pippa—which led to his rejection of her love, and a perceived betrayal—eventually directed the psychotic and deranged female assassin to Keenan's family, where she slaughtered them without mercy. Keenan had sworn he would avenge his family, and Pippa had fled—with Keenan in pursuit. He had chased her for a year... and three times came close to wiping her from the face of existence.

The first time he'd caught up with her, asleep in a sleazy, damp, rat-infested hotel on the decadent mining planet of Mistral. As he coolly aimed his silenced pistol at Pippa's sleeping body, revellers in the street outside disturbed the peace and she was instantly awake, Keenan kicked backwards by a stunning fast blow, and Pippa's athletic figure gone from the three storey window. Keenan fired off five shots at her dodging, fleeing figure in the freeze-cool night, but was hindered by the dark of the zero moon planet, the pounding rain, and the flush of blood in his eyes from a narrow cut across his forehead. It was only then he had realised Pippa had slash-razors in her boots. His mood descended into fury, and a brooding oblivion.

The second instance had been a chance encounter as he followed clues to her whereabouts on the busy, hedonistic pleasure planet of Tantalus IV.

Tantalus IV—or the *Theme Planet*—was an entire world dedicated to the pursuit of pleasure, an entire planet dedicated to enjoyment, fun and hedonism. The Theme Planet incorporated the very latest in high-tech rides, new drugs, sexual exploration and virtual stellar experiences. Ever wanted to be inside a star when it's born? Ever wanted to journey through a black hole? Ever wanted to ride on the backs of loveless and *technically dead* Stellar Dragons? Well baby, *now* you can...

Keenan hated the place, filled as it was with pleasure rides such as INSANE, MOTHERLODE, MONSTER MASH and BUBBLE GUTS. The marketing motto ran:

THEME PLANET!
it's better than drugs!
it's better than sex!
it's fun it's fast it's slick it's neat...
if you haven't been sick yet you soon will be.

And it was right. Keenan *was* sick—but not from the 'enjoyable' adrenaline junky rides; no. Just from the cacophony of noise and bustle and charging screaming teenagers—screemagers. Keenan had always thought he discovered his personal hell on the overcrowded industrial compact of The City; however, he had been wrong. Watching thousands of squealing, over-excited, caffeine-riddled adolescents covered in popcorn, candyfloss and puke, push and jostle their way around sunny walkways littered with half-eaten hotdogs and the odd discarded teddy-bear—on a *planetary scale*—filled him with a loathing for organic life that went far beyond Cosmic Joke.

As on any planet, Tantalus IV suffered from an underworld of criminal activity. Contacting the dreg-heads in command Keenan had bought information on inbound Shuttles, which in turn had led him to The Green Zone—or *Tranquil Park*. It seemed the parents of screaming, jostling kids needed a place to *relax*. The Green Zone was filled with flowers and trees and shrubs, gondola rides on calm waterways, soaring cable-car rides through snow-bound peaks. The architecture was ancient alien stone, spires and towers and curving paved walkways ascending gentle hills to blue-stone castles and orange towers. The *rides* were rides dedicated to relaxation; immersion games of gentle pursuit or carefree, lulling, tantric sex.

Stepping from the delivery zeppelin, and watching idly as this huge helium-filled vehicle soared away in an eerie, looming silence, Keenan had wandered down to the gardens and a map which said: YOU ARE HERE, and spread out a myriad of attractions before him across one thousand square kilometres of *chill time baby*.

Checking into a local hotel, Keenan had headed for the bar, dropped his pack at his feet, lifted his hand to call the barman and froze. To his right, in a curved leather chair, a small PAD computer on her knee, sat Pippa; clothed in a long floral-pattern dress, her dark shoulder-length hair held back with blue clips, she looked fresh-faced, eyes sparkling, stunningly beautiful. Keenan's breath caught in his throat. He was pole-axed by her femininity.

Stunned by her womanhood. He remembered kissing those sensuous lips. Remembered tracing erotic lines through the sweat on her flank. Remembered her dulcet tones tongue-whispering tickles in his ear... as she drew a matt Makarov from a thigh-holster and opened fire on him—

Keenan dived over the bar, Techrim in his fist. He returned fire, but she was gone. Like a ghost. A terrible, fleeting angel.

"You spill her drink, mate?" asked the cowering barman with a toothless but wary grin.

Growling, Keenan had sprinted after her... but the hotel lay in heavily wooded grounds. He searched for an hour before he found a trace of her passing; and by the time he reached the Shuttle Docks Pippa had already fled the planet.

The third time Keenan had contact with Pippa, it wasn't he who found her—but the other way round.

Hekkan Grall.

He shivered.

A strange, improbable world. A world of contrasts, of opposites, of salted wine, sweet main courses and bitter desserts. Of women with penis extensions, and men with triple vaginas. It was a place of acquired taste. And, on a fast-cruise across an endless warm green ocean, snow tumbling from cold-sun skies, Keenan's deck apartment—with a cloth shield roof—allowed him to watch the falling snow diffused with sunlight. Even at night.

When he had woken, in the darkness, sun and snow piercing fingers high above him through the black, the cold barrel against his head had sent a shiver reverberating down his locked spine.

The figure, a black outline in the dark, retreated a little. There came a *hiss* of breath.

"Pippa?" said Keenan, realising the game was now, ultimately, over. Within a few seconds he would be dead meat... for Pippa was a killer, and she'd pre-empted his hunt. She found him. "Shit." He had smiled in the darkness. A stray beam of green-sun cut a shaft across the room, for an instant illuminating Pippa's eyes. Then it was gone.

"I warned you not to follow me, Kee."

"But you knew I would."

"I didn't mean to kill them."

Keenan's humour left him. Anger flared. "But you did. And there's no forgiving that."

"Why won't you leave me alone? I'm *sick* of looking over my shoulder. Sick of being frightened."

"There's only one way you're going to stop me."

Her voice, when she replied, was dangerously low. "Yeah, Kee. I know that."

Keenan had tensed, waiting for the shot...

Which did not come. And then he realised; Pippa was crying. Hot tears coursed her cheeks. Her gun wavered. And he knew; knew if he drew out his Techrim he could take her. Blow her damned head clean off. End this scourge on his existence; on his *past*. And on his future.

But he did not. He could not.

Pippa had backed from the room; was gone.

Keenan had slumped back to his bed, and covered his face with his hands. He realised he, too, was crying and he hated himself for it. Why didn't you avenge us, daddy? asked Rachel in his dreams. Why didn't you kill the bad lady?

Keenan awoke scowling. He coughed, and rubbed at his eyes as he orientated on his surroundings. MICHELLE. Mission. Shit. "Can I smoke?" he asked, voice a growl.

"In here?" said Xakus, turning and raising a white eyebrow. Keenan stared into deep brown eyes.

"Yeah. In here. I'm feeling... a *need*."

"Would *you* like somebody smoking inside *your* belly?"

"Good point, but it doesn't answer my question."

"Let me put it this way, Mr Keenan. Have you ever seen a fifty-foot enraged bio-mechanical war machine rampaging across a city killing indiscriminately with a huge arsenal of military grade weapons? Would you like to?"

"A simple 'no' would have sufficed."

"Ha, a stupid question, no?" roared Franco, slapping Keenan on the back. Keenan's head swivelled.

"That's rich, coming from the resident Housewives' Choice."

"What's that supposed to mean?"

Keenan gave a wide smile, and nodded past Franco, to where Olga sat, her huge frame squeezed into the—seemingly—tiny chair. Olga's eyes were wide and filled with pure puppy-love. Her gaze was locked by chains of steel to Franco.

Franco grinned weakly. Olga lifted a hand and gave a delicate wave.

"Have you noticed a certain lop-sidedness to her smile?" said Keenan.

"It's the three missing teeth," said Franco, through his own, which were gritted tight in a rictus grimace that would have impressed Death's dentist. "Somehow, I don't think I'm going to get out of this situation with my dignity."

"I'm gonna have to agree with you on that one," said Keenan. He pulled free a home-rolled Widow Maker. Met Xakus's eyes. Cursed. Stowed the weed away. At the back of his skull, his recurring headache started to nag again. He rubbed the back of his head, wincing.

"At the next junction, turn left. Oo oo."

"It'll be asking for a banana next," hissed Keenan.

Olga shuffled towards Franco, and sat beside him. She placed a hand on his knee. Around them, a distant clanging and clanking and clashing of gears were the only noises to intrude in this comfortable, almost serene, hiatus in a world of violence.

"A. Haha. Ha." Franco's eyes betrayed his discomfort.

"Olga would like to thank you."

"For what?"

"Saving Olga's life!" She beamed. Squeezed his knee a little harder. And with a little more... *urgency*.

"Um. What? Back there with the zombies? When you got, shot? Ahh, 'twas nothing. Honest." He eyed her like he would a particularly manky cat. "Um. You can let go of my knee now."

"That bullet enter my flesh, and I say to myself, 'Olga girl, this is it! Ze zombies, they will feast on your brains! They will gorge zemselves on your generous rump!' Yes. Until my hero, my little ginger Franco, he came to ze rescue."

"*Actually*," said Franco, "*technically,* it was Keenan who rescued you."

"Fuck off," came Keenan's growl.

"Come on Keenan, help me out here!"

"You started this," said Keenan, looking suddenly evil in the glow of the bio-mechanical unit's cockpit, "so you can damn well finish it."

"That's hardly brotherly."

"I ain't your brother."

"You call me bro', sometimes, when we're in the shit." Olga's hand had moved up to Franco's thigh.

"Yeah well, that's because we're in the shit. This is different. This is your wayward stupidity at play again. You summoned Olga's affections, and you can deal with the consequences."

"Hey, I was only trying to sniff out some drugs! I was just, y'know, minding my own business! Like a good boy! I'm always a good boy! You know that Keenan! Come on man, it was the drugs I tell ye! It's not like *me* to go looking for women in odd and strange-smelling places!"

"Oh yeah? Well," said Keenan, smiling broadly, "you certainly gave *her* an addiction. Looks like you're going to have to satisfy it." With that, he moved away, over to Knuckles who had his eyes fixed rigidly on the screen showing the brutal exterior of this vast inner-city world—in all its desperation and accelerating decrepitude. Knuckles sat, open awe tattooed on his face.

"You OK lad?"

"Yeah, Keenan." He shivered. "Sorry. Felt like somebody walked over my grave."

"Happens to me every day," said Keenan, with a hint of bitterness. In his mind flickered the images of his little girls. Dead and gone, he told himself. Dead and buried.

"I thought I was dead back there." Knuckles was clasping his knees.

"It was a tough call," said Keenan, remembering the three GK AIs, and Nyx in particular. It had seemed to him, at the time, that there was something personal in the attack; a sense of *revenge*. But how could that be? Keenan had never before met the AIs. "Shit. Another puzzle." He shrugged away the concept, and patted Knuckles's shoulder. "Listen, you did well, lad. Really well. That idea with the fire extinguisher—genius. You might make the army one day."

Knuckles looked horrified. "Why on earth would I want to join the army? I have everything I need right *here*... in The City."

Keenan said nothing. A cynical part of him wanted to point out that The City, at least for the foreseeable future, was doomed. It was a ransacked shell. A desecrated temple. A biohell. Ground under the boots of a pirated, hacked, cracked and mutated biomod culture hell-bent on its own vain physical improvement—and instead, finding only a mutated version of *hell* inhabited centre-stage by the very people who sought to abuse their own organics at a genetic level. However, to point this out to Knuckles would be like kicking a kitten. Despite his streetwise rough tough image, Keenan could see, deep down under the young boy's onion-layers of panel-beaten hardness, ingrained cynicism and enforced maturity, he was still a ten-year-old boy, a ten-year-old orphan, lonely, weak, and in need of the simplicity of love and affection all children required. Keenan smiled grimly. And, in fact, exactly what he himself craved.

They sat for a while in comfortable silence, with only the grunting of Franco and Olga's locked stalemate interrupting the hum and buzz, the distant clanking, of MICHELLE's stomping advance across The City.

"Can I ask you something?" said Keenan, at last.

"Sure, Mr Keenan."

"Why do they call you Knuckles?"

A veil dropped in front of Knuckles' face, like a blast door slamming down a split-second before detonation. His eyes hardened. His face lost its boyish charm. He said nothing, but Keenan noted his hand, straying to a small velvet bag at his waist.

"It's OK," Keenan said, voice gentle. "If you don't want to talk about it, that's fine. Maybe another time."

"I'm... sorry, Keenan." Knuckles seemed to breathe again, and a red flush flooded his face. "I'm just... I, well, I lock my feelings away. In here." He punched his breast, over his gore-stained clothing. "It's how I survive in The City. Life has... not been kind to me. And I'm not used to sharing feelings. I'm not used to... talking to people." He grinned, then, and rubbed at a smudge on his gloss red boot. "Not unless it's to decode a small amount of cash from helk-fur wallets. Keenan—when we sort Mel out, turn her back into a human for Franco, decode this SinScript for the Quad-Gal military man, Stein-hauer; then, then I'll tell you."

"You listen a lot," said Keenan, eyeing the boy with respect.

"It's part of my trade," smiled Knuckles. "I'm a kid, yeah? Most of the time people forget I'm there. I blend in. A natural chameleon. But I'm there all the same. I listen. I understand. I've got a brain, and I know how to use it."

"You think Xakus will restore Mel to humanity?"

Knuckles met Keenan's gaze, and what the Combat K man saw nearly broke his heart. Knuckle gave a narrow, bloodless smile, without humour, and with—ironically—a hint of condescension. "Not this side of hell, he won't," Knuckles whispered.

KEENAN WAS JERKED from his weariness when MICHELLE halted, and the muffled clanking stopped. He felt the cockpit *roll* nauseatingly, as the huge bio-machine settled down, and he rubbed at weary, bloodshot eyes and wondered not just what time it was, but what *day* it was. Time, on the permanently darkened planet of The City, seemed to have little meaning now; it had simply become a question of passage.

Keenan stretched his back, wincing at bruises and strains which, in the heat of battle, had failed to exist. Now his body felt like a well-used punch-bag. He glanced over at Franco, who was asleep, snoring, with his head on Olga's lap. She was stroking his shaved ginger hair, and humming a soothing lullaby to the battered, middle-aged soldier.

"We are here," said Professor Xakus.

Keenan nodded, standing and prodding Franco. "Come on midget, time to move."

Franco sat up, glared at Olga, and gathered his pack, checking his weapons. He then glared at Keenan, his shaved head just a little tufty, his eyes filled with a distillation of anarchy. Then, finally, he glared at Xakus. "I suppose," he said, rubbing his goatee beard, "that we have to get out of this contraption the same way we got in?"

"You are correct," said Xakus, eyeing the small man.

"I just can't believe it. MICHELLE is gonna *shit* us out."

"You've got it all in the wrong context," persisted Keenan, shouldering his own pack. "This is disembarkation. It's like getting off a train. Climbing from a chopper. Hell, you've been down water-chutes in a water-park before now, haven't you?"

"Yeah, but they weren't full of shit."

"The only thing round here that's full of shit," said Keenan, "is you. Now *move.*"

Grumbling, Franco and the group followed Keenan into the narrow chute. The *feeling* was one of disorientation, as rings of what could only be described as *muscle* eased them one by one onto the pavement. Keenan was first free, and his Techrim covered arcs as Franco arrived, slumping onto the pavement in a heap, then wearily standing to cover Keenan with his Kekra, shuddering and shivering with massively repressed horror.

Olga, Knuckles and Xakus arrived, and Knuckles pushed forward to Keenan. His face was that of young boy again, obviously ready to see his friends—his *gang*. "Come on Keenan, let's go!"

"Not so fast."

"It's quiet," mumbled Franco.

"Too quiet," agreed Keenan. "Franco, take point. Knuckles, stay with me. This place was crawling with deviants the last time we were here; I don't see why it would be any different now."

They moved to the building, which still had security shutters in place from Mel's fortification. Franco gained entry using codes given him by Knuckles, and they stepped into the deserted sky-scraper's cool, glum interior.

"Let's move," said Keenan, and glancing back at Xakus he gave a short narrow smile. "I hope to God you can help Mel after all the garbage we've been through."

"So do I," said the large black man, voice soft. "Let me analyse her coding first. Then we'll talk."

They moved across the ground floor, past several zombies which Mel had slaughtered on her building flush. The lifts were still lit, and they climbed into a wide spacious interior. Franco hit R for ROOF. It triggered a distant memory; of being pursued through a mental institution during his breakout from Mount Pleasant. He grinned at the thought.

Music piped through tinny speakers as the lift hummed upwards. Ronan Keating's truly ancient *Life is a Rollercoaster,* the eternal re-re-re-re-recorded Quad-Gal hit, the one song in the entire Sinax Cluster which just never seemed to *die,* filled the ascending metal box with a surreal and ghostly presence.

Keenan tapped his foot in rhythm. Glanced at Olga, then Franco. He nudged Franco, and mouthed, *We found love, So don't hide it, Life is a rollercoaster, Just gotta ride it.*

Franco nodded, grinning back with wide drug-plate eyes, and mouthed, *Bugger off and suck dick you alcoholic arsehole.* Then he gave Keenan the thumbs-up, hoisted his Kekras, and stepped forward as the lift reached the roof.

Immediately the doors opened they knew something was wrong. The fire was out. Not even glowing embers remained. The roof was deserted. Franco stepped forward, wary, guns tracking, humour wrenched from him like a tooth.

"Mel?" he called quietly. Then louder. "Melanie!"

No reply.

Knuckles burst out, past Franco, and stumbled through the dead fire. He stopped, whirled, eyes scanning—then let out a little cry. He sprinted towards a large air-con outlet, and Franco and Keenan ran after him, skidding to a stop as Knuckles fell to his knees beside the neatly piled corpses of the children.

"No!" screamed Knuckles, pounding the floor with fists as tear-filled eyes raked the rows of tiny, pale-white bodies, like ribs in a dead and rotten behemoth. Bullet wounds glistened in the night-gloom across every child's torso. Eyes stared glassy at distant, cold, hydrogen-ringed stars.

"Franco, check the roof," said Keenan, voice quiet, and dropped to one knee beside Knuckles, his Techrim by his cheek. "Knuckles... Knuckles, we have to get out of here, lad. Whatever did this..."

"We need to find them!" He turned his tear-streaked face to Keenan. "We need to find them, Mr Keenan. Find them—" he hardened, "and kill them." Keenan nodded, and helped Knuckles to his feet.

"Come on." He grasped the lad's arm, lifted him up, eyes scanning the dead bodies of Skull, Sammy, Glass, Little Megan and the others. A huge weight fell from his soul, then, and a powerful feeling of meaninglessness encompassed him. Who shot these poor, orphaned children? What purpose did it serve? Keenan's face hardened. It served no purpose. It was evil in its purest form.

Franco returned, panting. "Mel's not here, Keenan. But I found this." It was a small grey unit, not dissimilar to the PADs Combat K used. Keenan eyed it warily.

"Could be booby-trapped."

"We'll soon find out."

Franco flipped free the lid and gazed at a black screen. A small red light blinked on off, on off, on off. The screen flickered, and a face materialised. It was lined with modest age, bore a neat black beard and unblinking brown eyes which seemed to smile with an internal humour.

"Voloshko," hissed Franco, heart thumping wild in his breast.

"That is correct, Mr Franco Haggis, ex-Combat K soldier and recently vacated patient from The

Mount Pleasant Hilltop Institution, the 'nice and caring and friendly home for the mentally challenged'." Voloshko sighed, as if all this really was a *drag*. "It would seem, Mr Haggis, that Fate has a sense of humour. You have hidden under my wings for quite some time, haven't you boy? Taken my pay, used my facilities, enjoyed the honour of serving under my banner? Then, when all I want you to do is terminate a scumbag named Slick for violating my delicate and fragile wife, you decide upon a route of disobedience and slaughter my men." He sighed again. His eyes were dark and hooded. He looked up, and a light source illuminated them; now, meaningful hatred replaced the gentle humour.

Franco stared with a grim, bitter look. "Get to the point, dickhead."

Voloshko laughed, a tinkling of ice cubes in a champagne flute. "As I said, Fate has a sense of humour. Sometime, I pull jobs for NanoTek. They asked me to recover... something. I recovered her. And would you believe it, her name is Melanie and she's your—" he laughed, "your *fucking* girlfriend." He moved close to the screen, so his face filled it from digital edge to digital edge. "If you want her back, Franco, you better come and pay me a visit. Although the compensation I require for your behaviour is... unorthodox."

"Where will I find you?"

"Why, at The Hammer Syndicate's HQ. Come unarmed. Or I might just cut Melanie's head off before you set foot across the threshold. Are we clear on that point?"

Franco nodded.

"One last thing."

"Yeah?"

"I left you a present. Oh, I see you already found it." He smiled a crooked smile, tutted, a click of tongue on teeth, and as the camera zoomed away he brushed a fleck of dust from his perfect pink crushed-coral jacket. "I do so *despise* children. So annoying, don't you find?"

The screen died. Franco stared at it for a long time.

Keenan touched his arm. "We've got to go to NanoTek. All roads lead there. They will have answers to questions. Solutions to problems. NanoTek holds the key to the puzzle."

"We're going to get Mel."

"Walk unarmed into a trap? Franco, use your brain, man. It would be suicide! Insanity! We need to get to NanoTek; Voloshko himself said he was pulling a job for NanoTek—they will have answers, Franco, trust me on this."

Franco whirled, staring deep in Keenan's eyes. "If it was Freya, or the girls, would you go and pay Voloshko a visit? Would you step unarmed into his *fucking* lair and face whatever bad shit he dared throw at you? Just for the smallest chance to rescue them?"

Keenan saw tears in Franco's eyes, and he grasped both Franco's shoulders in a powerful grip. "I hear what you're saying, brother. I hear it good. But you are side-stepping logic. Voloshko wants you dead, merely for some petty personal revenge. There is no compensation. There is nothing you can do there. If you walk in unarmed... he'll blow your damn head off."

There came a whisper of sound from the bodies on the ground. Instantly, Franco pushed from Keenan and knelt, scanning, until his lightly moving hand came to rest on Little Megan's inert form. Her eyes opened. She stared blind for a while, breathing shallow, ragged, then her head turned and she smiled a watery smile.

"You came back," she said, her voice an angel's whisper.

"We came back, little one," growled Franco, tears running freely down his cheeks and into his ginger beard. "After all, we couldn't be leaving you alone now, could we?"

"Where is Melanie? I like Melanie. She sang for me, Franco. Did you hear her sing?"

"I heard her sing," said Franco, voice crackling with emotion.

"Are you there, Knuckles?"

"I'm here, Megan, you little tinker." Knuckles eyed the purple hole in Megan's chest, and turned to Keenan. Keenan gave a sharp shake of his head in the negative.

"I missed you, Nuck. I missed the stories you used to tell. Will you tell me one now?"

"Of course I will, Megs." He coughed, but Little Megan had closed her eyes again. Her body gave a shudder, and she was still. Franco checked for a pulse, then hung his head, crying.

Suddenly, he surged to his feet. Rubbed savagely at spent tears. His head turned with a *crack* and he stared hard at Keenan. "I'm going after Voloshko.

I... understand it if you head out for NanoTek. You are right. It's the logical place to go. I will meet you there... later."

Keenan shook his head. Coughed. "No. We'll visit Voloshko together. The bastard has it coming." His voice was gentle. Smooth. An exhalation.

Franco cocked his Kekra. Patted Knuckles on the head. Scowled off over the millions of skyscraper roofs and points that formed the jagged, ragged skyline of the living *hell* known as The City.

"Let's kill us some urban terrorists," he said.

IT BEGAN TO snow, a thick, oily, grey snow which settled massively from iron-black clouds. Mr Ranger glanced up, face scrunching into a visage of absolute displeasure. "What's going on with this shit-hole's damn weather?" he muttered, then glanced down at the master controller in his gloved hand. A green glow bathed his palm, and he sat on the tailgate of the groundvan, fighting the urge to light another cigar. He was smoking so much his chest felt full of barbed wire.

Where were they?

His machines, his AI killers, his... *girls*.

He smiled at that, but the smile fell from his face like a tumbling mask. The GKs had lost (severed?) contact some three hours previously; presumably, they had entered some signal leak-free environment on their hunt for Combat K members Franco and Keenan... and the mutant, Mel. Still, the comms silence made Ranger twitchy.

Moans echoed down the street, and he glanced behind, into the van, which was loaded with all manner of shotguns—the D5, and the new D6 variant—sub-machine guns, pistols, grenades and even a couple of spare yukana swords.

"Come on."

And on they came, drifting towards him like elegant ghosts through falling oil snow. Lamia and Momos moved smoothly, but Nyx limped, her hips crushed, her gait that of a deformed human. Ranger whistled between his teeth, jumping from the van and rushing forward.

"What happened?"

The three GKs stopped, looked at him with matt black eyes, then looked *past* him to something behind. Ranger felt the birth of a shiver, and spun...

She was tall, with a voluptuous athletic physique. Her hair was dark brown, bobbed, hugging her face in the damp, snowy atmosphere. Her face was strikingly beautiful, her eyes a cold grey and locked on Ranger. Her hands were bare, arms folded across her chest as she leant against the side of Ranger's van.

"Do I know you?" he said.

"No. But I know you. I recommended your services to Dr Oz."

Ranger nodded, taking in her modest, integrated WarSuit—a new design he'd never before seen; and searching her for weapons. All he could see was a single yukana sword sheathed on her back. It was silver.

Ranger's eyes moved to the van, and his own stash of weapons. Dangerously out of reach. He smiled an easy smile. "Do you mind if I smoke?"

"I don't mind if you burst into flame."

"Is there a problem?"

"You have failed."

Ranger sucked on the cigar, shaking his head. "The GKs failed."

"You programmed the HuntScript."

"Still... I need to read their reports, to identify which environmental factors caused failure. Only then—"

"That's enough." Her voice was low, eyes fixed on him. "Nyx? Momos? Lamia?"

She glanced towards the three AIs. Ranger felt his heart leap, and he readied himself for action. What this *stupid* petty bureaucratic little Chief of NanoTek Security failed to understand was that Ranger had put an apotheosis clause into the script; he had given the machines *belief*. They thought he was their Lord. Their *God*. They would obey only him.

The woman met his gaze. She smiled. It was neat, and pretty.

"Kill him," she said, and Ranger turned, the controller still hot in his hand as the three GKs leapt at him, weapons out, blades singing shrilly as disbelief clouded his eyes and he felt the hot bite of metal through his flesh, peeling through skin, cutting muscle, crashing through his bones like a train-wreck and a scream welled in his throat as the AIs cut through him like butter, Lamia's arm slamming through his chest, twisting, pulling free his lungs so that he stood, swaying, staring at the twin bags of bloodied flesh skewered like ripe fruit on her blade. Strings of flesh and vein and tendon connected him to his excised lungs as a pain unimaginable ate acid through him, filling his brain with bright lights and a gushing roar like the ocean. *Impossible*, his brain tried to scream, as he floated out on calm black waters towards a boat that waited patiently to carry him away...

Ranger's corpse hit the ground with a thump.

The three AIs stepped back, Nyx twisting awkwardly.

The woman moved, boots squelching in Ranger's blood. She looked down into dead blue eyes. His mouth was open in shock, tongue lolling uselessly. Blood speckled his lips and face like pepper.

The Chief of Security glanced up at the three machines, which stood, motionless, awaiting their next instruction. "Get in the van," she said. "We need to repair Nyx's fractured pelvis hydraulics."

Lamia tilted her head. "What is your name?"

The woman smiled. "You have known me simply as 1. I am hardwired into your systems as The Primary. But I see you are learning quickly from your environment. If we're to have any kind of feminine bonding, I suppose you can refer to me by my birth name."

The GKs moved forward, feet clashing through Ranger's corpse. They leapt into the van, whirled, looked down at the woman expectantly. She smiled, but her eyes remained cold; grey, and cold; like a pall of nuclear ash on an extinct world.

"You can call me Pippa," she smiled.

PART III

SCOURGE

"Compassion is the basis of morality."
Schopenhauer.

CHAPTER 11
HAMMER & ANVIL

THE CITY PLAYED host to all manner of eccentric and esoteric architectural designs. Never had so many planetary engineers been let loose with such a wild and varied sandbox in which to pit their deviated experimental design-skills against one another in ever-escalating, extravagant and downright *odd* examples of building design.

The Hammer Syndicate's HQ was a concept and *reality* from one such nightmare imagination. It had been designed, originally, by a non-human organism, the term *alien* somehow having fallen from grace when humans constituted perhaps only two-thirds of The City's population. *Coogan III* was, in fact, half human, half Jandlin. Jandlin were highly intelligent sacks of protein with armoured scales and the ability to mould themselves into the shapes of other creatures, albeit still retaining their semi-translucent flesh. Not so much chameleons as base-level shape-shifters, the Jandlin had failed miserably in their chosen profession—that of subterfuge and covert investigations—because any attempt by a Jandlin to imitate another life form became nothing more than an embarrassing example of diplomatic stupidity. The Jandlin were far from bright, a situation not helped by having radial brains distributed around their inner skin sacks. Coogan III, by some miracle, was perhaps the only singular example of a child produced by Jandlin and human. After all, the Jandlin reproduced by sucking a mate *inside* themselves and constantly turning inside-out within one another until they imbibed, over a series of revolving generations, genetic information needed by the female to reproduce a moulded base-clone which could then be deviated by electro-stimulus into an altered genetic evolution. It wasn't easy for a human sperm to find an egg to infuse when said egg didn't, actually, exist.

The Hammer Syndicate HQ, viewed from the outside, was a three-hundred storey organic up-thrust, matt black, no windows, a wavering pinnacle of what on first glance appeared to be rock, but on closer inspection had its entirety of *flesh* held in a gently undulating, wavering, shuddering field. The walls moved as if summer waves rolled up and down their oceanic flesh contours. The summit was tapered, and usually ensconced in clouds. The HQ had no obvious doors or windows, and in the sunshine cast no shadow. However, in the current enforced darkness, it blended rather neatly with the night.

Within, Floor 698 was cool, dark, moody. Vertical drapes of primitive helk-fur tapestry decorated walls, and the floors were layered in metal-weave helk leather. Voloshko sat on a wide couch, reclining with a drink in one hand, a kube in the other.

"It's progressing with the perfection of a well-oiled machine," he said. He smiled, sipping at his drink as the person on the other end spoke. Voloshko nodded slowly, considering.

"When do you think you'll send them?"

He nodded again at the response.

"Yes. The timing would be... adequate. Talk soon."

He killed the communication, and glanced up, over, across the massive low-ceilinged chamber to where a low plinth of alloy-marble held the unconscious form of Mel. Voloshko stood, moved across the floor (which shivered ever so gently under his footsteps, as if he were walking across living, breathing, quivering flesh) and gazed down at the deformed monstrosity.

Her eyes flickered open.

Voloshko smiled. "Good morning, pretty one."

"Grwwll." She lunged, but wires around arms and legs, face and elongated neck, glowed suddenly, tightening. There came a stench of charred flesh, and smoke rose in tiny curls from her mottled skin. With a squeal of pain Mel slumped back to the plinth.

"HotWire," said Voloshko. He ran a hand through his hair, looking suddenly tired. "We find it works superbly against you... zombies." He smiled sardonically. "Not just pain, but a *promise* of fire and extermination. And even you, my beautiful little experiment, have enough self-preservation to understand the difference between life—and death."

Voloshko peered close. Mel growled again, a few inches from his face. He reached out, stroked her skin, observing with interest the incredibly fine mesh of wire which coated her. His hand dropped, brushing her breasts, with their huge plum-sized distended nipples oozing grey pus. Mel snapped at him, jaws grinding, and growled, lunged again, and the wires glowed orange. She thrashed on the plinth, Voloshko forgotten as the wires ate into her and filled her world with bright insect pain.

"We could have had *so much* fun, my pretty," he said, licking damp lips as his gaze lingered on her pus-drooling, quivering, raw, pink zombie vagina. He nodded, as if imagining some intimacy of the flesh. An image of sexual coupling of hardcore stamina. "Yes," he breathed, growing hard in an instant. "So much fun."

"Voloshko!"

Voloshko turned, eyes narrowed, and watched Dr Oz walk easily towards him. He glanced left and right, scanning for... something out of place. Despite their *business arrangement*, Voloshko trusted no man.

"Oz. You got my message."

"You have done well," Oz said, staring at Mel. "You retrieved our unfortunate mistake."

"She looks different to the others. More... *advanced*."

Voloshko caught the barriers falling into place behind Oz's eyes, as the sole owner of NanoTek gave a short nod. "The product of mistaken identity, I am sure. All that matters is that we have her." He slapped Voloshko on the back, and it took all of Voloshko's willpower not to take a gun and blow Oz's head clean off. Technically, they were in the same business. But even slime can hate slime. However, Oz was not to be underestimated. He probably had a wealth of military upgrades stashed in his pants.

Dr Oz spoke quietly into a PAD, and gave several codes. He glanced at Voloshko. "My people will transport her from here. Your finances are being transferred as we speak. I won't forget this. Your loyalty. It is appreciated." He lifted his finger, pointing at Voloshko as if he were... Voloshko smiled a bland smile on thin lips. As if he were a *normal* person.

"It's my pleasure to serve," forced Voloshko, voice tight, but the irony seemed lost on Oz. Four large Slabs entered from a distant door, and one administered a jab to Mel's eye. The needle slid into her eyeball and she screamed, thrashed for a few moments, then was still.

"Direct to the brain," said Oz.

"Primitive," said Voloshko.

"It will keep her sane, lucid, *and* controllable." Oz shrugged, then gestured to the Slabs who grunted, heaving Mel between them, and staggered off across the undulating flesh floor. Oz followed, and stopped at the door. He turned.

"There was something else?" said Voloshko. He was feeling irritable. Used, somehow. Abused.

Ironic, because that was usually how he himself operated.

For once, Voloshko did not know the bigger picture, and this irked him. After all, he *owned* The Hammer Syndicate. It was his gig. The City ran, partially, under his rule. He knew who was stealing what, who was fucking who, who lived... and who died. There were few to challenge his authority.

"Did you... kill the others?"

"We killed the children."

"No, the two men—Keenan and Franco."

"They weren't with the subject. Why? Do you need them taking out?"

"I have people on it," said Oz. He glanced around. "But I'd... lock your flaps, or whatever it is you do for security in this organic hive. It's possible Combat K might come looking for Mel."

"I am sure they will. Don't worry. My security systems are adequate," said Voloshko, voice cold, and he watched Dr Oz vanish into a rippling flesh valve. He glanced back to the bed where his wife, Melissa, lay. The very same wife who had *betrayed* him... an act which still tasted sour on his tongue, in his brain... and yet one he was willing to now overlook since her transformation into *deviant*. It was a sultry deformation he could not resist.

"Are you coming?" came the crackling voice of Melissa, the zombie, behind thin black curtains. Her outline seemed to shimmer, inhuman, as if lit by silver. Voloshko licked needful lips.

"I soon will be," he said, striding forward and loosening his tie.

* * *

Keenan stared at the Realtime TuffMAP™ (*the funky groovy way to find your way around the universe, dude!*) Franco stood close behind, D5 in wide steady paws, his eyes bleak and focused. "There."

"I see it," said Keenan, finger tracing the lines of the old underground tube system. "You know they're condemned, right?"

Franco gave a cold smile. "Yeah. But we'll find a way through. If they're still standing. First, we need weapons, Keenan. We need bombs, and guns, and armour. This is a savage gig."

Keenan gave a nod, stood, and folded the TuffMAP™ into his WarSuit. "We don't know if the old SPIRAL SP1_store still exists; maybe SPIRAL cleaned them out during their final war."

"No," said Franco, shaking his head. "They didn't have time. They were wiped out so fast the bastards couldn't even blink."

Keenan took a deep breath. "We take MICHELLE to the stores, tool up, then infiltrate The Hammer Syndicate HQ—possibly through the tunnels, if we can find an access point. That way we avoid the gathering zombie armies. Then we rescue Mel, take Xakus to NanoTek, restore Mel to full health and find out how to switch off these zombie deviants. *Then* we hunt down the kit needed to allow Xakus to decode the junks' SinScript. *Easy.*" His eyes sparkled, and he sucked in cool city air. "I always did like a challenge."

Franco slapped him on the back, barking a laugh. "Yeah Keenan. Just like the old days, hey lad?"

"Yeah, the old days," muttered Keenan, remembering the bad ones.

"Bah, you're a grumpy old git."

"It must be the people I meet."

"No no, Keenan, I swear, the older you get, the more of a miserable bastard you become. You'll stop celebrating your birthday soon; tell everyone not to buy you presents and lock yourself in the bloody toilet for the day."

"My *birthday?*" Keenan gave a cynical smile. "That's just something that happens to other people."

From the edges of the skyscraper came a buzzing sound, and five guns tracked Cam as he zipped up into the air, hovered for a moment, then dropped like a stone to sit solid and stable in the pollution before Keenan's face. Keenan held up a hand, and smiled. "It's OK. He's a friend." He squinted. "You are a friend, right?"

"Keenan, we need to talk. This is important!"

"Nice to see you, too, Cam. Been holidaying in the sun, have we? Machine, you wouldn't *believe* the shit we've been through in the last twenty-four hours." He stared at Cam's shell, which was battered and dented, and showed deep fresh surface scars.

Cam gave a little cough. Which was odd, because PopBots had no throat.

"So you've been in the wars yourself?" said Keenan, more gentle now.

"Yes," sighed Cam. "I found the battery upgrades I required, and repaired and charged myself. However, *something* sent a couple of HK PopBots to wipe me out."

"Hunter Killers? They're vicious little bastards."

"Exactly. I am not exactly *equipped* to deal with full-on military models. The fight was long and hard, I can assure you."

"Who sent them?"

"A question at the forefront of my mind," said the tiny little 'bot. "After all, I am nothing but a personal security device. Yes? Why expend the time, effort and cost of HKs on little old me?"

"You killed them?"

"I did," said Cam, voice distant.

"How?"

Cam spun, lights glittering red. "It's a long story, for another time. What's important, Keenan, is what's going on down there. On the streets. In the malls. With the... deviants. The *zombies,* as you like to call them."

"You've been monitoring?"

"Oh yes, and you're not going to like what I have to tell."

"Try me," said Keenan.

"This is how it goes. The zombies are humans and *other race organisms* that have taken biomod organic upgrades. These upgrades have then deviated the host system to produce a wide variety of mutations. You with me so far?"

"Hardly rocket science," grunted Franco.

"Some of us have a limited intellect," said Cam.

"Hey, you referring to me? Let me tell you," he pointed his stubby finger, "I might not have a triple degree in psykey... in sarky... in damn mind games, but I'm cleverer than a bloody sausage, I promise you that."

"A bloody sausage?"

"Don't be disrespecting the sausage. A hot-dog has more guile than you think."

Cam considered this, then, moving on, said, "It's incredible what one can witness from an aerial perspective out on the streets." Cam remained unperturbed as Franco made threatening hand gestures. "The behaviour of the deviated organisms is strange; some have grouped together, formed almost military units which have taken over SAM sites, military depots, communications towers; they seem to have learned from their surroundings, adapted, almost like machines, and some have created an unbreachable fortress down in DOG Town and CoreCentral. Quad-Gal Military could retake The City, but at a great, great loss. It would either have to use a mass infantry incursion—or simply clean huge sections of the planet of all life. But, of course, the Commandments would never allow such genocide to occur. Even mutations have rights; as laid down in the New QGL Scripts post-Helix."

Keenan stroked his stubbled chin. "We've seen as much on our travels, Cam. What you've witnessed, it means only that the deviated creatures are fighting to survive. They know the army could attack at any minute in SAM proof dropships; all they've done is throw up basic defences. Any rat fights when its back is against a wall."

"Yes, but I've also seen behaviour at odds with the group mentality. Some of these creatures are acting independently. However, the strangest thing of all are the... how can I put this? The *zombie* killers."

"You mean humans fighting for their lives?"

"No. There is a breed, or a strain, whatever you wish to call them, which are actively hunting down and destroying other deviants. They are awesome in their killing prowess."

"You think they retain characteristics?" said Keenan. "From when they were human? After all, Mel still seemed to have feelings for Franco despite being an eight-foot monstrosity. Maybe the mutations only mask certain character traits. Biomods turn a person into a monster, but inside, they still retain some human desires and needs. Or alien desires and needs. Or whatever." He rubbed his temples. "This is insane. It's turning my brain into spaghetti."

"There's one other thing," said Cam.

"Go on."

"The zombies are emitting... signals."

Keenan and Franco exchanged glances. "What does that mean?" said Franco, eventually. "Or am I being a short-arsed dumb ginger bastard again?"

"Each deviant emits a tiny, almost unrecognisable, but nevertheless *powerful,* digital signal burst. At a rate of about one burst per hour."

"What kind of signal?"

"They are encoded beyond my ability to decrypt."

"Wait a minute," said Keenan. "I watched you decode logic cubes in Pippa's skull when we lifted her from the prison planet, Hardcore. That was high-tec military shit. You're good at this, right?"

"I admit to having some skill in this field," said Cam. "However, the signal bursts from the zombies are far beyond my current skill-set. I hate to say it, but whatever data is being transmitted by the mutations, it's totally indecipherable. I cannot crack the codes."

"Where do the signals go?"

"A barren wasteland at The City's northernmost hemisphere. The one place The City's engineers will not build—where lines of latitude and longitude meet. Zero degrees, my friend."

"Convenient," said Keenan.

"Probably a relay point," said Cam. "Throws trackers off the scent. The signals are so advanced they could be bounced to a million other points before final destination. We'd never hunt them down, if that's what you've got in mind."

"How come," said Franco, voice measured, "these zombies are sending signals? They're not wireless radio stations, are they? I thought they were just people full of little robots gone wrong? Little bloody buggers rampaging through your sewage streams and turning your belly inside out?"

"That's incredibly mentally adroit of you," said Cam. "If we find out *why* the deviants are transmitting, we'll probably find answers to the whole screwed up debacle being played out on this devastated planet."

"Let's get moving," said Keenan, glancing over to where Knuckles was still crying over the corpse of Little Megan. Olga helped the orphan to his feet. His eyes were red-rimmed—and filled with a deep and burning rage. Keenan glanced to Professor Xakus, who seemed oddly aloof; cool, detached, staring out over the darkened city where distant fires burned and occasional gunshots shattered the oppressive silence. The City felt like a city under siege; a world of darkness and despair. Keenan shivered. "Xakus? You still with us?"

"Yes. We will reach NanoTek. I will discover what went wrong. This place has become an abomination. The biomods were never meant for this; they were supposed to save life, not destroy it."

Keenan's smile was touched with evil. "The lament of every bio-weapon engineer and scientist on every damned world between here and Ket. We didn't mean it. It was an accident. Pitiful."

"In this case, however, true," said Xakus, eyes full of silver tears.

"Tell it to the dead," said Keenan, his voice hard, head pounding and robbing him of sympathy and understanding. "The living no longer have time for excuses."

THEY STOOD ON the pavement. Rubble lay strewn in huge scatters. Franco stared constantly about, twitching, eyes gleaming, looking for trouble. The night was sable, skyscrapers and cubeblocks rearing and blocking out what few stars still shimmered. Again, thick oily snowflakes fell, coating the world in a slippery, evil-smelling grime. MICHELLE squatted against the side of The Happy Friendly Sunshine Assurance Company, and seemed to be preening herself, if that was the right word for a fifty foot tall biomechanical war organism. She stood when Xakus appeared, and leered down with several booming *clanks* from her great height. Franco squawked, and jumped back, cocking his Kekras.

"I... wouldn't do that," said Keenan.

"She bloody freaks me out," snapped Franco.

"She's our transport."

"Well, she's a bloody buggering freak if you ask me. I just can't be doing with these bio-methological transport vehicles. Why couldn't we travel in a tank like every other insane person? Huh? Answer me that!"

"She saved our lives," said Keenan. He lit a quick cigarette. Widow Maker entered his lungs and he sighed, staring at fingers gun-blackened by oil. Were they trembling? He would *kill* for a drink. "She got us out of that library. Smashed those GK AIs like they were toys."

"Ha!" said Franco, brightening. "She did that." He frowned. "I just wish we didn't have to crawl up her arse."

"It's not her arse," said Keenan.

"Yeah it is," said Franco, staring distantly into the cloud-heavy sky. "She's biological, innit? She's called MICHELLE. She's a she. She has a rear pipe. We crawl up the rear pipe. A rear pipe is an arse, ergo, every time we climb inside, we're giving her a good bumming."

Keenan stared hard at Franco. "I cannot believe we stem from the same biological race," he said.

"Ha! Listen buddy, I've had a lot of arse problems in my time. It's like, God, or some dude or geezer, has given me the perfect face—" he stared hard, challenging Keenan to disagree through the cloud of cigarette smoke, "but to compensate for perfect and finely chiselled features, he has forced me to endure all manner of arse infestations."

"Arse infestations," said Keenan.

"Aye. I had that recurring fissure during Combat K training. Had to have six-needle injections straight up bam! into the anal pipe. Ouch! Then I had those bowel problems, oh how the lads laughed every time I had to stampede to the bogs. Then I was cursed with that damned alien arse virus from Ket, which haunts me even now—whenever it decides to rear its ugly turtle head! It's like having a disease with its own artificial intelligence! When is it most inconvenient for Franco to have a shit? NOW!!! ATTACK!!! NOW!!! And then, as if to make a mere mockery of my humble existence, events transpire so's I have to travel around *inside* a giant arse! Do the gods have no end to their wicked sense of humour? Do they? Huh?"

Keenan drew on his cigarette, lips compressed, apparently lost for words.

"Listen Keenan," Franco puffed out his chest, on a roll, "you just haven't been afflicted like me, right? Oh no. Is there to be no end to my arse suffering? And you shouldn't mock, because you shouldn't judge a man until you've walked in his shoes."

"Or shit with his arse?" said Keenan.

"There you go again, with the jibes the jokes the mockery the put downs. I don't laugh at your funny face—"

"My *what?*"

"Or Xakus's frizzy hair, or Olga's bouncing titanic obscenity of a bosom. Oh no. And I didn't mock Pippa when she was part of the squad." He stumbled into silence. Rubbed at his goatee. "Shit, man. I'm sorry."

"It's OK." Keenan slapped him on the back, and stamped his cigarette butt under his boot. "Pippa's gone from my head. I have a funny feeling I'll never see her again. I'm over her. Her disease is gone from my skull, buddy. Her face has been erased from memory."

"I'll believe that one when I see it," mumbled Franco.

The group approached MICHELLE, and were absorbed into the war machine one by one, until only Franco stood on the greasy narrow street. Snow swirled around him, making his skin red with frost. He rubbed at his chilled nose, which was dribbling, and gave a short bitter laugh, glancing nervously at the desolation surrounding him.

"So you think you'll never see Pippa again? No mate." His voice was deathly quiet. "We'll see her again. Because she wants you, Keenan. She needs you like an orbital needs its host planet. Without you, she'll surely die."

He grunted, puckering his face and clenching his arse as MICHELLE, ironically, accepted him into hers.

XAKUS PILOTED MICHELLE with as much stealth as a fifty foot bio-mechanical war transport could muster; MICHELLE *crept,* clashing and grinding through the streets, squashing only the occasional stray zombie which crossed her path. Keenan stood behind Xakus as MICHELLE's scanners, using infrared, shifted from left to right and she halted with a clank, and a hiss of expelled gas.

"Down there," pointed Keenan, examining his TuffMAP™. "There should be an old warehouse, some kind of haulage depot. You see it? I'm sure the MonkeyMan has it logged."

"Turn left, oo oo."

Xakus nodded, and MICHELLE strode forward through the deserted district, huge metal boots cracking the road. They entered an area filled with massive decrepit warehouses. Many were crumbling, with shattered windows and half-destroyed roofs. Timbers and alloy emerged from walls like exposed bones. Bricks were absent, giving the impression of gaping maws.

"It's derelict," said Franco, who had crept up beside Keenan.

"Better for us, no?"

Franco rubbed his ginger beard. "I don't like it."

"You don't like anything."

"It smells fishy."

"No, Franco, that's just your food pack."

"Hey, there's nothing wrong with anchovies."

"I agree. On a pizza. But eating them from a jar? With a spoon? Franco, you're a culinary pervert."

"Where do you want me to stop, Keenan?"

Keenan peered outside. They'd reached the haulage depot's huge gates which hung from twisted, battered hinges as large as his torso. Beyond, a tightly packed swathe of SlamTruk cabs linked to TitanTrailers spun away as far as the eye could see, their long, corrugated flanks emblazoned with a colourful logo:

PORKY PAUPER'S FAST-FOOD BURGERS!
GO ON, BE A PORKER!

"It's too quiet," said Franco.

"Walk her through," instructed Keenan.

MICHELLE eased between rows of giant wagons, many with burst tyres, buckled axles and smashed flanks. Evidence of recent battle. Franco pointed out an arc of bullet holes down one truck, and as MICHELLE moved onwards, towards the depot itself, the signs and scars of war increased. A whole row of SlamTruks had been torched and sat, blackened, melted into the concretealloy. Others had been turned over, and yet more blasted into a fusion of melted, twisted steel and alloy, charcoal and blue, melded by the phenomenal heat of rampaging detonation.

"Someone's been having fun," said Keenan.

"Boys and their toys," observed Franco.

"Head towards the back, around the depot building. There should be an entrance to the old SPIRAL SP1_store. If we're lucky. And it's not been raided."

"They'd need entrance codes," said Franco. "Actually, how the hell are *we* gonna get in?"

Keenan smiled, and pointed at Cam. "We've got a special permit," he said.

THEY STOOD ON the flat expanse of concretealloy. A cold wind hushed over them. The oil snow had stopped, but the ground was slick with slush, treacherous, and the whole world seemed to have paused, a tableau of hellish desolation.

Knuckles shivered, and moved to stand beside Keenan. "I want to come with you."

"You want a weapon, lad?"

Knuckles glanced down at his rusted machete. "This seems a little... primitive. For those we are to face."

"You can't come into battle, Knuckles. You're..." Keenan stopped. He stared into the concentration of pain which made up the young orphan's face.

"Only a kid?"

Keenan gave a nod.

"This world has aged me. I am a man, now, I think."

Keenan said nothing, but moved to an almost invisible rectangle of alloy-concrete. Nearby, a huge, twenty-feet-tall TitanTrailer lay, twisted and buckled, broken almost in two. The bomb blast which destroyed the wagon must have been huge.

"Cam? Can you get us in?"

"I'm scanning now." The small PopBot rotated, blue lights flickering on his casing. "The codes are standard military issue. Should take me a few minutes to hunt down entry signatures."

"OK." Keenan lit a cigarette, and watched Olga sidling over to Franco. He pulled free his Techrim and checked the mag, then cocked the weapon and stared off over the barrage of battered trucks with their obesity-inducing logos. Franco was right. It was far too quiet.

"Franco?"

"Yeah boss?"

"You got those Kekras primed?"

Franco wrestled Olga's hand from his hip and gave her a stinging slap. She smiled coquettishly at him and mouthed the words, *my hero*. He frowned. "Yeah Keenan. You expecting trouble?"

"I can smell it," he said, voice a whisper.

His eyes roved across the massive open expanses of alloy-concrete. His eyes narrowed. Distantly, engines rumbled. Flashes lit the sky. Some kind of battle was being fought, and it was moving toward them, like a remote storm. Tracer lit the heavens, flashing green and purple like tiny, distant fireworks.

"We've got time," said Franco.

Keenan nodded.

"We're in," said Cam. There came a long, low buzz. Then a perfect rectangular outline of steel-concrete suddenly dropped into a ramp and lights sprang to life illuminating a stark metal interior. Keenan strode down the ramp, followed by Franco, Olga and Knuckles. Xakus remained outside, talking in hushed tones to MICHELLE. The giant bio-machine crooned, sitting down with a *crash* that put a twenty-foot crack in the yard.

Keenan felt nervous as his boots thudded the ramp. Then the room opened revealing a stock-pile of guns, ammunitions, rockets, armour, bombs, and every other ancillary piece of equipment a soldier could ever need.

Keenan smiled, relief etched acid on his face as Franco pushed past him and raised hands to the stark metal heavens a few feet overhead. He beamed a ginger beam, and said without a trace of mockery, "Let's offer up a prayer to our Host!

Porky Pauper! May The Plump One's Burgers Make
People Fat For Ever More! Amen!"

Keenan grabbed a gleaming, oiled MPK and
checked the mechanism. It clicked and clacked,
neatly. He slotted home a magazine, aimed at a distant target, and fired off a thirty round burst.
Smoke filled the chamber. The target, at the far end
of the underground store, sat battered and torn and
ragged under metal onslaught.

Keenan nodded, smoke stinging his eyes. He
pulled free his cigarette. Gazed over the group.

"Let's tool up," he said. "And go to war."

THEY EMERGED FROM the chamber carrying canvas
sacks. Franco and Knuckles had donned WarSuits,
but Xakus had turned down the offer of armour. He
was a scholar, an inventor, not a soldier, he said.
Olga had tried on various of the larger WarSuits,
but they buzzed and hissed in protest as she tried to
struggle into Permatex designed for squaddies, not
sumo wrestlers. Eventually, she resigned herself to
several Titanium-kevlar panels, strapped to torso,
arms and legs, and giving her the look of a giant,
somewhat obese, insect.

Keenan stocked up on ammunition, and carried
two MPKs, one slotted on his back, one slung
against his chest. He'd found fresh stocks of 11nm
ammunition for his Techrim. With this, he was
happy.

Knuckles found himself two slim Makarov pistols
and a small stash of ammunition. Olga had two D5
shotguns slotted against her back, and Xakus
turned down the offer of weapons with a weak

smile. "I am a pacifist, at heart," he said. "I abhor weapons of all kinds. I could never kill another man. Or... zombie." Franco couldn't bring himself to point out that MICHELLE was the most fearsome weapon he'd ever seen in his life; the irony knocked him out.

However, it was Franco, as usual, who behaved like a born-again hedonist. What he carried could only be described as an *orgy* of weapons. He had five D5 shotguns on his back, nestling in what he proudly nicknamed his canvas shotgun *quiver*, alongside a Bausch & Harris Sniper Rifle with SSGK digital sights. Two MPKs crossed his chest. Four Kekra machine pistols sat on his hips. Twin belts crisscrossed his chest sporting all manner of bombs and grenades, including infamous BABEs and SPUKEs. In his utility belt were myriad military-spec knife blades: flick knives, retractable knives, throwing knives, homing knives, exploding knives, poison knives, and even a couple with pre-programmable AI function. Finally, to round off his now incredibly stocky appearance, he wore tri-goggles against his head which could be pulled down over his eyes to provide infra-red, night-sight, recording functions, green-key and TIP (target identification priority) systems which linked to the AI knives on his belt.

Franco beamed.

"Like a kid in a sweet shop," drawled Keenan, lighting another cigarette. Snow swirled aimlessly in the air.

"Hey, I wouldn't want to get caught unprepared."

"That'll never happen," said Keenan, eyeing him up and down. "What are the goggles for?"

"They're not goggles. They're TRI-SPIES. All the rage, apparently."

"You mean they bring *on* rage," said Keenan, watching as they slipped down over Franco's nose for the third time. "Look, the strap's too long. Let me shorten it for you."

"No, it's already on its shortest setting."

"And there's me thinking you had a big head."

"Funny, Keenan. Amusing. Listen, it's the bloody army! Skimping on R&D. Either that, or all those SPIRAL buggers had huge bulbous skulls." He wrestled the goggles back onto his forehead, and switched on a beam. A red laser swept the group.

"Don't go pointing that where you shouldn't," warned Keenan, eyes tracing the skyline. The battle was definitely getting closer. Now they could hear a *crump* of explosions, and a muffled rattle of automatic gunfire.

"Who's fighting who?" said Franco.

"Not our problem," said Keenan. He glanced around at the rag-tag band, and gave an internal sigh. Gone were the simple days of solo infiltration. Keenan hated missions where he had to baby-sit. It made life *much* more difficult. "We ready? We tooled up?"

The group nodded, and moved back towards MICHELLE.

There, they halted.

Beyond her, perhaps thirty metres away, squatted five evil, matt-black HTanks, engines on silent stealth mode, huge, twin-barrel guns pointing directly towards the group.

They froze. Those guns were menacing.

There came a click, and a hatch slid open. A SIM appeared, poking his head from the oval and levering himself up on elbows. His eyes clicked as he focused on the group. His chrome-masked face and black armour shone, as if polished by somebody with a strong right elbow, an eye for anal precision, and a terminal obsession for that very special *Darth Vader* gleam.

Keenan heard Franco groan.

"You know him?"

"It was a while back," said Franco, voice hoarse, eyes roving for an escape route.

"I am Justice D," said the SIM. "The humans are to throw down their weapons and surrender immediately. The humans are not to make a fuss." He smiled, then. It looked wrong on his face. "Or Justice D will be *forced* to blow all life from frail human shit-sacks."

"WELL, WELL, WELL," said Franco, moving forward with hands above his head. "If it isn't my old chum Justice D. I remember you, laddie. You need to get yourself a sense of humour injection, and pronto!" Franco turned, and started making frantic facial gestures at Keenan... who gave a single nod of understanding.

The Justice SIM's face was a blank chrome mask. When he spoke, his lips moved a touch out of synch with his enunciated words, as if the SIM was a product of a badly dubbed Japachinese B-movie.

"I remember you, Franco Haggis. You helped slaughter a considerable number of my colleagues on the roof of the Razor Syndicate a while back. I remember it as if it was yesterday, loading slack broken punctured bodies into float-carts ready for reintegration in The Great Wheel." His mechanical eyes shifted, clicking. "And you, Keenan. You were part of that extermination group."

"Now!" snapped Keenan.

Keenan and Franco's guns roared, bullets screaming at Justice D who, without any sense of human unpredictability, and with all the imagination of a goat, was caught totally unawares. Bullets screamed off the HTank's hull in bright streamers of sparks; Knuckles and Olga ran for the protection of the depot buildings, with Keenan and Franco covering them, weapons juddering, barrels snarling fire, faces set in grim determination as...

As MICHELLE slowly awoke.

She stood, towering over the HTanks. Barrels squealed on ratchets, following her up as Justice D, still poking out of his turret and mumbling anally about how he'd been so rudely interrupted in his diatribe, and how you couldn't trust humans to listen to a decent sermon on rights and responsibilities of the SIM, dropped his jaw and leant backwards to fit the whole of MICHELLE's form into his false mechanical vision.

Go easy now, my little honey pot, thought Xakus as he backed away from the impending slaughter. *HTanks can be dangerous weapons depending on what shells they're carrying...*

Don't worry, thought back MICHELLE. *I have every angle covered. Go and join Knuckles and Olga. Me and the boys can sort out this little raiding party!*

An HTank fired, twin guns recoiling with a massive *boom*. MICHELLE slammed left, clanking, joints rolling as shells whistled past her flat vertical ears. She leapt forward, a huge fist slamming down to smash with terrifying force against the HTank's hull, shunting it down into the ground which cracked and buckled under impact. Revving engines, the other HTanks leapt forward, treads squealing, guns pounding. MICHELLE dodged the shells, grabbed one HTank by twin barrels, and rolling back, twisting, she hurled it away in a flail of broken flapping panels. The HTank connected with a wall of Porky Pauper SlamTruks, there was spark of ignition and a fireball raged at the sky carrying whirling SlamTruk trailers and parts of a destroyed and decimated HTank... and illuminating the whole depot and surrounding warehouses in eerie green firelight. Smoke rolled out like a nuclear pall, lit by flaming shards of molten metal. Noise slapped the sky.

More guns fired, and MICHELLE stomped down on an HTank with a huge cubic boot, again and again with rending, tearing squeals of compressing alloy. The HTank finally groaned, and collapsed into a buckled V.

The HTank sporting Justice D had reversed, hard, to lead the battle from the rear. MICHELLE leapt again, the whole Porky Pauper depot shaking as she grabbed an HTank in each mammoth fist and whirled them through the air to collide, with a thundering crash. Again and again she smashed the HTanks together, trailing cables and panels and squealing treads, as far below Franco and Keenan retreated, MPKs thundering until with a final, titanic crash the battered HTanks exploded and sailed across the depot, hitting the ground in a tangled mash of merging melting alloy, guns bent, wheels skittering free, fire pounding the sky. Fiery grooves scarred the depot's concretealloy as the mangled mess slid to a halt with a groan. Keenan and Franco looked at one another, ears ringing after the harsh metal onslaught. MICHELLE turned, as Justice D's final HTank *slammed* and the shell caught her in the midriff. Her hands fastened around the glowing ball, locked, for a moment, as her head snapped up in realisation. The shell detonated, and fire raged over MICHELLE, engulfing her in screaming, billowing heat. Below her metal boots concretealloy buckled, cracked, and formed irregular pools of molten metal.

Xakus surged forward...

Keenan grabbed him. "Whoa, pal. You can't go out there!"

Xakus strained for a moment. "I have to help her!"

"You can't help her," hissed Franco, voice low, Kekra against his cheek. "What you gonna do? Kill a tank?"

Xakus strained, and Keenan had to use both hands. "Wait!" he snapped. "Watch!"

The flames started to die down. As smoke and flames cleared, they saw MICHELLE was scarred, blackened, but still... alive. She had dropped to one knee, and with a creak her head lifted to fix on...

Justice D, striding through clouds of thick belching smoke. Metal debris littered the floor, twisted and buckled, reflecting the glow of flickering fire. He carried what looked like a long rifle, cradled in his arms. He seemed perfectly calm, tiny, out of his depth as he stared up at the fifty-foot bio-mechanical killer with something akin to a child's curiosity. MICHELLE towered over him, smoke billowing from her shrapnel-embedded shell. Her face snarled...

Keenan blinked. Something *clicked* bad in his mind. Recognition. "Shit," he snarled, MPK rising but it was too late.

Justice D lowered the IMS—an industrial molecule stripper, used predominately for hardcore demolition work. It reduced most materials to component atoms. The IMS was whining like a caged animal. Justice D and MICHELLE locked false eyes... digital to digital... and Justice D fired.

There was a *whump*.

MICHELLE's legs were severed at the knees, and she toppled forward with a look of surprise on her woven face. Her steel eyes hissed as panels slid across one another.

"No!" screamed Xakus, sprinting towards her.

"Franco?" said Keenan, voice steady.

"I'm on it."

Franco smoothly drew his Bausch & Harris Sniper Rifle; he steadied the weapon, and SSGK digital sights hummed. Franco released his breath, calm, and squeezed off a single shot. The bullet whirred across the clearing and slapped into one of Justice D's mechanical eyes, flipping the SIM backwards to lie, stunned, on the ground.

"Good shot."

"Cheers."

"He's not dead."

"I *know* that."

"I'll get us transport. Keep everybody together. *Here.*"

Franco winked. "I can do *that,* mate."

Keenan jogged off around the smoke-filled depot.

Franco aimed down the SSGK, watched Justice D push himself onto his knees. SIMs were notoriously tough; what Franco often called *hard bastards to kill.* He sighted carefully, knowing it was pointless shooting at the SIM's armoured hide, arms, legs, neck, and even head. Even a Bausch & Harris round wouldn't penetrate. But a SIM's eyes... Franco grinned. That was its weak spot.

Knuckles touched Franco's arm. "Is there anything I can do?"

"No lad. But it's a brave offer. Thanks."

"Why didn't the bullet enter his skull?"

"Because it's solid," grinned Franco, then glanced, worried, at Xakus. The old black man had run across the buckled, glowing, smoke-filled depot, kicking through bits of smouldering metal and savaged mechanism. He fell to his knees beside MICHELLE's huge, angular face. They seemed to be talking, but without words.

Franco relaxed, and aimed again. Justice D struggled to his feet, anger his mistress, and staggered towards the IMS. His intention was obvious: he was going to mow them all down with the devastating industrial weapon. Vaporise them into component dust! Franco breathed free, gave himself a single, permissible nod, and squeezed the trigger for a second time.

The bullet slammed Justice D's one working eye, shattering the high-tech optics and slamming off into the sky. Justice D hit the ground again, twisting, and this time the SIM groaned.

In the background, fire roared a symphony.

Green light shimmered, sending long shadows stretching over the scene.

Heat pulsed across the desecrated depot yard.

Franco strode past the dying form of MICHELLE, to halt at the SIM's groping hands. He kicked the IMS away, and it clattered over broken metal. At the noise, Justice D lunged for Franco, but the squaddie leapt back. He smiled at the ironic reversal.

"What's it like to live in fear, little man?"

"The human has blinded me! The human will die for this!"

"I think you've uttered your last threat. Buttered your last toast. And believe me, mate, you've eaten your last pork pie!" Franco turned, stared at Xakus who was weeping, rocking backwards and forwards, his hands on MICHELLE's dying, pain-filled face. The bio-mechanical war machine had leaked a lake of blood. Franco could see tubes and wire erupting like arteries from her severed legs; they were still pumping, gushing, foaming ersatz blood into the gutter.

Knuckles ran to Xakus, and helped the man to his feet. Franco joined them, and placed his hand tenderly on Xakus' shoulder. Behind them, the SIM started to squeal and wail, high-pitched feminine shrieks which shattered the ambience of the war-buckled depot as he pounded his fists against the ground in pure frustration.

"She died to save us," said Franco.

"I know that. But... I could never explain the bond between us. She was more human than human to me. I... loved her."

Franco nodded, knowing he did not have the words to ease Xakus's pain. Then he turned, and Olga approached. She pointed at the sky, through clouds of smoke. "The battle is growing close. It will be here soon. Then we know which sides fight, yes?"

"I think we have a bigger problem than that," said Knuckles.

"What's that, lad?"

The final, remaining HTank—which had shelled MICHELLE and given Justice D time to attack on foot with the IMS—revved its engines with a spurt of chemical exhaust. It had crept forward through the smoke, masked, hidden, overlooked. Closer and closer... until it stopped only a short distance from the group.

"Oh dear," said Olga, eyes wide. She cracked huge knuckles and squared herself. "Time to fight."

"Damn and bloody bugger! I forgot about that bloody badgering bastard!" Franco scrabbled in his pack for bombs as the HTank roared and charged, slamming and crunching through debris crushing and pounding and pulping everything under compressor tracks as huge twin guns turned, rotated, with an agonising precision to reveal twin black eyes locked on the group with a promise of violence and disintegration and death...

* * *

KEENAN CLIMBED THE ladder, rungs cold even through gloves. He reached the corrugated roof of the depot out-building, squinted through smoke, heard the rev of engines and sprinted with all his might, boots pounding the roof as the HTank sped below and he leapt, teeth grinding, fists clenched, landing on the HTank's hull in a crouch. He popped the pin from a BABE concussion grenade and dropped it through the open hatchway. There came a muffled *crack*. The HTank slewed sideways, missing the huddled gathering of vulnerable, shivering flesh, and grinding to a shuddering, juddering halt. The engine died. Keenan, crouched on the turret, glanced down at Franco who gave him a grim nod and thumbs up. Keenan aimed his MPK through the hatchway and bullets screamed, echoing and ricocheting in the HTank's belly. Smoke rolled up from the dark hatch. It stunk of death.

"I'm coming out!" The voice was gravelled, and filled with a heavy, guttural coughing.

Keenan took a backward step down the HTank's hull as the SIM appeared, bloody and tattered, torn and with one side of its semi-mechanical head caved in. Gore glistened, and blood had run out from beneath shattered mechanical eyes.

The SIM struggled out, and staggered across the hull of the HTank. It dropped to the floor, stumbled, and fell to its knees with Franco covering it with his Kekras.

Warily, Keenan leapt down into the HTank's interior, then reappeared. "It's clear."

Franco glanced at Xakus. "You want to kill it?"

"No."

"It helped murder... MICHELLE."

"I am a peaceful man," said Xakus, eyes filled with tears.

Franco lowered his gun, then leapt back as the SIM was suddenly slammed in half, the body sliding in two directions, melted flesh glowing, a cross-section of abdomen, bowel, spine, fat, flesh, all sliding and melding together to an accompanying aroma of roast pig.

Franco's head rose, slowly, to stare at Knuckles. The young lad's face was grim, tears on his cheeks streaking lines through smears of dirt. He held the IMS not quite pointing at the group.

"Drop the weapon, lad," said Franco, voice soothing.

"I had to kill it! It wanted us dead!"

"Sure you did, son." Franco moved forward, stepping over the slopped SIM corpse. He reached out, prised the IMS from Knuckles' knuckles, then glanced back at Keenan as Olga hurried forward to embrace the shivering child. Keenan nodded as a concept flickered between the two Combat K men—

Knuckles was a danger to himself, to the group, and to the mission. They needed to cut him free, but safely... The group dynamic had become too complex. And where they were going, deep into the heart of The Hammer Syndicate... well, they'd be lucky to walk out alive.

Franco moved to Knuckles. "Look at me, lad."

"Yes?" There was a snarl of defiance there; Franco smiled.

"You've proved yourself efficient. So I've got a job for you."

Knuckles' eyes narrowed. "You're getting rid of me."

"No lad. This is important."

"What do you want me to do?"

Franco eyed the approaching battle; he needed something to keep Knuckles occupied, to get him away from the battle and the huge concentration of zombies.

"We're heading for The Black Rose Citadel—NanoTek's HQ. But we can't infiltrate alone. There's a man, a Combat K man, Slick Guinness. You need to find him. Tell him what we're doing, explain about the corruption of the biomods. Tell him to round up any Combat K squaddies who still survive in The City—and to bring them to us, to The Black Rose. We'll need all the help we can get. Can you do that?"

"Where will I start?"

"I'll write down his address. Can you do this?"

"I can do it."

"Franco, why are you sending ze boy away?" scowled Olga. "He will die for sure!"

"No!" Franco glared at her. "You understand? We're heading to The Hammer Syndicate. And NanoTek. You've heard of those guys, right? And you'd want me to drag a ten-year-old into their lair?"

Olga nodded. She laid a hand on Knuckles' shoulder. "I will help him. I will take him to zis Slick Guinness. But I do it for you, Franco. Because you saved my life. Because I... have feelings for you."

"I am betrothed to another," croaked Franco.

"Still. I will wait for you. If it take eternity!"

Franco stared at her quivering bulk, and gave a weak smile. "Whatever you say, love."

An engine roared, and Franco glanced over to Keenan who'd hot-wired a Jeep 6X6. Fumes plumed from spluttering exhaust. Franco pointed to the vehicle. "Your transport."

Olga suddenly reached out, clasped Franco's cheeks between the iron grip of mighty hands, and planted a long and lingering kiss on his lips. Franco squirmed and grunted, kicking his legs as Olga lifted him from the ground, still kissing him, her eyes closed and mind lost in a faraway place of romance and pleasure. Then she dropped him, suddenly, and he hit the ground on his arse.

"Knuckles! Come! We have ze important mission, no?"

Knuckles saluted, giving Franco a lop-sided (and somewhat evil) grin, and followed his adopted matriarch to the Jeep. He turned then, staring at the three men, and the slow spinning battered PopBot. "I won't let you down," he said, and gave a single nod.

The group watched the mammoth figure of Olga reverse the Jeep with a clatter of crunching debris, and head off through rubble and smoke, heading away from the fast-approaching roar of battle.

An eerie veil descended through the smoke. Distantly, guns rattled. An explosion lit the underside of the clouds—and the sky suddenly ignited in a roaring sheet of flame, a nuclear umbilical between World and God.

"Will they be safe?" said Xakus, voice soft.

"Safer than with us," grunted Franco.

"That was a clever thing you did," said Cam, moving close to Franco. "You have probably saved both their lives. I doubt they will even find Slick Guinness; not in this insanity, this mess of a world. You have gone up in my estimation, Franco Haggis. You are a kind man. A man of honourable character."

"Bugger off, you little poisoned scrotum," said the old soldier, scowling.

"Also, I'm absolutely *certain* your plan had nothing to do with getting rid of a certain amorous member of the party."

Franco eyed the machine beadily. "I don't know what you mean. She chose to help him. She chose her own path."

"Olga would never have let Knuckles travel alone. And she had, on six previous occasions, shown signs of mothering the boy. It doesn't take a brain-box to work out the probable outcome of sending Knuckles on a mission."

"Like I said, I don't know what you mean."

The HTank roared into life, and Keenan popped from the hatch. "Time to move, guys. The BABE caused only superficial damage; this monster is still operational."

"Oh no," said Franco. "I remember what happened the *last* time you drove an HTank. You sent it over a cliff, all rolling down and smashing trees and ending up on its roof on top of a guard barracks! You were drunker than a skunk and singing a song about sausages!"

Keenan stared hard at Franco. "That was *you*, dickhead."

"So it was."

"Get in. And Franco?"

"Yeah boss?"

"Grab the IMS. We might need it later."

IN A DARK vault beneath the earth it waited, without power, without sense, without intelligence, without emotion, without instruction, without *focus*. It was one step away from death. Drowning and lost, deep below a catatonic state of sleep.

It rotated, a slow, aimless drifting on ionised currents which preserved its State.

There came a tiny, tiny *buzz*.

Voltage flowed through nano-circuits, rapidly expanding, rapidly accelerating until life and flow and instruction and need slammed the tiny machine and trillions of instructions slammed and it felt suddenly—

Alive.

A single pin-prick of light illuminated. White. Piercing.

#proximity series15000

#scanning perimeters... perimeters scanned OK loading files

#instructions received/ k5 integrate interface communications

#integrated received understood co-ordinates loading............

#uploaded all date structures OK

There was a low, deep grumble, like a minor earthquake. Inside the vault more pin-pricks of light glowed, and the hundreds, the *thousands* of machines illuminated one another in an eerie, eldritch witch-light.

#systems accelerating fully online OK
#sequences initiated; structures analysed
#destinations secured
#END.

Distantly, a door slid revealing light—and freedom. As one, the six thousand Detonation PopBots jostled and moved, lights blinking, feeding neatly out through the horizontal slot and speeding off up, into the sky, into the snow, into the night...

THE HTANK RUMBLED through long quiet streets and stopped, grinding stone to dust. The hatch opened, and Franco popped up like a mole from a hole, peering about myopically with his TRISPIES flickering through a myriad of different filters.

"Don't be seeing nuffink up here."

"The HTank's scanners work *fine*, Franco. Get back down."

"I'm just making sure," Franco said, testily.

"No, you're playing at being a superhero secret agent."

"Hey, there's nothing wrong with that! A man has to have his fantasy."

"I saw enough of your fantasies back at Porky Pauper's depot."

"What do you mean by that?"

"When Olga gave you that big snog."

"Hey, that was under *protest*."

"Didn't look that way to me."

"She grabbed my head! Lifted me off the ground! I kicked my little legs!"

"So what? From where *I* was standing, it looked like you were enjoying yourself."

"Get stuffed."

"Temper."

"I was *not* enjoying it."

"I'm sure you were using your tongue."

"I was *not* using my damned bloody tongue!"

"And I'm sure there was a little bit of trouser action going on."

"Meaning?"

"You know what I'm meaning. Down below."

"You think Olga's kiss *excited* me?"

"Certainly looked that way. Although maybe you were just twisted at a funny angle."

"I didn't get a hard-on, Keenan. That's slander, that is. I could have you sued. That's derogatory inflammation, mate."

"Franco, the only thing inflamed was your pants."

"I'll sue! I will! Don't push me! I'll sue!"

"You think you'd find a good zombie lawyer knocking around down here then, do you? Someone who could really get his *claws* into your case. Really get to use his *brain*."

"Very droll."

"Are you getting your arse down here, Franco, before a sniper picks you out as a big fat-headed peacock target? Gods lad, we're in the middle of a war zone!"

Franco dropped below, face sulky. Even Xakus was smiling at the exchange. The mood seemed to have lifted a little; an oasis in the midst of the storm. Cam spun close, and made a large sucking kissing slurping noise.

"I love to watch the course of true love."

"Bugger off."

"She'll be waiting for you," crooned Cam.

"I hope you rust."

"She'll never, ever stop loving you, baby."

"I hope you get *magnetised*."

"She'll hunt you to the ends of the earth!"

Franco swung a punch at Cam, but the PopBot described a neat swerve around swishing air. "Not catch me like that again, little Franco punchy. Oh no. I remember the *last time*."

"Yeah, well, you're just pissed because of the 'pub incident'."

"No. I'm just pissed because that's the way I *am*, it's hardwired into my motherboard, and you're the way *you* are, an annoying little midget with a comedy ginger beard, because you're a natural born muppet."

"Sticks and stones will break my bones."

"Hopefully," said Cam.

Keenan dropped some gears, and eased the HTank forward. Matrix drives hissed cold fusion and the machine crept through towering, darkened streets. Occasionally they passed groups of zombies, but none made a move to attack the HTank.

"Can't they smell us?" said Keenan. "Something's changed. The others were hell-for-leather bent on our extermination, HTank or no."

"Things are changing." Cam buzzed close to his ear. "These are the weak. The stragglers. The ones left behind."

Keenan stared at the PopBot. "Behind... from what?"

"The deviants seemed to have formed hierarchies. Groups. Armies. Maybe this is just a natural zombie selection, Kee. A kind of zombie evolution. Maybe these are simply the weak. Those left to die. Cannon fodder, yeah?"

"I know the feeling," said Keenan, who on several occasions had been abandoned by army 'officials'. *Expendable* was a word that tasted bad on his tongue. "So if we see a larger group of deviants, then they're the strong ones? The... selected?"

"It certainly looks that way."

"Shit. It's as if they're developing military habits."

"Freaky, isn't it?"

Keenan ploughed on, travelling several miles through deserted city streets filled with nothing more than corpses and debris. Black snow still tumbled, interjected by occasional rants of sleet and rain. The whole world, The City, seemed to be holding its breath. Waiting for something. Waiting for something *bad*.

As they closed on The Hammer Syndicate, they came upon a street of staggered, scattered, burning cars. The HTank eased through the fire, nosing blackened vehicles out of the way and grinding along, for another mile or so, before—following Franco's PAD directions—they entered a long, narrow, dark alleyway. Some kind of barricade had been erected at the far end. It was twenty feet high, made up of a teetering wall of cars interspersed with what appeared to be heavy industrial machinery.

Keenan's eyes flickered to his scanners... nothing. But then he *saw* them, a horde, silent and motionless, waiting beyond the jagged wall of steel and wood and iron and concrete.

"I see them, too," breathed Franco, leaning forward in his seat.

"They're not on the scanners, Cam." Keenan clicked in annoyance. "How the hell can that be?"

"I bet it's because they're dead," said Franco.

"Yes. No heat," said Cam. "They're the living dead. An HTank works on thermals."

"See!" beamed Franco. "I was right, I was. Bloody right! They don't call me Franco 'Mr Intuitive' Haggis for nothing, you know."

Keenan revved the HTank's engines. Fumes hissed from exhaust. "They don't call you that at all," he said quietly. "Cam, can you make out how many?"

"About..." the machine scanned with tiny clicks. "A thousand."

"Yeah? That many? Well, we need to get through. This is going to be damn messy."

"Let's hope they've no heavy artillery!" beamed Franco optimistically.

Beyond, the silence had risen through moans, risen in rapid steps to screams and howls and flames flickered leaping fast along the barricade in a sudden roar of ignition. Fifty foot sheets of fire *whooshed* into the air, orange and yellow and green, smashing windows in skyscrapers four storeys above. Glass tinkled down like crystal snow.

"What are they protecting?" muttered Keenan, revving the HTank again. Matrix engines hissed.

Several bullets whined through the dark, sending showers up the HTank's hull.

Cam spun for a few moments, clicking as he scanned. Then he said, voice low, "You're right, Keenan. They seem to be *protecting* an area. The zombies have formed a barricade in all the streets leading towards The Hammer Syndicate HQ."

"Why the hell would they do that? Why would they want to protect a *Syndicate,* of all things? They're the bloody criminals, aren't they? The bad guys!"

"I don't know," bubbled Franco, eyes rolling wild, "but I reckon we'll have some fun finding out!"

"Are you *insane?*"

Franco winked. And growled, "Better believe it."

"Hold on tight. We're going in."

"Be careful, Keenan." Cam's voice was a digital whisper, a bad feeling creeping over the machine. His scanners raged, sweeping back and forth over the barricade, the thousands of zombies and the heavy plant machinery embedded in the burning, roaring wall. Something was wrong. He could feel it in his silicon.

"We have no choice, my friend."

Keenan revved the HTank hard and with a grinding of teeth, slammed the massive, brutal twin-gun tank in a belching charging advance, forward... a screaming push towards the burning barricade and the thousands of howling, chanting, gun-toting deviants beyond.

At the last moment, Cam's scanners slammed him. His digital soul paled. And Cam *saw it*...

Death.

Waiting for them.

"No!" screamed Cam, but his voice was lost in the roar of the HTank's charge.

CHAPTER 12
DETONATION BOULEVARD

THE HTANK SLEWED at the last moment, turning sideways with a shower of sparks and showering concrete, to cannon into the wall of burning cars and metal. Deep clangs sang. The wall rocked, teetering dangerously. Fire rained down like burning hail.

Beyond, the zombies let out a massive roar, deep and reverberating and impossibly choreographed. It was as if they had a hive mind.

Through the HTank's thick, armoured walls, Keenan, Franco and Xakus felt the terrible heat of the raging inferno.

"What is it, dickhead?" snapped Franco, scowling at the bobbing machine. Sweat rolled down his face and dripped from his ginger beard. "We was about to have us a slurry when you went all screamy like a little girl!"

"Well, let me think," snapped back Cam. "Maybe it's two things. Maybe on the one hand it's the fact I've just located the old disused tunnel system that will lead us *beneath* the zombies without having to crush hundreds of potential humans under heavy HTank tracks. After all, they were once *like you*, and loathe as I am to admit it, *related* to you in a deviated and evolutionary kind of way."

"And the second reason?"

Despite the dark interior of the HTank, despite the confined space and despite the smell from Franco's sandals, it seemed as if Cam was grinning. "Ahh. That would be the modest yield atomic weapon I've just pin-pointed at the centre of the barricade. Which would, no-doubt, be triggered into detonation by something heavy, for the sake of argument shall we say an *HTank,* attempting to ram its way through."

"Good reason," said Franco, beaming. "Well done that PopBot. Congratulations. Seriously!"

"Well, they don't call me Cam 'Clever Bastard' PopBot for nothing, you know."

"Hey hey! I see what you did there! You clever little bugger."

"Charming, Franco. You are a true gentleman."

Keenan tore a hole in the nearest wall turning the HTank about, and powered back down the alley-way trailing bricks and with howling zombies roaring after them and sending bullets screaming from juddering hot-barrels. They seemed disappointed.

Cam directed Keenan, and with difficulty he negotiated the thumping, grinding HTank towards a nearby underground subway entrance. The HTank, squealing and sparking, dropped its nose and squeezed down a set of steep narrow steps amidst dust and a shower of rubble, and to the tinkling soundtrack of ceramic wall-tiles, bashed free to shatter against steelconcrete.

The HTank descended, entered a wall of darkness, turned left, then right, bright lights slashing out to cut a hole from the night pie. It descended, warily, down yet more steps with tracks grinding and squealing and concrete crumbling all around. They came to a set of aero-escalators, and the HTank ploughed on through, and down, destroying bubbles and rubber and grinding a huge curl of safety rail before it emerged in a shower of dragging sparks and flapping rubber.

In the confines of the cab, Franco hunkered down, peering at the control screens. "Watch that wall, Keenan," he said. He chewed his lip thoughtfully. "And that escalator there *don't hit it!* Shit man, you bloody buggering well hit it. Just watch where you're going *I said watch where you're going* shit man you nearly took out a cooling tower and that could have drowned us *and* you keep smacking into brick walls and that's just sloppy driving that is. *Watch out!*"

"What?"

"That, there."

"What, where?"

"*That!*" squeaked Franco.

Keenan halted, easing free of the accelerator, the HTank rumbling around him, and turned in his chair. He stared hard at Franco's innocent face.

"*What?*"

"Shut up, dickhead."

"I was just trying to help."

"Well, you're not."

"You *do* keep hitting things."

"The fucking HTank is wider than the fucking tunnel. What do you expect?"

"I bet *Pippa* wouldn't hit anything."

"Just shut up, you damn dribbling backseat driver."

Franco, ruffled, scratched his beard. "Well," he huffed, "I know when *I'm* not wanted."

"Really? Well you never take the hint."

The HTank ground on, lower and lower beneath the city streets. Eventually it levelled onto a platform and Keenan pulled a lever, drawing the ponderous vehicle to a shuddering halt. He slipped the hatch, popped his head into the stale, musty air of the deserted train system. He shivered as a super-chilled breeze flooded him. The place felt... ancient; desecrated, like a violated tomb.

He gazed around in the stagnation, looking carefully at moss-infested tiled walls, damp-blackened peeling posters, rotting, sagging timber benches; the place was a ghost shell, a relic of an ancient abandoned world. There were old posters for books, films, concerts, all caught in the stark glow of the HTank's lights. It was like stepping into the past. Keenan shivered again, dropping back into the relative comfort of the HTank.

"It's a dead world out there," said Franco.

Keenan nodded. "The whole city's dead. Well, undead."

Franco shivered. "Gives me the heebie jeebies."

"Franco, *everything* gives you the heebie jeebies."

"Yeah, well, that's because I'm a sensitive guy."

The HTank juddered forward, through the black, through the silence, and Keenan eased it down towards the abandoned rails where once, a millennium ago, underground trains thundered. "Cam, you sure this train system is dead?"

"I'm sure. Dead as a donut."

"You're absolutely *positive* now? I don't want to end up with two thousand tonnes of train up my arse when we're stuck out in No Man's Land. You hear?"

Cam, rotating with a gentle flicker of condescending orange lights, snorted, "*Trust me,* Keenan. I'm a GradeA+1 Security Mechanism with advanced SynthAI and a Machine Intelligence Rating (MIR) of 3450. I have integral weapon inserts, a quad-core military database, and Put Down™ War Technology! You think I don't *know* when there's a damn train due? This place has been deserted for a thousand years! All the DBs say so. And anyway, we only have to travel a few klicks. Should only take us five minutes."

Keenan nodded. He eased the HTank around, and with a giant *clunk*, down onto ancient rusted tracks. The aged metal squealed beneath the HTank. Keenan eased the vehicle away from the platform, and into the tunnel opening.

Like a hungry mouth, it swallowed them.

"I CAN SMELL FIRE."

Keenan glanced at Franco. "You sure?"

"Yeah."

"Since when did you train as a sniffer dog?"

"Trust me, Keenan, I can smell *fire!* It's behind us. It's approaching fast."

"What, you mean, approaching fast? Like a *train?*"

Franco shrugged, and cast a glance at Cam. "Ask Mr MIR 3450 over there."

"I assure you, there's nothing moving on these tracks."

Keenan had slowed the HTank, and suddenly realised that was a *bad* idea. He accelerated again, the lumbering behemoth pounding down the lines which weaved, gently left, then right; an underground umbilical from dead mother to abandoned abortion.

Something trembled. They felt it, rippling through the HTank's chassis.

Keenan shot Franco a glance.

Franco shrugged, as if to say, *Hey, who am I to argue with a PopBot?*

Gradually, over the heavy rumbling of the HTank, a noise intruded at the seams of hearing. It was metallic, insect-like, a constant, ululating low-level scream. Keenan glanced at the rear visual scanners. Behind them, glimpsed then lost on a bend, he saw a glow of orange.

"Cam," snapped Keenan, "Franco's right. There is something behind us. On the tracks. On fire. Remind me of your promise?"

"I guarantee," began Cam. But stopped. On the screen for all to see, and advancing rapidly towards them at a frightening speed, came a train, but not any normal train, this was an underground passenger *juggernaut.* It was massive, a blazing inferno of fire and pumping smoke which filled the tunnel, sucked along by its own mammoth burning vacuum. At the helm, at the train's controls, tiny behind cracked and ribbed plasti-glass, were five or six screaming, wild-eyed zombies.

"Aiee!" said Franco.

Keenan slammed the HTank's controls, and the vehicle lurched, accelerating on matrix with a howl of churning power. The train slammed at them, a glowing fireball, its elongated, pointed snout reaching out to touch their tail as they hurtled down the lines in sudden raging competition.

"We should have turned the HTank's guns before we entered the tunnel!" wailed Franco. "We could have blasted it!"

"Too late for that," snapped Keenan. Sweat glowed on his brow. He kept one eye ahead, one on the screen. The juggernaut train bumped them, sending the HTank careering wildly and scraping a scree of sparks from the wall. Bricks detached, flew off, bounced against the flaming train's hull.

"Two klicks ahead," said Cam, voice cool. "Our exit point."

"Not at this speed," snarled Keenan. "It's too close! We'd never get off the tracks!"

They hammered, a close convoy, the flaming passenger juggernaut howling like a banshee as it bore down on the—by comparison—miniaturised HTank. Fire roared. Somewhere, a detonation rocked the tunnel, deep down, a bass concussion the Combat K squaddies felt through their feet and stomachs.

"Don't like the sound of that," muttered Franco.

Keenan reached out, grabbed a digital lever, and pulled. It moved on slick gears. Before them, the HTank's twin guns started to lift, rising with hydraulic, ratchet thumps until...

"It'll hit the roof!" wailed Cam.

The guns ploughed into the tunnel roof and bricks exploded outwards, back in a stream of violent smashing destruction. The HTank slowed, its guns yammering, juddering, buckling, but the fire-billowing train slammed them with a violent jolt urging them on as the HTank's armour screamed and buckled, caught between the impaling guns and the force of the ploughing train. But the more the train pushed, the more the HTank's guns smashed through bricks and concrete above, screaming and growling, steel mashing bricks which flooded behind in an accelerating stream until...

The tunnel's roof collapsed.

With a roar like the ending of worlds a flood of debris slammed down, instant, flattening, impacting everything under the weight of billion-tonne buckling skyscrapers above. The train was caught by its mid-section, yanked to a sudden halt like a dog on a leash which sent the piloting zombies smashing and bouncing around the cockpit in a blender of living dead organics. The HTank, drunk, slewed ahead, bouncing from tunnel walls and slowing to a limping, buckled, squeaking halt as all around them the roar of collapsing tunnel boomed, and howled, and gradually, like a retreating, growling tsunami, subsided.

Keenan slammed open the hatch, lifted himself free, and jumped down to the tracks. Smoke and dust drifted over him. A roaring continued, muffled, as above an entire tower block shifted and realigned—sitting back and down on its haunches as it crushed the flaming passenger train in staggered compression crunches.

Franco hopped, yowling, across the red-hot hull of the HTank, his sandals poor protection against glowing metal. He dropped to the ground, scowling back at Keenan. Then he glanced ahead, perhaps twenty feet, where the platform—and their exit—waited patiently. Franco stared at the destroyed HTank, fully a half of its former length, its hull unrecognisable as a war machine. Its guns were buckled, cracked, glowing hot from their intimate integration with the tunnel's roof. The HTank groaned, and with a sigh of escaping gas and spurting hydraulic fluid, squatted down on its arse like a dying metal dinosaur.

"That brought the roof down," grunted Franco.

"As you can see," Keenan pointed at the platform, "we will be disembarking in one minute. If sir would like to step onto the platform? I'm sure Cam will escort us promptly from this *trap.*"

"Very neat, Keenan, very neat. Just don't milk it, lad. Nobody likes a smart arse. Reet?"

Franco led an ashen, coughing Xakus towards the platform. Cam followed, but Keenan gave a whistle—as one would to a dog.

Cam rotated; his black shell remained the same, but Keenan could tell he'd managed to irritate the Pop-Bot. He smiled, a grim baring of compressed teeth.

"I am not a canine," said Cam, testily.

"I thought you said there were *no* trains."

"Ha! What I *actually said* was that the lines had been deserted for a thousand years."

Keenan thumbed the wreckage, and the growling wall of collapsed tunnel behind. Dust was settling, making the raging inferno hazy and surreal. "You call that deserted?"

"Tsch Keenan, don't you think you're being a little picky?"

"Getting fifteen thousand tonnes of flaming engine up our jackass is being picky?"

"I cannot attest for every eventuality. An eternity crystal ball, I am not."

"Damn right," snapped Keenan, striding onto the platform and towards the skewed, buckled steps where Franco had wrenched free a rusted gate, which lolled on broken hinges, squeaking forlorn. "But you're certainly a ball. As in, a *testicle.*"

Keenan disappeared.

Cam surveyed the wreckage, his tiny AI mind whirring like precision clockwork.

"How rude," he said.

THE NIGHT AIR was chilling as they emerged. Green veins lit the clouds turning the sky into solid onyx. "Whats' the hell's going on with the weather system?" growled Franco.

Keenan shrugged. "The zombies have taken control. Could be anything. Who knows how a deviant's mind works. Well, maybe you have a vague idea."

"Listen Keenan. About this word. This Z word."

"Zombie?"

"Aye. I don't think we should use it."

"Why not? They look like fucking zombies to me."

"No no, it's more, well," he shuddered, "the more we see of them, the more I think of them, well, to be frank, I'm getting more and more uncomfortable killing them." He eyed Keenan beadily. "They were human, right? Deviated and mashed out of all recognition, I'll give you that, but still human at the core. And, if all this shit is down to biomods, then one day they might just get changed back. Zombie just seems the wrong word to use."

Keenan slapped him on the back. "Shall we call them *accidents*? Will that make you happy?"

Franco brightened. "Yeah. That's better."

"This got anything to do with Mel?"

Franco nodded. "I'm missing her, mate. I never thought a woman would get to me like this. I thought I was Mr Testosterone, a proper hero in tights, flitting like a star-struck magpie from one dangerous love tryst to the next."

Keenan stared hard. "You need some tablets, mate?"

"Aye, aye, I'll have one in a minute. What I'm trying to say, is, Melanie came to check my taxes, and I ended up wanting to marry her. It's a funny old world, ain't it?"

"She's a tax collector?"

Franco nodded. "Yeah. Why? What's wrong with that?"

Keenan grinned. "Oh. Nothing. I just thought, well, I thought you'd never paid any taxes."

"I haven't."

"And she's still alive?"

"That's the funny thing," said Franco. "Once I fell in love with her, I no longer wanted to blow off her head and bury her in a shallow grave. Call me Mr Old Fashioned, but that's just the way I am."

"So, you have used the L word then?"

"Shit. So I did." He reddened.

Keenan patted Franco kindly. "Take your tablets, there's a good lad."

Cam, who had headed off into the black to reconnoitre, emerged from the gloom trailing smoke. "It's up ahead," he said. "And by God, this Hammer Syndicate Tower is big. And not quite... *normal*."

"Not quite normal?" Franco's ear pricked up. "What's that supposed to mean?"

"Like you, Franco, it has to be seen to be believed. Follow me."

They trooped after Cam, Franco muttering in annoyance and hoisting heavy Kekras in gloved fists ready for any contact. He noticed Xakus starting to fall behind, and turning, dropped back to walk beside the ageing professor.

"You're doing well, old man."

Xakus smiled a weak smile, face ashen, eyes dulled. "This quest is taking its toll on me. I am not a soldier, Mr Haggis. I am not a warrior, not a fighter."

"But you built MICHELLE."

"She was not, primarily, designed for war, although I acknowledge it could look that way. I built her out of love, Mr Haggis. Love. But I find, worryingly, in this day and age one has to be able to protect oneself. Sadly, MICHELLE could not even do that."

"She died for a noble cause," said Franco.

"What? Discovering the root of this deviant problem? Helping to translate the junk's SinScript? No, I don't think so. You people, you could never understand MICHELLE. To you she was just some faceless, stony, emotionless terminator machine. But to me... I could see inside her, see the beauty within the mesh, the love within the shell." He stuttered to a halt, overcome by emotion.

They were walking down a narrow, roofed tunnel created from derelict buildings, their pace slow, wary, observant. The warzone had mutated. Ahead, Keenan halted and crouched beside a tangle of sharpwire, gun to his cheek, eyes roving, picking out every tiny detail. Like a machine he missed nothing. This was his environment. His world. Whether he acknowledged it, or not.

"It wasn't your fault," said Franco.

Xakus turned tortured eyes on him. "Oh but it was. I gave her life. And because of me, that life was taken. I killed her, Mr Haggis. I killed my true love as sure as putting a gun to her head and pulling the trigger."

Shit, thought Franco, rolling his eyes. And they think I'm mad!

Keenan turned, staring at Franco. "Seems we've a long way to go to find Mel. This is no simple infil."

Franco crouched, looking out across a field of sharpwire, towards—

"Wow," he said, and he meant it.

The Hammer Syndicate HQ rose for three hundred storeys, its matt-black, rippling, undulating edifice like nothing the Combat K men had ever witnessed.

"That's not a building, it's a bloody dildo!" snapped Franco.

"More importantly, how do we get in?" Keenan searched his friend's face.

"More importantly, do we *want* to get in?"

Keenan hissed, "She's your missus, mate. If you want to rescue her, you have to get inside that damn place. You work it out."

"How the buggering bugger am I supposed to do that?"

"That's where I come in," said Xakus, crouching beside them. He seemed suddenly infused with energy. His eyes had grown bright after their previous dullness; his face was ruddy, as if excitement coursed his veins. "This is an organotower."

"An orgasm *what?*" said Franco.

"No. A tower, formed of living semi-sentient over-stretched molecules. It's like a giant vegetable."

Franco stared at Xakus with incredulity. With care, he finally said, "Is that the best the bloody Hammer Syndicate could afford?"

"You don't understand. I'm not talking carrots and potatoes here; it's an organic material from the Triclux System; an alien, if you will. It has incredible resistant armoured properties, and the benefit of being self-rejuvenating."

"So a building that heals itself," muttered Keenan.

"Yes."

"But," persisted Franco, "ultimately, it's an alien vegetable. Right?"

"Yes."

"How come I've never heard of it? I've walked these mean city streets for years. I mean, a vegetable dildo, the size of a tower block! I'd have noticed! It's, um, something that would have caught my attention, I'm sure."

"This unit is very rare, very expensive, and the Hammer Syndicate don't advertise its uniqueness. You note the surrounding sharpwire of No Man's Land? The whole structure lies under a shimfield. Move a few metres away, you won't see it due to visual pressure waves."

"It's still a damn comedy vegetable," said Franco. "Can't we just take a peeler to it? Flush the bastards out that way?"

"I think you'll find it's a *little* more complex," said Xakus. "Cam, can you clear us a path through the sharpwire?"

"It will take but a few moments," said Cam. He sounded smug. "After all, I have a new-found advanced military status. I am, in fact..."

"Get on with it, gonad," snapped Franco.

"Your rudeness has reached cosmic proportions."

Cam eased ahead, spinning slowly, scanning, clicking. Then, low to the ground, he shot towards the organic wire and there was a soft *snap*. Coils sprang up, encompassing Cam for a moment. At the core, Cam *glowed*, a miniature sun, a mobile fusion reactor, and the sharpwire melted into molten droplets. Cam sped on, wire leaping up around him as he cleared them a path through the highly dangerous toxic deterrent.

"Ain't nothing organic getting through that," said Franco, in a grim and horrified awe.

"Reminds me of that thing we met. In the bunker on Terminus5. The Tangled." Keenan's eyes were hooded, unreadable.

"A similar technology," said Xakus, standing and heading out after Cam. His boots crackled on crisped strands of *dead* sharpwire. "Only this is more benign. It has no advanced AI elements like a coil of Tangled."

"You know your stuff," said Keenan.

"I used to work for NanoTek," said Xakus. "I did my bit of synthetic intelligence programming, bio-molecular engineering and artificial cell structuring. I know my control theory from my probability; my fuzzy systems from my hybrid neuroscience." He smiled a bitter smile. "You could say I'm something of an expert. That's why you brought the SinScript to me. That's why we're going to decode the son of a bitch up there."

"They have the technology?"

"There is a likelihood," said Xakus. "Hammer has always had a close relationship with NanoTek. They scratch one another's scabby backs, if you get my meaning."

"But this *is* an amoral syndicate, right?" said Franco. "I presume their relationship is financial?"

"Isn't every relationship?" said Xakus. "There is also the option that Hammer Syndicate are in on the biomod hacking business. The pirates and the coders, hey? They'd need serious bank-rolling to undercut NanoTek. And yes, NanoTek would like us to think it was some backstreet small-scale operation, some bedroom genius, because that way less people would trust the hacked biomods. Well, let me tell you, a biomod takes a lot of cracking. That could also be one reason why these people have taken Melanie. There's something different about her zombification. Something unique. Maybe their hackers want to examine her nanobots? Maybe Hammer Syndicate is on the brink of *war* with NanoTek."

"An interesting concept," said Keenan, voice cool. "Which would mean the Syndicate are stabbing NanoTek in the back, and using NanoTek's money to finance a planned coup d'état?" He scratched his chin in thought. Then grinned. "I love it when the big boys play rough. Let's hope you're right."

Cam, dripping hot runs of melted sharpwire, had reached a safe spot across the No Man's Land leading to the organotower. Keenan and Franco, running low and with weapons ready, set off across rough ground; a few steps behind, still wary of the destroyed biological menace, Xakus followed.

They stopped at the base of the tower. Cam positively *glowed* with pride.

"I bet they know we're here," said Franco, one Kekra against his cheek, his eyes scanning the seemingly deserted ground before him. Distantly, seen through a haze of debris and darkness and barricades, deviated humans patrolled with an almost clockwork rhythm.

"I guarantee it," growled Keenan. "After all, it was a polite invite." He took free his cigarette case, took a moment to roll some Widow Maker, then lit the bedraggled cigarette, breathing deep on fresh pollutant.

"Isn't this an inopportune moment for a smoke?" suggested Xakus, glancing up the sheer wall of the tower which rose, undulating, above them. Something was happening above. Slick orifices were beginning to open high up on the vegetative walls; Franco pulled a face of pure disgust.

"I'm facing the possibility of extinction," said Keenan. His face was grim, now. Set. "I can't think of a better time for a smoke."

"How do we get in?" said Franco, eyeing the puckering orifices high up the slick oily wall. They were making tiny slurping, kissing sounds.

"You're not going to like it."

Franco eyed Xakus, his face narrowing. "No more damn arse pipes, I hope."

"Not... exactly," whispered Xakus.

The orifices above suddenly disgorged huge, tuber-like limbs which thumped down with terrific force on the ground the group had recently crossed. They were long, slick, black, gleaming, narrow-stemmed appendages ending in flared, pulsing snouts, raw pink and sphincter-like in appearance. The limbs emerged with a sudden bursting energy, three, five, ten of them, flailing out above the group in apparent randomness like some panic-stricken octopus, before flopping through the air and slamming down against the earth with heavy, sodden booms.

Franco, covering his head, screeched, "What the hell's going on?"

"Cam destroyed the sharpwire. He's triggered the organotower's natural vegetative defence mechanism."

A limb flailed past, a breeze of proximity causing Franco's beard to ruffle. He scowled, aware he was within inches of having his head knocked clean off. "You call that a defence mechanism?"

"Looks pretty good to me," snarled Keenan. He turned to Xakus. "We climbing inside one?"

"You catch on fast," said Xakus.

"Hey, hang on a minute!" said Franco, "I ain't climbing up no more tubes, pipes, snouts or anal passageways. Are we clear on that? A man can only take so much anal abusage."

"Well stay here then, and let Mel suffer."

Keenan, with head low but eyes lifted, eased forward. Above, the limbs flailed. Xakus joined him, and pointed to where one swinging, flailing limb emerged from a puckering, sphincter mouth in the tower wall. "You see the bulge, high up? It's a nerve centre. Put a bullet in there and it'll be paralysed for a few moments. Enough time for us to climb in, I think. The limbs are hollow."

Keenan nodded and sighted down the MPK. A single shot cracked, and the limb fell to earth with a dull *thud*. Keenan bared his teeth, staring at the quivering, twitching mass of pink lips; it looked like an electrocuted vagina.

"After you, Professor."

Xakus crawled with care to the stunned vegetable flesh, and with slurps and squelches, eased back layers of what appeared to be human skin. Franco shivered, close beside Keenan.

"A man shouldn't have to go through this."

"What?"

"All this crawling around in tubes and stuff. A man has his dignity, y'know?"

"I thought you lost all *your* dignity back in the whorehouses, the bars and the prisons?"

Franco puffed out his chest. "What? Me? Listen, they don't call me Mr Franco 'Moral Fibre' Haggis for nothing, pal. A man has his morals, right? His standards. A man has his, y'know," he twitched, "sanity to think about. And crawling around in anal pipes and suchforth is just too much like a dodgy pulp SF novel. I shall complain, I shall."

"Oh, you shall, shall you?"

Xakus's kicking feet disappeared. The lips of the vegetative tube squelched shut. Jelly glistened. The flaps quivered like an epileptic vulva. Keenan nudged Franco. "This is us."

"Bugger!"

"Just imagine something erotic." Keenan grinned with his teeth. "After all, some of the shit you programmed in Immersion Consoles defies belief."

"Pippa went wild, didn't she?"

Keenan nodded. Sighed. "Yeah mate. She did." He shook his head. "Come on. Mel is waiting. I'm sure she won't mind you molesting a giant alien vegetable suction dildo in the name of true love."

Keenan parted the lips, and a stench of rotting cabbage washed over him. He nearly gagged; holding his breath, he took the weight of the heavy flaps and crawled inside.

Franco, kneeling, ducked as another live limb whooshed over his head. He stared around, eyes wide in disbelief, as distant machine gun chatter sang a metal symphony. "How can the same shit happen to the same guy twice? Huh?" He pulled free a small white tub, popped the cap, and eyed the rainbow pill. He pushed it into his mouth, where it sat under his tongue, slowly dissolving.

"Into the Lion's Pussy," he whispered, and lifting the cabbage-reeking flaps, he held his breath, squinted his eyes, tensed his muscles, and slipped, and struggled, inside.

FOR A FEW moments Franco fought with slippery veg flesh. He kicked and scrambled, clawed and fought his way into a tight black pouch. He glanced up—at where Keenan, with a tiny torch, grinned down at him. "I thought this would be right up your particular back alley."

"Get to fuck, Keenan."

They climbed, using ridges of vegetable-strand muscle as handholds. The tube was greasy to the touch, like a slick, ribbed onion, like crawling inside a hollowed leek. It was dark, despite the needle beams from torches, and the tentacle gave regular shudders as if threatening a revival that would surely kill them.

Franco tried hard not to vomit as he climbed. It wasn't just the stench, but the globs of purple jelly which rolled down the interior of the tubular walls, sliming over his hands and face, pooling on his shaved head and in his beard, covering him with an afterbirth of vegetable semen. But, to Franco, most disgustingly of all, the jelly pooled over his hairy, sandaled feet, squelched between his toes, tickling the undersides of his paws and making him slip and slide within the violated sanctuary of his own footwear. Franco *hated* his feet being touched, tickled or mauled. Not by human, not by alien, and certainly not by drooling vegetable pus.

They climbed; for what seemed an eternity.

It was a very long way up.

Franco mumbled profanity all the way.

With a final, tremendous grunt, which came not without sexual comedy merit, Franco slopped over what appeared to be a tiny volcanic mound and onto a rib- and muscle-ringed floor. It was pink, with gnarled green crusty knobbles, all gleaming. Franco lay, panting, shining under his coating of jelly and staring about with undisguised raw hatred.

"Damn that vegetable spunk slime," said Franco, face puckered, voice forlorn.

"Come on," snapped Keenan. "We've got a job to do." His weapon was slimed, his WarSuit also slimed; damn, even his EBH was coated with natural vegetable gunk.

Xakus, by some unwritten agreement, led the way. Unarmed, however. Keenan stayed by his shoulder, Techrim in one fist, MPK in the other, face grim. Franco, as ever, took the rear and squelched along miserably muttering obscenity after profanity after obscenity in the hope of a vegetable exorcism.

Xakus paused, dropping to one knee.

"Everything good?"

"Yes. These lower tunnels and caverns are the organotower's foundation structure; what gives it the ability to grow and regenerate, and also support the heavy bone tower chassis above."

"You sound like you know the place well," muttered Franco.

"I've seen the genetic blueprints," said Xakus curtly. "Taking this tower from its homeworld was not something with which I ethically agreed. I have a moral standpoint, you understand?"

Franco nodded, shuddering.

They moved on, through endless quivering tunnels which sometimes spilled into large caverns filled with slime and slop. On several occasions all three men retched, kneeling in the corridor and vomiting so hard they cried as blasts and waves of thick cabbage odour swamped them with a semi-poisonous gassing.

"Nice place you brought us to, Keenan."

"You've got sick in your beard."

"Damn and bloody blast!"

"Anyway, we're here to rescue *your* fiancée. It could be argued it's *your* damn fault."

"Have a heart!" said Franco, but Keenan was being sick again and Franco soon joined him.

Gradually, they left the lower bowels of the organotower and climbed a series of spiral staircases made of what appeared human, or animal, bone. Franco halted, halfway up, and fingered the smooth ivory surface.

"Definitely feels like bone to me," he announced. "How the hell does a vegetable grow bones?"

Xakus smiled a sick smile. "The organotower is a kind of alien genetic construction; and just because it's vegetable, doesn't mean it's a herbivore."

Franco stared hard. Realisation dripped like honey into his pill-addled brain. "You mean... you mean *it eats people*?"

"Digests is a better word. It has no mouth."

"And you brought us *inside*, you madman?"

"I was under the impression," said Xakus, voice tight, black features scowling in the eerie gloom, "that *you* brought *me* here; that you needed my help. I'm just a guide. A translator. A decoder. For the good of mankind, right? Help the war effort against the junks?" He laughed. "Damn that bastard Steinhauer. He's got me by the balls."

"I never did ask why you were helping," said Keenan, watching Xakus in the limited light provided by torches. Around them, organic walls filled with strips of muscle pulsated. Beneath their boots sat the reconstituted bone of the digested unfortunate.

"Let's just say I owe Steinhauer my life. He stopped NanoTek from... well, that's another story. A story of betrayal, blackmail and espionage." Xakus laughed. It was filled with bitterness. "You've always got to ask yourself the question, Keenan. Who do you trust?"

"I trust no man."

"I learnt that lesson the hard way. Come on. It gets more civilised above. Unfortunately, that also means we'll have company."

"The Syndicate?"

Xakus smiled. "That would be a reasonable assumption. And they'll be armed."

Franco cocked his Kekras. "Good. I'm sick of killing *unfortunate accidents* whose only crime was sucking the wrong pill at the wrong time. I want me some *real* payback."

"You know where they'll be keeping Mel?"

"Where else? Voloshko's Bedroom."

"Bedroom?" Franco frowned. "What do you mean, his bedroom? I don't like the sound of that!"

Xakus scratched at his matted hair. "Let's just say Voloshko is renowned for his... *esoteric* tastes."

KEENAN AND FRANCO crouched, waiting. The heat had increased to furnace level, and sweat poured from the men mingled with vegetable juice and dribbles of hardening vomit. There came a heavy, rhythmical bass sound from up ahead.

Cam disappeared, scouting ahead in an attempt to find Voloshko and *"to assess the level of threat for purposes of health and safety"*.

Xakus, who had called the halt, back-tracked to Combat K. He was shaking his head. "We can't go on."

"Why not?"

"It's too dangerous."

"Nothing's too dangerous for the men of Combat K!" beamed Franco. He pushed forward, eager. "Let me see!"

With Keenan by his elbow, Franco advanced. The floor was slippery with green jelly and a slime of organic dribble. Suddenly, the floor fell away into a large cavern supported by huge bones—what looked like giant *ribs*. However, it was the sight below that churned their stomachs.

"Is that what I think it is?" said Keenan softly.

Franco nodded. "It is." He blinked. Shivered. "It's... It's a... it's a fucking *disco.*"

Both men stared at the strange, sobering sight. Other than the encompassing bass rhythm it was a silent disco filled with ambling, bumping, aimlessly meandering zombies. Not hundreds of them, but *thousands.* They filled the chamber, packed tight, occasionally giving low moans as they squeezed past one another or nudged aimlessly and repeatedly at other zombies, or the walls, or the supporting bone columns. Above, coloured lights whirled and spun, strobe-lights giving short machine-gun bursts of white to turn the scene into a *rave, man, a fuckin' rave. Mad for it!* Franco and Keenan stared at one another, then back down to the insane spectacle arraigned before them. Suddenly, there came a *crackle* as music blared out, reverberating deafeningly throughout the chamber. It was Ronan Keating's *Life is a Rollercoaster.* Ronan was one of rock's *Eternals.* Like Cliff Richard, and Elvis, he would never die, down and down through millennia, songs reissued, rerecorded, repackaged and supporting the H-section undercarriage of popular contemporary music. Franco groaned. "I tell you, Keenan, even in a zombie-infested pit-disco inside an anal vegetable bowel-pit, you can't get away from Ronan." Bizarrely, the zombies started to amble faster, a kind of enlarged version of Brownian motion jiggling in their disco squalor amidst millions of whirling, coloured lights and zaps from the starship-sized strobe flickers. Franco felt himself going light headed. Quite *insane.* But then again, that might have been the drugs. Or lack of.

"What a *hell*zone," said Franco, voice hushed in awe.

"I don't know, it looks quite interesting."

"What, the brain-dead living-dead rotting-dead bopping to an insane tune with no sense of style, rhythm or élan?" Franco considered this. "Actually mate, you might be right. What concerns me, however, is how we get across. Any ideas, bro'?"

Keenan watched as a fight broke out, and three zombies bore another deformed biomod victim to the ground. They bit free his face, black blood arcing and dribbling, then fed on his brains until nothing more than a bone-ringed empty fruit-husk of a skull remained. The triumphant, and now partially-fed, zombies howled, lifting gnarled and broken hands in the air and drooling blood and mucus and gore. A cackle roared around the disco like discharging static, and several zombies attacked other zombies, feeding and drooling and caving in skulls to feed on the brains of their half-dead horribly deformed comrades.

"I'm going to be sick," said Franco.

"Yeah," nodded Keenan, "Ronan has that effect on me as well."

"There's no way across," said Xakus, appearing suddenly behind the two men and nearly getting a bullet in his brain for his trouble. He eyed the four barrels of Franco's Kekra, an inch from his nose, thoughtfully. "Franco, tell me you've got the safety switch on?"

"Nope. That would be silly."

"Doesn't a Kekra have a hairline trigger?"

"Yep."

"So you nearly blew my head clean off?"

"Yep." Franco leered at him. "So don't fucking sneak up on me, OK? Or I'll never find Mel, and brains are so *damned hard* to clean off the matt finish of a Kekra's quad barrel. You have to scrub and scrub for ages. You have to use a pan-scrub, and detergent, and *everything*. OK?"

"I hear you, Franco. Loud and clear." He stared at the milling zombies. It could be argued their aimless movements were a close approximation of any disco atrocity. Only zombies had an excuse. They were brain-dead mutations.

Xakus ran a hand through his white, frizzled hair. "This could explain why we've met so little resistance. I would suspect an organisation as powerful as The Hammer Syndicate of using biomods to enhance a lot of its employees. They certainly had the financial backing. So…"

"So when the shit hit the fan, and the biomods deformed their hosts, the deviation took the majority of the Syndicate's staff with it?" Keenan rubbed his stubbled chin. "Sounds possible. That's *if* it was the biomods. But I thought Hammer had something to do with the cracking and pirating? Providing a service to the No-Creds of The City?"

"Yes. But Hammer didn't expect the deviation. That came from… somewhere else. There's something *not quite right* here. The puzzle doesn't quite fit."

As they were talking, Keenan had been analysing the surroundings. He gestured with his MPK. "There's a way across." Keenan's voice was soft, face thoughtful. "Up there."

"Amongst the rigging?" Franco stared at him. "Are you mad? Amongst the lights and the strobes? Amongst the wires and the cabling? It's not designed to take somebody of my," he patted his rotund belly, "*advanced* metabolic stature."

"Look at the bolting on the mesh." Keenan scratched his chin. "It'll hold."

"Have you done a Risk Assessment?"

Keenan's scowl sank below contempt. Then he leant forward, staring down at the spiral staircase which led to the lower halls of the disco. "What I want to know, is, why did the zombies remain *here?*"

"Locked in," said Xakus. He gestured to the far doors.

"So somebody wanted to keep them here? Why?" asked Franco.

"We'll ask Voloshko when we meet him," snapped Keenan. He strapped his MPK to his back, moved to the edge of the stairs, and reaching up, started tugging at the edge of the ceiling mesh. After a few moments he peeled a panel free, which wobbled as he threw it to one side. He glanced back at the two men. "I'll go first. Xakus, next. Franco, to the rear."

"Why do I always have to go last?" mumbled Franco.

"Because you're armed, dickhead."

Keenan hoisted himself up, onto the meshed false ceiling, and squeezed between thick cabling and trailing wires. The mesh shook worryingly under his weight, but held, as he'd predicted. Warily, he eased forward, crawling past stacks of flaring, flashing lights which spun colours across his face and vegetable- and grease-smeared WarSuit.

Xakus climbed next, and leaving a suitable gap, followed Keenan out above the sea of gyrating zombies.

Finally, Franco had to run and leap, catching the edge of the mesh and hauling his bulk up, legs kicking frantically. He sat, panting for a moment, then realised he was being left behind.

"Guys? Hey, you guys? Wait for me!"

He started out, crawling hurriedly over the shaking, vibrating roof-mesh after the fast disappearing figure of Xakus. Behind Franco, unseen, several bolts jiggled and worked free of their L-shaped brackets and clattered like metal rainfall on the bone staircase below.

Far beneath, the zombies boogied.

FRANCO WAS SWEATING as he crawled. It stung his eyes, tickled his beard, and made him squint like an unconvincing D-list Hollywood actor in a cheap horror flick as the rubber-suited monster comes round the corner.

"Franco? Where the hell are you?" boomed Keenan's voice above the din of Ronan's warbling.

Franco froze. Keenan's voice was in the *wrong place* which meant *holy shit he'd managed to go and get himself—*

Lost.

"I'm here," he squeaked, eyes frantic and searching for a way through the forest of cabling, the barrage of flashing lights and the zaps of strobe which periodically blinded him.

"Where, lad?"

"*Na na na na na na,*" sang Ronan.

"Here! I must have taken a wrong turn!"

"There *are* no turns!"

"Listen, it's not my damn fault this entire mesh business is so confusing you know I don't like being locked up after what happened at Mount Pleasant with the testicles an' everything and it's just unreasonable for you to expect me to negotiate such a downright discommodious obstacle!"

"*Discommodious?* Just get your arse *over* here, Private!"

"Keenan, something feels *weird.*"

"That's because the whole damn ceiling is shaking! Get over here *now!*"

"Keenan, the floor's moving, the floor's tilting, oh my God oh bloody bugger and damn and blast..."

"Franco!"

There came a long, staggered cracking sound followed by a comedy hiatus, as if God wanted to extend this moment of pure and perfectly timed slapstick. Then came another, final, sickening crack.

A *whoosh* of air.

Franco felt his world *tip* and amidst flashing, coloured lights and flickering strobes and a sensation of rolling and whirling and falling he lashed out with desperate fingers as Ronan's melodic croon rattled around his skull like bone dice and a true horror and realisation struck him like a baseball bat in the face because if the ceiling mesh *did* collapse and there was a sea of zombies just waiting to feed on his brains down below...

Then they'd feed on his brains down below.

Franco blinked.

Ahh, he thought. *'Twas all a dream!*

His brain spun into nasty focus.

Actually, it *wasn't* a dream.

I shouldn't have taken that last rainbow pill, he thought amiably as a decent kick of euphoria slid like honey needles through his veins. He looked up. Oh look, he thought idly, my fingers are all white where they're clasping that nice bending flexing mesh ceiling. Then he looked down. Something heaved against his shoulder, and he shrugged at the static weight, thus dislodging a block of coloured lights which flashed and spiralled on its way to the dance-floor. Only it didn't connect, because there was a shambling zombie in the way. The huge block of lights flattened the zombie with a squelch, and continued to flash, whirling colours, spinning and rotating across ceiling mesh. Oh look, thought Franco, there's coloured lights on the roof and coloured lights on the floor as well and I wonder if they make a rainbow when they collide in mid-air? That's a nice concept. The sort of thing you could tell to small children. Rainbows. Na na. And look! The lights are shining on the zombies' faces. And the zombies' faces are all turned up to look at me. Haha. Franco gave a little wave. Only it was with the hand he was using to hold onto the flexing, wobbling ceiling mesh.

Franco fell.

It seemed a very, very long way down.

Long enough, at least, to sober up.

* * *

IN HIS TIME Franco had attended all manner of dodgy concerts, festivals, events and gigs. Franco quite often lost himself to the music, rocked out, and was one of those annoying individuals who liked to climb on stage and hurl himself into the crowd, happy in the knowledge they were crammed like sardines and would carry his considerable lopsided weight, sandaled feet kicking people in the mouth as he performed his personal dodgy group fantasy.

This fall, however, was the stage dive of his life...

Viewed from above, Franco fell spread-eagled, like a starfish, both hands clasping Kekra machine pistols, face in a kind of rapture of euphoric stupidity. Below, alerted by falling debris and a pulverised comrade, the mulling zombies looked up, soft moans emanating to mingle quite convincingly with the Ronan Keating backing track.

Into this sea of upturned faces, Franco fell.

He connected with a series of dull thuds, like tiny flesh detonations, but despite his modest height he carried some *serious* weight and his landing dropped several unfortunately situated zombies as effectively as any D5 shotgun blast. Like a sea of unloving flesh, the crowd of deviants parted, then surged back, undulated, a necrotic river, a pus-weeping ocean, and Franco went down and under with arms flailing and mouth a silent O of wonder and intrinsic, disbelieving horror...

Franco disappeared from view.

Kekras roared.

Slabs of zombie flesh spewed up and out in a chunk fountain, and despite Franco's earlier misgivings about these poor creatures being unfortunate victims of circumstance, he chose to momentarily ignore deeper philosophical speculation as the rancid snarling beasts homed in on his fresh, if not entirely functioning, brain.

"Keenan!" came his wail from beneath the sea of surging zombies.

Keenan, on the lip of the roof, chewed his lip, MPK wavering. "Shit." He couldn't fire into the mass. He might hit Franco! His head snapped back. "Xakus, get us down there!"

"Follow me."

They jumped down into a connecting corridor, sprinted down slippery spiral stairs, and came up against a locked bone gate, the bars wrist-thick and human-fat yellow.

Keenan poked his MPK between the bars, and the weapon screamed, fire ejecting from the barrel, bullets mowing down a field of scrambling, half-dancing, half-gyrating zombies and turning the zombie disco into a zombie *rave*.

"Franco!" screamed Keenan. He took a step back, analysing the bars. He smashed a side kick, but it did nothing more than leave a black rubber mark. He lined up his gun, and unleashed bullets which chipped and spat bone shards, but the bars held and Keenan gritted his teeth. "Bastard." He peered into the surging, heaving gloom.

Between the packed mass of scrambling deviants, he could see nothing...

FRANCO STRUGGLED, A turtle on its back. His Kekras were gone. Taken in the scrum like candy from a kid. A bloated face with no lower jaw leered at him. It could make no other expression. Franco slammed a right hook to its temple, knocking the zombie sideways with a grunt. Another face replaced the first, this one with maggots in its hair. Franco squawked, eyes wide, mouth open. He jabbed a punch to its nose, spreading gristle across yellow zombie flesh, then again, a right hook to the jaw which knocked the jaw clean free with a crunch. A bloated purple-black tongue lolled out, unrolling like diseased liquorice, to give Franco a slimy zombie kiss. "Aiiee," he said, grabbing the tongue and giving it a hard tug. The tongue came free in his hand and started struggling, and the zombie stared at him, eyes wide, drooling into Franco's screaming mouth. Thick zombie pus ran over his lips, across his tongue and teeth, into his throat. It tasted of rancid amputation. Franco gagged, stomach heaving as he whacked the zombie with its own bloated tongue, a comedy sausage, then clubbed it with his left fist, knocking it aside. Another, a woman this time, lurched over him, onto him, claws scrabbling for his brains. Distended blue breasts rubbed in Franco's face in a parody of the act he so loved, and grimacing, he bit hard and was nauseated to find a ripe nipple part like well-cooked meat and slide slug-like down his throat. No, he screamed at himself. This cannot be happening! Cannot be real! He felt her claws on his head making circular motions in an attempt to remove his skull-top like a PreCheese jar lid. He wriggled under the weight of pressing zombies, felt a hand on his crotch and fear slammed his brain like a train-wreck. No! Not his nuts! Anything but his nuts! Twisting and straining in renewed panic like a kitten in a sack, Franco managed to free a D5 shotgun from his pack-holster. The deviant's face stared up him, grinning through crooked black teeth. It licked mephitic lips. Franco scowled. "Not on my watch!" he snarled, and pushed the D5's barrel into the zombie's molten mouth. Teeth fell free, rattling like ivory dice. "Suck this." He pulled twin triggers, watched the face— and entire *head*—disappear in a smush of explosion leaving nothing but a wavering spine tip, charred and smoking and wriggling weakly. Franco felt his head suddenly wrenched to one side. He squawked. The hands above grasped him, screwing his skull with tenacity. The female zombie leaned across him, intent on her task, great rotten breasts suffocating him. Franco struggled, head smashing from left to right and back. Claws gouged a circle around his skull-top. This was it! Death by screw-top! Banishing Queensbury Rules, Franco thumped the zombie in the belly and felt her stiffen in shock. He rolled, wriggling, dragging himself powerfully from the rugby scrum of squirming bodies, and rolled onto his hands and knees and began to crawl in an accelerated comedy fashion. A zombie jumped on his back. Franco's head slammed up, back, a rear head-butt. The zombie disappeared, but left its upper denture embedded in Franco's head. He scrabbled at it frantically as he crawled. "Euch!" he muttered, finally levering the teeth from his indented skull with a crunch and bringing them before his disbelieving eyes. He stared at the yellow fangs, still attached to a broken upper jaw. "You dirty, dirty *bastards!* Horrorshow! Pure horrorshow!" He crawled like a maniac, veering left and right between legs, between zombies, as hands, claws and talons thrashed at him, grasped at him, tore his clothes and his damaged, sparking WarSuit. Fangs bit his toes and he cursed his sandals. His D5 made a rhythmical clattering as he crawled beneath the writhing zombie throng. And then he saw it! The exit from the zombie disco. They may take my life, but they'll never take my *freedomm!* He crawled, faster now. Hope burned like a birthed protostar in his breast. A zombie lurched before him. The D5 boomed, kicking, scattering the creature across the wall. And then he was free of the scrum, staggering to his feet and slipping and sliding on gore as he lunged for the exit—only to realise, with horror, that the exit wasn't an exit at all, but blocked by wrist-thick curved bars of bone, absorbed into the organotower and molecularly redistributed to create a prison cell *just for him.* "Oh how the Gods mock me!" he wailed. Franco slammed against the bars. Blinked. Saw Keenan. Saw the attached explosive. Saw the flickering red light.

Keenan snarled, "Get *back*, idiot!"

Franco whirled, and charged like a lunatic towards the lurching zombies who were taken by surprise as their quarry sprinted panic-fuelled into their midst... with a *click* High-J detonated. Zombies were thrown around the disco as if in a blender.

In their midst, knocked and bashed and churned, gyrated a *very* unhappy Franco Haggis.

* * *

FRANCO OPENED HIS eyes—to see Keenan standing over him, an MPK in one hand, Techrim in the other. A low growling, moaning sound came to his ears. Keenan glanced down. Grinned. Through gritted teeth, he said, "I'd get moving *real fast,* Franco. They're about to attack. Again."

Franco scrabbled up, pulled free a fresh D5 shotgun, and scowled at the wall of wavering zombies. Around him lay a platter of torn zombie body parts, a mish-mash puzzle of severed arms, legs, limbless torsos and decapitated heads.

"They've been pulled apart! And I was in that?"

"It would seem you're made of sterner stuff, Franco lad."

Keenan opened fire at the wall of deviants, then the two men turned and fled, slipping on severed fingers and toes, and the occasional ear. They made for the blasted, bone-bar exit. Franco suddenly stopped.

"What is it?"

"A gift. For my leedle friends." Franco rummaged in his pack, dropped a grenade at his feet, wiggled the pin at Keenan, then snapped, "Let's go visit Voloshko."

XAKUS GUIDED THEM up through the ever squirming interior of the organotower. They had evaded no less than six charging squads of mission-fevered Battle SIMs, and as they stood, sweating, and panting, waiting for Xakus to regain his breath, Keenan lit a cigarette and blew smoke over Franco. Franco had found a rag in his pack, and was scrubbing at his face, his beard, and his infected tongue.

"I feel dirty," he said.

"You are dirty," said Keenan, gazing at Franco's bedraggled exterior. "You look like someone who's just been mauled by zombies. Either that, or been to bed with them." He winked.

"Shut up! Ugh! It was just, slime, in mouth, breasts, blue pus, green pussy, ugh. Not tell. You. How bad. Feel. Want. Vomit. Insides. Out. Sheee*at*."

"So, one to tell the grandchildren, then?" Keenan finished his Widow Maker. He checked his weapon, they eyed Xakus who appeared exhausted, dangling at the end of his tether. As he pointed out, he was a professor, not a soldier. And this mission was difficult, physically and emotionally; even for veterans.

"I can go on," said Xakus, finally. "I'm just thankful the Battle SIMs have not taken up pursuit."

"That's the thing about SIMs," said Keenan, his eyes and gun barrel endlessly roving for fresh danger. "Theoretically, they make great guards; I'll be the first to admit they're a bastard to put down. But when the danger is real, and you need some genuine IQ, a Battle SIM is not what you want by your side."

Xakus nodded, and hauled himself to his feet. "It's not far. I'm sure of it. All these egomaniacs seem to nest at the summits of their respective towers. That's how this one was designed. In the organic blueprints, anyway."

Keenan gave a nod, checked his PAD. It was dead. Had been since they entered the organotower. Even Cam hadn't been able to explain the phenomenon, although in fairness, Cam himself had been behaving strange since entry. And now Cam had vanished, Keenan once again felt like a father waiting till three AM for his daughter to return from her first trip to a nightclub. He was filled with a subtle uneasiness. When Cam disappeared on side-quests—well, it always made Keenan twitchy.

The group moved on. The temperature was still rising, and Keenan felt his mood turning sour, more bitter, the closer he got to this man, this Minister, of The Hammer Syndicate. Back at The Happy Friendly Sunshine Assurance Company Voloshko had not just taken Mel, he'd had the rebel kids, harmless as they were, exterminated. Violence against children always sat bad with Keenan. It made him do things he knew he would later regret, but strangely, in a detached way, was a personal parameter of viciousness he could not change. Deep down, Keenan was a bad man, a vengeful man, a bitter man, and he acknowledged these character traits without remorse. After all, somebody had put down the fuck-ups, didn't they? And it sure as hell wasn't going to be the government.

Like a bad smell, Keenan's headache returned. A dull nagging, deep in his brain.

He smiled, a grimace of loathing. "Great. Just what I need."

"Shh." Xakus held up his hand. The group slowed.

"This is my gig. I'm here for Melanie!" Franco moved to the front, bristling with new weapons from his pack, although thankfully he'd ditched his

TRI-SPIES because they kept attempting to strangle him. Carefully, he peered around the corner.

The corridor to Voloshko's quarters was guarded by two Battle SIMs. Franco glanced up, then around. Did they know he was there? Was it a bluff? He chided himself. Battle SIMs didn't bluff. They didn't have the intelligence. Sweat niggled under his collar, a flexing maggot of fluid. Voloshko said don't bring any weapons. Hmm. But then, what nutcase would go unarmed?

Plan. Need a plan.

Franco rummaged, pulled free a BABE Grenade, slid free the pin, and showed it to Keenan. Keenan gave a nod, patted Xakus on the arm, and they retreated down the corridor a safe distance.

Franco lay on his belly, and eased himself to the corner. The floor beneath felt like human flesh, soft and wriggling and disgustingly erotic. It was so nauseating it made Franco want to puke. Again.

Extracting a tiny digital spy mirror from his inoperative PAD, he peered round the corner. One of the Battle SIMs shifted, heavy armour creaking. Franco rolled the BABE Grenade along the floor, then waited, arms over his head.

The SIMs, too long in domestic servitude, stared sullenly at the BABE as it rolled to a halt by their feet, silent and rocking on the veg flesh floor. They looked at it. Then up. They stared at one another, heads tilted in curiosity.

"I..." began one—as the detonation picked them up and tried to rip them physically and elementally into a million pieces. A deep concussive *boom* roared through the corridor, and Franco sprinted through the smoke, Kekras in hands, and almost toppled into the ragged hole blasted in the semi-organic floor. He skidded, arms flapping, and was almost swallowed by ragged lips of bomb-charred flesh. He gazed down into distant darkness ringed with blood-dripping ribs. The SIMs were bellowing and punching at one another as they fell, arguing, voices hollow and fading, fists like whirring spades. Bullets whined from combat carbines, panic tracer carving distant lines. Franco grinned to himself... he'd expected to have to finish them off with head shots. He hadn't anticipated the grenade eating the soft floor. He chided himself, aware he was supposed to be an expert in detonations.

"Do come in. I have been expecting you."

Franco's head slammed up, focused on... Voloshko. The man stood, wearing an immaculate crushed-coral suit. It was pink, and shimmered. His hair and beard were neatly trimmed, eyes dark in sunken sockets. Despite his appearance and obvious wealth, he appeared a little... tortured?

"Where's Melanie?"

"Ah, straight to the point."

Franco's Kekra came up, quad barrels trained on Voloshko's face. Voloshko did not flinch... and that made Franco wary. He edged forward, around the grenade hole, and into Voloshko's... *apartment*? Franco shook his head, eyeing the moody interior, the drapes of helk-fur tapestry, the metal weave floor.

Voloshko gestured to a wide black couch. "Would you like to sit? We need to talk."

"There's nothing to discuss. You took Melanie. You killed those children. I want Melanie back. Or you *will* die."

Voloshko smiled, but it was a movement with his mouth and not his eyes. When he spoke, his voice had changed. It was level, monotone, like a machine. "I don't think you *quite* understand your predicament, Franco Haggis." He moved, and seated himself. He picked up a drink. Ice cubes chimed. "Now let *me* explain."

There was a *boom*, and bullets ate the leather three inches beside Voloshko's head. Franco strode forward, face a snarl, and he halted gazing down at the Minister for The Hammer Syndicate.

"No, let *me* fucking explain it to *you*. This is the way it works. You're not fucking immortal, and you have no biomods in your blood *because* if you did then you'd be a deviant mess of organics, like all our friends out there on the streets. So you're human. And you die as easily as any other sack of flesh shit. You're acting cool because you think you invited me here, but you expected me to roll up like a good doggie wagging its tail, but no, I came in the, uh, arse way. You weren't expecting that. That's why you've got Battle SIMs running around like headless chickens. Stop trying to play the cool fucker and *tell me what you've done with Melanie!* Before I really lose my temper and start a little Voloshko Cellar of my own."

Voloshko licked his lips.

Franco's Kekra boomed again, and this time blood appeared on Voloshko's ear. A nick. A *warning*. A droplet oozed free, and dripped onto the shoulder of the pink coral suit. Ice cubes danced in Voloshko's glass.

"Next time," said Franco, "my aim might not be quite so true. I'm a little bit," he twitched, "tetchy."

"She's not here."

"Where is she?"

"NanoTek took her."

"What did NanoTek want with her?"

Voloshko smiled. "You'd have to ask them."

"You're lying?"

"Why? You're the Big Man with the gun."

"You're a bastard."

"I never claimed to be anything other."

Franco roared, and slammed a right hook that sent Voloshko reeling to the couch, blood spraying from smashed lips. Franco lifted his Kekra and fired ten shots off into the ceiling... then froze.

Blood rained down.

"Don't move," said Keenan, voice impossibly soft.

Franco licked his lips, and stared down at Voloshko. "What's your secret weapon, scumbag? You're way too cool."

Voloshko glanced up with his eyes, then eased himself back into a sitting position. He produced a white handkerchief and dabbed at his bleeding lips.

"Franco. I repeat, don't move. Don't look up. Just don't damn well move." Keenan was standing by the entrance to the Floor 698 apartment. Franco could hear, and *sense,* his tension.

"So," said Voloshko, and stood. He lifted the Kekra from Franco's hand and weighed the weapon thoughtfully. "You are, indeed, correct. A man such as I doesn't simply employ stupid Battle SIMs to charge up and down corridors. Things at The Hammer Syndicate are, shall we say, a little more sophisticated. You may now look up."

Franco looked up. His heart sank.

The high, dark ceiling—in its entirety—was filled with needle thin elements, spear-long, and glinting with nasty black sparks. As Franco watched, several of them curled back into recesses, and other long needle-thin lengths uncurled and wavered, then became rigid. Franco took a step one way. A hundred of the needles followed him, swaying slightly, as if caught by magnetic attraction... before becoming rigid again.

Voloshko moved in close to Franco. "It's alive," he whispered in Franco's ear. "AI. Sentient. You can forget The Tangled, forget biowire, forget sharpwire and veinthreads and ticklestrands. Above you lies the evolution of a technologically advanced synthetically living killer; it has intelligence far outweighing humanity, has no empathy or emotion, is loyal only to its master, and has a single one-core function. To kill. We call it a *skein*, but some of our tech comedians refer to each strand as a Spear of Destiny. Haha. They will have their little jokes. I, however, have absolutely no sense of humour."

"What do you want?"

"Want? Well, I know you are Combat K, Franco. I knew it when you worked the streets for me, all those long detached weeks ago. I knew it when you took out my men, the retards Keg and Tag. I've been watching you for a long time, Franco. Yes. Waiting." He circled Franco, still dabbing at his lips. "And I admit to being aggrieved when you helped that bastard Slick escape; and I was aggrieved when you evaded capture for so long. But, ultimately, it was a plan that worked out for the best. Didn't it?" He smiled. His dark eyes shone.

"Waiting for what?" said Franco.

"You were the bait, little man." Voloshko lifted his head. His gleaming eyes fixed on Keenan. "I needed you, and Mel, the whole thing, in order to reel in Mr Z. Keenan here. I feel that me and Keenan have some unfinished business."

"We do?" Keenan stepped forward, leaving Xakus in the corridor. Xakus, ashen, backed away; vanished like a ghost.

Keenan glanced up, watching the skeins of toxic wire waver and solidify, waver and solidify, as if in never-ending cycle, like metal hairs in a breeze. Taking a deep breath, he strode to stand before Voloshko, hands resting light on his weapon. "I do not know you."

"But I know *you,*" hissed the Minister of The Hammer Syndicate. He reached up to his face, took a hold of the skin, and peeled it up and back with a sudden violent wrench. What stared at the two men now was quite clearly not human. The head was small, circular, a tiny sphere of some black metallic substance... almost robotic, but not quite. It was organic. A synthetic machine built from odd old flesh. Eyes wavered on stalks, clusters containing millions of tiny black globes above a slit for a mouth. The slit smiled, and Keenan saw perfect little cubic teeth.

Keenan allowed a breath to leave his body. His eyes flickered to Franco... and he knew Franco was ready. For the battle that must surely follow...

"Yes," said Voloshko, voice husky without his ersatz human voicebox, clusters of eyes glistening and altering in size—some shrinking, some enlarging—in a rhythmical pulsation. "I am Seed Hunter. Like my brother, the man you murdered on Teller's World. The man you knew as Mr Max."

"I did not murder him." Keenan's voice was quiet. His head lowered. His eyes subdued.

"You—" Voloshko's head snapped right, to Franco, "*both* of you, you killed Mr Max as surely as putting a gun to his nerve-cluster. And now you will die. A horrible, long, painful death. It will take weeks. The skeins have been *programmed,* and we've been waiting for you."

He stepped back, a sudden movement. From the ceiling flashed a hundred *skeins*, needle thin wires which pierced Keenan and Franco, entering their flesh in a hundred separate places and worming under skin, into muscle, into faces and arms and legs and torsos...

Both men dropped to their knees, screaming, clawing at their faces, the air around them hazy with fluttering organic wire like strands of silk, synthetic killing *skeins*. Franco howled as wires wormed into and under his cheeks and stood out against skin like thick black veins, a web-mask on his flesh as the skeins burrowed inwards, sank deep towards his brain...

Franco toppled over, rolled to his side, vibrating in a spastic fit, caught in the throes of a slow and agonising death.

Keenan gritted his teeth, forced his head up, black wire writhing under his skin, in his cheeks, his nose, inside his eyes, wriggling stark against his cornea like microscopic worms. He glared at Voloshko, teeth entwined with black skeins, his tongue riddled with the poisonous killing wire and he spat at the Seed Hunter—

"Go—to—*hell*," he snarled, growling, hands clasping at the agony in his skull.

Voloshko smiled with his tiny mouth. "On the contrary. That's your religious belief, not mine. Enjoy the experience, Mr Keenan. And Mr Haggis? I have to say, it's been a pleasure."

Voloshko turned, and strode from the room.

CHAPTER 13
WIRED & WEIRD

THE CITY HAD once been a normal planet. It had equator, oceans, desert, arctic regions; and a gravity near-similar to Old Earth. 1.1 OEG. However, over millennia a thousand different species had built a billion different buildings, towers and skyscrapers and cubeblocks, all vying for life and light and towering over every and any expanse of the world which would take foundation. Then, a planetary engineer had the bright idea of *utilising* those areas not traditionally utilised; first to be decimated by the hand of the architect were the deserts—kilometre-deep foundations forced beneath the sand, huge areas fused into glass by controlled thermonuclear direction, sand dunes skimmed and buildings speedily erected. The seas fell next, pontoon support struts housing floating fifty lane freeways above roaring surf, with floating rig-decks acting as huge cubic boots for towering concrete and alloy and emerald structures. Finally, it had been the arctic which succumbed to planetary usurpation. Ice and snow were tamed. Icebergs used as flotation chambers. Skyscraper domes erected against freezing hailstorms.

Predictably, this planetary molestation caused havoc with the natural ecology. Species were rendered extinct in months. Natural resources could not fulfil the building quota, the geological shopping list, and so trillions of tonnes of raw materials were dragged low-grav down-side on MeshCables by orbiting freighters, and pummel-dropped into anti-grav clusters surface-side. This, combined with a realigning of the planet's natural ecology, in short, screwed up The City's weather.

Floods, heat waves, snowstorms, hurricanes, tornadoes, tsunamis, earthquakes, volcanoes... all accelerated in event and violence, which caused untold damage and, more importantly, *loss of revenue*. A reduction in the credit column. And so, over the next twelve years a system of climate control was gradually and experimentally dragged into place. Two hundred and fifty huge, orbiting WCS blocks monitored the planet's ecosystems, and were capable via skystreams of injected aeromatter of altering any advancing weather patterns that cost-programmed hard-wired AI controllers could predict. Which meant, overnight, threats to The City's stable economy and accelerating growth were killed dead. Like a miracle, like a god, The City controlled its own climate.

Which is a great state of affairs when sensible machines rule the roost. However, currently, twenty-five AI controllers lay crumpled, broken and dead, on the WCS Control Centre's nicely panelled marble floor.

And sitting at the controls, pus and drool spooling from green necrotic lips, eyes shining with a strange and curious intelligence, the zombies had taken their place. They had rotting, flapping boots on the desk. And were eating brains on toast.

THICK BLACK SNOW fell on the city. It was getting thicker as the climate grew colder, and colder, and colder. Ice settled on mammoth buildings, icicles lining high summits like evil, glistening teeth. Globally, liquids froze, and the colder it got, the more functional the zombies became. As if whatever controlled them *needed* the cold.

High up in the atmosphere, there came a *hiss* as something slammed north.

There came another... another... then thousands more as tiny black PopBots smashed through the snow in a neat, flowing formation which undulated around buildings and aircraft, weaved through the atmosphere, and targeted a very specific single location:

#proximity series15000
#speed 275 altitude 2370 beginning descent
#updated instructions received
#integrated/ received/ understood co-ordinates loading............
#uploaded all data structures OK
#attack sequence initiated

With a silent, flowing *hiss,* six thousand detonation PopBots dropped like ice from the sky, and locked unerringly to their target.

WITH SHAKING, WIRE-SQUIRMING hands Keenan lifted his Techrim, sighted, and as Voloshko exited the chamber, turning right, so Keenan started firing, the gun booming in his hands as he tracked across the organic vegetable wall. On bursts of fire, bullets howled across the chamber, punching fist-sized holes through the interior. With wire squirming in his face, Keenan kept on firing, shot after shot after shot, and he staggered to his feet as Voloshko reappeared, his fake human flesh ragged and scorched and holed and his tiny Seed Hunter's head lowered, globe-eyes fixed on Keenan with... annoyance.

"Why can't you just die in peace?" Voloshko growled... and charged—as a *detonation* rocked the tower. The walls shook, flapping like quivering, impacted slabs of flesh. From somewhere, cold air flooded the chamber in a downdraught dump. It smelt of ice.

Voloshko skidded to a halt as Keenan toppled over, foetal, his Techrim thumping across the floor. His eyes were closed, breathing laboured as the wires closed on his *heart* and started to squeeze tight in a fist of AI metal...

Voloshko's head lifted, turned, eye-clusters fluctuating as his senses screamed warnings... and *understanding* flooded him as the detonation PopBots began to slam the tower. Explosions howled like machine gun fire. Huge ragged tears appeared in the walls. The quivering organotower seemed to pause... in suspended shock... then *scream* in a silent wail of tortured despair.

"No!" snarled Voloshko. He sprinted to the gaping, ragged maw, stopping at the edge and gazing out and down over six hundred and ninety-eight floors. Thick snow fell. He blinked away ice from his cluster-globes. And saw them, more detonation drones, undulating towards him in a vast, awe-inspiring wave—

Only one man had the resources and the technology.

"Oz," hissed Voloshko, spittle at the edges of his thin-slit mouth. "You have betrayed me!" Oh the irony, he thought. Before I could betray you!

Voloshko whirled, in time to catch a *flash* at the edge of his vision—as Cam hurtled into the chamber, did a single fast circuit reconnoitre, then slammed at Voloshko with all the speed his upgrades and military combat training would allow. Cam hit Voloshko centrally between the eye clusters at about 70,000 pounds per square inch. Voloshko staggered back, stunned, head caved in with a crunch, and stepped backwards from the fluttering lips of his bombarded organotower with a stutter and a fall...

There came a *whoosh* of air.

Voloshko was gone.

More explosions rocked the tower, and Cam spun, sped to Keenan and Franco, and slammed an EMP through their metal-invaded flesh. Inside, the wriggling skeins halted instantly as electronic life was blasted into an electronic coma.

Franco groaned.

"Quick!" snapped Cam, "we haven't got much time!"

Franco opened his eyes. The tower rocked, and deafening squelches could be heard, deep and muffled. Past the quivering hole in the wall, through which a cold wind gusted, huge chunks of charred flesh fell.

"What hit me?" groaned Franco.

"You've got to get up! Come on! You've got to carry Keenan! The skeins have crushed his heart!"

Franco rolled onto his belly, pushed himself to his knees, stared in horror at the black veins standing out across the backs of his hands. "I remember." He spoke slowly, slurring a little. The wires were in his brain, interfering with motor function. "What happened... to Voloshko?"

"Took a long walk off a short plank. *Hurry up!*"

Franco staggered up, grabbed Keenan's arms, but did not have the strength to lift his comrade. Instead, he grunted and dragged Keenan, bumping his friend's body across the organic floor as he limped after a fast retreating Cam.

Xakus rushed in, grabbing at Keenan and helping Franco lift the stocky soldier. Between them, they staggered on.

"What the fuck happened to you, Mr Judas?" snapped Franco, glaring sideways at the old professor.

"I am a man of peace, not violence. I was stealing the machinery we need to decode the junk's SinScript." He lifted a small, colourless, glossy box, which gleamed and seemed to squirm in the black man's fist. "A CryptorBox. We all had our specific jobs to do. I did mine. Now let's move, and stop your moaning!"

"Hah!"

"We're near the roof," said Cam. "Voloshko has a squad of Apache choppers—if the damn DetBots haven't wasted them! We can get ourselves an airlift."

Panting, sweat gleaming on his face, Franco stopped, knelt, and was sick.

Cam swerved back. Dropped to Franco. "If you don't move your arse, soldier, we'll be dead in two minutes. There's thousands more detonation Pop-Bots descending on this tower right now! Do... you... damn well understand?"

Franco wiped his mouth with the back of his skein-infested hand. Subcutaneously, they gleamed. He nodded. Stood. Took his hold on Keenan.

"How long has he got?"

"Three minutes. Which is academic. Soon, Franco, we'll all be *sushi*."

Franco limped after Cam, up several sloped floors, and between him and Xakus they managed to get Keenan onto The Hammer Syndicate's roof. Cold air blasted them. The wind howled a mournful song. Snow danced diagonal jigs.

Deep down, beneath boots and sandals, more explosions detonated like muffled ordinance. The organotower shuddered. It swayed beneath them, and the whole chassis quivered constantly, as if in terminal seizure.

As Cam predicted, many Apache choppers were nothing more than glowing shrapnel, parts scattered like comedy dice across the hole-infested roof.

The two men staggered with Keenan towards an unmolested vehicle, skirting wide, quivering gaps in the floor showing twitching bone and gleaming gristle.

"Quick!" howled Cam. "The main wave is here!"

Deep below, near the organotower's foundation, hundreds and hundreds of detonations ignited simultaneously. The Hammer HQ swayed dangerously, a dying erection, and started to slide, slowly, flapping over in a slow-motion stop-motion topple—

Franco dragged Keenan onto the Apache, clambered into the cockpit, and slammed the starter. Rotors began a slow turn. In the back, Xakus unzipped Keenan's WarSuit and stared with horror at the mesh of wires beneath the soldier's bruised and inflamed skin.

"You perform heart massage, I'll extract the wires," said Cam.

The organotower, in its lazy slide, began to actually scream, a deafening, squealing, gnashing sound interspersed with millions of crackling, snapping bone cracks. Still the DetBots exploded, ignited, detonated, blasting flesh and gristle and sinew and bone. Fires burned. Raged. The stench of scorched vegetable flesh flowed up through the snow like a mushroom cloud.

"Come on, come on!" snapped Franco. The rotors were buzzing, dicing black snow.

Franco felt himself start to shift. Before him, the tower swayed and tilted in a nauseating parody. The Apache began a slow slide towards the edge of the bomb-blasted roof. Franco frantically tried to take-off, but the Apache gave a simple warning *buzz*. No, it seemed to be saying. Go and find another chopper.

Cam, rotating beside Keenan's chest, inserted a needle. Something glowed. Cam flowed inside, flowed with the dormant skein wires using their own micro-molecular pathways. He observed a spiral of thousands of strands encasing Keenan's heart, a black coil suffocating an electric motor. Tutting, Cam began to burn away the wires from inside Keenan's chest cavity; with digital winces, he tried to ignore the scorching of Keenan's actual heart fibres.

Outside in the snow, once again Franco tried to panic-leap the Apache into the air. Again, it buzzed at him and he scowled his legendary Franco scowl, all eyebrows and squinty hatred.

"Bastard machine! Fly you bastard of a bastard's bastard!" He thumped the console. "Come on, I say, *fly you bastard!*"

The Apache reached the edge of the roof, runners grinding. Below, in darkness and gloom and falling snow, the whole of The City seemed to rear up like a million-headed snake to mock Franco with each and every lisping head. Franco stared at his own ghost-reflection superimposed against the Apache's cockpit, a HUD mannequin. His face was nearly entirely black, hundreds of minute swirls beneath his face giving him the appearance of suffering a bizarre tattoo epilogue.

More detonations rocked, deep down below... and this time, they did not stop. On and on they boomed, thousands of final concussions slamming

the remaining fabric holding the monolithic structure in place. And with a shudder like widow's grief
the organotower, finally, died...

Agonisingly, it tilted.

The Apache slid free of the summit.

And with a scream Franco fell...

VOLOSHKO HIT THE ground *hard*. Six-hundred and
ninety-eight floors was a long way to fall. His body
slammed the earth, compressed, and within his
organic sack he felt the sickening crunches as his
bones and chassis collapsed, crushed, disintegrated,
many components ground into powder, floating
like dust in blood both human and alien: mingled
and combined. Voloshko felt his spine compress to
become an organic corrugation. He felt his skull
flatten, bouncing from concrete to give him instant
brain damage; a total pulping.

He lay, contorted at impossible angles, fuming.

He watched the organotower fall, as if in slow-
motion, through swirling black snow. It keeled over,
crunching through various other buildings and taking them down with it. The last of the straggling,
final detonations boomed through darkness until
only a gentle sound, as of running water, remained;
that, and the blanketing, muffled silence, of the
snow.

Voloshko tried to move. But his spine and limbs
no longer worked.

He settled his burning anger on NanoTek. On Dr
Oz.

Had Dr Oz discovered Volsohko's plans to over-
throw him?

Had Dr Oz realised Voloshko was behind the bio-mod hacking and piracy?

Or was the total annihilation of The Hammer Syndicate simply a cheap shot attempt at removing Keenan from the face of the planet?

It mattered not. The Hammer Syndicate had served its purpose. And NanoTek had used a premiere war machine to put the syndicate out of business.

Voloshko frowned, the look strange on his metallic face. He tried again to move, but could not. Frustration gnawed him like a maggot, eating his heart from the inside out.

Come on, he thought. Where are you. Where are you? What's taking so long?

A terrible thought flowered in his brain. If it was NanoTek who had betrayed the Syndicate... then maybe the *gift* was also a betrayal? A final mockery? A two-fingered salute to the most powerful ruling Syndicate on the planet?

Time. It was supposed to take *time*.

Voloshko relaxed. Sighed. He allowed his pulped and liquid mind to swim, drifting lazily back through long hot centuries, always hot, to the days with his brother Mr Max... and the others of their clan, their breed, their tribe.

He floated along distant timelines, half-forgotten. To their youth, on the planet which one day became known as Sick World... The world for the ill, the deformed, the dying and the dead. The place where he had *developed* his Seed Hunter abilities. The place where he had ceased to *be* human, instead having to wear a human skin which in itself mocked him with ersatz physiology. To masquerade as that which you had been born! The shame. The shame burned him...

He awoke, to find the burning was real. Inside his bones. Inside his metal bones. Inside his crushed spine. Inside his eyes. Inside his pulped and gooey liquid brain.

Carefully, the nanobots began to rebuild Voloshko.

Carefully, they began his restructuring.

"Aiiieee!" screamed Franco, waggling the joystick and slapping at buttons randomly. They slammed through the snow, the organotower falling after them, behind them, and then above them. Franco checked his rear-view mirrors. Shit. Yep. There it was. Several billions of tonnes of dead organic slab chasing him vertically through the atmosphere. Stubbornly, the Apache still refused to operate, despite rotors *whamming* round in a blur of slivered snowflakes...

"It's the red button, retard," came Cam's drawl.

Franco slammed the big red button, marked helpfully in white letters that read: FLY.

The Apache lit afterburners, banked, and screamed low through the city streets. Franco was pushed back in his seat, veined cheeks wobbling as far behind the organotower slammed the ground like a billion tonnes of raw meat on the biggest butcher's slab ever carved. Franco, fully awake now in fresh air and fresher fear, tugged and jerked on the joystick like an automaton as they smashed a random, insane dance ten feet from the ground following roads filled with zombies and burning, overturned cars.

"Arrrhh*hhh*!" he managed after a while, as he rounded a corner, rotors taking alloy shavings from the edge of a building, and yanked back on the controls to send them searing like a rocket up up into cold high brittle heavens.

A minute later, Franco finally had the chopper under his control, and hovering steadily, humming. He released a pent-up breath. Then he beamed, grinning back at Cam and Xakus. "I did it! I got us out of there! I'm a hero, I am! The man of the moment! I saved the day!" Then his eyes fell on Keenan, and he paled, despite the dead skeins beneath his own, quivering, rancid skin. "Will he be OK?"

"He's breathing," confirmed Cam, and even as the PopBot spoke Keenan's eyes flickered open. They were laced with black swirls. He focused on Cam, then Xakus, then a grinning Franco who bounded forward, dropped to his knees, and hugged Keenan.

"Whoa, mate," croaked Keenan. "I'm still a bit... tender."

"It'll take another hour to remove all the skein strands," said Cam mellifluously.

"What happened to Voloshko?"

"I helped him learn to fly." Cam sounded smug.

"And the organotower? Why the detonations?"

"They were DetBots. NanoTek's finest. We can only assume NanoTek had some grievance with The Hammer Syndicate and decided to go to war."

"Yes, I can confirm NanoTek certainly has the technology. It's a common misconception the computing giant is simply an over-exaggerated software house." Xakus sat, one hand run halfway through his bushed white hair, his face weary with exhaustion and fear. "NanoTek uses and abuses. Believe me, it has teeth. Whatever the reasons, it matters little to us know. We have the CryptorBox. I can use it to analyse the junk's SinScript... although it may take a little time, and I will need a massive power source."

"We have time," said Keenan. "It's a long walk to NanoTek."

"You still plan to invade?"

"We're going to stop this shit. We're going to find out what's gone wrong."

Franco lifted his hand. "Is it OK if I get these worms out of my eyes first? They're really starting to irritate. They're all itchy scratchy." He shivered, scratching his beard. "It freaks me out. I've never felt so... *wired* and weird before."

"Haha," said Cam. "Very funny. Anyway, we certainly need to remove the wires before they reactivate."

"*What?*" hissed Franco, eyes widening.

"I used an EMP. I disabled them. They'll... no, I just can't say it."

"Say what?"

Cam took a deep breath. "They'll be back."

"Put us down on that rooftop, over there," said Keenan, nodding. "We'll let Cam do his micro-butchery on us and we can re-group, and plan. I know what you mean, Franco, about feeling this shit inside my veins and my flesh—I feel like a doper permanently wired on a bad cocktail." He shivered. "I feel like every atom has been raped."

Franco went back to the controls, and eased the Apache through heavy falling snow. Warily, he touched down on the rooftop, and with Kekras primed, climbed out to secure the area.

"I can use the power source here to start decoding the SinScript," said Xakus.

Keenan nodded, flinching as Cam extracted wires from inside his eyeballs. Pain flared through him like molten metal. Through gritted teeth, he said, "Go ahead. Lets find out what the poisonous little junk fuckers are up to."

Xakus met Keenan's gaze. "You might not like what I find," he said, voice barely more than a whisper.

Keenan stared off through the snow, eyes stinging. He breathed deep. It felt good to be alive. Bizarrely, he thought of Pippa. Remembered what it what like to hold her. To touch her soft skin. Kiss her ripe lips. "*Hold me, Kee,*" she said in his mind, words a distant haunting echo.

Keenan shivered. "Not like it?" He laughed, his laughter the sound of an alien metal wind across a desecrated, dead world. "I'm betting on it," he said.

IT TOOK AN hour for Cam to remove every last strand of fried biological skein wire from Keenan, and a further hour to replicate the procedure on Franco. As Cam operated on Franco, Keenan gave himself painslashers, vitboosters and brain and heart stims from the Apache's medical box. Then he lit a burner, out beside the Apache, and boiled some water for a brew. Xakus had moved away across the skyscraper's roof, connecting the tiny Cryptor-Box to a 90,000 volt mains power cable, where tiny electric teeth burrowed through insulation like an electronic parasite, and stole power. Keenan watched Xakus insert the stolen SinScript. There came a massive bass whine from deep down below in the building. In its heart. In its soul. Emergency lighting around the rim of the skyscraper dimmed.

"Powerful, for such a tiny thing," said Keenan, walking to Xakus and handing him a pot of steaming coffee. Xakus took the drink with a nod of thanks.

"Size has never been an indication of power."

"Don't mention that to Franco. You'll hurt his feelings."

Holding his own coffee, Keenan climbed into the Apache and stared down at Franco, lying on his back on an unrolled sterile med-stretch. Cam was silent, humming, extracting wires from within Franco's flesh. As Keenan watched, a ten metre element was drawn slowly, painfully, carefully, from one of Franco's eyeballs. The little ginger-bearded soldier squawked in a long-drawn low-level agony, then blinked rapidly, eyes smarting.

"It'll hurt for a while," said Cam.

"Story of my life," snorted Franco, then looked up and saw Keenan. "Ahh. At last! The basic staple of the old-fashioned honest-to-goodness squaddie."

"Tea, five sugars?"

"Just how I like it." Franco struggled into a sitting position, took the brew and slurped tea down his WarSuit. "Ahh," he said. "Ahh. *Ahhhh*. That's good, that is. *Ahhhh!*"

Xakus appeared at the door, sipping his own coffee. "Look at us. We're all exhausted. Fit to drop."

"No rest for the wicked," said Keenan, voice low. "So many lives depend on it."

"You really believe you can stop this thing?"

"If there's a way," said Keenan. "I'll find it. I don't believe these *zombies* are the living dead; I believe whatever changed them can change them back. Something stinks here, Xakus, and I want to help clean up the mess."

"You're quite a humanitarian, for a soldier."

"He was never always that way," grinned Franco conversationally.

"Just because I can kill, it doesn't mean I like to. There was an incident, once, many moons ago. I torched a whole host of deviant bastards in Lakanek Prison. They were paedophiles, sex offenders, the abusers of babies. I burned them and they squirmed, squealing like pigs in napalm. At the time, I was filled with hatred. So much anger it consumed me." He sighed. "But as I get older, I realise violence and death are not always the right way. There are alternatives."

Franco snorted, tea coming out of his nostrils. "What? What's this? Keenan the do-gooder? Keenan the fucking cardigan salesman? Those paedophiles deserved to die. They murdered children! Why should they continue to exist? Hell pal, soon you'll be wearing hand-knitted jumpers and organising jumble sales! You'll be protesting for the release of scumbag murderers just because they've had a few human rights *constrained*. Ha! Get to fuck and suck hard on it."

"Calm down." Keenan was smiling. He punched Franco on the arm, playfully, and the rotund soldier yelped. "All I'm *saying* is this entire situation sits bad with me. Once, I would have torched the place. The entire planet! Now... we may have a different option."

"I don't think you understand what you're up against." Xakus sat across from Franco, holding his coffee, and Keenan settled down cross-legged.

"Have we got time for this? What about the Sin-Script?"

"I've set cores running to decode algorithms. It may take some time." He eyed Keenan coolly, and not for the first time did Keenan sense the *iron* in this old professor. Despite age, this man was not a weak-willed individual. He was a man to walk the mountains with. Keenan believed in his judgement: he was rarely wrong.

"Tell me about NanoTek, and Dr Oz."

"Dr Oz is slim, delicate, small. Nothing to look at. Nothing at all. He's bald, face a bit bland, you know, nondescript. In a crowd he would never stand out. He always wears a simple glass suit. It's only when he smiles that his face changes; he has little pointed teeth made of some kind of alien jewels. They say he has never taken his own biomods, but I think that's an urban myth. How could somebody so powerful keep away from self improvement? Why invent them in the first place?"

"Ouch!" Franco glared at Cam. "That bloody hurt that bloody did. Watch what you're poking! I don't like being poked like that! A gentleman," he smiled haughtily, "should not be poked."

"If sir would like to remove his own dormant biowire?"

"OK, OK, you gotta point. Just… stop hurting me! I hurt enough already, what with Mel being kidnapped an' all. And it hurts!"

"What about this Black Rose Citadel? NanoTek's HQ? Sounds hard to infiltrate. Sounds like maybe we should call in Steinhauer, get him to bring his entire QG army down here and forge us a passage. Then we'd have some fun."

"The HQ is an island. About three hundred klicks north of here. Anti-aircraft, anti-nuke, anti-everything. It looks like what it is, a military citadel; huge and black and foreboding. The roof is steeply pointed, the whole thing coated with biowire and veinthreads. Nothing living's going to infiltrate that way. But that's just the tip of the iceberg; the citadel extends *down*, down beneath the ocean for perhaps three or four kilometres. There are sea-corridors created from plasma, hubs with Octo-strands and VertClicks, like cylinders, dropping deep beneath the ocean. In the depths they have the GreenSource Mainframe, the hub of NanoTek's knowledge, technology… and wealth."

"I've got a really bad feeling about this Green-Source Mainframe," said Keenan, voice slow, caged, intuitive.

"And you'd be right to. Rumour suggests it's alive—not just a collection of processors, or even AI; but a real, organic, sentient machine. Rumour has it the GreenSource came from *somewhere else*. Made NanoTek what it is today."

"But you've never seen it?"

"Nobody has seen it," said Xakus, shaking his head.

"So it may not exist?"

"A possibility. You thinking of a distributed network core?"

"I'm thinking a single target is too neat. Also too risky for a company like NanoTek. Still, we'll find out soon enough. Have you got co-ordinates for the island?"

"Yes. It's no great secret. Gaining access is what's going to cause the problem."

"I think we'll go for the straightforward approach."

Franco grinned. "You mean knock on the front door?"

"Seems like the best way to conquer a citadel to me."

"Ouch!"

"Sorry!"

"Damn tennis ball!"

"I said *sorry*, Franco."

Xakus smiled, and jumped down from the Apache. "I'd better go and check on the decryption." Keenan nodded, and watched Xakus crunch off through black snow.

"What do you think?" said Franco.

"I like him. But I don't trust him."

"Me neither. There's something too neat. And we was sent to him by Steinhauer. That's not a great recommendation, my friend. Steinhauer has played us like prawns before."

"Pawns."

"Whatever."

"And you said "we was". Grammatically incorrect."

"Bugger off!"

"One last thing, Franco."

"Yeah mate?"

"Thanks for saving my life back there."

"'Twas nothing. I know you'd do the same thing for me."

"Always, brother."

FRANCO JUMPED FROM the Apache and rolled his shoulders. "Ahh!" he said. "Ahh! My flesh feels as good as new!" He turned and stared at Cam. "Good job scrotum ball!"

"A thank you would be nice."

"Hey, don't push your luck."

"I just spent an *hour* picking dangerous weevils from your flesh."

"Yeah but, like, that's your job. Ain't it?"

"Still, manners cost nothing."

"I agree," beamed Franco. "It's about time you recognised your own deficit."

Leaving Cam hissing to himself, Franco strode through the snow to where Keenan leant over the edge of the skyscraper, enjoying a cigarette and gazing into the vastness below. "What you doing, bro'?"

Then he saw the PAD in Keenan's hands, and he raised his eyebrows. "You sending?"

"Aye." Keenan nodded.

"What you sending?"

"An open Panic Burst. On the old Combat K frequencies. I've also sent one on Fortune's private number; if he still lives. I've not heard from him for a few years."

Fortune was a rogue mercenary AI wanted by the Quad-Gal authorities. Once hunted, Fortune travelled from hiding place to hiding place within the Sinax Cluster. Occasionally, and for the right fee, Fortune would act as NMH Bridge—Navigator, Monitor and Hacker. This gave whoever paid the right fees access to the Quad-Gal Military Factory Class Database, and Fortune could sometimes get Combat K out of situations by employing his awesome technical hacking skills. He had been quiet for a long time now. Privately, Keenan thought he was dead.

"You asking for help?"

"Yeah." Keenan grinned through a pall of smoke. "*Any* help right now would be much appreciated. That's if there's any Combat K guys left out in the smush."

"Olga might…"

Keenan held up his hand. "Don't even go there, Franco. I doubt very much she'll manage to find that which you sent her for. But—don't worry. If we escape this shit, I'll make sure you two get back together for a sweet reunion."

"That's not what I meant," mumbled Franco, face flushing red.

"Sure it's not, buddy. Sure it's not."

Keenan shut down the PAD and checked his weapons, then his WarSuit. Franco's was malfunctioning after his escapade with the disco zombies, but was still vaguely functional—and better than going in without any armour at all.

Cam buzzed over. "Keenan. I was thinking of journeying ahead, scouting out the land."

"Every time you say that, we end up in the shit."

"It's what I'm designed to do. And in all actuality, I don't foresee you having another contact before you reach the Black Rose Citadel."

"On a long enough timeline, we all run out of luck."

"Yes," said Cam, "but you have here a fine Apache Gunship. You know your destination. No. I am quite confident you are safe; I will zip ahead, gather what intel I can for a smooth and speedy infiltration. What do you think?"

"Go on then. Just don't get into trouble."

"I'll be careful," said Cam, primly, and dropped neatly off the edge of the skyscraper.

"That little yellow chicken-shit!" snapped Franco.

"You think he's scared? He's our *scout*."

"Yeah yeah, sure he is. Probably gone for some PopBot sex. Or something."

"You taking your pills?"

Franco popped a green one, and crunched it. It turned his teeth a frothy green and he grinned as if in the throes of a rabid, pus-drenched fit. "Better believe it."

From over by the power source, where Xakus worked with eyes and mind focused decoding the SinScript, there came a heavy bass *whine*. Both Keenan and Franco stared.

Xakus looked up.

"Something wrong?" said Keenan.

"We're out of power."

Franco snorted. "How can an entire *power block* be out of power? Don't be ridiculous!"

Around them, a sudden swathe of blackness washed over the buildings which remained illuminated. Dark flowed like liquid. Distantly, a variety of clunks, whines and growls emerged from machinery closing down, shutting down, *dying*. Darkness seemed to sweep a mammoth quarter of The City.

"Impossible," said Keenan, voice gentle, cool, eyes shining with understanding. Then, voice carefully measured, he turned and stared out over the black horizon where tiny zig-zags of purple flashed and yellow tracers streaked like strobes. "Xakus. Get your kit together."

"Why, Keenan? I can re-route..."

"We've got company."

Franco whirled, eyes straining. "Boss?"

"Get the chopper started. *Now!*"

Franco ran, leapt aboard the Apache and fired the engines. The rotors started to run, scything snow, and Keenan hoisted his MPK, checked the weapon, and lit a cigarette. Smoke engulfed him. Calmly, he waited.

Xakus, with kit packed, sprinted to Keenan. He handed the SinScript to the battered soldier for safe keeping, and Keenan stowed the valuable disk beneath his WarSuit. He laughed. Yeah, he thought. Until the next time.

"Have you seen anything?"

"Get in the chopper."

They slammed, screaming through blackened skies, rotors thundering, fire flickering from exhaust ports: Three Black Tiger KAZ Gunships, howling as they sped into view and roared over-head, rotors whirling, banking in close formation as Keenan sighted down his MPK and unleashed a long, hard volley of bullets, turning, tracking the choppers as they circled, banking steeply again, their targets now identified...

"Franco, I need that chopper!" roared Keenan. He changed mags, allowing the first heated alloy strip to tumble to the ground. It clattered brittle against concretealloy.

There came a whine, then a *whump*. Keenan stood, legs braced, teeth in a snarl, and unleashed another stream of bullets, watching the rocket detach from the Black Tiger and roar towards the roof... and his fragile shell.

Keenan rolled left and hit the ground hard amidst puddles of melted snow as the rocket slammed the roof thirty feet to his right—where seconds earlier Xakus had stood. A green fireball billowed, raged into the sky on a volley of erupting building chunks and severed cables. The explosion sent a wash of steam broiling over Keenan.

Keenan crawled as the Black Tiger Gunships smashed overhead, gunfire rattling. Bullets slammed Combat K's Apache; sparks smashed a firework display.

"Come on!" cried Franco.

Keenan leapt in the Apache as Franco thrust at controls like a mad monkey. Engines screaming, they leapt into the air and Keenan grabbed the heavy mounted machine gun, an EMF5000, and buckled himself in. His head snapped round. "Xakus, strap yourself tight. We're in the shit."

Xakus nodded, face drawn in fear, and struggled against physics to the far wall where he locked himself to the internal buckles of the machine.

"Going down," said Franco, who despite claiming to hate flying, was actually a pretty accomplished pilot, only superseded in skill by Pippa—although he would never admit it. Franco dropped the Apache from the summit of the skyscraper and roared towards the ground. "What's on our tail?"

"Black Tigers. Three of them."

"Bastard. Not the KAZ models?"

"Yeah. I think."

The Apache roared ground-wards and behind the Black Tigers were jostled into single-file due to the narrow streets; guns roared, and Franco pulled up, cruising along in a blur a few feet above street level. Bullets raked the streets. Stray cars were caught, punctured, lifted and tossed, hammer-blows which left them squatting on destroyed suspension and curling flames. Several exploded, and Franco banked, taking an intersection and whizzing between towering skyscrapers, flashing through balls of acrid smoke.

"I can't use the gun down here," shouted Keenan over the flapping, smashing noise from the open door. "We're too enclosed!"

Franco nodded. "If I rise above the streets they'll flank us."

"Here, we're a sitting duck."

Franco nodded again, slamming the chopper right down another intersection. Rotors thrummed, reflected from glass and alloy walls. In close pursuit, the lead Black Tiger growled, lurched forward, and started to gain.

Keenan grabbed Franco's pack, pulled free a BABE grenade. He pulled the pin, shuffled to the edge of the chopper so his legs were hanging out over the flashing, stroboscopic ground. "Make a left," he shouted.

Franco slammed them left, and as they banked Keenan squinted, tears streaming down his face in the slipstream, and hurled the BABE. There came a hiatus. Then a *boom,* and a blossom of purple flames. The three Black Tigers slammed through smoke. Machine guns roared, and bullets slapped along the Apache's flank.

"Hold on!" screamed Franco, and the Apache's nose lifted dramatically and they soared skywards, g-force pinning them in place as engines screamed and groaned and wall panels rattled. Reaching the summit of the nearest skyscraper block, Franco pulled a massively tight turn, soaring in an arc through the sky and coming around towards...

A wall of glass.

"No!" growled Keenan as they flashed towards the skyscraper, and Franco blasted an AAAM rocket. It detached, roared, and detonated a hole in the side of the skyscraper. The Apache slammed into the smoking maw and for a few seconds Keenan caught glimpses of flaming chairs and blackened desks, scorched computer terminals, internal walls and a flashing flicker of a bizarre detonated office. Another *boom* signified a second rocket and then they were out in the black, snow-swirling sky as Franco jiggled the Apache around...

"Get on the guns!" he screamed.

The three Black Tigers were arraigned, searching for the Apache. Keenan, gripping the EMF5000 in two sweating fists, unloaded a hardcore smash of bullets that streaked across the sky on trails of fire and cordite. Bullets ripped into the first machine, spitting sparks from rotors and sending it spiralling down in a stream of billowing, blue smoke...

In the punctured cockpit, Keenan had seen flailing, panicking... *zombies*.

You've got to be kidding, he thought.

Shit.

"The zombies are flying the choppers!" he snarled. "How's that possible? How, I ask you?"

He continued to fire the EMF in heavy bursts, but the Black Tigers had manoeuvred and missiles streaked towards Combat K. With a squawk Franco dropped the Apache out of the sky, cutting power and they fell, chasing the plummeting, spiralling Black Tiger out of control and heading groundwards at an incredible, terminal rate...

The damaged Black Tiger fell. And as it fell, zombies disgorged from the side door in what appeared an attempt at escape—and Franco screamed, suddenly, as a zombie flashed up at him, slammed the Apache's cockpit with a pus-riddled maw trailing ooze and slime, then slid free and through the rotors, distributing fine minced zombie cubes over a kilometre wide area.

"What the fuck was that?" snarled Keenan, shaken by the ferocity of the impact which had rocked the entire chopper.

"A flying zombie," yelled back Franco, hard on the vibrating, almost-out-of-control, controls. Below him, the Black Tiger disgorged more panicking, free-fall zombies. Only now Combat K's Apache was travelling faster, vertically, than the zombies could fall, and despite Franco veering left and right and spinning them around various axes, still more zombies splattered against the web-riddled cockpit windscreen with *thuds* and *crunches* and *cracks*.

"No no no!" muttered Franco, trying desperately to avoid this random sky-kill.

"What the hell's going on?" bellowed Keenan.

"It's a zombie apocalypse," spat back Franco, before wrestling control and veering the groaning Apache around on a wide arc that shaved the roof from an abandoned street-level juggernaut like a tin-top from a can of spam, and left the Apache without landing gear.

"Neat," said Keenan, voice dry and calm, eyes full of ice.

"Hey, they don't call me Franco 'Sky Captain' Haggis for nothing, you know!" Franco beamed optimistically, all of Keenan's considerable sarcasm lost on him.

"They're still on our tail!" said Xakus. The man, strapped tightly behind his X-BELT, was watching a wall scanner. "You can't outrun Black Tigers. They're the fastest combat choppers on the market."

"I *know that!*" said Franco, wrestling again with his dodgy controls and ignoring a swathe of red warning lights which decorated the console. "Why d'ya think I'm doing all the fancy piloting?"

They screamed through the streets at psycho low-level. More bullets roared from the pursuing Black Tigers. Then, there came a *whumpf*. Fire roared around them and Franco squawked like a head-hacked chicken as his entire rear-view was filled with an expanding blossom of fire. Heat smashed the men. The Apache groaned, rattling, and the tail-rotors started to smoke. Franco veered left, and the two Black Tigers missed the turn and disappeared in a blaze of billowing, grinding flame-throwers.

Franco slowed their wild onslaught, slowed with nervous care, and hovered for a moment near street level. Glass sparkled like snow across the ground. Franco checked damage reports.

"What hit us?" he said, finally.

"They've got anti-chopper *flamethrowers*," snapped back Keenan. "I thought you'd know?"

"How could I know that, eh lad? How?"

"Because it's been on the news," said Keenan, voice low. "KAZ Systems have been heavily criticised for their inhumane approach; but, seeing as the staff at KAZ are all *aliens,* they consider it an intrinsically dumb criticism."

"I never saw no news," said Franco. "Shit. Too much time in bed with Mel! Hey, better get us moving." Even as he spoke, a swarm of heavily armed zombies charged from a side-street with a roar. Limping and dragging and lolling, they attacked the hovering low-level chopper and started to hurl bricks and bottles.

Franco gave them a V-sign through the web-crackled cockpit. "Dickheads!" he shouted. "What d'ya think you're doing, throwing bottles at a damned armoured chopper? Go on, bugger off the lot of you!"

"*Franco!*" hissed Keenan, as a zombie lifted an RPG and shouldered the long, sleek, matt green military-grade weapon.

"Yeah yeah, OK, I'm on it. Don't get your knickers twisted all backside waywards."

The Apache soared towards the sky, zombies waving fists to become distant stick-zombies. The RPG disgorged and the warhead slammed towards them trailing fire and smoke. Franco twisted the Apache, and the rocket arced off into the distant sky like one of the world's largest, deadliest fireworks.

Franco turned and beamed at Keenan and Xakus, the Apache still climbing vertically. "See, compadre? What you panicking for? You're with the *smart* party now! Nothing can touch Franco 'Chopper King' Haggis when he's got his War Head on!" He beamed, congratulating himself on the metaphor. "You see what I did there? Warhead? War... *head*! My head? You see? Geddit? Ha! Now, all I need is to get those bloody Black Tigers in my sights..."

They slammed up from the jagged toothline of skyscrapers, just as two Black Tigers crossed their path. Franco's Apache smashed into the lead Black Tiger Gunship side-on with a devastating *crunch*, the Apache's nose poking into and *through* the passenger hold, through buckled side-cargo doors.

The two war machines *merged* with a scream of metal.

Franco stared, slack-jawed, as ten zombies glared at him through his web-riddled cockpit windscreen. They cocked weapons, and with chewed, severed fingers and lolling, pus-oozing jaws, levelled a bristling array of guns...

The two choppers, locked together in an unholy embrace, fought to travel in different directions. Engines whined and screamed. Exhausts spat fire and oil-smoke, ice-shards and matrix-spill. Rotors, spinning at 10,000 rpm only inches apart, set up a weird aural wailing as sound waves bounced and chopped between them. Suddenly, this gestalt machine entity began to jerk and wobble and weave across the sky in looping arcs, in the most un-balletic example of combat chopper flight ever witnessed above The City; the joining jerked and fell, lifted and spun, a spastic dance of screaming motors and wrestling controls. Franco fought with his Apache F52 Gunship, cursing and howling, one eye on the ten armed zombies who were growling and spitting beyond the spider-screen. However, he didn't need to worry. As the locked and mating choppers gyrated and pulled, dropped and whirled, so the ten zombies with aimed weapons were suddenly tossed about inside the hold like rotten, fuzzy tomatoes in a blender. They bounced and spun and slammed and thrashed. With wide eyes, Franco watched them disintegrate slowly before him, rotten limbs pulled free, heads bouncing from his cockpit, green pus spewing to swill first across floors, then walls, then ceiling. Occasional random bullets *zipped* and *pinged* as zombies head-butted one other into oblivion.

Franco patted his harness with relief.

The second Black Tiger had roared past the merged and buckled machines, lifting and banking, coming around with two zombies arming heavy machine guns. It levelled, watching for a moment for a clear shot... and then, obviously deciding it was willing to sacrifice its comrade in order to bring down the enemy Apache, the Tiger's guns opened fire...

Bullets roared. They slapped up the Apache's flanks, then on into the Black's Tiger's fuselage.

"Hey! Hey stop that!" screamed Franco, as the zombie mincer mashed and churned before his beady eyes. He was starting to feel sick. He tried again and again to pull the Apache free, jerking backwards, full-throttle, with engines roaring in a grinding, pumping frenzy. The Apache's nose-cone groaned, and tugged, and resolutely refused to budge.

Keenan, every few seconds, got the third Black Tiger in his sights. He squeezed the EMF's heavy triggers, watched bullet and tracer slam off across the night. Then, in their erratic dance, the gun would be pulled from his hands with a slick curse.

"I feel sick!" moaned Franco, observing the organic zombie blender.

"Get us out of this shit!" screamed Keenan, firing off more heavy calibre rounds. Several found their mark, and the Black Tiger leapt up into the sky, circling, aiming for a safe, clear shot. More bullets slapped the waltzing machines. More punctures appeared in both the Apache F52 and its unwilling lover.

"What's that smell?" said Franco, voice suddenly cool, head clear. An arm landed against his cockpit window. It only had one finger. A middle finger. It seemed to be giving Franco a final, mocking farewell.

"Aviation fuel," snapped Keenan.

There came a roar as the free and painfully dangerous Black Tiger unleashed a blast of industrial flamethrower over the two machines. Flames sped along the Black Tiger's tail and Franco, chirping and squeaking like a panicked budgerigar, wrestled with his controls and gnawed with his teeth. He slapped open his harness, sat back, and kicked out at his cockpit with both sandals. The arm with its offending middle finger vanished into the mire of pulped churned zombie slush. The cockpit folded over, and fell *inside* the enemy chopper. Franco scrambled out, onto his own machine's nose-cone. He could hear the roar of fire. He could smell smoke and hear the *ping* of superheating alloy. Bullets whirred and whined. There! There! He could see the ridge that trapped them! The alloy lip which ensnared their brave Apache! Franco scrambled down the nose cone, and around in a circle, a monkey atop a cracked and sliding cockpit screen which in turn floated atop ten mashed mushed zombies. Franco poked his MPK into the ridge gap and with a grunt, levered at the locked and battling choppers. The barrel of his gun groaned, then bent in a comedy U shape.

"Bastard. Bastard."

Panting hard, and with the temperature rising fast, in the gap between nose-cone and door-rim

Franco could see Keenan pumping round after round at the enemy Black Tiger through a funnel of flames. He scrambled back, bottom sliding on the gore-slippery screen. With both sandals, he slammed at the Apache's nose cone. Again, and again, and again.

As he kicked, grunting, sweating, he made the mistake of looking down. Several zombie faces were pressed against the underside of the battered cockpit, squashed and leering at him with lolling tongues and the permanent inebriation of the alcoholic dead.

"Aaii," said Franco, shuddering, and with a final surge of sandalled feet, he disconnected the two combat helicopters. There came a deep and heavy groan of stressed and twisting steel. The two machines eased apart, and Franco punched the air several times.

"Yes! Yes YES!"

And then he realised.

He was *inside* the enemy chopper, surfing a glass platter atop a sea of mulched zombie. The chopper was on fire. And, quite possibly, about to explode.

"No! No NO!" he squeaked, and ran, leaping from the buckled doorway to skydive towards his falling, out-of-control Apache F52. Behind, there came a *click* of detonation. The Black Tiger billowed into a raging howling screaming fireball, the nose turned towards The City far below... and began to suddenly accelerate in a smoking, fiery plummet. Straight at Franco.

Franco dived like an Olympic athlete, but his body was far from aerodynamic. Below, inside the

Apache, he could see Keenan fighting to free himself from his harness. Franco gave a wave, beard flapping in the wind, and watched Keenan return him a scowl of pure evil.

With a grunt, Franco landed on the Apache's buckled, battered nose cone, sandals slipping treacherously. "Yeah, baby!" he cheered. His nostrils twitched. He could smell smoke. Beard snapping violently, he glanced back. The fiery fireball of the burning detonated Black Tiger was gaining. Inside its roaring shell, there came further *cracks* of ignition as bullets exploded.

Franco screamed, clambered through the cockpit hole and into the Apache, grabbed the controls and veered them to the right and down, levelling out with a sudden thudding of rotors and an instant rush of cool, rhythmical calm.

They hovered.

Behind, the flaming Black Tiger disappeared to ground level and there came a *whumpf*. Flames roared a hundred feet high, broiling. Franco sat, breathing deeply, eyes saucer wide. He patted frantically at himself, to check he was still in one piece. Then he turned and beamed at Keenan.

"Hey hey *hey*!"

"You *dickhead*."

"What? I mean... *what?*"

"You *utter* arsehole."

"Hey, come on, admit it, that was a serious bit of adventuring, right? Couldn't have done it any better if I'd been a stunt man in the movies." He chuckled to himself. "Huh. I tell you something, they should give me a job in Holy Hollywood!"

"Yes," snarled Keenan, "as the *fucking tea boy*. The other chopper's coming round. Get us moving!"

"Right you are, boss."

They cruised, low, at a slow and manoeuvrable speed, waiting for the attack—which never came.

"We've lost him!" beamed Franco.

"Hmm," said Keenan, and by the look on his face it was clear he was unconvinced.

"Either that, or them damn zombies recognised in me a superior flight commander. I tell you something, Keenan, I would have made a great Luftwaffe pilot, I would! Untouchable! King of the Skies! Fighter Pilot *supremo!*"

"Have you finished?"

"No."

"Well *finish*. Now. And get us the hell out of here."

"North?"

"Yeah. To NanoTek."

"I'm on it." And, still muttering about superior flight skills, clever aerial combat manoeuvres, and how *he'd beat them damn zombies in a fair dogfight any day*, Franco—eventually—flew them north.

THEY FLEW FOR an hour, sometimes low through deserted city streets, sometimes *whumping* over armies of zombies. After several incidents of RPG tracking, Franco avoided close confrontation with battalions of tooled-up deviants.

"They're getting more frisky," said Keenan, as they passed low over yet another collection of maybe ten thousand zombies. They milled around, armed to the backbone, eyes on the heavens and the stench of fresh brain scooting overhead.

"You think they can smell us? Even from down there?"

Keenan shrugged, smoking, eyes on the damaged readouts from the Apache's battered and cracked console. "Mate, I wouldn't put anything past them. One thing's for sure; they're a damned sight more advanced than any living-dead creature has a right to be."

Xakus remained silent, withdrawn, often closing his eyes and resting his head back against the wall. After their recent near-death experiences, and the death of MICHELLE, Xakus simply wanted this mission finished. He had lost his sense of humour.

They flew through heavy falls of snow, then out under crystal clear heavens. Cold wind howled into the Apache F52 through a vacant lack of cockpit windshield and the three men pulled on heavy thermal jackets which ignited with a chemical *click*.

After a while, the world seemed to fall silent.

It was as if they had left the zombies behind.

Mile after mile of vacant, blank, cold, dead skyscraper scrolled beneath them. There was no life here, no movement; nothing. They had entered a ghost town, a dead world, a planet of lost dreams.

"We getting close?" said Keenan, after a while.

"Yes," said Franco. "Not far now."

They sped out under fifty-lane highways which soared, veering above a vast and choppy ocean gleaming like black glass. Huge thick crystal struts with a fifty-foot diameter soared from beneath the ocean, supporting arcing bridges and walkways and elevated cubescrapers. The giant support plinths glittered with twinkling lights.

"This place is surreal," said Franco, finally.

Keenan nodded. "An echoing underworld," he said, smoking and sipping at a coffee from the Apache's CoffeeChef™—perhaps the only single item aboard the vehicle which hadn't been battered, bashed, scratched or scorched in some way.

"It's spooky all right. Reminds me of Teller's World."

"Yeah, and that *other place* after the K Jump." They both fell into a brooding silence, contemplating the Zone they'd travelled after the jump from Teller's. By all rights, they should have been dead. In all reality, they carried a splinter to another place in their souls. It made them not quite human. But then, that was another story...

Keenan leant forward, catching a glimpse of something nestling in the Apache's foot-well. Franco had cunningly draped a jacket over the item in disguise. "What's that?"

"Nothing."

"Franco?"

Franco looked shifty. "'Tis nothing boss. Honest injun."

Keenan made a grab for the jacket, and Franco made a grab to stop him but Keenan was too quick; the jacket whipped away to reveal...

"Is that the damned IMS Knuckles took from the SIM back at Porky Pauper's juggernaut depot?"

"Aye."

"And what do *you* want with it?"

"Protection."

"*Franco,* it's fucking *dangerous,* mate. You *know* why they made them illegal. Because if some moron got hold of one, he could do some real fucking damage! It's about the only thing that'll get you ejected hardwire offworld from The City, for God's sake! It is their one Statute Law. Gods, they see an IMS as far worse than any suitcase nuke."

"Yeah? So? Well? Danger is my middle name! Reet?"

"An IMS was the one thing that managed to stop MICHELLE dead in her tracks. It's one serious piece of industrial hardware, and I'm not too happy about you smuggling the bastard with us. It's bad enough to think you've got a gun. But *that!*"

"I like to know I'm tooled up," persisted Franco. "I just wished I'd had it to hand when those choppers attacked me. Did I say me? I meant us."

"What, so you could have destroyed half a city block? Franco, it's lethal with a capital L. We're supposed to be on a covert infil. What were you thinking? That we'd eat our way into NanoTek's HQ through a few klicks of solid concrete?"

"Hey, that's a bloody good idea!"

"And that's why *I* plan and *you* fly."

As they argued, the water beneath them became increasingly choppy. Little white waves spun jagged detail across the ocean's ice-rimmed surface. Above, a fifty-lane freeway servicing the NanoTek HQ on mammoth crystal supports sat, desolate and forlorn; a deserted, abandoned road to nowhere; a Highway to Hell.

"Any sign of Cam?" Franco was cheery. Optimistic. It was galling.

"No."

"Any message from Steinhauer?"

Keenan checked his PAD. "No."

"What about Pippa?"

"Why would Pippa contact me?"

Franco stared at Keenan. "We-*elll,* I bet she knows we're here, and I bet she wants to see us, *and* she did used to be your bird."

"So?"

"So, you had some, y'know, fun times together."

The Apache F52, battered, bruised and scorched, started to make a rattling, banging sound. It was unhealthy, in a mechanically failing kind of way.

"Our past relationship is irrelevant. She wants me dead. I want her dead. You could say our love is over."

"Ahh, it's never over 'til the fat lady sings."

"What kind of garbage statement is that?"

"I heard it, I did."

Keenan sighed, and Franco took the Apache down low over the waves. Rolling ocean crashed beneath them, the chopper's rhythmical passage bouncing from a vast seascape.

Franco tapped the Apache's scanner. "Damn and bloody blast."

"Something up?"

"It's broke."

Keenan snorted a laugh. "What, the scanner or the whole fucking machine?"

"Don't be like that, Keenan. This baby has taken us to hell and back! She's reliable! Hard-working! And when she wants to kick arse, she can really kick arse!"

The rocket seemed to come from nowhere; it slammed the tail section of the Apache howling in a raging, expanding inferno that ate the combat chopper's rear end and sent rotors whirling and screaming off across the ocean, where they skimmed, and struck down with super-heated *fizzes*.

Alarms shrieked, and smoke poured into the cockpit.

"Abandon ship!" wailed Franco, but before they could do anything the Apache stalled and dropped from the sky, like a bird hit by a bullet. It struck the ocean with harsh impact, black waters slamming aside as Combat K grabbed what they could, struggling into packs as freezing ocean rolled away and then surged inside and the Apache began to quickly sink...

There were hisses, clouds of smoke and steam. The fireball at the machine's tail-end was extinguished. Smoke rolled through a crisp clear night.

Keenan gasped, losing his cigarette. He struggled free of the Apache's cabin cell and trod water, which chilled him instantly. There came a *crackle* as his thermal jacket adjusted—the one thing keeping him alive in such a chilled environment. His narrowed eyes roved the black sky, searching for the enemy, and he hoisted his MPK around and above his head, trying to keep the weapon dry.

"Reliable and hard-working?" snorted Keenan, as Franco swam towards him. They both watched as the Apache, bubbling merrily, sank below the rolling ocean and was swiftly claimed.

"Help," said Xakus, who was struggling, some feet away.

Keenan swam to him, eyes still sweeping the sky. Something had brought them down. Had it been an automated system, like Steinhauer had warned him about, or another aircraft? Either way, Keenan was feeling twitched.

"What's the matter?"

In the dark, Keenan couldn't see shit. He blinked, attempting to adjust his vision to ambient light. Below them, the Apache disappeared, a huge fountain of bubbles erupting on the surface of the ocean.

"Shrapnel. From the explosion." Xakus was grimacing in pain, and Keenan grabbed him to stop him going under. Waves lifted them, undulating, and dropping them savagely into a trough. Xakus spluttered on black brine.

"Are you bad?"

Before Xakus could answer, they heard the rotors of the Black Tiger KAZ Gunship. It cruised, low over the ocean, search lights sweeping left and right. It slowed near their crash zone.

"Bastards," snapped Keenan. "Well, that answers *that* question."

The combat chopper was lit internally by an eerie green glow. They could see the crowd of zombies, lolling, pus-strewn faces searching for survivors.

The chopper circled, rotors thumping.

"They found us, then," observed Franco. "I knew it. I *knew* we should have stayed and hunted them down. I did, I said to you, we should have stayed and hunted them down. I did."

"Franco, shut it."

"Yeah boss."

Keenan became suddenly aware Xakus had passed out. He grasped the man tight, and realised in anger he could no longer fire his weapon. If he let go of Xakus, the professor would sink...

"Shit. Shit." Keenan gritted his teeth, eyes narrowed and fixed on the circling, zombie-filled helicopter.

"Don't worry," whispered Franco, bobbing on a rising wave, then splashing back down into a trough. "I'm on it. I'm the man, the dude, the guy for the gig."

Searchlights swept.

There came a *whine* from the chopper... and Keenan found himself debating the issue of his own survival when suddenly, from the water beside Franco, there surged a barrage of bubbles and the long grey barrel of the IMS.

Keenan started to mouth the word "No!" as Franco hoisted the weapon and unleashed hell and fury at the searching helicopter. The IMS whined, and there came a *whump* as molecular disintegration lashed through the heavens and the chopper slammed right, banking sharply, warning systems screaming. Keenan could hear onboard shrills from weapon detection systems; the chopper's AI knew what an IMS *was,* and the destruction it could bring.

The Black Tiger opened fire, miniguns howling and Keenan ducked under the ocean, down into a cold obsidian muffled world dragging Xakus with him. Franco slammed the IMS around, charged it again, and unleashed a scream of energy which cut through the Black Tiger's runners and sent it spinning off through the dark under-sky. Franco, grinning like a maniac, muttered to himself, "Bastards! Blowing us from the sky then wanting to come down here with dirty guns and pick us off when we're bobbing on the sea well we'll have to see about that because Franco Haggis is here to save the day and he's not taking none of your crap and believe me this weapon is a *bad ass* weapon and they don't call me Franco 'Happy Detonation' Haggis for nothing!" The IMS howled, and reality seemed to warp and wobble around the industrial demolition tool. Inside the Black Tiger, the zombies were fighting and screeching. The IMS beam slammed through the Black Tiger, first cutting it in half vertically, and, as Franco waved the Industrial Molecule Stripper around in his calloused powerful hands like a madman with a chainsaw, horizontally. The Black Tiger, effectively quartered and spitting showers of sparks and outpourings of fuel, toppled in cubes into the ocean where the fuel flared and the wreckage ignited, burning atop the rolling waves.

"Ha!" said Franco, switching off the IMS with a *clump*. The machine vibrated for a while in his hands, then was still. "No bugger's going to mess with this redneck!"

Keenan surfaced, dragging the unconscious form of Xakus with him. He glared at Franco. "You finished, idiot?"

"Idiot? Moi? I think you will find, Mr Keenan, that once again the wily and wonderful Franco has saved the day! He has disposed of the dastardly enemy! Spliced their little attack chopper into pieces! Saved us all from a sound and jolly buggering!"

Keenan paddled close, until his face was inches from Franco's. Then, so close the glare of nearby fires burning on the ocean reflected crazy-lights in his narrowed eyes, he growled, "Take a good look around, you drug-infused moron."

Franco licked his lips. Had there been something he'd overlooked? There couldn't have been. He was Franco! And Franco never, well, rarely, well, sometimes, well, *many times,* made mistakes. And on this occasion he'd been super careful! He'd been sure of his actions! Hadn't he? After all, they were out at sea. What could possibly go wrong?

Franco turned, paddling in the black ocean. Overhead, the fifty-lane freeway veered in a climbing arc soaring high into the heavens and blocking out the stars. Franco stared hard at the freeway. Perhaps a kilometre across, it was vast, epic, a monument of world-class engineering skill. An example of man conquering nature, and imposing his Will over the World.

Franco opened his mouth to say something.

Then he closed it again.

He squinted.

One of the fifty-foot-diameter crystal support struts had a narrow, glowing line across its base. Franco stared hard at that line. Stared at it for a long time.

"No," he said. "I couldn't possibly have."

Keenan was by his ear. "I think you'll find it's much worse than *that,*" he hissed.

Franco peered again, myopically. The next support strut had four glowing criss-cross marks on its flank; simple orange lines, like scars of molten glass. Franco looked to the next strut. And that, also, was marked.

"That *can't* have been little old me," he said, finally, uneasily.

"What fucking *range* setting did you have on the thing?"

"Only about..." Franco stopped. It was fifty metres, right? He'd clicked it to fifty metres. 50.0m. He stared down at the dial. He felt something curl up and die inside his belly.

It was set to *500* metres.

Franco looked up. Up. *Up.*

Above, several glowing lines of molten steelconcrete criss-crossed the fifty-lane freeway. Even as he watched, the titanic mega-structure gave a long, low, agonising groan. It was a concrete dinosaur, dying. A Ket-i World Warrior in the throes of global agony. A behemoth ready to *awake.*

"No! Shit! Keenan! It wasn't me! It can't have been me! I mean, even *I'm* not that stupid!"

Keenan was swimming hard, dragging Xakus behind him by the scruff.

"Hey? Where you going? What you doing, Keenan? Come back!"

Franco started paddling after him.

Keenan turned. Glared at his friend. "Swim, you idiot! When that lot comes down it's gonna drag a whole load of shit under the ocean! We need to get out of the suction radius."

"Hey, relax, it's not gonna fall! Don't be silly! Don't be a crazy fool!" Franco swam on, a beady eye peering back over his shoulder. Already the pillars had started to shift, minutely at first, molten edges screeching in a torturous, long-drawn out *wail* which became gradual agony to the ears and made Franco want to vomit.

"It just *can't fall!*" he whispered.

A sound like thunder began. The two men powered through the ocean, heads down, entire strength focused on swimming now; and swimming *fast*.

The thunder warbled and rumbled through the heavens, growing louder and louder and louder and louder. Behind, dust and chunks of concrete started to fall, tumbling from the slow-motion undulating freeway. Huge splashes echoed across the ocean. Waves rammed Keenan and Franco, and they both swam faster in accelerating urgency. Franco's arms pumped like pistons and he overtook Keenan at a rapid crawl, then stopped, grabbed hold of Xakus, and helped tow the unconscious professor after them.

"I think it's gonna fall," he gulped at Keenan, spitting out water.

"You don't say."

"Where we going?"

Keenan nodded. "There's an oil-carrier platform over there. I think we'll be safe. That is, unless the fall creates a fucking tsunami to wash us to our well-deserved deaths."

"You mean you *don't know?*"

"I'm a soldier, Franco, not an expert in hydrodynamics."

They reached the platform, which was rusted, greasy, and bobbing wildly as more and more chunks fell from the towering, swaying, kilometre-wide freeway. Keenan climbed up, hauled Xakus after him, and dumped the man on the corrugated deck. He helped Franco to scramble, little legs kicking, aboard. Keenan traced around the dark edges, and found the platform linked to something beneath the sea by wrist-thick chains.

Keenan rolled Xakus to his back, then rolled him over, locating the wound in the man's flank. Beneath, a rib was broken, and a ten inch gash, not too deep, had been carved in flesh from the explosion aboard the Apache. Keenan found his medkit and applied field strips, effectively gluing the professor's flesh together. He turned the man's thermal jacket to full. Out there, in the ice-laden ocean, they were all beginning to freeze.

As he finished his work, Keenan looked up, watched the freeway teetering around in the darkness, then slowly topple sideways, pillars sliding apart with gruesome growling sounds, disintegrating neatly, a billion billion tonnes of steelconcrete sliding under the surging water carrying abandoned cars and juggernauts, and twenty-carriage ultra-coaches.

Grimly, Keenan injected Xakus with painkillers and nutrients, and spat discharged stingbots into the rolling, seething ocean.

"Bad habit, that," said Franco, watching uneasily as a fifteen trillion dollar building development sank in a surge of bubbles and churning black.

"You're the bad habit! Franco, are you sure want to continue on this mission?"

"I must rescue Mel." He sulked.

"Well, in that case, you do exactly what I tell you, when I tell you. Or I'm going in alone."

"You can't do that! I have rights!"

"Oh yeah? Well for the first time in history, Franco, I'm going to pull rank on you. Now, you do what you're told. And that's a fucking order. Understand?"

"Mnmnffmnf."

"I said, UNDERSTAND?"

"No need to shout. I get it. It's got. Up here. In my skull." He tapped his head.

The platform rolled violently, pulling at its clanking chains which stretched, screeching and dripping iced brine. Where the freeway slice had tumbled beneath the waves, the sea surged and bubbled as if boiling. Distantly, buoys clanged. The ocean seemed to roar, and it went on for a long, long time…

And was gone.

The ocean fell still. Eerily still.

Xakus groaned, sitting up, touching his side tenderly. His fingers explored the repair strips, then he rubbed at his head and accepted the water canteen from Keenan.

"So we survived, then."

"Just," said Keenan, throwing Franco an evil glare.

"We're not far. From the entry point. You still want to go in the front gates?"

Keenan shrugged. "I kind of get the feeling we're expected. I'm starting to feel like this is… a test. Although what kind of test, I'm not sure. One thing that's certain is those zombies keep turning up with unerring regularity; and well-tooled, for such a bunch of deviated twisted individuals. This is starting to feel like training school." He gave a sick, twisted smile.

"Come on," said Franco. "We've a long swim ahead."

They slid into the ocean, which had grown calm now Franco's embarrassment had disappeared, and gazed off into the darkness. They could not see the lights of NanoTek's Black Rose Citadel HQ; but it was out there, squatting in the gloom, in the night, in the blackness... ominous, and waiting, like a giant maw for their impending arrival and a necessary feed.

THE SWIM TOOK an eternity. It was cold despite thermal electronic jackets, and portentously dark. The sea was filled with debris. Packets and tins, slimy boxes, skank-filled bottles. Combat K swam through filth; gradually, they absorbed the scum of The City.

During the monotony of swimming Keenan thought back, drifted back to a better life a good life an early life when everything had been... well, *right*. His children. Shit. Rachel and Ally. Their sweet faces. Their sweeter smiles. Giggling and clinging like loose monkeys to his arms, begging him for sweets or SLAM music or glitter shoes. And... Keenan no longer swam though an endless cess-pit of churning toxic ocean; he was back with his wife, and children, when there was still manic hot love between them and she held him round the waist and laughed at some small joke, lifting up under his arm, coming round, arms drooping over his shoulders, kissing him. He could smell her perfume. Still smell her perfume. It was powerfully erotic. And... then the image crashed down around him and he realised with a start rain was falling on the ocean in thick black droplets, probably containing oil or some other toxic contaminant.

Around the three struggling men a storm arose, swift and powerful, slamming at them with predator ferocity. And in the storm Keenan could see Pippa's face and he realised; she was poison in his blood, in his veins, in his heart and in his soul. She always had been. Always would be. He remembered Hekkan Grall. *I should have killed you then,* he thought. *I should have ended both our miseries. Either that, or died in that bed under cold green sunlight.*

In bitterness, he swam on.

Franco, on the other hand, was reliving happier memories. At first he thought of Mel, of their chance meeting down to a certain lack of tax contribution, and the wonderful acceleration of sexual intimacy that followed. In truth, Franco had never had such an intimate and deep relationship (despite being married, twice) and he savoured every nuance of post-coital chatter, every syllable of ear-whispering delight, every instance of tongue-teasing exploration... right up to the point where Mel transmogrified into an eight-foot zombie deviant with dubious body odour.

Franco blinked. "Shit."

"What is it?"

They stopped; were treading water. The darkness seemed infinite. Out there, they were terribly alone.

"I was having a good ol' daydream; then I remembered Shelly."

"The first wife? The one who cleaned you out?"

Franco nodded, face bitter. Then he brightened. "Still. I look at the positives, right? At *least* she set me on the road to sexual exploration with all manner of deviants." He beamed.

"Franco, you'd find happiness in cancer, joy in a brain haemorrhage, ecstasy in instant death."

"Aye." He thought. "I'm the man who put the tit into hepatitis." He beamed. "Still! All those STDs are gone now and solved! No more itchy scratchy for this sexual athlete!"

"Come on," growled Keenan. "We've got a long way to go."

"Aye."

"And Franco?"

"Aye?"

"Keep your thoughts to yourself in the future, there's a good lad."

"I CAN SEE IT!"

Keenan and Franco stopped, treading water and nudging at bobbing filth in the darkness. Silence reigned, except for the roll of the ocean, and the occasional slap of water. Sometimes, in the depths beneath them, a huge and bass grumbling could be heard, almost *felt,* like some titanic machine roaring in subdued and muffled operation. Now, however, this mechanical leviathan had receded. Even Xakus with his knowledge of The City could not explain the aural phenomenon.

Keenan squinted. "Yes," he breathed, feeling at once a terrible fear and apprehension, but at the same time an excitement at stretching for the climax of the mission. Would Xakus decode the SinScript and decipher why the scourge of invading junks desired Galhari? Would Mel change back to human and be fit and healthy, and ready to marry her beloved Franco? And would NanoTek own up to having a hand in the terrible deformations caused by their deviated unsafe biomod technology?

From their ocean platter, NanoTek HQ, the Black Rose Citadel, was ominous indeed. Xakus had said it was an island, but had not emphasised its sheer *scale*.

The Citadel was a fortress island, a vast, sheer, black-walled monstrosity that reared high and impenetrable and covered the twenty-square-kilometre island in its rocky entirety. In the gloom, the massive slick walls gleamed, gloss, solid, smooth, without window or hand-hold or any possible means of ascent.

"How can we climb that?" said Franco, in awe.

"They have gates, right? A means of entry? Up on the freeway bridge?"

Xakus smiled weakly. "Yes, there are bridge connections to the mainland, but these retract into the body of The Citadel leaving nothing but a smooth and impassable wall. However, this rarely happens. I assumed these bridges would be open, but looking now," Xakus glanced back over his shoulder, then tracked across the dark ocean, "it would appear everything has been shut down. They've closed everything. NanoTek has retreated into its bomb-proof shell."

"We need an air infiltration, then," said Franco.

Xakus shook his head. He was shivering, and his teeth chattered despite electronic thermal aid. "No. The shell analogy was a good one; the whole place is built to withstand aircraft, bombs, nukes, the lot. It would take serious industrial weaponry to carve a hole in NanoTek."

"Like an IMS?" Franco beamed, waving the Industrial Molecule Stripper around dangerously; the two men ducked.

"No," snapped Xakus. "They thought of that, also. The walls are covered in a type of sub-atomic electronic mesh; it can absorb an IMS beam and re-distribute to source."

"You mean it bounces it back on the user?"

Xakus nodded. "Yes. Very effective."

"Are you sure?" Franco was scowling.

Xakus gestured at the distant citadel. "Try it. Even from this distance, it *will* work."

Franco stared at the Black Rose HQ. Finally, he said, "No."

"Good choice. The only way I can think of gaining entry is beneath the ocean. The HQ descends for two or three kilometres, although my clearance never allowed such immersion. Down there, beneath the black, there are long flowing sea-corridors, hubs, OctoStrands and VertClicks. There's a city down there, gentlemen; a city dedicated to technology. A world dedicated to the human upgrade." He smiled, his face the mask of the sardonic, and tinged by the twitch of the insane.

"The GreenSource Mainframe is down there?" said Franco.

"Right at the bottom." Xakus nodded.

"And Mel! Let's not forget Mel!"

"Who could forget Mel?" said Keenan.

"Hey, what's that?" Franco was peering up. Keenan squinted, following the ginger squaddie's gaze. From the core of NanoTek HQ a tiny filament, a silver strand, wavered off up through bunch-fist clouds of iron and carbon; it undulated gently, describing a sine wave, then disappeared into a seeming infinity where, if one concentrated hard enough, at strand's end a tiny sparkle glittered like a star.

"It's a SPIRAL port," said Xakus.

"That's impossible!" snorted Franco.

"Is it?"

"What? Here? *In* NanoTek?"

"They're the richest conglomerate in the Quad-Gal," said Xakus. "The glittering thing at the summit, what you probably think looks like a star, that's the SPIRAL EYE, the bit that fires ships up near LS. Further down, but dark so you can't see it, is the dock itself; only NanoTek have gone one step further, and another umbilical connects the dock directly to the HQ."

"How big is this dock?" asked Franco, squinting.

"Big, Franco. Very big. Plush. Like an opulent city, in fact, and reserved purely for the admiralty of NanoTek. Probably weighs in at a million tonnes. It's suspended using AGE anti-gravity engines, the most powerful engines ever built. By NanoTek, of course."

"So, that there little silvery wormy thing, people slide up and down it?"

"Sort of. Just think of it like an express elevator. From the space station to the HQ passing a thousand different levels. Only, it's a *very* fast lift, capable of taking not just people, but cargo, freight—weight and mass matter not. Using a by-link to the AGE engines, they can drop a million tonne Shuttle down one of those lines."

Franco nodded, watching the wavering filament strand which described a faint sine wave through the thunderous, storm-filled heavens. "The wonders of modern technology," he snorted, and sulked, thinking of what modern technology had done to his Melanie.

Keenan extracted his PAD. "Cam, do you copy?"

"I've got you, Keenan. Gods, did you guys see that horrible display of urban terrorism a few hours ago?"

"Urban terrorism?"

"Some fanatical bastards blew the connecting freeway to NanoTek's HQ! NanoTek are in real panic! A real big zombie army has gathered, a warhost on the march towards NanoTek's HQ— and now NanoTek think the zombies have got hold of nukes, or something, and destroyed the main connective. They've closed the Citadel tighter than a bank vault of politician's porno photos. Your path in *would* have been straightforward; now, it's been compromised by whoever blew that freeway. We'll have to improvise, gentlemen. I'll be with you in ten. Don't move. Out."

The PAD went dead. Keenan glanced sideways at Franco.

Franco whistled softly.

"You hear that?" Keenan said.

"Hey! See! It was those pesky urban terrorists that blew the freeway! Nothing to do with me, lad!"

"Nothing to do with..." Keenan's eyes were wide.

"It must have been one of those, y'know, coincidence thingums. The urban terrorists *just so happened to strike at the freeway at the same time I had my unfortunate accident with the Industrial Molecule Stripper*." Franco smiled. It was a wide smile in a flat face devoid of true understanding.

"What's it like? Being you?"

"It's great, mate. Thanks for asking."

Cam arrived, as promised, ten minutes later, skimming low over the choppy ocean. He circled them, sensors scanning jagged horizons, then dropped low to hover beside Keenan's head. Something trailed from Cam's shell, held in tiny metal grippers. It looked like oily metal rope.

"It's been a long, hard slog," said Cam heroically.

"You find a way in?"

"Ye-*eessss,* sort of."

"Meaning?"

"'Tis a route fringed with peril and danger."

"Have you been sniffing hot oil again?"

"Listen, when a GradeA+1 Security Mechanism with advanced SynthAI and a Machine Intelligence Rating (MIR) of 3450, with integral weapon inserts, a quad-core military database, and Put Down™ War Technology gets on a job integral to the success of a Combat K mission, he *does not* sniff hot oil. OK? Now, this is the plan."

Cam explained the plan.

Keenan and Franco stared hard at the little Pop-Bot.

Finally, a few moments after Cam had finished, Franco snorted. "That's insane," he said.

"Fine words coming from a frizzy ginger midget with an addiction to rainbow pills!"

"Hey, less of the frizzy. I shave it off now."

"What do you think, Keenan?"

Keenan, treading water, and shivering violently despite his WarSuit and thermal-tek, was rubbing at his chin. His eyes gleamed. "Seems we have little choice if we want to get inside. Are you sure it will work?"

"Aye, Keenan. I've been analysing and hypothesising since the terrible hooligan destruction of the freeway put a new challenge before me. I admit, a submarine would be preferable, especially one of those new HunterShark K12 models with aero-flux turbo-fans and Mercedes quad-impellers; but we ain't got one."

Keenan looked at Xakus. "You can do this? Including the bit with Cam?"

Xakus nodded, eyes weary. "I have the technical ability, once the *merge* takes place, but it's... highly dangerous. For both me and Cam. Joining with an AI always is."

Keenan nodded, accepting the danger.

"How will we breathe?" said Franco.

"These." Cam ejected three tiny silver globes. "Oxyjets, with a concentrate of titrapsyche-oxygen. "Just keep one in your mouth whilst submerged. I stole them. *Before* the Black Rose Citadel closed down and I had to cut a PopBot sized hole to escape."

Franco nodded, and popped the long silver pill into his mouth. The three men took hold of the thick rope attached to Cam's shell.

"So, we going down?" Franco's eyes gleamed.

Keenan pointed at him. "Don't fucking start!"

"I was just…"

"No, Franco!" Keenan inserted his Oxyjet. It gleamed, entwined with his teeth. Against the lapping dark ocean Keenan's eyes were pools of poisoned mercury. Focus hijacked his face. His concentration was total. "Cam. Let's do it."

"Yeah boss."

Cam plunged beneath the ocean; there was a surge of bubbles and frothing water, and the three men tensed, preparing themselves as the rope uncoiled with a hiss.

Suddenly, they were dragged violently under, and down down towards a cold and bottomless pit.

CHAPTER 14
BLACK ROSE CITADEL

CAM SPED, SPIRALLING into the depths trailing bubbles. Towed, like fluttering ragdolls, Kecnan, Franco and Xakus hung on for life. They descended into ink black. Above, any still-visible lights were immediately extinguished. And it got very, very cold.

Keenan and Franco's WarSuits instigated extra thermal settings, and even Xakus's thermal electronic jacket clicked and buzzed. But as they went deeper, and the world got colder, so heat circuits started to fail and the three men began a rapid descent towards the beckoning door of death...

Cam halted, bubbles spurting from his casing, and the three men floated down to stand on a huge globe. Squinting through blackness, they saw spidery arms, like rubber tubes, disappearing off into the gloom.

"We can use this as an EntryShell," said Cam, his electronic voice carrying weirdly to warble through the ocean. Other than his squeak, the world was filled with an oppressive, heavy silence. As if the three men slept under a very great weight.

"What—is—this?" bubbled Franco, uncomfortably.

"A coolant system. Xakus, are you ready? To do what we... discussed?"

Xakus nodded, boots planted on the globe. Cam moved towards him, bubbles hissing in a burst stream. He bobbed by Xakus's head. Two tiny filaments drifted from his black case. Xakus took the filaments, placed them against his skull... and *shuddered* as they flowed through skin, bone, and into his brain to merge with his prefrontal cortex and hypothalamus. Xakus's eyes closed.

"Are you comfortable?"

"There is a lot of pain."

"For me also. You must blank the pain. It will interfere with our cortex bond."

"Yes."

"You must show me the NanoTek organic codes. Then I will sneak us through the walls of the EntryShell."

"Yes."

Xakus concentrated. Cam watched the spirals, memorising billions of patterns, swirls, colours, sounds, experiences; they all mashed and merged, to form a Whole and the Whole was a password. Cam formatted a section of his own brain, and optimised it to match the brain of the human organism to which he was joined. Then, he took the data and shuffled it into memory slots and riffled it at speed; he then cross-matched more data with Xakus. It had to be perfect. He would only get one shot at this illegal and highly treacherous entry attempt...

If he got it wrong, it would erase his mind.

"You still OK?"

"Yes."

"Describe how you feel?"

"Light-headed. Weak. Cold."

"No pains in your spine?"

"No."

"Good. I have the password. Wait."

Cam spun, still connected directly to Xakus's brain. His voice wobbled through the ocean. "Keenan. Franco. Focus. Hold Xakus. We're going in. Be. Warned. It. Will. Be. Wild. Inside."

The two members of Combat K took hold of Xakus, and suddenly all three men and Cam sank through the black globe, as if absorbed into quicksand, or through an incredibly sticky, black rubber-gel. Keenan caught a last glimpse of the oppressive ocean and the wavering, rubbery tentacles as he was *accessed* by NanoTek and allowed through their esoteric organic password system. Organically entered. Merged. Genetically accepted. Mechanically decrypted. Given. Access. Entry. Inside.

Everything went black.

Keenan felt movement, then a sudden insanity of pressure, as if being smashed by the wall of a tidal wave... and he was gone and lost and slammed, flowing through thick black gunk and Franco and Xakus and Cam were all torn away and smashed away and gone as Keenan was buffeted and forced into a long dive through a horizontally pressured cooling system. A roaring filled his head. Pressure waves slapped him, sending pain coruscating through every atom. His eyes squeezed shut, but his head was full of pain with intense pressure, and Keenan sped along a winding, twisting route of tubing until he was ejected, arms and legs kicking, eyes trying to blink free gunk, through a waterfall of pressure-*release* and down a long trailing fall towards a deep oily basin. He fell for a long time through cold air, peppered by gunk spray, blinded, and hit the surface with a splash. He went under. He sank, deep, then with a snarl of anger he kicked out, kicked up, struggling and forcing his way past a deep centrifugal suction and up to the edge of what felt like cold hard stone. Keenan hoisted himself up, and slapped down onto the surface of the walkway, shivering. He spat out the Oxyjet and lay, panting, wheezing, head full of stars, blood full of adrenalin, head full of confusion.

Keenan rolled onto his side. Glanced up into gloom, where high above it seemed to rain oil. Several pipes emerged, feeding into this huge cylindrical chamber. Keenan lay on a narrow concretealloy lip circling the interior of the cylinder. Metal walls reared off above him. Before his eyes, the pool of gunk was thick, gelatinous, and a central whirlpool spun denoting interior suction.

"Franco?" he hissed. He could see nothing moving in the pool. "Cam?"

No response.

Keenan stood, checked his weapons, glared around.

He was alone.

He fished out his PAD. "Franco? Cam? Copy?"

Silence.

"Bastard." Keenan—and Cam, who had formulated the plan—hadn't anticipated the force of the cooling system with which they merged. It had quite literally ripped the group apart. And that meant... Franco, Cam, Xakus, they could be anywhere within NanoTek. They could be dead...

Keenan was on his own.

He breathed deep, calming himself, and narrowed his eyes, moving cat-like around the cold metal cylinder. Gunkfall pattered around him, splashing his boots. He scraped it from his eyes, and found a metal ladder.

NanoTek. Dr Oz. GreenSource Mainframe.

Keenan wanted answers. He wanted them now.

He started to climb, up past the oilfall of gunk and—he blinked, *hundreds* of pipes which fed into this huge, towering cylinder. That's a big cooling system, he thought. What the hell does it cool?

He clambered up the ladder, hands and boots gunk-slippery on slick rungs. Up and up he travelled, until the pool into which he'd fallen was nothing but a distant dot. He shuddered. He was lucky. He'd emerged low, and hadn't taken a dive from this kind of height; the impact, WarSuit or not, would surely have snapped his spine like a dry twig.

Far up on the greased ladder, Keenan paused. He tilted his head, sure he'd heard a rattle of gunfire. He fished out his PAD again, and tried to contact Franco. Nothing. He set it to scan, but it simply blipped at him in the negative. It would not, or could not, formulate a map.

"Bastard."

Keenan carried on, slipping and sliding up the rungs, gunk-spray tickling him. Finally, he spied an access corridor high above, and gritting his teeth, muscles burning, hands raw despite his gloves, he powered on, boots squealing on slick metal and threatening to toss him back into the devastating pit.

He finally slammed down into the low-ceilinged access corridor, and realised it was little more than a rectangular pipe. Coolant gunk churned through a gully down the middle of the corridor. Keenan realised this meant, despite its access pretensions, it was still operational as part of the cooling system.

Rolling to his knees, he started to crawl. Fast. He wasn't sure how much time he had. The metal floor beneath him was slippery, and it was probable it was used as a pipe, either an overflow or runoff of some kind. If a jet of gunk caught him there, in that place... he'd be forcibly ejected like a bullet, fall like a suicide jumper, and compact as readily as any meat pie in a groundcar crusher. *Son of a bitch*.

Keenan slid and slipped along the bowed floor, and saw a horizon approaching. Tubes fed in at roof height, with injectors pointing directly into Keenan's emerging, snarling face. He squeezed past the evil narrow nozzles to find himself balanced on a high gantry overlooking a vast, vast warehouse. At Keenan's level, a sea of matt black steel rushed away, support beams, H-section, alloy, ironanium, spirals and tubes and blocks and cable-carriers.

Keenan moved carefully, warily, from the access tube and dropped down onto a thick, H section beam. He crouched, grabbing hold of a tube over his head, and stared down into the heart of the NanoTek HQ.

At one far end, huge juggernaut SlamTruks were beeping and revving engines, reversing into a swathe of loading bays as wide as any average city. Some were leaving with spouts of churning acrid fumes. Keenan shielded his eyes, staring, trying to make out what they were... unloading? There were long crates. Cranes worked, whining and banging, unloading the SlamTruks and dumping crates onto skeeters and blobs.

Keenan's gaze swept the vault, from the loading bay to the...

"Holy mother of God."

Keenan's jaw, quite literally, dropped.

Half of the vast, titanic chamber was full of zombies.

They stood in ranks, row upon row upon row, crammed and silent and stationary; thousands upon thousands of deviant, broken, buckled, torn, pus-weeping figures. Keenan crept along the beam, keeping low behind thick tubes, to get a closer look. Reaching a junction, he stood, balanced high above the sea of motionless zombies, turned, and leapt onto an adjacent beam. He caught his balance, steadied himself, then moved out over the ranks.

They're a battalion, he thought.

They're an army.

What the hell are they doing here?

Keenan frowned. Who'd want an army of zombies? They're slow, (well, slower than any trained soldiers), they're useless, they moan and dribble and fight amongst themselves. But then, he thought, look at them now! Happy as puppies. Docile as dopers. Not an ounce of aggression amongst their ragged... torn... exteriors.

Keenan frowned. Something was wrong. Something, far down below him, didn't fit. It wasn't right. Like a clever puzzle designed to fool the brain, Keenan fought against what he was witnessing; then he relaxed into the game, allowed his eyes to play over the scene, around the edges of the vault, and he realised and smiled a bitter, sour smile. That was it. The discrepancy. The mind-fuck.

The zombies were organised by *deformity*.

So, there stood a rectangular battalion of zombies with sloping shoulders and distended jaws. Then, arranged neatly next to them, another battalion with buckled ankles and twisted claws. Another, seven feet high with eyes popped out on quivering stalks. And on and on it went, the zombies, although clothed differently, were *arranged*. And, Keenan was damn sure zombies didn't arrange themselves like that. And they certainly didn't stand docile and... *waiting?*

These zombies were not the wild, random creatures he had seen out on City streets. These were well-behaved. Conditioned. They seemed to be obeying... *orders*.

"Ha!"

"What you doing here, pep? You not look like maintenance staff. Are you maintenance staff? Give me your name and rank serial, so I can check if you maintenance staff, silly little pep staff straying out of the main service route where only maintenance staff are allowed."

Keenan's heart sank. What? Up here? *No, it couldn't be...* But it was. Keenan turned. The voice belonged to a Justice SIM. A Justice SIM with an MPK *machine gun*... Keenan smiled weakly. "Hi," he said cheerily. "I was just looking for the cooling chambers. I had a routine maintenance job to do. Should I not be up here? Sorry. Sorry!"

All the time he spoke he was moving towards the SIM... which frowned, mechanical eyes clicking, face impassive and emotionless. "We don't have any cooling chambers," said the SIM. Its gun snapped up. "You stand there, pep, you illegal, you illegal immigrant, how you get in? You not able to get in? I'm scanning now... you not have..."

Keenan's Techrim *boomed*, three times, and bullets kicked sparks from the MPK which smashed from the SIM's gloved hands and went sailing out over the sea of motionless zombies, a few bullets rattling from a hastily trapped trigger. Fire blossomed from the barrel. The gun turned. Keenan ducked as bullets *whined* overhead, pinging erratically from metal beams.

The SIM charged him...

Keenan fired off a few more shots, scrambling back, but the SIM's armour absorbed bullets with little jelly *whumps*. A fist slammed Keenan's face, and he ducked a second swing, dropping to one knee, powering a blow to the SIM's groin which *cracked* metallically. The SIM kicked out, the blow lifting Keenan and sending him staggering back. A second kick sent his Techrim flying out after the falling MPK. Keenan glanced down, watching his trusted weapon disappear. Below, none of the zombies had moved; none looked up. None seemed the slightest bit interested in the fight taking place over their heads.

The Justice SIM *smiled*. And that was unusual. They normally didn't have the personality.

"I'm going to make you hurt, pep."

"Come and show me, dickhead." Keenan was edging back across the beam. A quick glance told him his retreat was blocked by waist-thick pipes. He'd have to go for his MPK holstered on his back... and even then, he knew, the fight would be a hard one—

SIMs didn't die easy.

He went for the MPK as the SIM charged, but it was too fast. Keenan lashed out with a combination of punches, all of which connected and rocked the SIM. It staggered, then smiled, eyes clicking. It pulled out a long knife from an embedded compartment at its waist...

Keenan was grappling, trying to pull free his MPK, but something had trapped it against his pack. Had it been the fall? The rush through high-pressured cooling tubes? Whatever, the gun was jammed, wouldn't tug free, and Keenan dropped to pull a slender knife from his own boot. In comparison to the SIM's blade, he might as well have held a toothpick...

Man and SIM faced one another.

Keenan was sweating, and he wiped it from his eyes.

The SIM started forward. Slow. With care.

Keenan retreated, until his back slammed the pipes. They vibrated with a hollow, clanging reverberation.

"I'm going to gut you like a fish, pep. Your kind are inferior, pasty, so weak and brittle and easily broken. You were the template for the SIM; yes, but look now how superior we are! And yet, still you are arrogant little man, patronising, think you so superior. You... *humans*... you make me sick."

FRANCO FELL DOWN and slapped along through thick gunge, flapping his arms like a madman. "Aarrghie!" he screamed as the pressure spat him, and he sucked in a mouthful of gunk that made him choke and splutter and splurge. Everyone was gone, Keenan, Cam, Xakus. He flowed like a drug in an arterial system, slammed along at a fair old rate spreading his own special brand of Franco *high*. "Get me out!" he screamed. "Get me out of this place!" He zig-zagged through more pipe junctions. "Get me out! Get me out of this trap!" He sped and rushed, hands flapping, trying to slow his accelerating insanity. His hands juddered from the insides of the rubberised pipes and were nearly ripped off at the wrists. "Get me out! Get me out of my brain!" And then, as the speed seemed to shiver and hum through every single vibrating atom of Franco Haggis, making him weep and scream and wail and want to die with every pounding pressing crushing second, so—a miracle happened.

"Get me..." he began.

And it did. It got him out. Ejected him like a bout of diarrhoea from a colitis-riddled giant. Franco sailed onto a metal platform, high in the air, and rolled over and over and over again, rattling to a stop and staring down at knurled alloy. He was panting. He was sweating. His WarSuit was making funny erratic clicking noises. Franco glanced right, to where gunk poured under high pressure and fell into a velocity well far below. If he'd gone down with it, he would have been instantly *crushed*. *Thanks be to God!* he praised.

His head turned the other way. To see gleaming boots. "Ahh. Haha. Yeah, right, sure, it was never going to be *that easy*, right? *Bugger.*" His eyes blinked a few times, and his depth of vision returned. Behind the boots were... metal legs. Three sets. They looked solid, well-crafted, *sculpted,* even, in a kind of sturdy, efficient, robot-killer kind of way.

Franco looked up, sheepishly.

He blinked.

And blinked again.

A hand reached down towards him. Franco took the hand, and allowed himself to be helped to his feet. A big, beaming smile smacked like a kipper across his face. His eyes went wide, glistening in happiness. His nostrils twitched involuntarily at her natural perfume. The scent of the wild *woman*. The aroma of the *sexy* bitch.

"You are one lucky son of a bastard," said Pippa, still holding on to Franco's gloved hand. "Three feet less, and you'd have gone into the grav, your whole body compressed to the size of a pin-head."

"Pippa!" he roared, and embraced her in a swathe of gunk-smeared clicking WarSuit. There came three hardware *clunks* and Franco met the eyes of the GK AIs, Nyx, Momos and Lamia. There came a rush of noise, like ice-hail on a windscreen, like machine gun bullets against corrugated steel, and five thousand needles rippled across Nyx's arms and torso as her sculpted head lowered, and the discs of her eyes fixed on Franco.

Franco held up a hand, palm outwards.

"OK, OK, no need to get frisky, doll." He took a step back, and looked Pippa up and down. "By God, girl, it's damn good to see you! And I don't even mean that in a sly sexual way, although of course, you know how it is with little old me, and if you do change your mind you know I'd be the first one to jump into a bath of hot marmalade with you, despite being on a mission to save my beloved Mel!" He grinned. Slapped her on the shoulder—at the same time she slammed cuffs around his wrists.

"It's good to see you, Franco." But the smile wavered, and disappeared from her face. "It's a shame things have changed for the worse. I have a new job now."

Franco stared at the cuffs incredulously. He tugged at them, not quite believing they were there. "What? WHAT? What's this, Pippa? Who do you think you're betraying? What you doing here in NanoTek? And with them bloody buggers who tried to smash us up back at that library?" Franco's face relaxed. He released a breath. He nodded. "So. The Big Boys got you on payroll now, eh girl?" He grinned, only this time it was removed from the grin of friendship he'd offered a few seconds earlier.

"This is my job," said Pippa, stiffly.

"This is *me,* Franco." He shook his head. "What the fuck's going on in your head, girl? After all the shit we've pulled? All the hardtime missionwise we went through? Pippa, you've got your head on all backside fucked."

"This is my *job*!" she snarled, moving close to Franco, cold grey eyes narrowing. "How can you criticise *me*? After the K Jump went wrong, after we went to... *that place.*"

Franco's voice was cool. "I just know we all had to be strong," he said. "It was a bad time. But we worked together to break free. We worked as a team. We are a *team.*" He eyed the three advanced AIs standing dangerously languorous behind the woman. "But I see some things have changed, right? Killing Keenan's family... well, that's fucked with your skull. Now you've took up with some new slick fresh-oiled meat." Franco leant over, and spat at the AIs. They did not move. "Man-murdering meat-*fuckers.* I thought MICHELLE ragged you all over the place. A shame to see you still standing."

Pippa took a step back, gestured to the AIs. "Take him."

Momos and Lamia moved, like flowing liquid, smooth and seductive animation that was not lost on the horn that was Franco. They grabbed him, roughly, one under each arm. Their heads turned, the matt black discs of their eyes fixing him; enamelled jaws smiled on sliding greased pistons.

Pippa strode ahead, down a high-roofed, alloy-floored hallway. Behind, the gunk from the coolant system faltered and suddenly dried up; as if a simple tap had been turned. A passageway closed. A job well done.

Franco dragged along, boots bumping. "Pippa! Pippa, don't do this! We're still a team… hey? Still Combat K! You can never change what you are! Never kill what lies in your heart! You were *born* Combat K. And you'll *die* Combat K."

Pippa halted. Turned. Smiled a tight, cold smile. She eyed the GK AIs with cool compression. When she spoke, her voice was melting ice over frozen alcohol. "Nyx, Momos, Lamia—if the," she savoured the word, "*prisoner*… speaks again… then hell, please feel free to kill him."

She strode off, boots clacking down the hall.

CAM FELT HIS strands ripped free from direct contact inside Xakus's brain; and as the old professor slammed off down a pipe, Cam knew instinctively that the old man was dead. Sadness swamped him—for a nanosecond—until reality kicked his small AI brain into gear and he focused on his dangerous situation. It was a massive surprise to be swept away, each of them jerked in different directions and sent spinning down separate coolant pipeways. Cam spun fast, at first trying to fight the flow, then relaxing into a current too powerful for his motors to drive against without burning out, or at least becoming seriously damaged. Cam flowed, zipping down pipes, along pipes, even *upwards* if his gyroscopes were to be trusted. He coolly logged his direction, speed, co-ordinates. He monitored for Keenan and Franco... but, worryingly, could find nothing. Had the pressure killed *all three* men? Cam cursed in machine code.

He sensed the vertical cylinder full of gunk before he was in it; it slammed his sensors with its power, its pressure, its ferocity. With a sudden intuition Cam fought his direction of flow, realising instantly the danger into which he was being sucked... only too late, he was squeezed through an ever-narrowing complex network of tubes, the pressure building and building and building and he was forced unceremoniously into the cylinder where he was dragged down and fed into a circular loop. Gunk compressed his shell with a *crackle*. Under intense pressure, Cam started to quickly become very, very hot, and he fed heat to his outer-shell and allowed the coolant to do its job. But, conversely, it didn't seem to be working. Cam felt himself growing hotter, and hotter, and hotter as he spun around the base of the cylinder in an entrapped circuit. His motors whined, trying to eject him from the drag. He could not escape. With the heat build-up reaching 600°C Cam started to feel the extremities of circuits malfunctioning. Growing desperate, he began to pump heat into the surrounding coolant and suddenly realised why it wasn't working as his synapses slowed and his multi-core CPU began a binary twitch. The coolant outside was *hot*. Hotter than *him*. Which probably meant he was near the core of whatever was being cooled. Cam tried to think. Images jagged across his sliver-spitting memory. He thought of Xakus.

Which path did the dead man's body take? Had it been compressed? Or maybe boiled, like a lobster in a pot—the current fate being applied to himself? Cam cursed again, and with a final, heavy-duty surge he attempted to escape the coolant cycle in which he was trapped... at the same time, cycling through a million blueprints until he found one, and it stopped, revealed to his inner senses:

Ahhh, he thought.

So *that's* where I am.

Inside The Sump.

The base of the entire cooling system for NanoTek HQ.

Cam strained harder, his actions tinged by an edge of atomic panic. With a *pop* one motor burned out, smoke pluming from Cam's case to be absorbed by coolant. Then another died.

Then a third.

Working now at under 50% efficiency, Cam limped around the bottom of the central coolant cylinder known as The Sump—like a dying goldfish with one fin going round in circles at the bottom of a bowl. And the only problem with being a dying goldfish at the bottom of the bowl was that, well, all the other goldfish were cannibals, and it was only a matter of time before they clocked terminal distress and closed in for a good ol' feed.

Warily, Cam scanned his surroundings.

And with a jolt, realised he wasn't alone...

THE SIM ADVANCED on Keenan, whose arm came back and sent the narrow blade speeding with unerring accuracy to pierce under the SIM's left mechanical eye. The SIM went down on one knee, letting out a gasp. But, despite the knife piercing its brain, it glanced up, mouth a sour line, and bared its teeth at Keenan... who charged, growling, and leapt, both boots smashing the SIM's face. It toppled back, sliding to one side, legs cartwheeling over the abyss and pulling its body after it. The SIM slithered across steel, nails dragging along metal with screeches, then with an outstretched arm it fired a line which whipped around Keenan's legs and brought him crashing to the ground. The SIM slithered off the high H-section walkway, the line buzzing from its forearm as it swung, pendulous, and Keenan grunted with pain, hunched, taking the SIM's weight.

"Bastard," he hissed, and again tried to scrabble for his MPK. Again, he could not work the weapon free. Slowly, he slid in several painful jerks towards the edge of the walkway, his locked boots kicking and pushing. He glanced down at the SIM, which swung. It was laughing.

"Let go!" he snapped.

"What?" The SIM looked up, Keenan's blade protruding from the front of its face like some bizarre sculpture. "And deprive myself the satisfaction of knowing you, too, will die in the fall?" The SIM chuckled again. It was an evil, binary sound.

Keenan glanced around, panic rising within him. The line was growing tighter and tighter about his ankles, just below his WarSuit, cutting off his blood-flow. His boots, whilst solid, did little to halt the compression of three hundred pounds of SIM.

Then he saw it. The SIM's knife. He leant, grunting, and almost lost his grip on the precious ledge. He stretched, muscles screaming, and shuffled millimetre by millimetre towards the curved, gleaming blade—and salvation.

Keenan's fingers closed around the weapon. With a triumphant scream, the blade slashed down, only to bounce from the line. Savagely Keenan hacked away at taut fibres, but it simply would not part.

"TitaniumIII, an interwoven mesh line," said the SIM conversationally, from where it swung above the frozen zombie army. Blood had run down its face, giving it a blood mask in an inverted V.

Keenan stared down, past the SIM. Still the zombies were motionless, despite the battle above. It's as if... they're dead. Laughter welled manically in his throat, in his brain, vying with the intensity of pain in his ankles. Keenan hurled the SIM's knife, but the SIM twitched to one side, and looked down, watching the blade flash over and over to half-sever a zombie's head far below. Still, the distant, deviant creature did nothing. It stood, head hanging half-off, lolling to one side and showing pink sliced tendons and a lode of squidgy neck fat.

"Pull me up," said the SIM.

"Get to fuck."

"Or we both die."

"Then we both die," snarled Keenan.

"I am prepared to meet my maker. He stamped the back of my neck with a laser logo. However, Mr Keenan, are you ready to meet *your* fictitious God?" The SIM laughed long and loud, but Keenan caught the sound. The laugh was fake. Ersatz. A

SIM had no emotions. It didn't know how to laugh. Its comedy was a mimicry of the human shell it so despised.

"How," said Keenan, staring down, "do you know my name?"

The SIM gazed up, mechanical eyes clicking. It did not speak.

"What game is this? Tell me what's going on."

"The simplicity of the human mind. The simplicity of human trust. It's what will instigate your downfall as a species, Mr Keenan. It's the factor that will doom your race." The SIM smiled. Its teeth glinted with blood.

Keenan worked his way into his WarSuit, and pulled free his PAD. Now it was his turn to smile. He activated the laser, and then glanced down at the SIM; it shrugged.

"Even your PAD laser won't cut through Titanium-III interwoven mesh line," said the SIM, voice almost smug, blood-masked face curled into a snarl of contempt. "You really are pathetic."

"Who said anything about cutting the line?" growled Keenan, and directed the high-intensity short-range beam. Leather and armour sizzled, followed by the stench of cooking flesh as the laser ate through the SIM's arm. There was a squelch, a moment of hiatus, then arm and SIM parted company. The SIM fell, clutching its cauterised stump, tumbling down over and over and over to eventually slam the ranks of motionless zombies far below. The SIM spread itself over quite a large area.

"I *hate* fucking bureaucrats."

Keenan pulled up the line still attached to the severed arm and WarGlove, and with a grimace he
unwound the leash from his numbed feet. He tossed
the arm after the splattered SIM, then stood, and toppled over with a cry. His legs wouldn't take his weight.

Keenan crawled along the beam, and watched
tiny stick-men in white coats rush to the splattered
SIM. They glanced up at him, and he resisted a sardonic urge to wave with grinding teeth.

So much for covert entry. But then, the SIM knew
his name. Which meant...

"There he is!" Bullets whined, slapping sparks
from the beam. "Don't move pep motherfucker, or
I'll cut you in half!"

Keenan glanced left, then right. Ten SIMs had
moved onto adjacent beams. They all bore guns,
trained on Keenan's trapped and helpless figure.

"OK, OK." He rubbed at his useless legs, realising that even in death the splattered SIM must be
laughing. He'd condemned Keenan as readily as
cutting off the soldier's feet.

Two SIMs worked their way to Keenan. They
removed his weapons, bound his hands with raze-
wire, and took his weight, shuffling along the beam
and into a wide corridor. The walls and floor
gleamed like polished granite. The SIMs surrounded Keenan.

"What now?" he said.

The butt of an MPK smashed his head, dropping
him to the ground where he glared up, through
blood and strings of saliva.

"The pep not talk or we put bullets in the pep's
skull. The pep is to accompany us to The Palace. If

pep try to escape, we have permission to kill the pep. If pep try to be funny wise-guy, we have permission to kill the pep. If pep try to take our weapons, we have permission to kill the pep."

"OK, dickhead, I get the idea." Keenan climbed to his feet, spitting blood and a sliver of tooth.

"Wise-guy shut up. Wise-guy need to walk. Now! Or..."

"Yeah yeah, I heard. You have permission to kill the pep."

The SIM leered close to Keenan, and poked an MPK barrel against his teeth with a *clack*. "The pep learn fast," growled the SIM, and nudged Keenan along with a growl.

FRANCO WAS DRAGGED for what seemed like miles by the GKs, and it hurt his neck to keep his head up so in the end he stared at the passing floor tiles. They changed in colour, radiating through the spectrum from yellow to pink to red to green to blue and finally, to black. Tiny inset jewels sparkled deep in the black. Ever the mercenary, Franco wondered if he'd be able to get a knife inside to prize one free.

With a violence of shock, the GKs dropped Franco to the floor and he banged his nose. Pain flared through his skull, and he felt blood roll down his nostrils. "You buggers! You could have warned me! That was bloody buggering unfair, that was!"

He rolled to his side, and realised nobody was listening. The GKs had their backs to him, smooth black bodies resting and at ease. And that made Franco's blood boil. "Well, of all the damn and bloody buggering cheek! Those little stick-men can-openers!

I'll bloody show them, I shall!" He surged to his feet, and for a long, long moment all thoughts of violence and damaged pride were expunged. Franco stared from his high vantage point in... awe.

Pippa turned. She gestured to Franco, and he staggered forward, arms tight behind his back, and stared down at...

"This is The Palace," said Pippa, voice a gentle hum. "Beautiful, isn't She?"

"I'd rather have a naked fat whore..." began Franco, but his voice petered out. He had to admit it. The Palace, at the core of the NanoTek HQ, was stunning indeed.

The chamber was big. No, BIG. From their high vantage it soared away as far as the eye could see, and it took a while for Franco's beleaguered brain to work out it was at about 1:5 scale. He squinted, recognising some areas from vid, but unable to put names to them.

"What's that one, there? It's from Old Earth, right?"

"That is Babylon, Mr Haggis."

The voice oozed from behind, and the man walked with precise steps as Franco turned. He wore a glass suit, and was small, slim, a delicate man. Franco eyed the bald head, the brown eyes, and then, as Oz smiled, the pointed, gleaming teeth. They shone red. They dazzled. Franco calculated their worth with the practised eye of a jajunga thief.

"The other proud cities you see ranged before you, in perfect miniaturised scale, are London, New York, Cairo, Sparta, Alexandria, Rome. It took my historians twenty years to assimilate the data need-ed for this model; they travelled the Quad-Gal, visited tens of thousands of planets, talked to rela-tives of relatives of relatives who had once *walked* our ancient birthplace, cradle of humanity, *Earth*, and had been witness to stories passed down through thousands of generations. It took my engi-neers another *ten years* to build the place. If you look, you can see each city is divided by a natural rolling plain, a barrier, so to speak. Each sector has its own micro-climate, its own miniaturised people and animals... although nothing as populous as those real cities would have possessed during their correct existence."

"You're Oz, right?"

"Your intuition astounds me."

"Where's my Melanie?"

"All in good time, Mr Haggis. You will get to see your beautiful little Melanie very soon, although my, hasn't she grown up recently? *Matured*, you might say, into an almost perfect killing machine."

"What did you do to her?"

"Me?" Dr Oz smiled. The smile was worth a bil-lion dollars. "I did nothing. I simply allowed vanity and greed to perform the invitation; and the nanobots did the rest."

"So the biomods *did* transform people into zom-bies!"

Dr Oz laughed, nodding his head as he steepled his hands before his chest. "Ah, now I see why Quad-Gal Military think of you as such a prize pos-session, Mr Haggis! A specimen worth treasuring, no less! Although I, obviously, have my own mis-givings regarding this whole venture."

Franco glanced sideways at Pippa. "Is he taking the piss?"

Pippa said nothing; her grey eyes were as blank as the matt metal disks in the sculpted, sweeping faces of the GKs.

Franco snarled, and fought at his bonds; but they held. Oz tutted, as if disciplining a particularly naughty child. He turned back, gazing out towards the sweeping granite corridor which led to this, his Palace; then held up a finger to his lips. Ruby sparkles edged like gaseous blood around his fingers.

"Say hello to your friend," said Oz, as, at the end of the corridor a squad of SIMs came into view. They dragged with them a limping, bruised Keenan, and marched him unceremoniously along the expanse to dump him at Oz's feet.

Keenan crawled onto his knees, hawked a mouth-ful of blood, phlegm and saliva, and spat it onto Oz's polished boots. He grinned upwards through the bruises of his beating at the hands of the SIMs. It had been an eventful journey. "Hey, if it isn't Dr Fucking Oz. We meet at last, you metal cripple." He eyed the man's diminutive size. "You're bigger than I thought you'd be."

Oz smiled an easy, rolling smile, and reaching down, helped Keenan to stagger to his feet. "I must apologise for your... treatment at the hands of the SIMs. It was not what I anticipated." He made a swift and complicated hand gesture, to something just out of sight. There came a sudden *blast* in the corridor and the ten SIMs were picked up and thrown violently down the entire length, bouncing from walls and the floor and ceiling, whirling and spinning, limbs cracking, bodies breaking, skulls pulping as they were snapped away in a terribly vicious violent instant.

Keenan and Franco blinked, then looked at one another. Keenan released a slow breath.

"That's a pretty good weapon," he said, voice low.

"I agree. I designed it. It's in the walls. As a deterrent, you understand. Now, follow me."

Dr Oz moved towards the edge of the horizon which looked out, and down, across this— his miniature, created world. In the distance a false sun was rising. Sunlight sparkled across desert and jungle, cities and snowscape. "I had to synchronise the sunrise and sunsets, obviously," said Oz, "although different climates are handled at ground-level using mid-level ion filters and hydrogen scales. Please, step up onto the black circle."

Keenan and Franco glanced down. Before them squatted a circle of metal, and Oz moved to the forefront. Keenan glanced over his shoulder, where Pippa and the three GKs had eased forward, hemming the two Combat K soldiers in and brandishing MPKs with a honed and honeyed threat.

Keenan feigned to see Pippa for the first time. He gave her a nasty smile, and winked. "How's it going, Killer?"

Pippa prodded him in the back with her MPK, and he stumbled forward, growling. Franco followed, as did the GKs, until the small group stood atop the smooth metal circle.

"I call this my flying carpet," said Oz, and a tiny device materialised in the air at waist height. Oz reached forward, and skilfully manipulated compressed air controls. The disk lifted and eased out, sweeping and dropping low over a range of desert dunes. Aboard, they could smell hot sand and baking heat. "The Sahara," said Oz, by way of explanation. "It could be said I am obsessed by our heritage, by Old Earth. This is a personality flaw to which I openly admit. After all, Earth was the primus of our creation, yes? The point from which we stemmed. The original sperm and egg for our decadent species." He smiled, teeth glittering blood-red in a face ravaged by power.

The disc hummed, lifting and zooming over rolling dunes. Swiftly the landscape altered, blossoming and morphing into greenery as trees suddenly burst like a fresh scented carpet beneath their feet.

"I want to see Melanie!" snarled Franco, scowling at Oz.

"As you wish."

The disc accelerated and veered, banking, and after a few moments of incredible high speed they approached a looming city of dark, sodden stone. A cold wind arose, and rain lashed at the group on the levitating disc making all except machine shiver. Buildings slammed beneath them, and Oz slowed the disc, passing over miniaturised haystacks and muddy fields, past tiny hovels with straw roofs and cattle and pigs rooting around in timber enclosures. They approached a castle, a magnificent edifice—despite being in miniature—and it appeared

deserted. On the outskirts, tiny people fled screaming, their voices squeaking and surreal as they
waved minute pitchforks and sticks.

Keenan peered down. "So, are they real? Or pro-
jections? Or what?" He lifted his head, eyes
connecting, staring hard at Oz.

"We grow them in VATs, a similar technology
used thousands of years ago for the Slabs. Only this
time we don't breed soldiers, just little simplistic
men and women, and cows and pigs and chickens.
However, do not think of them as flesh and blood,
like you or I. The genetic codes used here are organic vegetable-based. After all... I wouldn't like to
play at being God." He laughed, as if enjoying a
private joke.

"So we really are scaring the shit out of them?"

"Yes." Oz nodded. "In their simple, vegetative
minds. But then you might as well try scaring a car-
rot, or a cabbage. If you grab one, bite it in half,
they taste like tomato juice."

"You mean you've tried?" Keenan met Oz's
brown, glassy stare.

"Oh yes. I consider it quite a delicacy. And *so
amusing* to see little women running around on
your plate as you sprinkle them with salt and pepper."

"You are one sick fucker."

Oz held out his hands. "A product of humanity,"
he said, voice dry with dark humour.

The disc lifted, soaring over castle walls trailing a
stream of rain-water. In the wide courtyard below,
lying flat on a stone slab, was Melanie, all eight feet
of her mottled deviated flesh, sagging pus-filled

orifices and macho, staggered jaw. Her eyes flickered open as the disc settled on the ground, and she sat up, warily, hands and feet bound by HotWire which had scorched vibrant rings like dark tattoos on her skin. She moved carefully, as one afraid of very great pain.

"Melanie!" roared Franco, leaping forward before anyone could stop him and launching himself at the eight foot genetic mutation. He charged, barrel-chested, across the cobbled courtyard and fell against her, his head pushing to nestle under her elongated neck with her small head and distended features.

"Grwwlll? Ranco! Ou Ame!"

"Of course I came! I would never leave you! We are to be married! And I'm not just some low-life dirt-box scumbag with weak moral fibre who gives up just because his girl has turned into a... turned into a... had a misfortunate accident! Reet?"

"Awww, Ranco!"

As everybody watched the reunited couple with a curious mix of sympathy, tense apprehension and sheer out and out *horror*, Keenan moved, he moved fast and hard, and performed that thing which he did best...

The act of violence.

Keenan rolled right, fast, away from the GK AIs, coming up behind Oz in a *nanosecond* and looping his wire bootlace over the man's head, drawing it tight with one fist whilst holding the man's head encircled in his free arm. Everybody froze. Dr Oz struggled, but Keenan tugged the cord tight and Oz gurgled, one leg kicking out spastically as blood flowed beneath the wire. He halted his movements. Keenan smiled, and patted him.

"Good boy."

Nyx growled, lowering her head, poisonous fangs glistening with tox. Keenan eyed her over Oz's shoulder, glad of the flesh barrier between him and certain, instant death...

"Wait." Pippa held up her hand. Keenan watched the three GKs visibly relax. They had been about to spring, an attempt to rip him limb from limb... but that wouldn't have saved Oz.

Keenan nodded. "Bright girl."

"Not bright, Keenan, I've just seen you pull this trick before." She lowered her eyes to Oz's purple face. "His boot laces are TitaniumIII paracord; if he tugs any harder, he'll decapitate you. Relax, Keenan. Don't do anything rash. We have all the time in the world."

Keenan's steel biceps loosened their pressure and Oz choked, snot and saliva erupting from his nose and mouth, spilling to glisten down his chin.

Keenan leaned forward. Pressed his lips against Oz's ear. "Listen carefully," he said.

"Don't kill me! You have this situation wrong!"

"I do?" Keenan gave a low, evil chuckle. "That's funny. I thought I understood it completely."

"No! It's a test! This is a test for Combat K! To check you still have the old magic."

Keenan glanced at Pippa, then across to where Franco was frantically trying to fight off an accelerating frisky monster. He licked his lips. Time had *slowed* into honey-treacle.

"I don't believe you," he said. "That's just too neat. Too easy an escape route for you, my friend."

"Why do you think we took Melanie?" snarled Oz. "We knew Franco would come after her, and drag you with him. We knew he wouldn't let Mel suffer… it's in his character profile. It was a chosen pathway for Combat K."

"Shit, and there's me thinking I came to NanoTek to decode the junk's SinScript. And, of course, to find out what caused the genetic fuck-up slurry on the planetside streets out there."

"Wait!" Franco had escaped Mel's advances, and trotted over to the group. Mel came close behind him, her eyes fixed glinting on the three GKs. She growled, tiny black hackles rising on her corrugated neck. Franco prodded Oz in the chest. "What the *hell* did you do to my girlfriend? Explain!"

"OK, it was an accident," said Oz, voice wavering, hands clenched into claws as blood flowed down his neck and stained the collar of his shirt. "There's a little boy, a bastard street-urchin called Knuckles. He mugged a woman in the street—a simple enough crime—only she wasn't just any normal woman out shopping for shoes; no, this was Christiane Solomonsson, fresh off the SPIRAL dock shuttle and heading for a meeting with Ministers from Quad-Gal. She had her case hard-wired to her arm, but Knuckles cut through the cord and stole it. Inside was a tiny bottle of biomods. *Very, very* advanced biomods. The template for, shall we say, a super-soldier."

Keenan, Pippa and Franco turned, and stared at Mel. She growled, staring right back.

"So you turned my bird into a mutated super-soldier?" snarled Franco. "You dickhead!"

"No, the biomod KJ-X elements should have remained dormant... only, when the altered, pirated biomods reacted out in The City, and everybody started to change, to deviate, then *everything* went wrong. Melanie became a prime deviant. PriD. One of the most powerful genetic soldiers NanoTek ever designed." He stared at her, eyes gleaming, face twisted into... pride, despite the cord tight around his throat; an umbilical of death leading straight to Keenan's fist.

Rain lashed the group, and distantly thunder roared. Keenan glanced up and around at the micro-climate. He shivered. He was deep under the sea, in some madman's personal play-pit. A sandbox for the insane. Never had he felt so estranged from reality.

Franco took a threatening step forward. His head lowered. His expression dropped into the sub-zero temperatures of cold ice fury. "Oz. Change her back."

"I cannot," said Oz.

"Grwwlll," growled Mel.

Franco's eyes met Keenan's. Keenan nodded. "Change her back. Or you *will* die."

"Then you'll have to kill me!" snapped Oz. "It's an irreversible process! The PriDs are not designed to fluctuate at will between human and military killer... they are simple fucking machines designed to destroy all life. You understand? There's a war coming, Franco, and NanoTek will be at the forefront of military supply! We are employed to design *soldiers*... but nobody gave us instructions what to do with them when they finished the job. They're not supposed to *turn back*."

"Soldiers? Who for?" said Keenan.

Oz smiled. "Why. For the Quad-Gal Military. Who else?"

"I don't believe you. QGM are an ethical outfit; they would never condone the deviation of existing human and alien species. They have compassion. They have... morals."

Oz shrugged. "You believe what you want to believe," he said, voice level. He licked his lips, tongue rimed in blood. "And I *know* what I know. I have the paperwork in my office. Signed, stamped and sealed. In triplicate."

"What about the others?" said Franco, voice cool now, eyes hooded.

"What others?"

"The zombies, *NanoTek Man*. Out there on the streets. Out there in The City. The *millions* who are fighting and murdering and killing! What about them? What happened with the biomods? What changed them? What in the name of God went wrong?"

Oz closed his mouth, jewelled teeth giving a tiny *clack*. He stared back at Franco. He did not reply.

"Talk, damn you!"

Oz remained silent, his eyes moving over to Pippa and the three dormant GK AIs. Oz smiled then, an eerie, blood-shadowed expression which fired a warning shot through Keenan's brain like a lightning bolt...

Behind Oz, Xakus appeared from a turret stairwell, his face blank, his eyes fixed on Keenan and the drama unfolding in the castle courtyard. His boots thumped cobbles and he moved forward, easily. Keenan's eyes dropped to the MMS Xakus held; it was slender, a beautiful, curved weapon with a horizontal magazine and tiny, glowing blue lights. Keenan had only ever seen one before, and he still remembered the devastating charges it could pulse across a battlefield, destroying tanks, aircraft, pigs, armoured crawlers, *anything* that got in its way. It was deeply illegal throughout Sinax.

"That's a Military Molecule Stripper," said Franco from the corner of his mouth.

Keenan nodded. "We thought you were dead."

Xakus shook his head. "Merely… disabled."

"Hey Professor, point that thing at the GKs," said Franco, gesturing at the sculpted AIs. "Don't be waving it near me, *my* beard doesn't need that kind of industrial trim!"

"No," said Keenan, voice gentle.

As Xakus moved forward, so the MMS came to rest aiming squarely at the Combat K men.

"Sorry Keenan. It's a long story. Take the loop from Oz's throat; it's hard for him to call me off when he's got no head."

Franco glared at Xakus. "What? Where? When? What's going down, man? You were here to help us! Steinhauer sent us to *you*! Said you were to be trusted! You were going to decode the SinScript…"

"I am to be trusted." Xakus grinned. He no longer looked weary. His eyes sparkled with energy. In fact, the harder Keenan stared, the more he realised Xakus wasn't quite as old as he claimed… or maybe, now, he was simply showing his true agenda. "Only not by you. Now, Keenan, step away, before I turn this devastating example of military brutality on your Combat K buddies."

Keenan tensed, and Franco glanced at him. For a split second he thought Keenan was going to cut Oz's head free and launch into a bout of hardcore violence; so he readied himself, mentally and physically...

Instead, Keenan freed the loop from Oz's throat, staining his gloves with blood. Oz turned, looked up into Keenan's eyes, and smiled, stepping back as the three GKs surged into life and leapt forward, guns aimed at Keenan and Franco.

Again, the fickle tables had been turned.

"I'm getting damn sick of this," muttered Franco.

"Rwwll."

"What's that?"

"Rwllwl rwlw."

"Aye."

"What happened, Xakus?" said Keenan, voice soft. "They offer you more money than Steinhauer? They offer you a big fat pension fund to bring in Combat K. Gods, when we broke our Prohibition D order we really dredged up some scum."

"No," said Xakus. "You misunderstand. Steinhauer sent you to me for a reason. I have not *betrayed* Steinhauer. In fact, we'll let him explain it himself."

From the same arched stairwell doorway that had disgorged Xakus stepped the stocky figure of General K. Steinhauer. He was smiling, and ran a hand through grey hair, pursed his lips, as if in thought, then rubbed at the pock-marked skin of his cheeks.

He strode forward, large frame carried with power, grace, élan. He stopped several metres clear of the group, as if gauging their strength. He glanced at Dr Oz, and the two men had a moment of unspoken communication. Steinhauer smiled at Keenan.

"Well done, my lad."

"Who you gonna bring out next, my mother?"

"You have travelled here, through this genetic mess, for a reason."

"Which is?"

"QGM need Combat K reformed. We have a series of highly illegal, immoral and dangerous missions, and we need you to lead specialist hard-ops teams out there in the field. You are the best. Combat K's best. Without a doubt. Your record is untarnished…"

"What about Terminus5? We nearly melted the fucking *planet*."

"You did not err," said Steinhauer, voice powerful, gaze iron. "And I admit to you, here, now, that you were exploited by a politician whose rank far exceeds mine. Nevertheless, Terminus5 is irrelevant… a bad dream."

"Not to me it isn't," snarled Keenan. "My family were *murdered* whilst I served time for that bullshit. And now you try and tell me Combat K are the best, and you've got a whole series of new and exciting missions lined up. Well, fuck you Steinhauer." He turned, glared at Pippa. "And fuck you as well, bitch."

Pippa's lips narrowed, but she did not respond.

"Wait, wait!" Steinhauer stepped forward, went as if to put his hand on Keenan's shoulder, but thought better of it. "You, and Franco, working your way across The City to this place... it was a test, my lad. To check you were still the best. You've proved you've given up the alcohol, and you don't let your family's deaths get in the way of a mission. And Franco, he has proved he's not as insane as he looks. Combat K are ready."

"What about the SinScript?" Keenan's eyes were cold, his gaze that of a desolate ice tomb. "You gonna tell me next you set up the junk's invasion of Galhari?"

"No, that atrocity is real, unfolding, a drama we cannot stem." Steinhauer's voice was stern. "We will decode the SinScript in a few short moments— only the GreenSource Mainframe can do that. After Xakus failed to decode the SinScript using the CryptorBox we came to realise nothing else in Quad-Gal had the computational power to unlock the junk's secrets. The SinScript is a device designed by a different age, an ancient people."

"Leviathan's people?"

Steinhauer, again, exchanged glances with Oz. Then back to Keenan. His eyes were trusting, open, honest. He smiled, like father to son. "Listen to me, Keenan. You, and Franco, and Pippa, you helped Emerald... one of the few remaining Kahirrim, a servant to an extinct GODRACE. I know it was not your intention; but you were duped, by the man known as Akeez." He laughed. "This game, Keenan, this game is bigger than both of us. QGM, with the help of the politician Kotinevitch, has assembled the largest WarFleet ever seen across the Four Galaxies. We knew this day was coming. We knew, one way or another, in this century, or the next, or the next, that Leviathan was going to rear its ugly head. This gameboard has existed for a hundred thousand years. A *million* years. It is unfortunate the dice have rolled in our lifetimes."

"To be brutal," said Keenan, "what the hell has that to do with us?"

"You were there," hissed Steinhauer, eyes glowing. "You *saw* Leviathan. You survived. And more than that; Emerald called you *Dark Flames*. That is more than a simple label. It means you are special, Keenan; Combat K is special. You—the three of you—have part of the alien in your blood, and as such, you may see things, do things, that no other mortal can achieve. We have monitored you on your journey across The City; few humans would have survived such odds."

"What about the junks?" said Keenan. "They are Leviathan's army?"

"Yes. But they are weak, and old; in the SinScript are their plans for expansion. They are a hive-mind creature; each and every one linked by script. When one dies, they all suffer. When one kills, they all rejoice. They are a walking, talking, breathing *bacteria*. Keenan, we must stop them before they wipe out more life in the Sinax Cluster. We must halt their conquest and decode their plans."

"I don't like being used," said Keenan. His eyes were bleak. He glanced right, to Pippa. "And I don't think my… *comrades*… like being manipulated, as well."

"Certain protocols had to be observed."

"Yeah?" Keenan cast his gaze across the group. Across Oz, Xakus, Steinhauer, the AI machines relaxed with weapons, then over Franco and finally, to Pippa. She gave him a short, cold smile and Keenan frowned. He did not understand that smile.

Steinhauer sighed, turned, and nodded to the GKs. The AI machines sprang at Pippa, who leapt back, suddenly, but was caught off-guard, surrounded instantly, and punched to the ground with stunning force, brutal betrayal. They stripped the woman's weapons, carefully—she carried a small arsenal—then Nyx stooped, lifting the dazed ex-member of Combat K and gazing down to where a trickle of blood stained the corner of her mouth. Nyx carried Pippa, and dumped her at Keenan's feet. Franco, beside Keenan now, glanced back to Mel, who gave a low slow nod, and Franco felt the situation escalating into insanity...

Pippa groaned, and pushed herself to her elbows. "What the fuck's going on, Oz? I thought we had a deal?"

"You are surplus to requirements," said Dr Oz, gaze focused. "You have served your purpose. You controlled the GKs. You proved yourself against Ranger. And the *others*. So many others. Now, it's time to return to your military unit. Your natural brood. Time to reform Combat K. Whether you like it," he smiled, "or whether you do not."

"*What?*" Pippa laughed, and spat on the cobbles. "You've got to be kidding, right? You've got be fucking *insane*. I'm not working with these two lunatics. Ever. Again."

"I'll second that," said Keenan. "I'd rather put a bullet in her skull than work missions with the murdering bitch. She killed my wife. My two little girls." He met Pippa's gaze. "I'd rather rot in hell for all eternity than touch her flesh. She is abomination to me."

"And what about me?" said Franco, holding out his hands, palms outwards. "Eh? Eh? Nobody's asked *my damn opinion in all of this!* Huh, I tell you, some people are so *rude.*"

Nobody spoke.

"Fuck you all," said Pippa, eyes hard like frozen, interstellar hydrogen.

"You will co-operate," said Steinhauer. "Combat K will reform. And Combat K will carry out missions for QGM and NanoTek." His face had gone hard. Gone were paternal smiles, the easy manner, the ambience of fatherhood. It had been replaced with iron. No compromise. "All three of you *will* co-operate, because you have been implanted with spinal logic cubes. If you do not work together, then you all die. If one of you," he bared his teeth in a smile, "kills another, then again, all three die. Horribly."

"I'd rather die," snapped Pippa, voice tombstone cold.

"Be my guest," said Steinhauer, and handed her a black Makarov. Pippa stared down at the grease-gleaming 9mm weapon in her steady hand. "Kill yourself."

Hush descended. Pippa's arm snapped up, gun levelled at Steinhauer. He grinned, and it was a grin too full of base understanding to be ignored.

"I should add." His voice was little more than a whisper. "I, also, am immune. As are all QGM Commanding Officers. After all." He coughed. "We wouldn't like our little war machine to suffer the embarrassment of a mutiny. Would we?"

"So they've trapped us?" snapped Franco, glaring around. "We work together, or die together?"

"Neat, isn't it?" drawled Steinhauer.

"I should have known not to trust the army!" said Franco.

"And you would have been right."

"What the bugger *are* spinal logic cubes?"

"AI detonation charges," growled Keenan. "Small, but powerful enough to blow you apart. When did you do it, Steinhauer? When did you infect my spine?"

"You were the easy one," said Steinhauer. "The junks had poisoned you. You needed an antidote. We slipped you the logic cubes when you were out cold."

"And me?" said Pippa, eyes chilled, grey, hard.

"During entry to NanoTek. Your medical. Your…" he smiled, "jabs."

"Hah, but I was the most difficult, yeah?" snapped Franco, eyes gleaming. "You not fool old Franco without a fuss!"

"On the contrary," said Steinhauer. "We got you when you were drunk and lying in the gutter. It took no great feat of imagination. And that was why you once more had to prove your mettle by crossing The City in its state of emergency; only… we assumed you would stop at Voloshko and The Hammer Syndicate. We didn't think you'd get this far."

Keenan released a slow, calculating breath. He turned to Oz. Smiled a weak smile. "This was all your plan?"

"No. I am simply a pawn of NanoTek Corporation. We make weapons and biomods. It's that simple."

"And what about the biomods rioting through the population?"

"An unfortunate accident."

"Bullshit."

Oz shrugged. "You always look for the complex, Mr Z. Keenan, when the basics are staring you in the face."

"What about the warehouse?"

"What warehouse?"

"The vault. Where you store your army of controlled zombies. You going to tell me that's an unfortunate accident, as well? You people, so arrogant, elevated to God by Power and staring down your narrow little noses at reality. This stinks, Oz. NanoTek stinks, Quad-Gal Military stinks, the whole fucking game is corrupt like a bloated corpse. And I, for one, am no longer playing."

"Then you will die."

Keenan shrugged. "We all die. Some of us had incentives removed a long time ago."

"Well, let me tempt you."

"How?"

"The GreenSource Mainframe. It... *she*... is the most powerful computer ever created. She is NanoTek's seventh wonder of the Quad-Gal. And she has news for you, Keenan."

"Oh yeah? You gonna tell me I've a long lost twin? Or maybe you're my fucking father? Wait, let me guess, me, Franco and Pippa are all triplets separated at birth, and we've come into a fabulous inheritance and only if I step into the GreenSource Mainframe do I qualify for a GOV funded pension when I shuffle off my mortal titanium-coil."

Silence descended. Still, fine rain fell. The sky had darkened. The three GKs moved, uneasily, swaying, organically shifting, as if waiting for an order to... kill?

"The GreenSource. It is predictive. It can tell you about your family. About their killer."

"Right. Sure mate. Like I haven't heard *that one* before."

"Pippa didn't kill your family. At least, not in the way that you think."

The snarl froze on Keenan's face. Then he relaxed, eyes glazing into contempt. "You're too late, pal. She already told me. Already spilled her guts into an unholy stinking heap. Pippa was released from prison days before me. She went to my home in a fit of jealousy, and murdered my wife and children. Not you, not any GreenSource Motherfucker, none of you can change that."

"Ask her," said Oz.

Keenan laughed, glanced at Pippa. She was shaking.

"Well, bitch?"

"I... don't remember."

"You don't remember? Hell girl, I'd sure remember sticking a pair of scissors into a child's eye. Try thinking *harder*. Actually, don't bother. Here, pass me the Makarov, and I'll end all our damn suffering right now. I've nothing to lose, and I will not be a pawn of QGM *or* fucking NanoTek."

"Hey guys! Wait!" snapped Franco. "Wait a god-damn stinking minute! *I* don't want to die. You two can slot each other if you want, OK, great and dandy, but don't be bloody taking me out with you! I'm an innocent victim in all of this! I'm not part of your sordid little argument. I don't deserve to die! I've got... so much more to give!"

Pippa stood, smoothed down her black uniform. Then she moved to Keenan, and looked up into his face. "When I was arrested, they found me uncon-scious in a back alleyway. They took me to the Urban Force Station; sat me down, pumped me with nar-cotics and coffee. They showed me the footage taken from Freya's apartment... it was, *horrible*. Unholy. Evil. And I watched myself stalk through that house, killing, killing, killing..." She covered her face, cheeks streaked with tears. Then she moved her hands. Looked up. Her eyes were dark smudges. "But I don't remember any of it, Keenan. I swear. The psycholo-gists pronounced I was traumatised and suffering short-term memory loss due to the... murders. But I do not, truly, remember. All I know is I woke in that alley covered in the blood of your children."

Oz stepped between them. "GreenSource can give you the *truth*."

Keenan chewed his lip, staring into Pippa's cold but beautiful eyes. She reached out, touched his arm. And he did not pull away. Again, he was pic-turing her on the beach on Molkrush Fed. The day their unholy love blossomed...

The pain returned. Keenan's head spun, pounding him with hammers.

The world, and reality, seemed suddenly distant. Viewed through frosted glass.

None of this can be real, he thought, bitterness eating him.

None of it.

He looked at Pippa. She tilted her head, staring at him. She was as unreadable as ever. An enigma.

With a howl, a SLAM Cruiser breasted the castle's wall and landed a few metres away on cold spurts of hydrogen. Oz gestured, and the GKs, with bristling guns, escorted and prodded Keenan, Franco and Pippa onto the bobbing loading ramp, followed by a lumbering, submissive Mel. Steinhauer followed, and Oz smiled at Xakus, giving a single nod. "You did well to bring them here."

"Thank you. And you are still good for your promise?"

"We can repair MICHELLE using every technological advancement available to us. When this scene is played out, MICHELLE will be collected and delivered to our labs."

"That's all I require."

Dr Oz nodded, and with his face impassive, turned and boarded the SLAM Cruiser. The ship *roared* and slammed up into fake atmosphere, rising swiftly through clouds and then *above* the ersatz plaything of the greatest computer genius ever to stalk Quad-Gal.

On the ground, Xakus watched the SLAM Cruiser disappear; then shivered under a pepper of light rainfall. He pondered on the recent journey;

MICHELLE, the battles, Keenan and Franco, the
SinScript. He shivered again. Now it was out of his
hands. Yes, he had been loyal and truthful up to the
point when MICHELLE had given her biomechanical life... and it had been that point when
NanoTek, with perfect timing, struck. When Professor Xakus was at his most vulnerable...

Burning just a little with shame Xakus turned to
head back to the stairwell and his disc moored on
the battlements. From there, he would direct engineers to MICHELLE's location.

Xakus froze.

There, in the archway, stood a junk. It had blood-
red eyes in an oval face. Its skin gleamed, metallic,
like pitted old metal smeared with bad oil. The lipless mouth opened, a stream of flowing mercury,
and a forked tongue flickered. Xakus realised the
junk was laughing.

Xakus scrabbled at his belt for his pistol as the
junk lifted a long Thump Rifle and a single shot
cracked across the cobbles, reverberating hollow
from stone. The heavy calibre round entered
Xakus's forehead, exploding his skull from the back
of his head in a million pieces to rain down, slowly,
like fluttering snowflakes. One knee folded, and
Xakus's body collapsed and leaked a thick red flow
between the grooves of neatly machined ersatz cobbles.

In silence the junk turned, retreated, and disappeared into a fake and fast-falling darkness.

CHAPTER 15
GREENSOURCE

CAM FROZE, SENSORS screaming. The Sump gurgled. He could smell the stench of his own burnt-out motors. What am I going to do? he screamed in fast-time binary. What can a little trapped PopBot like me with three burnt-out motors possibly *do* in this situation when... he gulped in digital... when *surrounded* by five of the latest and most efficient and deadly prototype NanoTek designed and manufactured K1LLBots? The best of the best. The elite of the PopBot hierarchy. Prototype. Awesome. Cam had read the glossy magazine literature whilst waiting for his upgrades.

Cam watched the K1LLBots as they circled him in the sludge. They kept wide, scanning him, attempting to decipher his level of threat. They recognised he had upgrades. K1LLBots were wary; intelligent. They did not underestimate. But—when they exploded into violence, Cam knew—they really *went for it.*

Help.

Mummy.

Cam wondered if he dared try his remaining motors, but logic dictated that if seven motors couldn't extract him from this mess, then four had absolutely no chance. Zero. Nada.

Bollocks!

Sometimes, often, Cam wished he hadn't been fitted with a Profanity Chip. He believed they were crude and unnecessary, especially in an AI as refined as he. However, on occasions like this, surrounded by five deadly K1LLBots and trapped limping in the bottom of an inescapable coolant sump, he was glad he had.

No. He was *fucking* glad he had.

The K1LLBots buzzed, and started closing in, circling faster and faster and faster... Cam felt a digital scream well in his digital throat and he wondered if NanoTek K1LLBots would be susceptible to bribery or empathy but deep down he knew they would not, and anyway, really, considering the awesome speed with which they were accelerating and what was that noise? Oh look all five K1LLBots had just extricated high-tensile triglium cutting saws which buzzed and whirled amongst the sludge and, most importantly, were able to cut neatly through a simple Security PopBot's outer shell...

Cam knew he had three seconds to do... something.

Anything!

Fast.

* * *

THE SLAM CRUISER sped above the miniature world, lights cutting down through a fast-scrolling darkness. The SLAM turned, banking swiftly, and flipped through a phase-screen into another, vast, subterranean chamber filled with... nothing.

Keenan peered out of the circular portal, out and down into an apparent infinity of space.

"I don't like this," muttered Franco, staring forlornly at the HotWire bonds around his wrists.

Keenan and Pippa had been similarly restrained, the Makarov neatly returned from Pippa's shaking hands to Steinhauer's holster. "Wouldn't like a little girl like you hurting herself," he smiled, as he eased free the weapon. She'd glanced back, then, towards Nyx who held Pippa's own yukana sword against the back of the Combat K woman's neck. Pippa snarled something unprintable.

Keenan watched as a vast, black, nothing trailed past. The space killed any feeling of speed. "Hey, Oz. Big place you have here."

"NanoTek came late to The City," he said, rubbing at the wound on his throat so recently inflicted by Keenan's homemade bootlace garrotte. "By the time we arrived, there was very little surface land remaining, at least not in the vast cubic areas we required. It meant building either up into the sky... or down here, under the ocean, beneath the rock. I like it down here. We've bought a million square kilometres. Ready for expansion, you might say."

"Expansion?"

"NanoTek is in a state of permanent expansion," said Oz, quietly. His eyes glittered. Red light danced in the hollow of his mouth. "It is the way of things. The Nature of the Beast."

"Hey, dickhead, why so much empty space here, then?" Franco was scowling, and fiddling with his HotWire bonds. Beside him, Mel was crooning softly to herself, rocking, apparently lost in some kind of canine zombie song. Her drool was pooling in her lap.

Oz turned, regarding Franco as he would something on the sole of his finely polished shoe. "The City has esoteric building regulations. Not even a galaxy-spanning multi-armed conquering conglomerate such as NanoTek can avoid the pointless pencil of bureaucracy forever. Let's just say there have been *interesting* planning meetings. And some men, stiff-collared paper-shuffling arse-sniffing bureaucrats... well, they don't know when to back down. Even when it threatens their health." He smiled, a dark, blood-oil smile.

The SLAM Cruiser cruised through wide tunnels, narrow tunnels, twisting tunnels, vast empty caverns, caverns filled with underground lakes sporting gentle ripples sparkling under the SLAM Cruiser's lights. Franco shivered, witnessing these vast stretches of underground water; he'd had a bad experience in one, once; it had left him mentally scarred, or at least, riddled with scar tissue on top of all the other mentally unbalanced wreaths of scar tissue. Some spaces were filled with glowing dust, through which they glided, the SLAM Cruiser's jets retracting and engines silencing to avoid risk of explosion... then on, they moved, ever on and subtly *down*.

Suddenly, the SLAM Cruiser tilted and dropped vertically. The occupants were slammed back in seats. Mel growled long and low, jaw making cracking crunching sounds as she, apparently, chewed her own teeth. She seemed distraught. Unhappy.

As they fell, Keenan nudged Franco and gestured to the portal. Franco peered out. They dropped, following a flowing smooth black tunnel towards the bowels beneath The City... and there, running parallel with their descent, was the same thick silvery umbilical they had witnessed from outside the Black Rose Citadel HQ.

"That lead up to the SPIRAL dock?" said Keenan.

"The Line? Yes. SPIRAL port technology is incredibly complex; if not meticulously controlled then it becomes a danger to us all. We are dropping through a hermetically sealed environment. Freefall."

"The GreenSource Mainframe controls all this?"

"Yes." Oz locked his gaze to Keenan. "And *so much* more, my little cooperative Combat K man."

Keenan was just about to speak, but the SLAM Cruiser slowed with rapid deceleration, dunk-engines whining, as they slipped through sealant-envelopes.

And there, below them, spread the GreenSource Mainframe.

At first glance it appeared to be a giant series of towers built from crystals of deep, rich green. The base was perhaps fifty metres across, and rose in jagged leaps, ragged steps, to a single inch-wide pinnacle which connected, via a narrow circular platform, to the Line leading straight up to the distant SPIRAL dock. NanoTek's express elevator to the *stars*.

The SLAM Cruiser decelerated further, and banked, and Keenan saw the Mainframe stood on an island of rough volcanic rock; to all sides there was a moat of nothingness, a desperate fall veering away and inducing instant vertigo. Deep, deep down the circular well could be seen the glow of magma, which broiled and churned in restless agony.

The SLAM Cruiser banked again, then levelled, and touched down on the platform at the tower's base with a metallic compress of suspension. The ramp fizzed, and Oz was the first one off the vehicle, watching as GKs prodded Keenan, Franco, Pippa and Mel from their cosy intimacy in the narrow hold.

They clumped down the ramp, to stand on uneven volcanic rock. All gazed up at the sheer magnificence of the rearing green towers, topped with that silvery, spidery strand of Line. And yet— yet something *strange* filtered into Keenan's mind. The image was wrong, somehow disjointed, as if the GreenSource Mainframe didn't quite inhabit the same time frame. It seemed to jerk, and jump, in infinitesimally small steps and he turned to the others. "Do you see it?"

"See what?" barked Franco.

"The tower. Stuttering, like a badly copied vid."

Franco stared hard at Keenan. "I think it's *you* who needs a pill, good buddy."

"Have you noticed the *colour?*" said Pippa, voice low.

"What about it?"

"When we visited Ket, and broke into the Inner Sanctum of The Metal Palace; we found Emerald, yes, but she seemed to be linked to a gem. Remember? Franco wanted to steal it. The tower looks like, hell, it *is* the same sort of thing. The same... mineral."

Combat K observed the GreenSource Mainframe. And felt, eerily, that it observed them back.

"You must enter the portal," said Oz, moving up close behind Keenan. Keenan glanced back, saw the poison dripping from Nyx's fangs, the steady hold on the yukana, and he glanced around at the other GKs with weapons trained on the unarmed and helpless Combat K soldiers. The unwilling unit reformed.

"I kind of felt you were going to say that."

"There." Oz pointed. There was a circular orifice, at floor level. Keenan nodded, and moved towards the organic lips. He turned, made eye contact with Franco, then with Pippa.

"I have a feeling this is where I discover the truth," said Keenan.

"Grwl," said Mel.

"What did she say?"

"She said that sometimes the truth is best left dead," translated Franco.

Keenan stared hard at the ginger squaddie. "You got *all that* from one growl?" Franco started to moan an explanation, but Keenan held up a hand, and rubbed at his temple as his headache returned to pound him. But this time, unlike during previous occurrences, it came flooding into his skull with a vengeance, washing over him, down through his entire being like a raw riot of fire. Keenan paled, and felt like he could vomit. "It's OK," he managed to say, through pulsing waves of sickening nausea. "OK, Franco. Stop!"

"Good luck." Pippa's voice was low.

"I thought you were trying to kill us? With those bastard... *things*. What changed?" Keenan was breathing deeply, laboured, obviously suffering agony.

"I..." Pippa shook her head. Looked at the ground. "Shit. It doesn't matter."

"She trusted Oz," said Franco. "But he stuffed her. Ain't that right, girl? At least with us you know Uncle Franco will look after you." He leered at her bosom.

"That's what worries me."

Brittle.

Chatter.

Insect chatter.

All wrong. All wrong.

Broken glass. Cracked crystal. Shards, piercing, brain.

Humans.

Feeble humans.

Come to me.

Keenan.

Come to me.

Keenan turned, head pounding, and pushed forward into the GreenSource Mainframe.

In silence, the machine accepted him.

I MEAN YOU *no harm. Relax. Come further in, deeper in, there will be no pain I promise.*

Keenan pushed on, as if through a thick shock-gel. It encompassed him, filled his mouth and nose and ears and anus, pressing into him, flowing into him, exploring him without his consent, a liquid, machine rape. And then, as if suspended in fluid, Keenan floated upwards through layers of green—dark and sombre at the base, then up through gradual lightening shades until he hung, suspended, arms outstretched near a central light source.

He kicked around, idly, swimming in streams of ichor, turning over and rolling and soon losing himself, wondering which way was down. It no longer seemed to matter. Keenan laughed like an idiot. Giggled like a child.

Welcome.

"You wanted to see me?"

Yes. And you require my services.

You need me...

The voice was definitely female, yet deep and powerful, almost a song. It filled Keenan with instant liking, instant calm; like a trusted mother-figure, a strong maternal embrace which took him back and back drifting down decades to the long, echoing, cosy months in the womb. He was a babe again, cherished and nurtured, fed and loved; and he sank, shamelessly, into the enveloping loving warmth, into this secure and total environment.

And I need you. Your help.

"You need my help?" Idle surprise. "You're the most powerful machine ever created. What could *I* possibly offer you?"

Not just you, Zak, but Combat K. You are special, all three. Your talents lie... beyond that of simple mortals. You are soldiers, yes, and twisted, yes... but you have been to places, seen things no mortal should ever witness. After Emerald, and the K Jump, you cruised the twisted millennia of space. You were changed by that, Zak. You were shifted.

"Only my mother called me Zak."

I am your mother, and your lover, I am a total part of your chemical now. I am inside you. Like Emerald was inside you. And I can see the channels she carved; I can see the route to the Dark Flame... that element which so upsets the Seed Hunters.

"What do you know of Seed Hunters?"

You are in their prophecies. The Dark Flame will destroy them. That is all I know.

"You are being helpful. But nothing is ever given freely. What do you want with Combat K?"

I want Combat K to work with Oz, and Steinhauer. We are building an army, Zak Keenan. Constructing a warhost from the deviant twisted morally corrupt individuals who inhabit this decadent place; the biomods have done their job, turned human and alien forms into powerful soldiers who are learning to fight, learning to kill. Honing their skills upon one another. Weeding out the weak breeds from the strong. When the biomods changed them, it deformed them physically, making them stronger, more immune to disease and biological and chemical warfare. But they are as children again; they must grow, must be nurtured. Combat K can help us do this. Combat K can help to train the deviants. Combat K can control the zombie host.

"It was a function of the biomods to change these people *on purpose?*"

It is an integral function of the NanoTek biomod, yes. It can be instructed to rearrange a genetic organism into... thousands of different compositions. What we have done in The City is create a sandbox, an experiment, from which we can choose and select, and identify the stronger definitions of deviation template and evolve the warhost from that baseline. You felt the pulse, knew of the signals emitted by each deviated organism, each biomod infested zombie. Cam, your PopBot, instructed you on this. This regular pulse—well Zak, it is data. Feedback. We call it product registration. It has allowed me to monitor the mutations and decide which is strongest, fastest, and ultimately the most competent for my... purpose.

"So the entire population are guinea pigs? There must have been a more humane way?"

Certainly more humane. But no way this fast, nor efficient. Out there, Keenan, on those corrupt streets there are billions of unwilling specimens, organic templates which I can deviate and mutate and play with... by doing this, on such a mass scale, I can accelerate military production from ten years to ten days. It was a sacrifice I was willing to make. All I had to do was appeal to vanity. And ego. And greed. And lust. The rest was simplicity personified.

Keenan's recurring headache, a dull and aching throb, again expanded to fill his skull. He gasped, and realised too late something was wrong with him, an organic element deep inside, something deeply truly *bad*...

It went *click* inside his head.

A *chord* changed in his soul.

And the skull pain vanished.

Keenan realised he could see behind the lies of the GreenSource Mainframe. In his heart, the Dark Flame blossomed, eating away at the lies, burning away the poison. And for long moments Zak Keenan stared out from his weak and pitiful organic shell. He could see—

Everything.

Like a machine, cold and clinical, he surveyed the GreenSource Mainframe and recognised its inherent evil. Keenan blinked. Felt the SinScript within his WarSuit and he delved through its shell and harnessed the power of the GreenSource to decode a trillion trillion combinations and he smiled, for within that fleeting moment he understood. The GreenSource could decode the SinScript *because* the GreenSource had created the SinScript.

NanoTek had programmed the junks.

NanoTek was a servant of Leviathan. And it was using Quad-Gal Military against itself...

This biomod deviation is for the greater good, lied the GreenSource Mainframe, failing to recognise this subtle shift in Keenan's physiology, failing to understand that he was a machine detached. *Leviathan comes. Before him spread the scourge of his ancient army, the junks, seeding planets with disease and toxins, turning worlds into jungles of biological hazard fit only for his next beautifully corrupt generation...*

Keenan calmed his breathing. He understood with clarity. It slammed his brain like an axe-blade. Punched his heart like an electric storm. The *truth* and the *shift* and the *Dark Flame burning* came from Emerald, the Kahirrim, the *alien*. A gift. From the time she entered Keenan, down on the planet of Ket; the time she flowed with him, merged with his blood and fluids, there, she had recognised the seed in him, the seed of the Dark Flame, the seed so desperately sought by Seed Hunters and from that time that merging that joining he had suffered with a dull, deep ache in his skull...

Kiss me, Emerald had said, *and I will know you, understand you, I will delve your deepest desires and fears and needs, I will flow with your saliva and blood and semen, I will be a part of you and you of me, fluid, joined, together for an eternity...*

Keenan pictured her, locked deep within her vault by the Ket-i warrior clans; her beautiful black skin contained emerald green veins; dark ringlets tumbled over her finely honed imitation body. The image flickered, transposed in Keenan's head with the hybrid killing machine she could become. And Keenan felt something crack in his brain, a broken egg, a yolk of truth and total understanding which flowed free and into his mind and into his bloodstream. When Emerald possessed him, flowed with him, joined with him, *merged* with him, so she had left something behind, some residue of her alien self, some substance clinging to the inner walls of his organic shell that had subtly *changed* him.

I can see Eternity, Emerald had said. *I can see beyond Time. I can see the pulse of The Galaxy Soul.*

And Keenan *understood.*

Like molten hydrogen, thoughts flowed into his brain with the simplicity of binary. Doors opened.

Lights illuminated. The pain had vanished. In its place, came machine truth. A digital epiphany.

The SinScript unfolded before his very eyes.

He flowed with the code, and he became the code.

There was a lot in there. Death, disease, torture, suffering. A million year promise.

Keenan flowed to the machine core.

And the instructions glowed.

The SinScript's core read: Destroy Quad-Gal.

"No," whispered Keenan, brain colder than frozen hydrogen. Despair swamped him. What could he do? What could one simple soldier do against an army of such vastness, such longevity, against ruling alien gods, and against a creature capable of destroying an entire galaxy?

Keenan opened his eyes, breathed deeply, and lifted his hand. GreenSource ceased speaking. Now, it realised there was something wrong and Keenan felt the underlying current of animosity and pure digital hatred.

The GreenSource Mainframe was not *created* by NanoTek. It was not a machine.

It was old. *She* was old.

And *she* was alive.

GreenSource was a part of Leviathan. NanoTek were a construct, a front-man, a puppet, a marionette, through which She could channel the biomods and change the organic life-forms of The City into...

"No more lies," breathed Keenan.

Leviathan sought to change the people and aliens of The City into a new breed, a new army. They would become the next breed of *junks*... more powerful, more deadly, more toxic. From there the army of poison would spread disease and pestilence and death across the entirety of Quad-Gal, turning it into a dark and terrible place... as they had, once before, a million years ago.

Here, and now.

This was the beginning.

This was a Prologue to War.

Keenan's eyes snapped open as he floated within GreenSource and he became aware that *she* had become aware and he smiled, a detached machine smile, and she understood his new found talents imbibed from a dead alien species. Keenan felt himself mentally accelerate, images flickering into his brain, The City sprouting the perfect deviant army, the army flooding out into Quad Gal and invading hundreds and thousands of planets and species and life-forms spreading toxicity only *this time* it was a mechanical and electronic toxicity and the disease *was* the biomod and it would spread and consume and eat its way through men and women and the alien species throughout Sinax Cluster—discarding the weak, the genetically incompetent, but *swelling its ranks* with every conquered world every poisoned system every desecrated life-arm and within months the scourge would be unstoppable.

Leviathan would riot through the Four Galaxies...

He would *feed*.

And he would destroy.

Keenan blinked as the *blast* of hatred from Green-Source slammed him... and he was ejected downwards with such force he thought his bones would snap, arms and legs flapping useless as he was wrenched from the liquid interior. He erupted, gasping, from the quivering orifice, soared over the gathered group, snarling as he turned the ejection into a roll, landing and coming up fast on the very brink of the precipice leading down down to broiling molten magma. Keenan teetered for a moment on the edge, boots showering a cascade of brittle rock and glancing down at the distant orange glow.

GreenSource had tried to kill him...

He whirled. The GKs had tensed, legs bowing, five thousand needles erupting across Nyx's arms and torso. Momos drew both yukana swords, and Lamia had transformed arms and legs into blades which shimmered, a hallucinogenic whirl.

Keenan licked his lips, eyes connecting with Franco, then Pippa. Pippa gave him a single, solid nod. In that nod came the bond; the old connection. The old magic.

Despite their hatred, Combat K were one.

And they had a job to do.

The voice of GreenSource boomed from staccato towers. "Kill them," she snarled, all gentility gone as her voice rose to an inhuman, wailing shriek. "Kill them all!"

"Wait!" snapped the powerful command of Steinhauer. "What's this? What's going on?" His head snapped from Keenan to Dr Oz, then back; and as his eyes met Keenan's there was a question there, confusion, and in that split second Keenan realised Steinhauer's intentions were honourable; he really, truly believed he was helping Quad-Gal Military, believed that Oz and GreenSource were enemies of

Leviathan and the junks... instead of the World
Eater's benefactor.

Oz rolled fast, yukana sword slamming horizontally through Steinhauer's legs, just above knees.
The blade exited on a fine spray of blood, which
rolled down the black blade into streamers against
volcanic rock. Steinhauer screamed, his organism
separating into three discrete parts. Femurs severed,
he tried to step forward, thighs parting with crisp
clacks from knee joints as he toppled onto the rock
with blood pumping a river...

Combat K smashed into action... with an automatic precision which made them what they were.
Pippa charged Oz, who slashed the hissing yukana
at her throat. She twisted, rolling fast with the
blow, HotWire bound arms flashing up. The
yukana parted the wire, which fizzled and gave a
small *pop*. Pippa rolled, hit the floor, lashed out
with boots and swept Oz's legs away...

The GKs spread out. Their guns yammered, and
Keenan dived, grabbing the Makarov from Steinhauer's holster and flinging it to Franco. He yanked
Steinhauer's MPK, still connected to the screaming,
legless man with paracord, and opened fire on the
GKs which danced back, sparks momentarily flashing across black alloy frames. And Keenan realised,
with a nasty shock, they were trying to protect the
GreenSource Mainframe...

Franco caught the Makarov, also opened fire. He
ran towards the SLAM Cruiser, diving inside and
grabbing their packs. He pulled free a G Knife, slit
his binding HotWire, then shouldered his pack and
sprinted down the ramp.

"Keenan!"

Keenan caught the blade, MPK still howling sending roaring scythes of bullets into and past the GK AIs, bullets impacting with soft *whumps* in the walls of GreenSource. Keenan sliced his own bonds, then glanced down into Steinhauer's tortured face.

Steinhauer seemed about to speak... but he slumped back, and was still. Keenan watched the life-light die in his eyes. Sorrow ripped through him. They had shared their moments of animosity, of differing opinions. Squabbled like kids on occasion. Steinhauer thought Keenan was a renegade, a psycho and a loose cannon. Keenan thought Steinhauer was an army bureaucrat, a bastard with a pencil shoved up his arse. But they were both still Combat K; brothers. Keenan's head lifted. His eyes were dark, glinting evil under the surreal green light of the Mainframe.

Franco skidded next to him, panting, and they focused on the GKs. All three machines were motionless. Waiting?

Pippa knelt on Oz's chest, yukana against his throat. Blood trickled from a fresh cut.

They had reached an *impasse*.

"I assume the Mainframe is a baddy?" Franco said, voice low, eyes never leaving the GKs.

"It's part of Leviathan. An extension." Keenan grimaced. "We have to destroy it."

Franco glanced up at the mammoth, kilometre-high structure, with its jagged towering peaks, its green-glinting, crystalline, splintered towers. He hoisted a fistful of grenades. Grinned a bad grin. "I predict a riot?" he suggested.

"Damn fucking right."

Dr Oz's voice was cool and smooth under the pressing yukana blade. "If you all lay down your weapons, you may just survive this encounter. GreenSource will not tolerate your misbehaviour." He watched from his prone position as Franco sidled to Mel, and with the G Knife, parted the HotWire which imprisoned her. She unrolled in height, stretched muscles long compressed by deviant pyro-wire, and her small, mottled head lowered on a long corrugated neck and she grinned at Dr Oz, then leered over towards the three GKs.

Mel took a weaving, threatening step, and Franco skipped back, out of her way.

"I think she's pissed!" snapped Keenan.

"Are you surprised? Look what they did to her! Now she has somebody to *blame*."

Franco fired a few more shots from the Makarov. "Keenan, you out of ammo?"

Keenan nodded.

Two things happened at once. The GKs, black, glossy, thin-limbed, sculpted, roared in high-pitched digital mimicry, the sound of tortured bandwidth, and moved fast... charging Keenan and Franco with weapons rippling, poison dripping from long slim jaws containing row on row of needle-thin teeth. Beneath Pippa, Oz squirmed and *flowed* away from her, standing to stare at her suddenly off-balance, kneeling figure.

Franco pulled a BABE grenade pin, yanked back his arm, but it was too late as the GKs sprinted fast, jaws clacking, and they would be on him in an instant mashing, tearing, injecting...

Pippa swept out the yukana, but Oz leapt the sweep with incredible agility, dodged left, then right, avoiding the hissing blur of blade. He accelerated, was beside Pippa, arm slamming down and making Pippa gasp at the impact. She head-butted him, and Oz's jewelled teeth impaled her head drawing blood. She slashed out, yukana singing, but Oz ducked and twisted, side-kicked her in the belly with stunning force, tossing her backwards across the volcanic rock platform to roll, dangerously close to the edge.

"Aiie!" screamed Franco as the AIs were on him, bringing up his arm before his face as something large, and brown, and thrashing and growling connected with all three GKs in one terrific launch and sent them spinning like skittles across the rock, thin limbs rattling, poison arcing like incontinent piss. Mel stood, brutal, massive, glowering, and growled back at Keenan and Franco who exchanged worried glances. Mel ran at the GKs, and Momos rose, twin yukanas whirling, but Mel stepped between them, swaying, claws lashing out and grating against alloy.

"She can't kill them all," said Keenan.

"We have to help her!"

"No! We destroy GreenSource."

Franco turned tortured eyes on his friend and brother. "I... have to help her."

"This is her sacrifice," snapped Keenan. "Focus. Bombs?"

Franco grasped his pack before him. "Enough High-J to put a Shuttle into orbit."

"Let's do it."

Pippa danced with Oz, blade hissing and slashing, balanced on the edge of the precipice. Franco turned eyes on her, again wanting desperately to help his friend...

"Just do it, Franco," snarled Pippa, shaking sweat from her shoulder-length black hair. "I've got this fucker sorted."

Her eyes met Keenan's. He ground his teeth. Gave her a nod. Without her, they could not destroy GreenSource... Without Pippa, without Combat K *as one,* they could not free the people of The City from their biological entrapment.

They were a machine.

A simple, well-oiled unit.

Franco ran, a few steps behind Keenan. They reached the edge of the GreenSource Mainframe, took hold of the soft, jelly-like substance, and started to hoist themselves up, boots and sandals kicking into the moving, rolling substance, hands grabbing and tearing as they climbed with grim faces and clamped, tortured jaws.

They climbed for a few minutes, powering up the flank of the widest tower. Below, Mel was battling with all three GK AIs, her claws pounding and hammering, jaws twisting and grinding. The two men paused, glancing down. Mel picked up Momos, and with a roar flung her into the abyss. Momos twirled, black-enamelled limbs glittering as she fell, and disappeared into the molten lake far, far below.

"Atta girl!" roared Franco.

"Keep climbing."

"I'm shagged, Keenan!"

"Keep *climbing!*"

"But Keenan, it's like climbing up a great mound of wobbling tits!" said Franco. He considered this. "Actually, I suppose in some ways I should be mightily thankful."

"Be thankful," snapped Keenan.

They pushed on, faster and faster, faces red, sweat dripping, muscles screaming with fatigue.

Below, Pippa was not faring well. Oz had grasped one of Momos's discarded yukana swords and they duelled, blades clashing and ringing, sparks flying.

In her years of violence, Pippa had fought many opponents. Only a few had been her better. But here, now, in this place, Oz was a demon, skilled like nothing she had ever experienced. Pippa fought with every ounce of talent and strength and experience, used every trick she knew; and still Oz played with her, a cat with a hobbled bird, a shark with an injured fish.

She was outclassed. And, bitterly, she knew it.

Blades clashed, discordant music. Pippa leapt back, Oz's yukana a hair's-breadth from her face, then she closed on him and his sword opened a line across her ribs, making her gasp; but she was in close, too close, her sword twisted at a strange angle and she reversed the cut, blade sliding through Oz's neck in a bright spurt of arterial gore. She stepped neatly away from her dark, death-lover's embrace, ripped her sword sideways, viciously, and decapitated Dr Oz with all the savagery of the betrayed. Panting, bathed in sweat and blood, she dropped to her knees, her yukana clattering at her feet, hands clasping her opened rib-cage with a yelp. Blood pulsed through her fingers and she twisted, peering down at her sliced uniform and the pale, exposed flesh—her interior flesh, and yellow fat sub-strata—beneath. She could see the ivory of exposed bone. She shuddered.

"That son-of-a-bitch," she mouthed. And realised. Something was... *wrong*.

She glanced up. Dr Oz's body had failed to fall. It stood, headless, swaying, as if modestly inebriated, the bloody, black-bladed sword still clenched in Oz's neatly manicured and almost *effeminate* fingers.

Pippa looked over to the severed head. It was glassy eyed. Dead.

Why doesn't the body fall? she thought.

More blood pumped through her fingers, oozing.

Why doesn't the fucker collapse?

Her eyes passed Oz's oddly behaving corpse, watched Mel batter the GKs, holding one in each powerfully bulging arm and swinging them round and round by their ankles to finally slam against one another with a clash and crash of buckling TitaniumVI casings and a scatter of loose rivets.

Pippa winced.

Looked up again.

And allowed a deep hiss through wet lips. She gritted her teeth and reached slowly forward, searching for her sword.

A dark mist had appeared, rising from Dr Oz's neck. It swirled up, billions of tiny particles coalescing and forming slowly, agonisingly, into the shape of Oz's recently departed head. Artistically, like metal melting over a wire-work mesh, Oz's head reformed, flushed slowly with colour, and was suddenly *real*.

He blinked. Gasped. Touched at his own throat as if testing reality. Then, he lowered his head, eyes staring out at Pippa with new, refreshed, rejuvenated life.

"A wonderful thing, these biomods," Oz said.

MEL, DESPITE APPEARANCES, was fighting a losing battle. In the raging inferno of her mind something started to register. It was a weakness; a weakness flooding through her system and she realised, as the GK's slender jaws tore at her, ripping flesh, tearing skin, snapping her bones... she realised with a dawning, primeval understanding that the AIs were gradually *poisoning* her...

Mel grabbed Nyx in a head-lock, rolled with the flailing machine kicking legs and slashing sparks from volcanic rock, then with Nyx's head in both clawed hands she bashed the machine's skull repeatedly and violently against the rock. Five times, six times, Mel felt it buckling under the might of her superhuman deviated muscles...

Lamia landed on Mel's back, blade-arms attempting to cut Mel's throat but Mel twisted fast, catching the blades in claws and attempting to bend them, to snap them—as Nyx hit her in the lower back at full charge, buckling Mel who heard several of her own spinal discs *pop* and crack and she grabbed both machines, hatred a bottomless well and they were a symbol of NanoTek a representation of the monolithic corporation who had abused her and deviated her and changed her from a sweet human woman into... this.

With a GK under each arm, Mel roared and charged the edge of the abyss. She leapt, both machines thrashing against her, slicing her, cutting her, and all three fell suddenly, swiftly, into the dark.

For long moments, all was silent.

Then, a scrabbling sound came from the edge.

In the green glow from GreenSource towers, stones rattled. Something moved at the edge of the precipice. Something black, and enamelled, gleaming against a lip of volcanic rock. Moving fast, accelerating with thumping hydraulics, a teardrop head appeared with matt black discs for eyes, and a long thin-limbed arm reached up as Nyx dragged her battered AI body from the pit.

She crawled on battered, twisted legs, then stood. One arm had been torn free, and the shoulder joint trailed organic-looking tendons. Her head swivelled, staring at where Pippa was about to die... then looked up to the frantically climbing figures of Keenan and Franco.

Nyx sprinted, leapt, and with swift, elegant movements, and leaving a trail of toxic poison from rows of needle-thin teeth in her wake, she began to climb.

FRANCO GLANCED DOWN. Saw Mel go over the edge with the two kicking, thrashing AIs. "No!" he screamed, face suddenly stunned, eyes wide in disbelief.

Keenan grunted, and halted his ascent.

Franco's head slammed up. "What is it?"

Keenan had both arms, up to the elbow, trapped inside the GreenSource tower. As Franco watched,

Keenan was *yanked* close to the wall, where suddenly his face pressed against the glutinous substance and the tower itself started to drag him in...

"Shit," hissed Franco. "Wait Keenan! I'm coming! Don't get sucked in! Franco will save the day!" He took a great handful of jelly and felt a curious twisting motion; with a squelch it sucked in his hand, his wrist, then twisted him in up to his elbow sending pain shooting through his joints. Franco yelled in surprise, pain and fear. Then felt his sandaled feet suddenly overwhelmed, sucked at, pulled *into* the tower... where it twisted his knees against their joints and made him howl and yammer in pain...

"You've got to get free!" screamed Keenan. "It's a living organism! It'll absorb us! Digest us!"

Franco struggled and pulled with all his strength, one hand flailing uselessly. But what can I do? he thought, mind wild, thoughts a chemical slurry. What the hell can I do? Look at me! A useless midget! "What shall I do?" he screamed, but Keenan could not answer. His head had been sucked into GreenSource.

He was suffocating.

CHAPTER 16
THE OLD MAGIC

CAM COUNTED THE seconds. Each speeding *tick* and *tock* seemed to last an eternity.

Three seconds.

The K1LLBots were closing, saws buzzing fast and bright and jewelled, and Cam could acknowledge by their formation, and the angle of their circular, spinning attack, that they intended to split him into apple slices along his globular latitude...

Two seconds.

What was it that Gunnery Sergeant Reznor always used to say? Other than *clean that floor, maggots,* of course, and *sort out that puke, maggots.* What had it been? Cam hummed nervously, trying to remember. If he'd had fingers, he would have drummed them against a solid table top.

Oh yes.

Let's get the job done.

One second.

So, thought Cam, I'd better get that job done. Suddenly, he ignited his external jets. Fire billowed in a high-intensity stream, slamming out and over the K1LLBots and Cam felt their pulses of confusion and sudden fear as they realised—Cam wasn't trying to *burn them,* because they were pretty much fry-proof... unless... no... hell, he was trying to ignite the coolant. Cam had analysed the cooling sludge. It consisted of trimethyprene hydrogen5 chloroxide. A superb coolant, unless it reached 1024°C, whereupon it became an unstable chemical compound which would instigate a fiery chain reaction capable of spreading through the entirety of the coolant system...

In other words, Bad News.

Cam dodged, whirling, around the charging K1LLBots, still emitting his fire and monitoring the surrounding temp. Come on, come on he hummed, The Sump's current dragging him around in a wide arc and sending him streaming back towards the core base. The K1LLBots whirled, tracking him, unsure what to do now. Because, if Cam *did* ignite the coolant, then surely they'd all...

Cook.

Ho hum. Cam grinned. Or would have, if he'd had a mouth.

1022°.

Dum de dum de dum. Round and round we go. Fire scorched. The trimethyprene hydrogen5 chloroxide started to squeal like a live thing. It glooped and bubbled. Cam clucked with annoyance. Come on baby! Let's get this party started!

1023°.

Hey hey, gotta time this one *just right...*

1024°.

There came a *whump,* and Cam had timed his circular projection so the explosion of pressure *thumped* him up from the bottom of The Sump, up and up through narrow passageways riding a wave of thrust forced *out* by the chemical ignition of all those billions of gallons of coolant. Cam rode the wave like an expert surfer. He screamed in joy at cerebral superiority, as behind him, deep deep down and far behind, the K1LLBots were crushed and compressed and burned into tiny molten pebbles which dribbled into little more than a chemical imbalance...

"Weeeee!" squawked Cam, aware that only a few inches behind heaved enough pressure and heat and chemical irregularity to squash him like a Vitis Vinifera under the stomping feet of an experienced grape crusher. He slammed like a bullet from a gun. A sperm from a testicle. A SPAW from a spawning barrel-tube. And his atomic heart *sang...*

CAM FLOWED. AND as he flowed, he thought to himself, I wonder what the cooling system cools?

Soon, his question would be answered.

Because it cooled the GreenSource Mainframe.

PIPPA CRAWLED TO her feet, watched Dr Oz swinging the black-bladed yukana. She backed away, fear eating into her. She'd won. She'd cut his damn head off! And now he'd gone and had the bad grace to grow a new one.

Oz attacked, a blistering assault, sword hammering left and right, whirling, cutting at Pippa's legs then slashing up past her face and reversing to cut her head from her shoulders... she stumbled, back again, sweat stinging her eyes, hair lank, aware of the terrible drop behind. She could imagine that furnace of lava far below; it was ready to eat flesh from her bones.

"You should be dead!" she snapped, pointing, unable to contain her fury.

Oz considered this. His smile glittered like alien jewels, which it surely was. "That's the thing, dear Pippa. When I employed you to be my Chief Security Officer... well, I didn't explain, did I? However, it should have been self-evident. My *position* was prominent on the job description proforma."

"What the hell are you talking about?"

"I'm not just the *head* of NanoTek. I am NanoTek. I *embody* NanoTek. I have become... shall we say, 100% *enthused* with the business. Why live on in an organic state, when there is something so much better?"

"You're made completely from nanobots?"

"Yes. That would be correct. And hey, it could even form an interesting ice-breaker at parties."

The sword slammed for Pippa's neck, but she twisted in a blur, an inhuman shift, her own blade up, a shower of sparks sparkling through the green gloom. She rolled her wrist and her own blade slid down in a shower of sparks, severing Oz's arm just below the elbow. Both arm and yukana clattered for a moment, rolling, then toppled from the precipice and into the abyss.

Oz clucked in annoyance as his arm swiftly reformed, running like melted plastic. "Such a waste of a fine weapon! Now I'll have to use my damn hands!" With a snarl he leapt at Pippa, and her blade slammed up cutting neatly through his groin, separating his testicles, and embedding with a wrist-wrenching *thud* deep in his stomach, up to the hilt. However, Oz ignored—or did not feel—the pain, as his hands closed on Pippa's throat and they went down, Pippa's head rammed back to slam rock, stars filling her mind, blood pumping and booming and pulsing in her ears. Oz's fingers were iron crushing her windpipe. She blacked out for a moment. She could smell magma, deep down below. Magma and... something else. Something metallic. The aftershave of the biomod. The cologne of the false human.

The stench of NanoTek.

Embedded in Oz, the hilt of Pippa's yukana dug against her own abdomen as he writhed atop her in a parody of love. She began a wild struggle, fists slamming Oz's head. One blow broke his cheekbone, Pippa's knuckles compressing his head into a distorted shape; it instantly reformed. Another blow smashed his nose, but the biomods inside Oz, fully in their stride now, primed and running at 100% efficiency, reanimated his flesh and aligned the broken bones in an instant. Pippa started to panic. Blow after blow she cannoned into Oz's head, each one massaged back into apparent human perfection by the rampant nanobot technology flowing through the man—and that which had *become* the man.

He's a creature made from a trillion microscopic robots, screamed her brain.

How can you fight that?

How can you kill it?

Some things are hard to kill.

But some things are impossible...

Deep red light danced behind Pippa's eyes, and she could no longer see. She suddenly heard a choking sound, and realised it was her own dying voice. In a fresh surge of panic she slammed blow after blow into Oz's head, then reached down, pushing her arms between their struggling bodies, and grasped the hilt of the yukana. She tugged, attempting to wrench the weapon sideways, but with instantly rebuilding muscle contractions Oz held the blade tight, using pure muscle control, his teeth gritted, his bones grinding as the single-molecule blade bit and tore and cut and deep within Oz the biomods fought to repair the grinding wounds as quickly as they occurred...

I am going to die, realised Pippa suddenly.

I am going to die here.

A sudden urge to cry swept over her. She remembered the good times on the beach on Molkrush Fed, running through sand with Keenan, hand in hand, warm and full of life and thinking their new future was secure, optimistic, filled with eternal hope and a deep understanding and love which would carry them onwards and forwards for ever and ever and ever... *Pippa tumbled into a well of blackness and remembered Keenan's lips brushing her neck her breasts her belly I love you he said words echoing bright and metallic down long corridors of fiery*

*history and she smiled she remembered that perfect
moment and knew she would die floating on a cold
cushion of that memory... Amen.*

KEENAN WAS SUFFOCATING, squirming in agony,
head compressed and the jelly of the GreenSource
Mainframe forcing its way into his mouth and
throat, down his oesophagus and into his belly. It
spread out there, like a cancer, and started to eat at
his insides and he wanted to scream in pain, in raw
hot agony but he had no air and no voice, and he
tried to punch, to kick, to fight, but every avenue of
defence or attack had been taken away from him.

FRANCO, THRASHING IN panic with his one free
hand, tried to stretch behind himself to his pack,
but he could not reach and he tried to kick but his
sandaled feet were trapped and held and he cursed
and sweated and scowled, and tried again to reach
his pack and realised, with sudden dawning relief
that he had grenades on his bandolier. "Hot sugary
dog dick!" he ejaculated, and pulled a grenade free
with a *pop*, but then wondered what he could do
with it. Explode it? What, and kill them both? His
faced dropped into an imitation of a tortured stone
gargoyle. No, he had to risk his freedom and life on
a long shot... growling, Franco pulled free the pin
with his teeth, and with a *crack*, his repaired false
tooth fell away, tumbling down with Franco staring
forlornly after his involuntary dentistry. "Bugger!"
Far below, the *tuff* bounced from Nyx's scrambling
shell with a tiny *cling* and Franco stared goggle-
eyed at the machine. He shook his head. Not good,

not good. OK, he thought, scowl growing darker and darker, and he plunged his free arm into the jelly and... released the grenade.

Trapped now, he waited and prayed. He peered over his shoulder, and could see the enamelled shell of Nyx growing closer. Needles rippled along her back and one remaining arm. They shone, like the glistening points of five thousand hypodermic needles... which took Franco shivering and twitching right back to his living horror at Mount Pleasant, his incarceration at the depraved and unhappy Mental Institute.

"Bugger! Bugger! Needles! Come on!"

He wiggled his fingers, feeling the jelly growing tight, and hoping hoping hoping the explosion wouldn't kill him, or Keenan, or both of them because... well, then they'd *really* be fucked.

The *boom* was muffled; distant.

Franco blinked. He could smell explosives.

However, nothing happened.

"No!" he wailed, realising his last chance long shot had failed. He would have beaten his fists, if they hadn't been trapped in a wall of computational jelly. "No no no! Bastard bugger bastard!"

Below, Nyx growled, and surged on up...

CAM EJECTED ON a spurt of hot gunk, and fell, spinning, motors whirring, until he halted, suspended above a mammoth cylinder. Below, the gunk began to bubble. Geysers of steam erupted. Cam's scanners scanned. All around him, irrational lights flickered and flowed up tarnished walls. And inside the PopBot's tiny brain, it clicked.

The GreenSource. The gunk cooled the Green-
Source.

And the hotter she got, the more confused she
would become!

Cam shot off, scanners searching for Keenan...

FRANCO HEARD A sound. Like blood rainfall.

Before him, practically *around* him, the Green-
Source Mainframe shuddered. Huge waves
pounded and pulsed through the behemoth. And
Franco realised he could suddenly move his fingers,
his hands, his wrists, his arms, and he pulled back
with *squelching* sounds of extraction as the Green-
Source malfunctioned, saw Keenan erupt
backwards above him gagging and reeling, retching
a long stream of green jelly vomit which poured
past Franco and bounced from Nyx's hull below.

"Franco?"

"Yeah mate?"

"Pass me a bomb."

"Sure mate."

Franco held up a BABE, and Keenan pulled the
pin, squinted, paused—a hiatus of intricate timing—then dropped the grenade. They both
watched, twisting to look down, as the small globe
fell, spinning, and *detonated* with a savage harsh
scream. Nyx was flung from the tower, sailing out
and down, legs kicking madly, to hit the ground far
below in a crumpled heap. Again, the tower before
them shuddered. The GreenSource Mainframe
seemed to be suffering.

"Let's climb."

"Sure thing, Boss."

"And Franco?"

"Yeah Boss?"

"Thanks."

"No problem, Boss."

They climbed. GreenSource shuddered several times as the two Combat K soldiers continued their ascent. The walls were no longer soft and malleable; they'd hardened, as if the Mainframe was trying to establish an outer shell of protection.

"It's coming again," said Franco.

"*What?*" Keenan stared down. Nyx had uncurled, and was once more climbing the tower far below. This time, however, the GK was moving with inhuman speed, claws finding exceptional grip on the tower-wall now that it had solidified.

"It looks a bit pissed, mate."

"Good. Come on."

They climbed, sweat streaming, muscles cramping, the glow of the Line leading to the SPIRAL dock growing closer. Finally, the two weary men hauled themselves onto a narrow circular platform near the summit of the central tower. It squelched, compressing organically beneath their feet.

Franco scratched his beard.

"I don't understand."

"What?" Keenan was peering up.

"It'd be better to blow the tower from the base, right? Unless you're thinking of separating it from the Line." Franco was casting his experienced eye over proceedings. He scratched his arse. "I mean, detonation'll only commit limited blast damage up here..."

"No," said Keenan, eyes gleaming.

"Eh?"

"I'm thinking of something more… drastic."

"Explain please?"

Keenan grabbed the Makarov from Franco's belt, and started to fire; bullets slammed down, bouncing from Nyx's sculpted—and slightly twisted—skull. The machine snarled at the two men, blank eyes focused on them, head tilted to deflect the bullets… Yet still she climbed. At that moment, she seemed totally unstoppable.

"We have to ride the Line," snapped Keenan. "There! Run!"

They sprinted for Line Base, Franco's sandals slapping, Keenan glancing behind. Nyx leapt, and landed on the platform with perfect balance. Her incisors grew in length, and ripples of needles pulsed down her back and arm. Claws flexed.

Keenan stepped into Line Base, and shot up, accelerating with a gasp.

Franco glared at Nyx, and pointed at the machine. "When this is over, lass, I'm gonna fuck you up for what you did to Mel. You hear me, calculator brain?"

Nyx roared, a metallic, shrieking scream, and pounced…

Franco stumbled back in panic, into the Line Base. He shot up, following Keenan high through the smooth vertical tunnel of rock, accelerating at a phenomenal rate and gasping, breath knocked from him for a moment as his beard streamed in the wind-flow and he giggled, suddenly, at the insanity of the *rush*.

Nyx looked around. She seemed to be listening to an internal voice.

Kill them, said GreenSource.

Nyx stepped into the Line.

With a *hiss*, the advanced prototype AI machine flashed upwards, head raised, lights glittering from matt eyes... and with CPU set in closed and locked pursuit.

STEINHAUER GROANED, COUGHED, and blood ran down his chin in a thick pulse. His eyes flickered open. He breathed. Pain pumped through him like some evil narcotic. Everything was fuzzy, and tinged with green. He levered himself up on elbows, aware of a choking sound to one side. He squinted, blinking, trying to focus. He could see Pippa. She was being strangled by Dr Oz.

With a great force of will, dragging severed stumps behind him, Steinhauer began to crawl. Clawed hands scraped rock, snapping two fingernails. His teeth ground, filling his mouth with enamel pepper. He glanced down, and almost wailed as he saw the bloody streamers of skin which followed his slug-like, wavering trail.

Steinhauer pushed on. His mind calmed, and started to scroll with clarity. He should be dead. But he wasn't. And he knew why, although he had never experienced the sensation through long years in the military. As a General, he'd been infused with basic Military Grade biomods, 1st generation, non-AI, programmed to keep him alive, channel energies, heal tissue, cauterise wounds. And that had happened. Despite the pain, and fear, and horror, the military biomods had sealed the stumps of his legs... or at least, slowed down the rate at which he would expire.

He was close now. Could see Pippa's face, a pale and drawn puppet, jerked and shaken by the powerful grip of Oz—like a dog with a bone. Steinhauer pulled free a semi-automatic CNP 1mm—a Compact Nail Pistol—from inside his uniform. With a shaking hand web-tattooed with his own gore, he aimed.

"Hey, Oz."

Dr Oz turned, a swift movement, lips drawing back into a snarl over ruby teeth.

Steinhauer squeezed the trigger, and held it hard. Needle bullets, tiny, whipping, flashing needles, gleaming bright with silver light, slammed from the pistol and riddled Oz's face. Oz screamed, scrambling back, but Steinhauer, up on his stumps now, teeth grinding in agony, staggered forward in jerking stump-steps, gun wavering but held true despite his fatigue and blood-loss and pain. Hundreds of needles distorted Oz's face, ripping his visage apart, tearing at his brain, puncturing his eyes, splattering his face into twisted rubber platters of stretched spaghetti. The gun clicked, an empty click, and Steinhauer reloaded the CNP, then turned to Pippa. He fell forward, onto his hands, and began to crawl to her white, deathly-still body.

Oz, face distorted, head exploded into thick octopus-leg tendrils, lurched forward and grabbed Steinhauer by the stumps. He threw the legless man *hard*. The CNP 1mm clattered. Steinhauer flew, slapped the ground, and rolled fast to an unconscious halt beside the SLAM Cruiser's ramp.

Slowly, Oz's face, misted and hazy with a cloud of a million nanobots, eased like moulding putty back into shape, torn strands of flesh pulled in and healed, popped eyeballs sucked together and organically reformed. Oz coughed, and his hands came up, pressing at his features as if surprised to find them whole.

With a grunt, he pulled Pippa's yukana from his stomach with three painful jerks, and looked down as the flesh melted together and his own blood coated his hands like gloves.

And, holding the blade, tip to the floor, he moved in to finish the job.

KEENAN AND FRANCO accelerated into the sky. The Line left the cover of the NanoTek HQ, and suddenly, through transparent walls darkness flooded their vision interspersed by a million fires. They were flying. They were *soaring*. Distantly, out over The City's ravaged battle-scarred streets, ranks of zombies merged, coalesced, gathered with roars, all drawn towards the NanoTek HQ as if summoned by some unspeakable force, drawn to this, their Creator, a Monster returning for a final Feed.

Keenan glanced down at Franco.

"You see it?"

"What?"

"The zombies! They've formed an army! They're marching through the streets to NanoTek!"

"What do they want?"

"They're coming home to sleep! They're the new junks, Franco. NanoTek have created an army for Leviathan!"

As the two men flashed into the heavens above The City, both Keenan and Franco could see the tens of thousands of zombies filling and packing the streets, flooding like a necrotic tide over ravaged highways towards the Black Rose Citadel.

"How many?" shouted Franco.

"Half a million, I reckon," yelled Keenan. "But there'll be more to come. Many, many more."

They ascended. And gazed down, dumb-struck with horror.

They had to stop the zombies.

They had to destroy the GreenSource Mainframe.

Franco, eyes narrowed, mouth a slit, bile in his brain, was suddenly nudged by instinct, and he glanced down.

Nyx was there!

He yelled, a sound of pure panic, and stamped down with his sandal, slapping against the AI's head with a metallic thump. Again he kicked, and again, and Nyx stretched up with gleaming claws and grabbed his ankle.

"Help! It's got me! Keenan, it's got me!"

Keenan turned, hair streaming, rolled so that he was facing down towards Franco. The Makarov sang in steady hands still scarred by a webbing of subcutaneous pathways from his brush with toxic biowire... bullets thumped on trajectories of howling fire, slamming into Nyx's face which stared up at him, eyes emotionless, jaws working soundlessly on black enamel hydraulics. Five bullets, ten, fifteen. One of Nyx's eyes cracked, then fluttered away leaving a tiny wriggling stalk of alloy. Franco kicked out with his free sandal, slapping at Nyx's head again. More bullets crashed down on the AI's TitaniumVI skull, and suddenly it released Franco, falling back down the Line until it steadied itself and glanced up—ready to attack...

"Shoot it again!" shouted Franco. "Shit man! Go on! What are you waiting for?"

He met Keenan's gaze.

Keenan smiled. It could have frozen nuclear fire. "Out of bullets," he mouthed.

They both watched, powerless, as Nyx growled, seemed to shiver, then stretched herself out, elongating slim alloy limbs and *surging* to dive up the Line after them...

MEL CLIMBED. THE rocky wall was jagged, and she struggled with her long claws and her own physical bodyweight, but scrabbling and scraping, distended jaws chewing at air, working spasmodically like a dog with a bone, Mel climbed and climbed, ascending towards the green glow high above. Below, magma churned. During the climb the lava seemed to be growing in molten discontent. Mel shrugged. She didn't understand such things. All she knew was that Franco, her beloved, was somewhere up there... and she couldn't leave him to *die*.

Claws raking rock, Mel finally heaved her bulk over the edge of the precipice, and dripping blood from a hundred wounds torn in mottled torso and thick corded muscles, and with tiny head bobbing, black pebble-eyes narrowing, she turned to see—

Dr Oz.

The man responsible for the creation of the biomod "human upgrade".

The man, then, responsible for her present condition.

As deviant...

Mel lowered her head. Saw Pippa, unconscious, beyond. She glanced left, tracking for Nyx, but couldn't locate the escaped AI. Mel growled, a low, low rumbling which started in her bowels and travelled up through her belly, to finally emerge through cracked and distended jaws...

Mel leapt, snarling, and Oz whirled, the yukana hissing out, causing Mel to rear backwards. Oz slammed the blade down, but Mel moved far faster than he'd anticipated. She grabbed the black sword, and flung it off where it clattered against the far wall, and toppled down end over end into molten magma.

Distantly, the blade sizzled, and vanished.

Mel grinned at Oz. Then charged him. His fists came up, delivering a cracking right hook that shook Mel's small head but she rolled with the blow, long neck crackling, claws lashing out and grabbing Oz and picking him up, hoisting him high above her head where she strained at him, bending him and he screamed as his spine *cracked* and snapped and then was almost instantly repaired by the nanobots. Holding his feet, Mel slammed Oz against the rocky ground and his head caved in, then melted back into shape and she lifted him once more, slamming him down, where again his head caved in. Brains splashed volcanic rock. Mel lifted him, and the wounds healed and Oz screamed, "No more! No more!" but Mel slammed him down a third time, and his head detached, rolling away and disappearing under the SLAM Cruiser. Mel tossed the limp body aside and moved to Pippa, stooping, staring down at the injured woman. Pippa lay in a wide pool of her own blood.

Behind Mel, there came a *crack*.

Mel stood, confused, and turned to see Oz on his feet, head swirling, engulfed by a black mist, flesh melting, skin and skull forming into a solid, perfect rendition of that which he'd just lost—

Oz smiled a dark smile. His eyes glittered. He rocked his head sideways, and there came the *crack* of realigning vertebrae. "I *wish* you people would stop *doing* that!"

He leapt, even as Mel leapt, and his boots slammed Mel's head sending the mutated woman reeling back, claws scraping grooves in the rock. Blow after blow followed, rocking the large deviant and she bellowed, snarling, pus and saliva spraying out under the pounding onslaught of Oz's fists and shoes. Suddenly, he dropped to the ground, hand groping and lifting the CNP 1mm dropped by Steinhauer.

"Bitch," he snarled. "I should never have created you!" He fired, a screaming stream of needles hurtling into Mel's body, ripping and tearing. Blood splashed the slippery rock. She charged Oz, screaming, and picked him up above her head, mighty muscles curling, to hurl him towards the Green-Source Mainframe... where he was half-absorbed, then violently ejected...

PIPPA GROANED, AND pushed herself to her elbows. She coughed, and pain slammed her throat. She breathed oxygen, and it was the sweetest flavour she had ever enjoyed. No mind it was laced with the stench of blood, and pus, sulphur, and distant scorched rock. It was *honey*. It was *nectar*. Sweet and oh so necessary.

Pippa rolled to her feet, and clutched at her opened side. She swayed, almost collapsing, and focused on the battle a hundred metres away. Mel and Oz were rolling on the ground, pounding each other, and she watched for a while as one of Mel's weighty claws punched clean through Oz's head leaving a gaping ring of skull-bone, face and brain totally demolished, claws flexing at the back of his hollowed out skull. Mel pulled out her fist with a sickening *squelch*. Instantly, Oz's features reformed and he was *screaming*...

Maybe the biomods had seemed like a good idea, she thought. At first. But here, and now, she read the agony on Oz's face. She shuddered. His soul was tortured. His spirit was broken. Sometimes, she thought, it's better just to die.

Pippa gathered herself, and jogged across rock towards the SLAM Cruiser. She glanced up, but could see no sign of Keenan, nor Franco. But she knew. When they came, they'd be moving fast... and Hell would be on their tail.

KEENAN SLAMMED TO the top of the Line, and with a *hiss* it slid him neatly sideways and deposited him on a sterile tiled floor. His sweeping gaze read the chamber. The SPIRAL dock was large, circular, the hub a suite of desks and screens for checking in and out, but currently deserted of staff or customers, presumably due to The City's state of emergency and martial law under QGM instruct. The ceiling was high, vaulted, and covered by a single flowing liquid plasma screen, currently set to a serene silver lake effect where gentle ripples curved out, flowing across the ceiling and promoting... *calm*. Rows of traditional seats were set in eco clusters, along with comfortbubbles and against one wall a high row of Swallow Couches. They filled the majority of space. Keenan's head turned left as Franco stepped from the Line close by, and running to the wall Keenan delivered a powerful sidekick which shattered safety glass. He pulled free a hefty steel fire-axe, tossed it to a dazed Franco.

"Deal with the AI. I'll plant the explosives."

Franco tossed back the axe, which Keenan grabbed from mid-air.

"Hey, why don't *you* deal with the AI, after all, I'm the damn and bloody detonations expert! I'll plant the explosives!"

Keenan hurled back the fire-axe, and snarled, "Because *I* know where the detonation points are, idiot, and I haven't got time to fucking explain!" Keenan hoisted the pack of High-J, and sprinted away. Franco stared at the long gleaming axe in his hands, then turned as Nyx stepped from the Line... He swung the weapon with a mighty roar, and it bounced from Nyx's head, slamming the AI back into the Line booth with a shower of sparks. Franco heard a growl. He gulped.

Nyx sprang from the booth, hammering into Franco and sending the man stumbling back, axe held up between them both, poisoned jaws snapping frantically at his face. Franco cracked a right-hook, shaking Nyx's head, then another as he was forced back, stumbling over a seat and landing heavily on his back with Nyx atop him. Poisoned needles rippled across her torso, and man and machine wrestled for a few moments, face to jaws.

Franco watched glooping poison glimmer above him from rows of razor teeth. Then, as he stared, hypnotic, a snake before a charmer, a long umbilical detached, lazily, and started to fizzle the alloy floor by his ear.

Franco began to struggle like a maniac.

But Nyx was too strong...

KEENAN HALTED, PANTING, and wiped sweat from his eyes. Four points of explosion would do it. He knew how SPIRAL docks were constructed. They were built using AGE anti-gravity engines placed equidistant around the dock's perimeter in order to stop the structure's sheer weight tearing itself from low orbit and crashing into the world below.

Keenan's eyes scanned. *There*. He kicked through the unauthorised access door, ran down a short corridor, and stopped, glancing left, sweat whipping from his hair. He could hear a *thrum*. And smell the acid of an organic engine. He moved on, and the heat was incredible now, and still rising, as he came to a large room. At the centre, pulsing, was an AGE. It looked like a giant, red heart, a muscle, beating, the very *pulse* of the SPIRAL dock. Some spiritualists said an AGE was the detached heart from a long-extinct alien species. Keenan didn't know. All he did understand was they were awesomely powerful, and nobody truly understood their origins, despite what academics might argue.

He ran down galvanised steps, boots echoing, and knelt. He planted a High-J charge. Set the control timer. Activated a quad-synchronicity circuit. Then switched it on.

The High-J beeped. A small blue light glowed.

Keenan turned, and sprinted for the exit...

"GOD, YOUR BREATH stinks!" said Franco, snarling up at the AI's face close above. It was beautiful, he realised, lovingly sculpted and yet—inherently *evil*. False life. False life *created* to remove real life, which was just plain wrong, if that made sense. It made sense in Franco's head. But then, he was a madman.

"You are destined to die, Franco Haggis!" said Nyx, voice powerful, mature, more full-bodied woman than machine. Franco gawped, mouth open, as they struggled around the barrier of the fire-axe.

"You can speak?" he squawked.

"Fool. Of course I can speak." Nyx released her grip on the axe, and punched down at Franco's head. He twisted, her knuckles grazing his cheek, and her fist went straight through the tiles and embedded in the floor. The AI tugged at it, but her one remaining arm was locked in a mesh of under-floor piping.

Franco wriggled out from under the snarling, kicking machine. Nyx's head slammed left, single black eye focusing on Franco as he hefted the axe and weighed it thoughtfully.

"Look, I'm sorry about this, love."

He swung the axe with all his might, and the blade *clanged* from Nyx's head, veering off and clattering against the floor with such *shock* that Franco dropped the haft. He picked it up again, blowing on his vibrating fingers.

"Hot damn! That hurt!"

"I will poison your soul," hissed Nyx.

"Look, I'm not too happy about axing a lady in the head, if that's any consolation."

"I will curse you to eternity, human!"

Franco looked at the machine thoughtfully. "Aye," he said. "But then, I'm the one with the axe." He slammed the hefty blade at the machine again, and Nyx squirmed around the pivotal point of her trapped fist; sparks flew, and Franco leapt back from snapping jaws and clutching feet-fingers. Again he struck, and again, dancing around like a madman waving the axe, then blundering in and thumping the hard-forged axe-head against Nyx's battered spine and abdomen and legs and distorted skull. TitaniumVI was tough. But it could only take so much. Franco noted it was starting to *flake*.

"I need something stronger!" he muttered. He ran off, clutching the axe like a prize, eyes scanning the SPIRAL dock for something he could use to kill Nyx. "Shit. SHIT! Bugger. BUGGER!" Completing a circuit of the lounge, he came to the reluctant conclusion he was going to have to bash on with the axe until he finally bludgeoned her to death. It, he corrected himself. He ran back to where Nyx was pinned, then stopped, mouth open, tongue lolling out.

Nyx had gone.

Are you sure this is where you left her? teased an internal dialogue.

Yeah! I mean, I *think* this is where she was.

*Are you sure? Are you 100% sure? Crazy boy?
Dog dick? Madman? After all, you had all those
weird imaginings at The Mount Pleasant Hilltop
Institution, the "nice and caring and friendly home
for the mentally challenged". Remember the pills?
Remember the electrodes? Remember your testicles?*

"Argh!" shouted Franco, as his eyes fell on the
jagged hole in the floor. He ran forward, battered
sandals flapping, and dropped to his knees beside
the tangle of mashed alloy. It was this movement
which saved his life.

Nyx's needle-knuckles slashed the air millimetres
from where his head had been, and Franco rolled
fast, axe sweeping out and knocking Nyx's legs
from under her. The AI rolled, came up, leapt at
Franco—

He lashed out, and the axe slammed Nyx's head.
She took the blow well, rolled and spun around,
then grinned at him. Poison glinted on fangs.

"You're already dead," she said.

"What?" Franco slammed the axe, which whistled past Nyx's face.

"I injected a fine toxic air-mist. Tricklium III. You
breathed it in when we wrestled over the axe."

"Bollocks!"

"Trust me." Nyx's metal face was almost serene.
"You have approximately five minutes. It works
more slowly in mist form. Injection is far—more—
effective."

She leapt, and Franco staggered back. The axe
rapped against Nyx's shoulder. Sparks leapt,
sparkling in Franco's panic-filled eyes.

"You're lying."

"Why would I? In a few moments you'll feel the sickness. It will rage through you, and you'll vomit your insides out through your skull hole. That alone will make you beg for death as your body tries everything it can to eject the poison. I am told it is excruciating. Then comes paralysis. And, if I choose not to kill you, but instead watch the drama unfold, you'll twitch like a rabid epileptic until the poison crushes your insides for the final minute of your diseased and worthless life. You *will* suffer. It will be bad. Torturous, even. But then, why invent a poison which is fun?"

Franco, listening, had been continually backing away.

Now, he ground his teeth, turned, and ran...

Nyx's laughter followed him as he reached the Line booth. He stopped. The AI wasn't following. It had turned, and was trying to locate Keenan. And that could only mean...

Pain jabbed Franco in the belly, then washed out through him. He gagged, and, as Nyx had explained, sickness napalmed his system, smashed through him with the ferocity of a powerful narcotic. He fell to his knees, dropping the fire-axe from shaking, useless fingers. He vomited on the tiled floor.

Franco heaved and heaved, pain wracking him, tears blinding him, and he realised his vulnerability and grabbed the fire-axe, covered in his own vomit, and lifted it shakily to his chest, casting about, searching for Nyx...

Something rattled across the floor. Franco tried to focus, then dropped suddenly and covered his head with sick-stained arms.

Nyx glanced down.

The BABE Grenade explosion picked the AI up and flung it like a rag-doll across the entire dock lounge. Nyx connected with a pillar mid-way, folding around it with crunches of compressing alloy, then veering off at an angle, legs flapping, to hit the far window with a thud. Nyx slid down the transparent wall in a crumpled heap of alloy.

Keenan ran to Franco, dropping to his knees and grasping his friend. "What's wrong?"

"It poisoned me," gasped Franco, eyes wide.

"Come on."

"I'm going to die, Keenan," he gasped. "I've four minutes left. Shit! And not a babe in sight!"

Keenan nodded, face grim, and helped Franco stagger to his feet. Swaying like drunk brothers, the two men tottered to the Line booth, Franco still trailing his axe.

Against the far wall, Nyx uncurled and stood in a fluid motion. Her eyes met Keenan's.

"Fucker," she said.

Keenan dragged Franco into the booth, and the Line slammed them down as, in a musical harmony, four sets of High-J, in perfect synchronicity, detonated.

The explosion was louder than Nuclear.

Louder than War.

And to Keenan's ears, as they howled down the Line towards the GreenSource Mainframe far far below NanoTek's Black Rose Citadel, the savage detonation of anti-gravitational engines seemed louder than Death itself...

FIRE AND SHRAPNEL raged. Ate. Exploded. Vaporised. Consumed. Engulfed. Heat and fire savaged through the SPIRAL dock. Engines were smashed and boiled into nothing in the heart of a screaming radiation-filled fireball. With perfect unity, all four High-J bombs detonated. All four AGE engines *died*. And the SPIRAL dock, weighing in at just over a million tonnes, tilted, slowly, one edge going down in a searing, thousand metre wall of flame which lit The City for a hundred miles. More secondary explosions rocked the internals of the dock, deep muffled concussions, but despite their size and ferocity, they were miniscule in comparison to the might of the dock itself, its sheer titanic *mass*. Listing now, one end dropping, gravity grabbed the huge station nearly two kilometres up in the sky and flung it like a rocket towards the world below. Towards NanoTek. Towards the GreenSource Mainframe... and the miniscule, pathetic, fragile creatures known as Man.

Across The City, the raging battles of zombies, SIMs, Slabs, humans, all those still fighting or hiding from estranged zombie individuals—all paused and stared at the illuminated sky. Fire raged and broiled in the heavens. Night turned to day. Green light and white light flashed, side by side, in an apocalyptic firestorm which vaporised the clouds and the darkness, and for some strange reason, to those who peered upwards, seemed to herald a new, clean, beginning.

The SPIRAL dock fell, massive and silent, fire raging behind it like a detonating trail of solar radiation.

Below, The Black Rose Citadel waited.

NanoTek waited.

And the whole planet seemed to hold its breath...

KEENAN AND FRANCO rushed downwards, Keenan in grim silence, Franco heaving occasionally, face gaunt, lips blue and trembling. Far above Keenan *felt* more than heard or saw the SPIRAL dock begin its rapid descent. And he knew: knew he should have given them more time, knew he should have given them a larger window of escape... but that would have meant leaving the High-J susceptible to Nyx, and God only knew what other agents of the GreenSource Mainframe were on the prowl. No. This way was best. Even if it meant, ultimately, their own demise.

Keenan saw Franco begin to topple, losing his ability to stand, and he grabbed the squaddie's loose, flopping arm. "Stay with it, buddy," he muttered.

Franco said nothing. His eyes had closed.

Down they slammed, and above them something *big* was shaking, vibrating, and Keenan peered up and could see, distantly through the tunnel of the Line, that the whole edifice was *collapsing* and chasing the two men, the two instigators of its annihilation, down towards their inevitable deaths...

Franco's eyes snapped over. "We're gonna get squashed!" he snapped, voice quavering.

Keenan nodded. "Maybe."

"You'll have to leave me."

"I ain't leaving anybody."

"Keenan!" Franco grabbed his comrade's War-Suit, and shook him. "I can hardly stand! You can't help me down those GreenSource towers. We won't have enough time!"

"I'll make the time," said Keenan.

Franco laughed. "Stupid fucking heroics. You're being the dumb and useless stubborn bastard I always loved. But listen to me, Keenan, and listen good." Keenan stared hard at his insane friend, ironically, in these last few moments leading to his tox-filled death, more lucid than most supposedly sane men. "Your girls wouldn't thank you for your sacrifice."

"That's a cheap shot."

"It's all I have."

"I'm not leaving you, Franco. If we die, we die together."

Franco said nothing. He passed into unconsciousness, body trembling as the poison from Nyx spread through his glands and arteries. His legs began to kick.

Above, a million tonnes of SPIRAL dock, in accelerating descent, began to roar...

MEL WAS DYING. Not just from the poison injected by the GK AIs, but from Dr Oz. He was wearing her down. Even now she could feel her strength leaving her. A genetic eight-foot mutation super-soldier she might be, but even one of *those* could only fight for so long. The two grappled, and Oz slammed Mel to the rock. He stood over her, shirt and glass suit torn in long jagged ribbons, one shoe lost, his tie tattered confetti. But he was grinning, in triumph, in superiority, in majesty.

"I made you," he snarled. Blood mixed with his saliva. Behind one of his eyes something twitched. "I created you! I created the biomods! I fucking *own* you!"

He took a deep breath. Mel, shivering and broken, weak and exhausted, lay there and bled.

Oz lifted his hands above his head, hands curled into claws. He knew what he must do. He would rip out her heart. Imbibe her core biomods, absorb them into himself. Then he could shift their code and she would die, writhing, on the rock. He, however, would become stronger. A Combined.

Suddenly, Oz heard the sound of screaming engines, and whirled, too late—straight into the accelerating nose cone of the SLAM Cruiser. It rammed him at a phenomenal rate, lifting him grunting from the platform and propelling him across the chamber, across the abyss, and spreading him across the rock wall. He screamed, a long loud wail as his body, his flesh, his intestines, spread out in a colourful flat blue platter and his eyes met Pippa's calm, cold, grey gaze in the cockpit beyond.

Pippa stared deep into Oz's biomod replicated eyes. She increased the pressure of the SLAM, watched his trapped body writhing and curling, black mist forming and reforming his mashed bones and broken spine and spread flesh, focused as he squirmed and screamed and thrashed, pinned against the wall, unable to break free...

"Have a nice day, fucker," she said, and hammered the SLAM into reverse. The Cruiser backed up, leaving Dr Oz spread across the wall, his flesh writhing like albino cobras, then with wide eyes he tumbled forward and fell, flailing, struggling, into the magma far below.

Pippa breathed deep. Blood pulsed down her flank. She blinked, almost passing back into the realm of unconsciousness. Wearily, she banked the SLAM Cruiser, watched warning sensors flicker above the console, and her brow contorted in confusion. The readings told her something near a million tonnes in weight was accelerating towards them at an incredible speed...

The puzzle clicked into place.

She understood what Keenan had done.

She sped to the platform, leapt free, grabbed Mel and helped the huge deviant crawl into the hold trailing thick arterial gore. Without lifting the ramp, Pippa sprinted, gritting her teeth, wincing at the warm flood down her own body, and pointed the SLAM's nose to the sky, climbing the height of the tower in a few heartbeats and levelling, ramp touching down as Keenan emerged from the Line booth, reached back, and pulled a frothing, kicking Franco after him...

Keenan dragged Franco up the ramp, and his eyes met Pippa's for the briefest of moments.

"We need to go down," he growled.

"You do what I think you did?"

"*Now!*" he snarled.

Above, the SPIRAL dock connected with NanoTek HQ. There was thunder, deeper than anything Combat K had ever experienced. But, rather than slowing the titanic station, NanoTek's Black Rose Citadel crumbled like brittle, pulverised sand. NanoTek slowed the SPIRAL dock's descent. But it did not halt it.

With crashes and screams, of rock crushing rock crushing rock, so the SPIRAL dock ploughed downwards with an incredible, mounting pressure, compressing and crushing everything that stood in its path, slamming through alloy and steel and titanium and glass and rock, crushing, compressing, folding, destroying, and Keenan grabbed Franco to stop him tumbling from the SLAM as Pippa turned the machine's nose *down* and they sped towards the broiling, agitated magma...

"Hello!" said a small voice.

"Cam! Where the hell have you been?"

"I had an altercation with a few K1LLBots." The machine, battered, bumped, limping, nevertheless hovered by Keenan's head. "We need to move fast; the falling station is compressing everything into a pulp..."

"You don't fucking say?" snapped Pippa.

"It's forcing the magma level to rise."

"Will this Cruiser take lava?"

Cam, lights glittering under a dried husk of black coolant, said, simply, "No."

"Cam. Franco's poisoned. Can you help him?"

"I will try."

Pippa dropped them, levelling just above the broiling sea of red. It popped and fizzed, hissing beneath them, swirling with a glow which burned their eyes.

"There!" pointed Pippa.

"A tunnel."

"It must be a way out!"

"It can't be. Or the lava would take it."

"Do we have any other option?"

Keenan glanced up. Rocks were falling from the top of the cavern, many larger than a house. They thundered, dust and rock tumbling, and the Green-Source Mainframe was shivering, its flanks rock solid now in an attempt to protect itself...

As Keenan watched, it seemed the world slammed down through the cavern's roof. One instant, a shaking, dust-pouring image. The next, something huge and black appeared and filled his vision in its entirety.

"Go!" he screamed, and Pippa powered them into the lava tunnel, spinning low over rolling magma, banking left and right with ferocious skill as above and around them the world shook and Pippa hissed, through gritted teeth.

"We'll have to go under," she said, voice suddenly calm. She closed the ramp. It locked, with a tiny click.

"Cam says the SLAM won't take it."

"To hell with Cam. We have no *choice!*"

Even as she spoke, waves of lava boiled up, rolling out, washing over them. Pippa thrust herself back in her seat, fear etched like acid on her features. Then, reading her scanners, she nodded, once, and dropped the SLAM Cruiser beneath the molten sea...

Everything descended into a calm, orange glow.

All noise, all vibration, all destruction, vanished.

Franco looked up, from where he lay on the floor. Cam had ejected two thin tubes, and was filtering Franco's blood. He stared hard at the little machine.

"What the hell are you doing?"

"Dialysis."

"Die whatastasis?"

"I'm filtering your blood. Lie still, I don't want to pump you dry."

"Hey, no little alloy gonad is pumping *me* dry!"

"Lie *still*, midget, it's hard enough filtering the massive amounts of toxin from your body without you rolling around like a lunatic." His voice dropped an octave. "Anyway, there's so much shit in your system, its replicating, its an organic semi-synth poison; sentient. It's fighting me. Don't get your hopes up, Franco."

"Thanks for putting my mind at ease." Franco beamed. "Hey! Where's the noise? We escape? We free? I'm so glad everything worked out. How long have I been out?"

"About four minutes," said Keenan, voice a monotone. He glanced sideways at Pippa.

They both stared at the wisps of smoke coming from the SLAM's console.

"What's that orange glow?"

"Magma."

"How's that, then?"

"We're *under it*," said Keenan.

"Is that safe?"

Keenan grinned, a deaths-head grin. "Hell mate, we're about to find out."

"The scanners aren't working," said Pippa, finally. "Everything has shut down. I don't know which way to go. All the sensors are burned to shit. It's just too hot down here, Keenan!"

"This is a SLAM Cruiser, not a space vehicle," chastised Cam.

"Just filter his blood," snapped Keenan.

"I'm trying my best," sulked Cam.

"Will you two *stop* arguing! I'm trying to navigate!"

Silence descended.

They watched, from the SLAM's cockpit, as fire raged across the Cruiser's nose-cone. Gradually, the burning began to move towards them. It was a worrying sight.

Franco shuffled into one of the pilot's seats. "Should it do that?" he asked, face grey with poison.

"I—don't think so," said Pippa.

"We're going to die down here, aren't we?" said Franco.

Nobody answered him.

"Pippa?"

"Yeah Franco?" Her gaze was focused on the scanners, dials and display screens. She glanced up. Looked into his eyes.

"We've probably got a few minutes," he said, hopefully.

Pippa stared at him. "You've *got* to be joking."

"Actually, I was deadly serious."

"You're not putting your toxic dick anywhere *near* me, Haggis."

"Well, it was just a thought."

Outside, suddenly, everything went black. There came a *clang*. Sound seemed to return, hissing through the SLAM Cruiser as metal started ticking, and pinging, and buckling with crunches of cooling, superheated alloy.

Then, lights illuminated. Bright magnesium lights.

"What's going on?" muttered Pippa.

A voice crackled over the speakers.

"Hi there!" it said. "Thought you guys might need a ride."

It was Knuckles.

"Knuckles!" shouted Franco, delight swamping his face. "How d'ya get down here, lad?"

"We've been tracking you for days, using the old Combat K channels. But you lost us when you came down into this shit-heap. None of the scanners would work. We picked you up again when you dived under the lava... thought you might need a lift."

"Who's with you?"

Another voice came over the speakers. "You sent a little kid and a back-breaking rugby woman to do your dirty work! Franco Haggis, you should be damned ashamed of yourself!"

"Slick? You old dog!"

"Well, you saved my arse, mate. It would be rude not to try and return the favour."

Keenan leant forward. "Can you get us out of this pit?"

"Sure," drawled Slick. "But you'll have to hang on. We're in a lava flow; it's gonna take some powerful thrust."

"After what we've been through, it'll be a walk in the park," muttered Keenan, and slumped back in the pilot's chair. He glanced over and grinned at Pippa. "Looks like we made it, girl."

"We?"

Keenan shook his head, glancing away. Bitterness flooded him then. Bitterness, and a hatred he knew would never, ever leave him. How could it?

Pippa had murdered his babes.

THE CLASS I Marine Frigate burst from a dark, rolling ocean with low-level engines screaming and trailing spray, steam and falling chunks of volcanic rock. It banked at a slow speed and hovered for a few moments, blue lights sweeping.

NanoTek's Black Rose Citadel was no more. The SPIRAL port collapse had completely crushed it, pushing it down beneath the rock and earth, caving in the entire island and causing tidal waves to heave out from the point of impact triggering anti-tidal defence screens to slam up from abandoned promenades the length and breadth of downtown City Shores.

Carrying Combat K like a baby in a womb, only in this case a corrupt and cynical baby high on the adrenaline of finding itself far from simple in-uterus comforts, the Marine Frigate, huge and black and angular, banked again, and rose above the smoking, shattered devastation that was NanoTek's crushed and pounded HQ.

Keenan, Pippa and Franco stared down at the city-wide wreckage.

"We sure gave them a sting in the arse," said Pippa, voice soft.

Keenan nodded. "I don't think NanoTek will forget our names in a hurry. I don't think I've ever seen such a fucking mess. It'll take the engineers months to sort out the wreckage. Years!"

"Ha!" snapped Franco, who was beginning to look more himself. Colour had flooded back into his cheeks, but Cam was still working hard hunting down every last trace of poison from the ginger squaddie's polluted system. "Nothing that couldn't be sorted with a dustpan and brush. Don't know what you lot are moaning about! My *bedroom* looks worse than that after a night on the piss!"

"Yes," said Pippa, head turning to survey Franco. "But you won't be doing *that* anymore. Not now you've met Melanie." She nodded towards the sleeping, injured mutation.

"Ahh. Yeah. Right." Franco glanced back, to where Melanie snored off her excessive bout of violence. "Um. You know before, that little thing I said to you?"

"You mean about wanting to go to bed with me? Because we were all about to die?"

"Yes." Franco considered this. "I think you may have misunderstood my intentions."

"No no," said Pippa, watching QGM Shuttles and Hornets slamming through the skies, roaring high overhead. "I think I understood you quite clearly."

Franco's eyes widened. "Hey, please don't tell Melanie!"

Pippa sighed. "Cam. You finished with his blood yet? Only," she wriggled, "I think my insides are about to fall out."

"Oh my God!" snapped Cam. "You poor girl!"

"It's OK, Cam," said Keenan, taking Pippa's hand. "I'll see to her."

"You sure?" she said, head tilting.

Keenan nodded. "I'll sew you up. Only, don't get too friendly. I've still got a bullet with your name on it."

SLICK BROUGHT THE Marine Frigate down on the towering, abandoned, fifty-lane highway. All were awake, except for Mel. Cam had worked feverishly on her injuries, cauterising wounds and bone-welding breaks. Finally, he gave her a massive sedative and, with Franco holding her claws as her eyes flickered and closed, she fell into a thankful sleep.

Frigate legs clanged, cracking the highway. After engines had died to a muted after-roar, the Frigate's belly opened and Combat K stared out into a new, rising dawn.

"Wow," breathed Franco, hopping down the buckled, lava-scorched ramp, and out into a fresh new world. "It's beautiful!"

"QGM are on the ground at last," came Slick's voice over the ScreamSpeaker, as he checked his scanners and PAD. "They finally thought it was time to restore order! Bastards. Maybe it had something to do with Steinhauer's Panic Burst, hey? Shit. What a mess."

Keenan nodded, and followed Franco outside, boots clumping on the smashed, rubble-strewn highway. He glanced down, at the decimation of The City stretching away for as far as the eye could see. Fires burned, barricades smouldered, but he could identify no signs of the zombies which had infected the planet like a plague. "Beautiful?" Keenan laughed. "I wouldn't go that far, Franco," he said, surveying the aftermath of an atomic blast.

"But we're *alive!*" beamed Franco, and did a little dance, sandals flapping.

"Only just."

"You're missing the point!"

"Am I?"

"Yeah. We always pull through! We always surge ahead. After all, we're Combat K... we're the *smarty party!*" He did another little shuffle, then punched the air in glee.

Pippa emerged, holding onto her tightly bandaged side. Her clothes were in tatters, the gleam of her white, neat, tightly-bandaged flank somehow at odds with the desecration of her current wardrobe.

"Franco's right. It is beautiful."

Keenan grunted, and turned as the Marine Frigate disgorged its crew. Knuckles ran forward, and gave Franco and Keenan a big hug. Behind him strode Olga, freshly attired, beaming with a face-wide smile and licking her lips in anticipation of meeting a still-breathing Franco. Finally came Slick, followed by a motley crew of rag-tag ex-Combat K men.

Keenan shook Slick's hand. "It's good to see you, mate."

"And you."

Keenan grinned past Slick. "I see you there, Chicken. And Clinty Eastwood! I thought you died five years ago? Still smoking those cigars? And you Bob Bob, you wily old bastard." Bob Bob grinned at Keenan, and rubbed at a custard stain which marked his worn and faded combats.

"We have a stowaway," said Cam, emerging on a stream of ionised air. His battered shell spun, lights flickering. He looked far from being the polished, immaculate PopBot of a few days earlier.

"Oh yeah?" said Keenan.

"Steinhauer. But he's nearly dead."

"He saved my life," said Pippa. "He must have crawled up the ramp during the fight!"

The Combat K men carried the battered, unconscious shell of Steinhauer from his hiding place in the SLAM Cruiser, and away to the medical deck of the Marine Frigate which towered above them on their vantage point across the elevated, curved highway.

"That bastard has a lot to answer for," snarled Keenan. "He played us as pawns. Do you believe we've got logic cubes in our spines? That we are *required* to cooperate?"

"I've got the feeling it was true," said Pippa, voice hushed.

"Well, we'll find out what he wants, soon enough. When the bastard awakes." Distantly, as if in a dream, he could hear Franco trying to push Olga away.

"One kiss," she was saying. "For little Olgy Wolgy."

"No! No! Listen, the missus is asleep in there, and I'm warning you, she's an eight-foot deviant with a love of fresh brains! You'd better be careful! She'll not like you mauling me! I'm an honourable man, I am. I am betrothed to be married!"

"Ahh, for you, Franco, I would battle all ze deviants in Hell itself!"

Keenan strode to the edge of the freeway, and leant on the bounce barrier. He patted at his battered WarSuit, dipped his hand inside, and pulled free a buckled, battered, but miraculously intact tin of Widow Maker tobacco. He balanced the tin on the barrier, and started to roll a cigarette. A cool breeze ruffled his hair. Distantly, the destroyed crater of NanoTek rumbled.

Knuckles moved to him. "Did you destroy the GreenSource Mainframe entirely?" he said.

"Yeah."

"How can you be so sure?"

"I can feel it. Up here." He tapped his skull. "Back on Ket, when the Fractured Emerald alien entered me, she left me with a gift. She gave me an ability to... *see* certain things. Unwittingly, the GreenSource unleashed this ability—freed me of a mental restriction. Now, I can feel it... feel *her*. She is crushed down there, under a million tonnes of shit. Exactly what she deserved."

"Listen. Something's happened to the zombies." Knuckles rubbed his hands together, then one strayed to the velvet bag at his waist. "When you blew the SPIRAL dock, when you pulped Green-Source, all the zombies lay down in the street. As if going to sleep. Slick has received intel from QGM; apparently, very slowly, the zombies are changing back!"

"Into people?"

Knuckles nodded. "Yeah. It's a miracle!"

"Not a miracle," snorted Keenan. "A function of technology. The biomods, without instruction or command, are reverting that which they deviated. GreenSource told me NanoTek were experimenting on the whole damned city; the whole planet was a

testing ground for zombies and their different deviated definitions. The aim was to create and select
the strongest and most lethal forms of toxic killer.
GreenSource was building a new junk army." He
laughed. He sounded bitter. "A new pestilence to
replace the old, and powered by a deviant microscopic technology that would spread like bacteria
across a million conquered worlds! I just love science. It's so clinically amoral."

Knuckles shivered. "That's bad, Keenan." He
leapt up to sit on the barrier, and glanced off over
the ruins, hair in disarray, eyes sparkling. He kicked
his red gloss boots against the barrier with *thumps*.

Keenan sighed. "Anyway, how are you doing,
lad? I'm here moaning like a geriatric with back
pain."

"It's been... an adventure! And I've learnt a lot of
lessons in the last few days."

"Haven't we all?"

"Are you referring to Pippa? I thought you two
were enemies? Ready to kill each other the instant
you met? I just watched you talking. You could not
mistake the body-language." Knuckles gave a
cheeky grin, but his eyes were old; older than *death*.

Keenan stared at Knuckles for a long time. Then
he ran his hand through matted hair, took a long
drag on his smoke, and sighed. "I think I never truly
wanted her dead. I loved her... once. Hell, I still
love her. But I can't forgive her. And here? Well, she
came good in the end. Combat K were forced into
a reunion; and it looks like for the immediate future
we have no choice in the matter. Without Pippa,"
Keenan gestured across The City, "well, all those

people out there, they would still be deviants. Walking dead-meat. She played her part." His eyes were filled with pain. And confusion.

"I believe you don't really know how you feel." Knuckles's voice was gentle. He was still rubbing at the velvet bag, hung at his waist.

"Maybe you're right, lad. I'll think on it." He laughed. "Anyway, that bag you carry. We made a deal, didn't we? Although you were right. We never did change Mel back to human."

"You decoded the SinScript?"

"Yes. I used GreenSource."

"And what does it say?"

Keenan grimaced. "Destroy Quad-Gal."

"That's... *bad,* Keenan."

"Tell me about it."

"Hey, he'll be OK, Knuckles," said Pippa, approaching to place a hand on Keenan's arm. She forced a smile to her mouth, although her eyes were still dark, hooded, the eyes of an unreadable killer. "We'll look after him now."

"I can't even look after myself."

"So, go on, what's in the bag?" said Pippa.

"The knuckle bones of my parents. They were killed three years ago. That's why I live on the streets. I keep them as... a reminder. One day, I will find my parents' killers. I will exact a terrible revenge!" His eyes shone, full of unshed tears. "And I will never forget my friends, Little Megan, and the others; all those killed by The Hammer Syndicate." He eyed Keenan thoughtfully. "I have a lot of revenge left in me."

Keenan nodded, and smoked.

Knuckles moved off, filled with melancholy. Olga, tired with Franco's rejection, gave the lad a bosom-engulfing hug.

"Sounds like he has the perfect family history to join Combat K!" said Pippa, shaking her head.

"Yeah, well, the lad came good in the end. Who knows what the future has in store for him."

"We're a brutal species."

"It's in our nature," said Keenan.

"Yeah, but one day, maybe, we'll change."

Keenan eyed her warily. "I doubt it," he said.

Franco arrived, rubbing at his bristling beard. He patted Keenan on the back, and the three of them stood there, Combat K, together, watching the destroyed world of The City through cynical eyes.

Keenan leant over the barrier, staring at the vast scene of total desolation. "There's a war coming," he said, voice barely above a whisper. He turned, stared at Franco and Pippa. "When we unleashed Leviathan, on Teller's World, we thought we'd put it back in the cage. But we didn't, did we? We failed."

Pippa's eyes were glittering. She took a deep breath. "We need to put this thing right," she said.

Keenan nodded, turning to stare back over The City.

"Yeah, but how do we do that?" said Franco. "After all, there are so many pubs to visit? And I've got a wedding to go to!" He beamed. "I'm the groom!"

"Yeah mate, well, you better get married fast. We have to stop the junks," said Keenan, smoke drifting from him like ribbons. "And they know it."

"But *how do we do that?*" said Franco.

Keenan looked at him, laughed, and slapped him on the back. "We have to find out where they come from. What spawned them. Where they've been hiding. Where they were *born*. And more importantly, how to stop them. Only then can we tackle Leviathan."

"Where they were born?"

"Yeah," said Keenan. "And I know where to start. I've seen it. In a dream." He laughed. "An alien dream."

"Where's that?"

"Sick World," said Keenan, and flicked his smoke into the fresh ripening dawn.

"AND HERE ON City Newsnight, I'd like to welcome English Teacher Ellie Midget, formerly of POSH Town's *Blessed Hilda's Perfect Educational Emporium* and, apparently, formerly a reconstituted mutation *zombie!* Please, can we give Ellie a huge round of applause."

[Studio audience: applause].

"Actually, I'd just like to point out I was the *Head* of English at *Blessed Hilda's Perfect Educational Emporium*," said Ellie, face compact, voice somewhat stiff.

"Well, many apologies for *that* monumental cooooooooock up!."

[Studio audience: laughter].

"Now, tell me, many people have been wondering just how *horrific* it actually *was* for you, being turned into a zombie and having your genetics squished and squashed arseways and bumward?

Would you be willing to comment on life as a zombie?"

"Well the funny thing is, Eamon, that for much of the time it was actually quite *enjoyable*."

[Studio audience: hushed silence].

"You mean, eating people's brains was *enjoyable?*"

[Studio audience: laughter/ increase volume +12].

"No, no, not like that, what I meant to say was, on occasion, well, being a zombie, it wasn't something horrible to eat somebody's brain, because brain gloop smelt so good, like the best of sloppy puddings, and once you dipped your claws in it was a bit like having a *Matrix-Choc Sicko Cream Egg...*"

"Eating brains was like eating a chocolate egg? Why, you sick, sick perverted woman!"

[Studio audience: sigh of horror].

"Hey, you keep twisting what I say, you bastard!" Ellie lunged across the table, and with squeals of rupturing flesh and bone, long claws ripped from the ends of her delicately-painted nails. With one deft swipe, Ellie Midget removed the summit of Eamon's cranium, straddled him—before any of the security guards had even *moved*—and was dipping her long, oak-gnarled claws into the TV Presenter's yummy blue goo before anybody could even say *resurrection of the zombie curse*.

As they dragged Ellie Midget from the studio, her legs kicking, her mouth rimed with fresh brain, she thrashed and struggled and squirmed and shouted, "It's not my fault, I tell you! You bastards! None of this is my fault! It was NanoTek! All NanoTek, I say!"

* * *

BLACK AND WHITE NEWS CLIP
The City's Premier News Delivery Service
[available in: print, TV, vid, mail, dig.bath, ident.implant, comm., kube, glass.wall, ggg, galaxy.net and eyelid transpose— all for a small monthly fee].

News clip GG/11/12/TBA:

Quad-Gal Unification Peace Forces have issued a statement regarding recently deviated zombie creatures and their return to supposedly "normal" human status after the desecration of NanoTek's Black Rose Citadel HQ and the biomod central controlling structure, the GreenSource Mainframe. Despite all known zombie fingers returning to human status, there have been several subsequent outbreaks of violence around rejuvenating areas of The City. It appears that, in a few instances only, those who succumbed to the pirated biomod curse [Legal disclaimer: we are in no way blaming the NanoTek Corporation for this instance of semi-genocide, and totally uphold the view that it was the fault of all hackers and pirates who deviated biomods in the first place]— well, many ex-zombies have had moments of minimal relapse. On five occasions, heads have been opened and brains eaten.

There is no reason for panic or alarm, and we are *sure* that the biomod deviation is non-transferable from human to human or alien to alien. And remember, just because somebody was once a zombie, this should not affect their employment rights! Several restaurants have been found carrying <NO EX-ZOMBIE!> admission policies; this sort of prejudice will not be tolerated by QGM Inspectors in The City environment. We believe in Equal Opportunities for all! Being a zombie is NOT, we repeat, NOT the disability it once was.

So. Be safe. Stay indoors. And whatever you do, carry a weapon—and shoot for the knee-caps.

News clip: END.

THE PENTHOUSE SUITE atop The City Waldorf Astoria was perfect. The best of the best. 10 STAR+. It took more than a zombie massacre on a planetary scale to slow down *these* lucrative money-making hoteliers!

The lights were dimmed. Champagne v3.7 chilled in a TitaniumVI bucket. Rose petals (synthetic_real to a grade of 7!) lay scattered across plush floral bed covers and the thick Helk-fur carpet. Music played, a harmony by the famous Quad-Gal composer, Muzo the Third.

Even the air smelled fresh. A miracle of filtration, as outside fires still raged from the zombie rampage.

The QGM Briefing was scheduled for 0700 hours, led by a drugged-up but nevertheless switched-on hover-wheelchair incarcerated Steinhauer. He informed the remaining veterans of Combat K that they had a job to do. And they were leaving The City in 12 hours rimwards out of The Cluster.

By 0810 hours Keenan was driving round in a commandeered buggy looking for a Holy Man and a ring. By 1120, Franco had a suit, Mel a dress, and by 1300 hours they were at the marble_cast Church of the Blessed Walrus, itching in starched fabrics, pew-seated guests staring in ill-disguised horror as Mel strode up the aisle, all eight feet of mutation, talons cracking the stone flags, Olga her lemon-scented bridesmaid. Mel's white dress still looked like a meringue.

"Are you sure you want to go through with this?" muttered Keenan, Best Man in starched monkey-suit, from the corner of his mouth.

"Of course!"

"But she's an eight-foot zombie, mate."

"Hey, I am a man of my word! I am an honourable fellow!"

"OK pal. It's your future."

The following few hours were a blur of romance, of cars and confetti, of Champagne v3.7 and heartily shook hands. Everybody patted Franco on the back and wished him the best. And that he'd survive.

"Didn't she look lovely in that dress!"

"A movie princess!"

"More beautiful than any catwalk model!"

Pippa caught the bouquet.

Now, as The City descended towards night in a frenzy of rebuilding, clean-up operations, and an effort to return some semblance of normality to a rampant warzone, so the Penthouse Suite's door was kicked open and Franco made one damn valiant effort to carry his huge and bulging, growling, pus-stinking, heavily-muscled bride across the marital threshold.

He managed one, staggered, half-sandaled slap, then dumped Mel unceremoniously on the carpet. "That'll have to do, chipmunk. My back's giving me hell!"

"Ranco! Ow Omantic!"

"Yeah yeah, I know."

Mel ran to the bed, claws tearing carpet, and reclined amidst petals, talons curling seductively around a glass of chilled Champers. She patted the covers beside her. Franco paled.

"OK." He sighed. "Love, you've been waiting for this for a long time, haven't you?"

"Es." Melanie made a crackling puckering kissing sound.

Franco stuck out his lower jaw, rolled his neck, cracked his knuckles, and switching off the light, climbed onto the bed. "Let's get it done, then," he said.

ACKNOWLEDGEMENTS

Thank-you to Sonia, for putting up with the manic depressions of a depraved semi-alcoholic writer. Thank-you to Joe and Olly, for being such fine little boys and always making me laugh.

And a big sloppy kiss to all at SOLARIS, basically for being such an entertaining bunch of deviant transmogrifications.

ABOUT THE AUTHOR

Andy Remic is a British writer with a love of extreme sports, kickass bikes and sword fighting. Once a member of an elite Combat K squad, he has since retired from military service and works as an underground rebel fighting bureaucratic oppression wherever he finds it. He does not condone the use of biomods, and urges human- and alien-kind to rebel against the market-oppression of nihilistic mega-corporations.

Biohell is his fifth novel.

You can discover more about Andy Remic at *www.andyremic.com,* and read his pointless dribbling on his blog at *andyremic.blogspot.com.*

A COMBAT-K NOVEL

ANDY REMIC

The new master of rock-hard military science fiction

WAR MACHINE

ISBN: 978-1-84416-522-3

Ex-soldier Keenan, a private investigator with a bad reputation, is about to take on the biggest case of his career. To have any chance of success, however, he must head to a dangerous colony world and re-assemble his old military unit, a group who swore they'd never work together again...

SOLARIS SCIENCE FICTION